The Midnight Swimmer

EDWARD WILSON is a native of Baltimore. He studied International Relations on a US Army scholarship. He later served as a Special Forces officer in Vietnam. He was decorated for his part in rescuing wounded Vietnamese soldiers from a minefield. After leaving the Army, Wilson became an expatriate and gave up US nationality to become a British citizen. He has also lived and worked in Germany and France. He is the author of three novels, *A River in May*, *The Envoy* and *The Darkling Spy*, all published by Arcadia Books. The author now lives in Suffolk where he taught English and Modern Languages for thirty years.

EDWARD WILSON

The Midnight Swimmer

Arcadia Books Ltd
15–16 Nassau Street
London W1W 7AB

www.arcadiabooks.co.uk

First published in Great Britain by Arcadia Books 2011

A catalogue record for this book is available from the British Library.

ISBN 978-1-906413-99-6

Typeset in Minion by MacGuru Ltd
Printed and bound by
CPI Group (UK) Ltd, Croydon, CR0 4YY

Arcadia Books gratefully acknowledges the financial support of Arts Council England.

Arcadia Books supports English PEN, the fellowship of writers who work together to promote literature and its understanding. English PEN upholds writers' freedoms in Britain and around the world, challenging political and cultural limits on free expression. To find out more, visit www.englishpen.org or contact
English PEN, Free Word Centre, 60 Farringdon Road, London EC1R 3GA

Arcadia Books distributors are as follows:

in the UK and elsewhere in Europe:
Turnaround Publishers Services
Unit 3, Olympia Trading Estate
Coburg Road
London N22 6TZ

in the USA and Canada:
Dufour Editions
PO Box 7
Chester Springs
PA, 19425

in Australia/New Zealand:
The Scribo Group Pty Ltd
18 Rodborough Road
Frenchs Forest 2086

in New Zealand:
The GHR Press
PO Box 7109
McMahons Point
Sydney 2060

in South Africa:
Jacana Media (Pty) Ltd
PO Box 291784
Melville 2109
Johannesburg

For all my former students with fondest thanks.

Mama take this badge from me
I can't use it anymore
It's getting dark too dark to see
Feels like I'm knockin' on heaven's door …

Bob Dylan

Already darkness, and the end is in sight:
Ophelia crying in an empty hut.
And Hamlet walks to and fro with white headband
in order to be recognized by the Ghost in the gloom.

'On the Sea-Shore, Smell of Iodine'
Regina Derieva

PART ONE

Near Brentford, Essex. March, 1962

Galen's body was uncooperative, even resentful. It seemed to want to stay curled up on the back seat of the Ford enjoying the after-effects of a bottle of single malt whisky laced with sedatives. It's the sort of cocktail you have when you are worried about losing your job and when your love life is a complete mess. At least that was the back story they were hoping to spread. People usually don't commit suicide when life is smelling of roses.

Catesby and Bone were wearing surgical gloves. The plan was to leave as little evidence for the forensic team as possible. It was part of the game. Catesby put his arms under the corpse's shoulders and began to slide the body off the red fake-leather seat.

'Get his legs, Henry, and don't bloody drop them.'

'Who would have thought he was so heavy?'

In life Galen had been a small man with soft features; he seemed to gain most of his nourishment from whisky and porn. Catesby, who had ample experience shifting cadavers, was surprised at the body's heaviness. Maybe, he thought, it was the weight of all those secrets that he was taking to the grave.

'I can't see the footpath,' said Bone.

'Okay, let's swap positions.' Catesby looked at the gravel beneath his feet. It seemed shiny in the moonlight. 'No, don't. If we put him down here his suit might pick up grease from the car park. Just go straight ahead.'

'I see a signpost.'

'That's it.'

Catesby knew that the footpaths of Weald Park were well marked. He often stopped there for his sandwiches when driving between London and his home in Suffolk. The landscaping of the estate, including the lake and deer park, had been carried out in the eighteenth century in the style of Capability Brown. The result was a setting of exceeding beauty and peace – the perfect place to dump a body.

'Can you manage, Henry?'

'I'm fine,' said Bone. He seemed to have got his bearings.

'You ought to come here during the day. It's the sort of place you would like. You could bring your sketchbook.' It wasn't often that Catesby had the chance to patronise his boss and order him around, but body disposal was a job where the field operative was in charge.

The footpath was wide and well trod which was why Catesby had chosen it. He didn't want the cops to pick out suspicious footprints or disturbed undergrowth.

'How much further?' said Bone.

'There's a beech grove off to the left – we'll take him in there. You ought to see the bluebells in the spring.' Catesby had once made love there. The woman had told him she'd always dreamed of making love on a bed of bluebells. Beech forests were picture-book romantic. They were dark and private, but had little undergrowth to catch the hems of dresses.

'Turn off here. Don't let his feet drag.' They continued for about ten yards. 'Here is fine. Lay him on his back.'

'Enough heavy lifting for the day. Would you like a drink?'

'Are you talking to me?' said Catesby.

'Very funny.'

'I thought it was.'

Bone reached for his hipflask and passed it over. He never laughed at Catesby's 'jokes'.

Catesby sipped the brandy. It was good stuff, twenty-five-year-old VSOP. Bone even had a bottle from 1812 and had once let Catesby have the tiniest sip. It was pale and had lost all its flavour. 'Not for drinking,' explained Bone at the time, 'I keep it for its rarity. But now you can say you've tasted brandy looted from Napoleon's stores.'

Catesby looked down at the body. Only the collar of Galen's white shirt and a tiny glint from his glasses were visible in the gloom. He seemed already to have melted into the earth. 'Can't we just leave him the way he is?'

'No, the drug that killed him won't show up in the post-mortem – and the whisky and barbiturates he's ingested aren't sufficient on their own to cause death. If the pathologists mess around long enough they just might discover traces of VX. It's not likely, but we can't risk it.'

'I think we should just leave him as he is.'

'No, we've already decided. You didn't forget the knife, did you?'

'No.'

Catesby reached in his coat pocket for the American switchblade. It was sealed in an envelope so it wouldn't pick up fibres from his clothes. He tore the paper open and removed the knife. 'I suppose you want me to cut him?'

'You've got steadier hands and better eyes.'

'By the way, was Galen left-handed or right-handed?'

Bone picked up both dead hands and compared them. 'Right-handed, the fingers are slightly thicker.'

Catesby carefully put the knife in Galen's right hand and moulded the fingers around the handle to leave fingerprints.

'Cut the veins in the wrist lengthwise.'

'How the bloody hell do you expect me to find them in the dark? In any case, you can't get veins up on a corpse.'

'Just find the two tendons at the base of the palm – slash up between them.'

The knife was sharp and easily penetrated the flesh. Catesby opened a deep gash about three inches long.

'Now,' said Bone, 'comes the hard part. Do you want to go first?'

'Okay.' Catesby leaned over the corpse and started doing closed cardiac heart massage. When amateurs try to make an assassination look like a slit-wrist suicide they often forget that dead bodies don't bleed. 'How's he doing?'

'It's coming out, but only a trickle. Pump harder, but don't crack a rib.'

The two men worked in turns. It took nearly three hours to push out enough blood to create a credible suicide scene. Both men were covered in sweat.

Bone wiped his brow and said, 'I'm sure that's enough.'

Catesby reached into his coat pocket for the theatre props: an empty whisky bottle and pill packets. They had already covered the items with Galen's fingerprints. He arranged them next to the body. And then for the *pièce de résistance*, a pair of frilly women's knickers that he draped over Galen's face.

Bone stared at their handiwork with his hands in his pockets.

'I think,' said Catesby, 'the knickers are too much.'

'Leave them. It means the Americans will do all the more to keep it out of the papers.'

'They're not going to believe it in any case. If he was going to top himself, why didn't he do it in his own flat?' They had, in fact, considered staging it there, but there were access problems and too many nosey neighbours.

Bone shrugged. 'That's not our problem. It's a problem for the coroner. Let's go.'

They made their way back to the cars. Bone had followed Catesby in an Austin 30 with fake number plates in case they got spotted by a curious member of the public. The plates traced the car to a minor East End villain. They obviously had to leave Galen's big left-hand drive Ford – with its US Diplomatic Corps number plates – near the scene of death.

'The setting is quite apt,' said Bone as he slid into the tiny Austin.

'Why's that?'

'This is where Claudius defeated the ancient Britons in 44 AD. I suppose you could say we've got our own back.'

Catesby looked at Bone in awe. He suspected, not for the first time, that beneath Bone's polished exterior of Whitehall mandarin lurked the soul of a wily rebel.

Berlin. October, 1960

Back then, Catesby didn't even know that Galen existed. Like a lot of these things, you only see the connections through the hindsight telescope. But it wouldn't have made any difference. Catesby wasn't the playwright, he was just one of the players – like Andreas, Katya and Zhenka. Sure, you could improvise a bit if you fluffed your lines, but the final act was still going to be the same. The prince was still going to die.

It didn't take Catesby long to realise that Andreas was a sleazy spiv. This wasn't a rare species in post-war Berlin. As soon as the shooting stopped, chancer spivs like Andreas popped up all over the city like mushrooms after a wet summer. They were still popping up fifteen years later. As an intelligence officer, Catesby had grown to like the Berliner spivs. They were honest about being dishonest. They were easy to handle because they were primarily motivated by money and pleasure. Sure, they could be cruel and vicious too – but maybe that was just a form of pleasure. The worst characters to deal with were agents with political axes to grind. They had secret agendas that you couldn't control.

It was much more difficult to be a spiv in East Berlin than West Berlin. Basically, there was a lot less stuff to nick and fewer rich people to cheat or buy your black market swag. For this reason the spivs in the East usually turned to the spy game.

To be fair, Andreas didn't really want to be a spiv or a spy. He wanted to be an actor. He went to drama school and wore a black roll-neck jumper and a fake leather jacket. He tried to hang around with the Bertolt Brecht crowd, but they didn't want to hang around with him. Andreas wasn't too popular with his drama school tutors either. They thought he was lazy and ideologically unsound – or as one suggested, 'an arrogant little bourgeois shit'. In due course, the school director convened a meeting where Andreas was told that 'he needed to become better acquainted with the working class'.

Catesby didn't think that two years in an opencast coalmine had given Andreas more respect for the proletariat, but it certainly gave him more respect for the power of the authorities. Catesby actually approved of the DDR's way of dealing with problem students. But this, like many of his views, was one that Catesby had to keep under his hat. In fact, even saying DDR, shorthand for Deutsche Demokratische Republik, had become a problem. Catesby had been told not to call it that in front of Americans. The Yanks always called it East Germany. When Brits said DDR, American eyebrows were raised. It was as if using the country's official name suggested being 'soft on communism'. It was the ideological version of 'tomaytoes' versus 'tomahtoes'.

Andreas never made it big as an actor so he became a whore. He liked his new job better than acting. There were no boring lines to memorise and he was paid a lot more, but not by the women he made love to. He was paid by the MfS, the East German secret intelligence service.

His first assignments were exchange students whom he was supposed to recruit to spy on their home countries when they returned. But his most important seduction happened quite by chance. At first, he was drawn to her by attraction and desire. It never occurred to Andreas that she was going to be part of his job as an MfS 'Romeo' agent. She was simply an elegant woman he had met at the debut of a film in which he had had a small role. She seemed lonely, sad – and quite bored with the party. Andreas knew that she was a Russian, but only later did he discover that she was the most important Russian wife in Berlin.

The affair began a week later. The woman had invited Andreas for tea to an address in East Berlin's most exclusive quarter. The address turned out to be a large and luxurious flat. The first thing that Andreas noticed when he was let in was a pair of black army boots in the entrance hall. His disappointment grew when he saw a Soviet Army officer's greatcoat hanging from a hook above the boots. The shoulder boards on the coat bore the rank insignia of a lieutenant-general. Disappointment turned to curiosity. The coat obviously belonged to one of the highest ranking Soviet officers in the DDR.

The woman saw Andreas staring at the military apparel. 'They're my husband's, but he's not here. He's always working. We are alone.'

Andreas followed the woman into a sitting room where a samovar was bubbling on a sideboard. It wasn't long, however, before the tea things were pushed aside and the pair were writhing with passion on the sofa. Andreas soon had her dress up around her waist and was about to have her then and there, but she stopped him. Her face was flushed. 'No,' she said.

'No?'

'I mean not here,' she said. 'Let's go into the bedroom.'

The rest of the afternoon was the maddest and hungriest love-making that Andreas had ever experienced. The woman clutched him with an almost deranged yearning as she finally shuddered to a prolonged orgasm. And it wasn't long before they began again. Andreas was a little frightened by her passion. He felt that she was never going to let go. But after an hour of rosy madness she did let go and pushed Andreas away a little so she could see his eyes.

'You must think,' she said, 'that I am a little strange.'

'Strangely wonderful.'

'In a way I have been very lonely. Today was the first time … the first time I had an orgasm in years.'

'Why?'

'Don't ask, I'm not going to tell you. And do not think that I've been completely unhappy.'

'But not for so many years …'

'Do you believe me?'

'Yes, of course.'

The woman smiled bleakly.

'I don't even know your name.'

'Katya. It's a short form of Ekaterina.'

'Your husband …'

'Don't talk about my husband.'

'Sorry.'

'I'm sorry I snapped at you.' She looked away at an ornate mantel clock that featured a nineteenth-century hunter and his hound. 'I think you must be going now.'

'Will we meet again?'

She kissed him.

As she led him to the door Andreas looked once more at the Soviet greatcoat with the lieutenant-general's insignia. He knew he had to see her again.

Andreas reported his tryst with Katya to his MfS agent handler the very next day. If she had been an ordinary Russian woman with a husband who had a dreary post in trade or transport, he would have kept the affair to himself. But he knew from the uniform that her spouse must be one of the most important Soviet officers in Berlin.

'He must,' said Andreas, 'be at least a corps commander.'

The agent handler was going through a large file. 'What did you say the address was?'

Andreas told him again.

The handler turned another page in the file and ran his finger down a list. Suddenly the MfS man's face turned white.

'What is it?'

'Fuck.'

'You found him.'

The agent handler looked across the desk at Andreas. 'You've just been shagging the wife of Yevgeny Ivanovich Alekseev.'

'Who's he?'

'He's head of the bloody fucking KGB.'

'In the world?'

'No, silly, in Berlin. The Russians call him the *rezident*. It means chief of the *rezidentura*, the KGB station – and the Berlin *rezidentura* is one of the most important stations in the world. This guy, Andreas, is one big fish.'

'Should I continue to see his wife?'

'That could be scary – I'd better clear it with the boss.'

The op request went straight to the desk of Mischa Wolf, the Head of the HVA – the foreign intelligence branch of the MfS. In fact, it was Mischa's film director brother, Koni Wolf, who had recruited Andreas in the first place. The brothers enjoyed a symbiotic relationship. Mischa protected Koni's artistic freedom and Koni provided Mischa a steady stream of B to Z grade actors to serve as 'Romeo agents' and 'honey traps'.

Mischa twirled his reading glasses and looked out the plate-glass window of his Normanenstrasse office over the dreary cityscape of Berlin. The important thing was that Andreas was not an official MfS officer. He was an IM, an *Inoffizieller Mitarbeiter*. The IMs were a small army of 'unofficial' part-timers who were paid in cash and favours. They were often recruited to do dirty tricks for which the

State could deny responsibility. And when it came to seducing the wives of high-ranking Soviet officials stationed in East Berlin, the lack of a formal connection to the MfS was essential. Maintaining fraternal DDR/USSR relations was important, but so was knowing the secrets that Moscow was keeping from Berlin. In many ways spying on allies was just as important as spying on enemies. Mischa decided to authorise the op.

As soon as Andreas's agent handler received the go-ahead, he arranged a series of training sessions. The first step was to teach Andreas how to use a Minox miniature camera for copying documents. Ideally, there should be a four-legged copy stand to keep the camera in place, but this would make concealment and speed difficult. Andreas was instructed to hold the camera as steady as possible and to use any available light from a lamp or window.

'You're shaking too much,' said the handler as they tried a few practice snaps.

'I can't help it.'

'Try breathing out, it helps keep the hands steady. We teach snipers the same technique.'

When the training was finished Andreas was given a new Minox B that could be traced back to a factory in West Germany by its serial number. There was also West German film to use with it. If Andreas was caught, the camera's origins would suggest he was working for a Western intelligence agency. But, of course, Western agencies supplied their own agents spy gadgets of East bloc origins for the same reason. The agent handler knew that the bluff and double bluff procedures fooled no one in the trade, but it was vitally important that nothing in Andreas's possession pointed back to the East German state.

Oddly, Andreas found that his new role as a honey trap whore gave him more confidence as a lover. It meant that he was no longer, as he had felt before, the inferior, less attractive partner in the relationship. It also gave the lovemaking a certain slightly kinky frisson. At first Andreas had felt that Katya was using him, now he felt that he was using her. Otherwise he would have fallen hopelessly in love with her.

Katya was so intelligent that Andreas sometimes forgot that she was also beautiful. Yet he found her intelligence unsettling. Katya wasn't just an intellectual who embarrassed him with her learning, but a sharply perceptive woman. When Andreas suggested they have a lovemaking session at his flat, as his MfS handler had urged, Katya firmly declined with a knowing sparkle in her eye. She wasn't a fool. Ekaterina Alekseeva hadn't been married to a KGB general for fifteen years without learning a few trade secrets. She wasn't certain that her lover was a spy, but she was certain that Andreas's flat would have a secret camera over the bed that had been installed with or without his knowledge. In the espionage swamp of Berlin there were predators lying in wait behind every bush – and Katya knew she was a trophy prey.

At first, Andreas was more than nervous about making love in the marital flat. He was terrified that at any moment the bedroom door would fling open and Lieutenant General Alekseev would be waving a black Makarov 9mm automatic in his face. If he wasn't executed on the spot, Andreas suspected that he would be bundled off to the huge Karlshorst compound where the Soviets enjoyed extra-territorial sovereignty. What awaited him there would be far worse than a bullet between the eyes – or legs. But as the months went by, the door remained closed and their lovemaking remained undisturbed. Andreas began to realise that Yevgeny Alekseev was *un mari complaisant*, a husband who turned a blind eye. It certainly explained the separate bedrooms and the fact the *rezident* was seldom at home even in the evenings. It then occurred to Andreas that Katya was, in fact, using him more than he was using her. The realisation made him angry, but it also made him love her all the more. He now knew that his love was hopeless and that he must do whatever was possible to profit from the affair before it ended.

Andreas found Katya the cleanest and most hygienic woman that he had ever been with. She spent a long time in the bathroom preparing herself for lovemaking – and she always fragrant – and a long time in the bathroom afterwards too. As Katya luxuriated in the bath bubbles of a pre-coital *toilette intime*, Andreas took out the camera and searched the bedroom for things to photograph. Katya was just as tidy with her things as with her body and never left paperwork lying about, but there was a writing desk with a locked drawer. The lock proved easy to pick – his MfS handler had taught him that skill as well. The top drawer contained letters from her mother and siblings. Andreas, who had studied compulsory Russian in school, wasn't fluent, but he could see that the letters were about family news that was mostly boring. Nonetheless, he photographed a selection of the letters; then opened a second drawer.

This drawer was more promising. It was full of photos – many of which seemed to have been taken at embassy receptions and *dacha* parties. Andreas was certain that the photos might identify high-ranking friends – as well as hitherto unknown KGB officers. He was sure that his agent handler would be impressed. Andreas snapped furiously until the roll of film was exhausted. When he heard Katya stirring from her bath, he hid the camera in the lining of his coat.

When Katya emerged from the bathroom she wasn't as made-up or slinkily dressed as usual. She was wearing a dressing gown and her hair was done up in a towel. She spent a long time looking at Andreas with her head cocked to one side – as if she were inspecting a plucked hen on a butcher's hook, a hen that had been there too long and gone off. Finally, Katya went over to the chair where Andreas had draped his coat. She went through the pockets and then felt the lining until she found the camera. Without saying a thing, she opened the camera and took out the film cartridge. She flicked open the cartridge with her thumbnail. She stared hard at Andreas as she unwound the film and exposed it. Katya crumpled up the ruined film into her fist and said, 'I'll burn it later.' She then picked up the camera and handed it to Andreas. 'I'm sure your boss will want this back. I wouldn't want you to get in trouble.'

'I'm sorry.'

Katya sat on the side of the bed and buried her face in her hands. Andreas sat down beside her, but without touching. He knew there was nothing he could say. Suddenly, he felt her stir next to him. Katya had slipped the dressing from her shoulder and exposed her nakedness. Her eyes had turned to cinders. She grabbed Andreas by his hair and pulled hard. 'Come on,' she said twisting his head downwards so that his face was in front of hers, 'fuck me. You get paid for that too.'

The relationship continued, but things were never the same. Andreas realised a gulf had opened between them – and that the coolness and distancing were completely on Katya's side. He began to feel the desolate pain of making love to someone who no longer loved him. Her coolness, of course, made him love her all the more. Andreas began to wonder if her continuing to see him was a form of punishment and revenge.

Andreas never told his agent handler what had happened. The handler, meanwhile, was becoming more and more disillusioned with a 'Romeo' who didn't deliver results. 'When,' said the handler, 'are you going to start using the camera? We're not paying you to get laid, you know.' At first, Andreas had been paid double the average DDR wage for a pleasant job that only took three or four hours a week. But his stipend as an IM had dwindled to less than beer money. In fact, Andreas began to have serious worries about his future life. The DDR offered full employment in return for subsidised housing and food. But it was not a society that tolerated the work-shy. Andreas feared that his agent handler would report him as useless and lazy. He knew that he would be forced to take on a job in a factory or building site. His previous experience with the proletariat, his two years in an opencast coalmine, had not been a happy one. Maybe, he thought, it was time to pack up and leave for the West. The only thing holding him back was his love for Katya. And the only thing he loved more was money.

A common characteristic of spiv Berliner IMs like Andreas was their lack of loyalty and ideological commitment. Every agent handler, both East and West, knew this was a fact. None would have been surprised to learn that Andreas hated life in the DDR – and that he wanted to live in the West and drive a soft-top Mercedes. He was shallow. Which was fine, for it also meant that his moves and motivations were all the more predictable. But the big problem with greedy spies like Andreas was their tendency to go in for 'double dipping'. A double dipper wasn't a doubled agent. A double dipper was simply someone who sold the same intelligence to more than one agency in order to maximise profits. It happened all the time in Berlin in the days before the Wall. It was a very risky business, but one that paid huge returns if you got away with it. Andreas's agent handler knew that his Romeo was a potential double dipper, but he still didn't have anything to double dip with. The handler decided it was too soon to put Andreas under surveillance.

The next time he visited the flat it was obvious that something was wrong. Katya was in a strange mood – and Andreas could tell it had nothing to do with him. She didn't even seem to notice that he was there. At first, Andreas thought that maybe she had taken a new lover. When he asked her, she simply shook her head and said, 'No.'

'What is it then?'

'Nothing.'

'Why are you so strange?'

'Can't you just let me be?' She smiled, but it was artificial. 'Let's get in bed.'

The lovemaking was perfunctory. Katya seemed completely uninvolved, as if she were on another planet. As soon as it was over, Katya got out of bed. Andreas tried to embrace her, but she pushed him away and went into the bathroom for her post-coital wash. Andreas sat on the side of the bed feeling both confused and desolate. When he heard the sound of Katya vomiting behind the bathroom door, Andreas felt relieved. It explained why she had been so out of sorts – she wasn't well. He listened to the toilet flushing, the bath water being drawn and then Katya sliding into the tub.

Andreas noticed something strange. Katya had left her writing desk open. He listened to the sound of her splashing and soaping in the tub. She couldn't be watching from the keyhole. He had a quick ransack of the desk drawer – and realised there was nothing there that he hadn't seen before. There was, however, a letter that she had begun to write – but it went no further than, *My dearest brother...* Andreas touched the paper: it was tear-stained. Something bad had happened.

It was then that Andreas noticed a book that was lying on Katya's bedside table. He picked it up. It was a collection of Mayakovsky's poetry – a favourite, apparently, of her husband. There was a bulge in the middle of the book – as if a bookmarker had been inserted. But it wasn't a bookmarker, it was a letter. Despite his poor Russian, Andreas knew that he had hit the jackpot as soon as he read the first words. It was too good to be true. It was certainly far too good for his MfS handler, the mean bastard had cut his wages. Andreas decided then and there that only the West had pockets deep enough to pay for this gem. His love affair with Katya may have been doomed, but money was a balm that would soon soothe his broken heart.

Catesby hated his office in the bowels of the Olympic Stadium, Berlin. There were no windows and no – *Gemütlichkeit*. It was the German word for 'cosiness', but the full sense of glowing warmth conveyed by the expression was untranslatable. It was funny, thought Catesby, that Germans, who valued *Gemütlichkeit* so highly, constructed buildings that completely destroyed it. Their national character had more internal contradictions than Marx's theory of capitalism.

The Olympic Stadium had been built for the 1936 games – and was the largest building in Berlin that had survived destruction from the '45 Soviet onslaught. Consequently, the British had requisitioned it for their headquarters during the occupation and were still there. Catesby's own office had been a physiotherapy room. He imagined that it had been used for massages as well as more exotic forms of manual manipulation. At certain times Catesby was sure he could detect the lingering scents of massage oils – camphor, chamomile, clove and sandalwood – still emanating from the concrete walls. He closed his eyes and imagined the fit toned bodies being kneaded, pummelled and slapped. How many of those toned athletic limbs had survived intact the storm of shell, bullet and flame?

Catesby looked at the standard-issue Ministry of Supply clock on the bare wall. It was just after nine in the morning, but it might have been midnight. His office bunker registered neither time of day nor time of year. Catesby looked at his desk diary. It was one of his mornings devoted to meeting his field officers. He only gave them five minutes each which was a good discipline for them. It meant they had to refine and summarise their intelligence findings into a presentation of about three hundred words. Young Gerald was his first appointment. Catesby pressed a button on his desk that flashed a green light. The office door opened.

'Sit down,' said Catesby, 'and speak softly. I've got a terrible hangover.'

'This might need more than five minutes, sir.'

'BINDWEED?'

'Yes – and it looks certain that his claims are genuine.'

Gerald handed over the document ledger. The red cover and yellow stripes indicated the contents were Delicate Source: UK EYES ALPHA. Catesby began to flick through the folder.

'As you can see, sir, he's only provided us a few taster samples. He's demanding a lot of cash for the full range – far more money than I'm authorised to hand over. But BINDWEED might be worth every pfennig.'

Catesby nodded agreement. He trusted the young field officer's judgement. Gerald was one of the best in his cohort. He was shrewd without being cynical. He was thorough and conscientious without being a bore. And Gerald was a team player. One of the worst duties of a junior SIS officer was being part of the British liaison team that inspected areas in East Germany where Soviet military exercises had taken place. It was literally a shit job. Soviet troops were not issued toilet paper. As a result, the mock battle areas were strewn with ill-smelling intelligence treasure: letters, supply chits, sections of field manuals and even code books. Gerald never complained – and always provided extra rubber gloves for his forgetful colleagues.

Catesby looked up from the file. 'He won't hand over until he gets the money?'

'That appears to be the case.'

'Shit.' Catesby closed his eyes and rubbed his forehead. Berlin was an espionage strip joint full of con artists. The Americans made things worse by throwing around money like drunken sailors in a whorehouse.

'We might, sir, be able to bargain BINDWEED down.'

'I think I had better deal with this bird personally. Can you arrange a *treff*?'

The DDR authorities were making noises about it, but they still hadn't done anything. There were rumours, however, of plans to build a barrier called 'The Anti-Fascist Protection Wall'. But it was only a rumour. In the autumn of 1960 it was still easy to move around the city, although vehicle crossing points were fewer and document checks more frequent. Nonetheless, the easiest way to get to East Berlin was simply to take one of the U-Bahn trains that regularly crossed under the border. And this was exactly how Catesby preferred to travel to the Soviet sector.

In Catesby's view, the best place for a *treff* was East Berlin. The streets were far less crowded which meant it was easier to do a counter-surveillance check to make sure you hadn't 'grown a tail'. If you had grown a tail, the best thing was to abort and go home. But it was always a good idea to get rid of your tail whatever you did. You could do this by changing U- and S-Bahn trains at busy stations like Alexanderplatz. But Friedrichstrasse was the best because there were always lots of 'Wessies' around who popped over to exchange hard currency for cheap DDR coffee and booze – especially *Rotkäppchen* sparkling wine which was as good as non-vintage champagne.

Catesby tried to look the part. He had a full wardrobe of DDR-manufactured clothing – and a large selection of fake DDR IDs. But he tended to leave those behind because if he got caught using one it could create a serious diplomatic incident. In any case, he preferred flashing his genuine British ID and demanding his full rights as a bona fide member of the Allied High Commission. They were allowed to go anywhere without asking permission. Although from time to time someone got shot doing so – and no one ever said 'sorry'.

On the way to meet BINDWEED, Catesby had borrowed a 'wife' from the Abteilung 4 of the BfV. The BfV was a West German internal security agency modelled on the American FBI. Abteilung 4 was its counterespionage section. Catesby didn't like working with the BfV because he wasn't sure where their loyalties lay – Washington or Bonn – and to what degree they had been penetrated by Mischa. But he didn't mind borrowing an occasional BfV 'wife' as cover disguise. Catesby encouraged his agents and watchers to operate as male/female couples whenever possible. A fond, or not so fond, couple looked far less suspicious than a bloke or a pair of blokes wearing trilbies and overcoats. MI5 had considered the practice for their own surveillance teams, but rejected it when the real-life wives complained. Ideally, thought Catesby, an agent going to a *treff* ought to take along a kid and a dog as well – but that was probably over-egging it.

The 'wife's' name was Jutta and she seemed realistically bored with her 'husband'. She was about ten years younger than Catesby and a little too pretty to be a likely Frau Catesby. She was an entry grade operative and didn't seem too happy about doing overtime on a Saturday. As they did an SDR, Surveillance Detection Run, along the banks of the River Spree Catesby regretted not having come alone. The secret of an SDR was to appear 'normal' and they didn't look like a normal couple. Mischa certainly wouldn't have paired them. And she kept looking around – which was amateurish – to spot a 'watcher'. Jutta had been trained to use TEDD. It was a procedure the BfV had picked up from the Americans. The acronym stood for Time, Environment, Distance and Demeanour. The idea was that you could spot a watcher if you saw him more than once in a different environment at the same distance – and acting oddly. TEDD was total crap. No professional surveillance operative would give him- or herself away that easily – unless they worked for MI5.

'If,' said Catesby, 'you look around once more I'm going to throw you in the river.'

Jutta grabbed Catesby by the arm and pushed him towards the water. 'I'll throw you in first.'

'Sorry,' Catesby smiled. He was beginning to like her – and they were looking more normal too. 'If you want to check for surveillance, pretend you're pointing out something to your partner.' To demonstrate he touched her elbow and pointed back up the Spree, 'Look at that beautiful swan.'

'Where?'

'There isn't one – I just wanted to check the bridge to see if anyone followed us. Small bridges like that are called choke points – you can use alleys or woodland paths too. It makes it more difficult for a surveillance team not to show themselves.' Catesby paused. 'But if they are well trained and large in number – in Moscow the KGB have been known to assign 200 to a single target – you will never get rid of them.'

Jutta stifled a yawn.

'I'm sorry if I am boring you – or sound patronising.'

'You can't help it.'

Catesby smiled. He always seemed to say the wrong thing even when he meant well. It had been like that with Petra. The memory pain came back as if a knife had gone into the front of his brain. He closed his eyes.

'Are you all right?'

'Yes. Just a bit of a migraine.'

'Men don't often get them.'

'It must be something else then.'

The girders of the Friedrichstrasse rail bridge and the huge barn of the rail station loomed ahead. It was their destination and – with casual clothes, rucksacks and sensible shoes – Catesby and Jutta looked just like an ordinary East Berlin couple heading to catch a train for an autumnal walk in the countryside. When they got to the eastbound platform for S-Bahn Line 3, there were families and couples in similar dress.

The S-Bahn, 'fast rail', covered both halves of Berlin, but was controlled by the East German government and ran on rails that were mostly above ground. They had been waiting only a minute when the next train arrived. There was always plenty of space if you got on at Friedrichstrasse. Jutta took the window seat and stared at the grey urban landscape as the train wheezed over the bridge that crossed the Spree.

The second stop was the busy Alexanderplatz, and the carriage filled up to standing room only. A lot of the new passengers were Russians, presumably heading back to their base in Karlshorst, but as they were in civilian clothes Catesby didn't know what their functions were. Ordinary Soviet soldiers seldom went out on the town in Berlin; they didn't have the money. A Russian of about forty towered over their seat. His clothes smelled strongly of tobacco and he was staring at Jutta as if he recognised her. She seemed to feel his eyes on her and this made her stare more intently out the window. Catesby tried to control his paranoia and reasoned that the Russian was just a lonely man in a distant country looking at a pretty girl.

Suddenly, the Russian nodded at the rucksack Jutta had on her lap and said, '*Spazierengehen*?' He had asked if they were going for 'a walk'. The Russian's German was clear, but heavily accented.

Jutta nodded, '*Ja*'.

The Russian carried on speaking German, as if he were a schoolchild rehearsing for a test. '*Deutschland*, very pretty.'

Catesby nodded and smiled.

The Russian smiled and continued. 'I come *Deutschland* first time in 1945. *Deutschland* not pretty then, *alles kaput*.' As the train pulled into the next station, the Russian made a sweeping gesture with his arm. 'But today, *Deutschland* is very pretty everywhere.'

Catesby was relieved. The Russian was just being friendly. His open demeanour suggested he was probably a driver or a cook rather than a security type. He just wanted to practise his German. Catesby kept smiling and nodding, but noticed that they were only as far as Warschauer Strasse. There were still four more stops before they got to Karlshorst – where, presumably, the Russian would disembark. Time for lots more German lessons. Catesby began to mentally rehearse his cover legend in case the Russian started to ask questions. His name was Karl and he had been a soldier in France – which, at least, was half true.

As they pulled away from the station, the Russian reached deep into the pocket of his coat. Catesby stiffened and thought he had been wrong about the friendliness. He expected to see a revolver emerge – but it was only a packet of cigarettes. The brand was called *Orbita* and bore an image of a red sputnik whizzing around the earth.

Catesby pointed at the sputnik and said, 'Belka and Strelka.'

The Russian nodded vigorously. At first, he seemed pleased that his new 'German' friend remembered the names of the two dogs that the Russians had launched into space and safely recovered the previous summer. Then the Russian stopped smiling and looked at Catesby with what seemed a slight turn of suspicion.

Catesby felt his stomach do a queasy flip. Had the Sovs actually announced the names of the bloody dogs or had he heard about them in a top secret briefing? He couldn't remember.

The Russian continued staring at him. His lips were moving as if he was rehearsing another German sentence. Finally, the Russian said, 'And there were forty mice – and two rats as well. All come back safe and healthy.'

'*Wunderbar*,' said Catesby.

Jutta half stifled a yawn with undisguised boredom.

The Russian extended the cigarette packet to Catesby to offer him a fag. Catesby shook his head and touched his chest. 'I don't smoke. I've got a lung problem.'

The Russian looked hurt. He hadn't understood the words, only the refusal of proffered friendship. He seemed to withdraw into himself, and he stood aloof and silent for the rest of the journey. At first Catesby felt guilty for having loosened the fraternal bonds between the people of the DDR and their Soviet brothers, but then he remembered that was part of his job.

When they got to Karlshorst all the Russians and a number of Germans got off the train. Catesby looked over Jutta's shoulder to see through the window. The name of the station was also displayed in Cyrillic letters as if it were a terminus of the Moscow Metro. There were Soviet soldiers in uniform on the platform – and Catesby could see the tops of army trucks parked under the birch trees in the station car park. Karlshorst was not a normal Berlin suburb.

For some reason the train remained stationary. Catesby was worried by the unexplained delay. He half expected to see a uniformed Vopo, an officer of the 'People's Police', enter the carriage to check IDs. During ID checks the Vopos usually worked with a partner from the MfS, State Security Service, who was always dressed in a smart black leather jacket and grey trousers. The MfS types must have watched a lot of Bogart films, but they never pulled off the sardonic sexiness no matter how much they tried. Catesby was relieved when he finally heard the electric motors wheeze into life as the train started up and began to move.

The carriage was now only a quarter full. As the train pulled out of the station a huge tank park full of T-34s was visible behind a chain link fence topped with barbed wire. Behind the tanks were grim rows of barracks in red brick. After Karlshorst and its dreary suburban backcloth, the train passed into a landscape of heath and woodland. The woods were mostly stunted pine and birch. The stops – Wuhlheide, Köpenick, Hirschgarten – were more village than suburb. The countryside between them had turned from sparse scrub into thick dark woodland. After Friedrichshagen the carriage was nearly empty.

'It's the next one,' said Catesby.

'I know,' said Jutta as she buttoned up her jacket.

Rahnsdorf was a completely lonely station in what seemed to be the middle of nowhere. Catesby and Jutta were the only passengers who alighted on the platform. Rahnsdorf was, thought Catesby, the ultimate 'choke point'. No surveillance team could follow you there without giving themselves away. And none had.

Once the train had wheezed away down the tracks they were completely alone. An eerie silence embraced them. Catesby loved silence. But he knew that some people feel threatened by it. They need to break silence with senseless talk or a radio station or a phonograph. He could see that Jutta was one of those. They descended the platform and crossed the tracks to a rusty gate. The gate squeaked when Catesby pushed it open and a jay screeched a harsh warning cry from the forest.

Jutta grabbed Catesby's sleeve. 'What was that?'

Catesby paused. It took him a few seconds to remember the German word for the bird. Finally, he said, '*Eichelhäher*.' The lapses in his fluency worried him; he didn't want to get caught out. It had already happened once. The jay worried him too. They were exactly the same species as English jays, but they looked larger and sounded so much fiercer. Maybe they had more to be fierce about. Or maybe the twentieth century had provided so much carrion to their diet that the jays had changed into loud-beaked carnivores. Catesby felt a chill run down his spine.

They crossed the unpaved potholed road that gave vehicle access to the station and set off down a forest path. In summer the path would have been crowded with Berliners carrying beach towels and picnic baskets as they headed towards the beach at Müggelsee, the largest of Berlin's several lakes. But now, on the first Saturday of a cold wet November, the beach path was empty and desolate. They walked along in silence, their feet muffled by a damp carpet of pine needles. Catesby kept his eyes on the path ahead. He was looking for the agreed rendezvous marker. He spotted the three stones sooner than he had expected – and was annoyed at the obvious way they were arranged in the middle of the path. He quickly kicked them apart and into the undergrowth. He shrugged his shoulders. You couldn't expect 'walk-in joes', untrained assets who thought they had something to sell, to be experts at tradecraft.

Catesby stopped and waited. Jutta continued walking until she was out of sight and out of earshot. It was important that she didn't eyeball BINDWEED; it was all strictly 'need to know'. And she didn't need to know anything. Catesby regretted bringing her along. He checked his watch; he was early. He decided to carry on down the path to make sure Jutta was out of sight. He walked about fifty yards, dipping in and out of the cover of the trees, and still didn't see her. Suddenly, he spotted something pale and low in the undergrowth. Catesby quickly and quietly retraced his steps. He didn't want Jutta to know he had seen her squatting for a pee.

When Catesby got back to the RV point there was still no sign of BINDWEED. He shifted nervously and wished that he had brought a gun. Both sides liked to play the kidnap game. Finally, he heard a branch snap and someone clearing his throat. He stared hard at the trees and saw a figure emerge who was dressed in a long black coat, town shoes and a flowing white scarf. BINDWEED looked far too urbane and bohemian to be a credible presence in the middle of a wood. Once again, Catesby frowned at the lack of tradecraft.

BINDWEED looked closely at Catesby and smiled. 'You look familiar,' he said, 'have we met before?'

'I'm sure we haven't.'

'My name,' said BINDWEED shaking hands, 'is Andreas, and that's my real name.'

There was, in fact, something familiar about the young man's face, but Catesby couldn't place him. The problem with the spy trade was that there were too many faces – from photo files as well as real life. More than one innocent civilian had been gunned down by mistaken identity. And on one occasion Catesby had accidentally brush-passed a secret document into the pocket of an unsuspecting stranger. He then had to mug the poor guy to get it back.

But this time Catesby was sure he had the right person. 'What have you got for me?'

Andreas leaned close. His breath smelt of menthol. 'A guy who called himself Roger said I should meet you here and that you might want to do a deal.'

Roger was Gerald's cover name.

'Roger,' said Catesby, 'thinks you might have something to sell, but we both think you're asking too much. You've got sixty seconds to convince me that it's genuine and that it's valuable.'

Andreas delivered his pitch. It was terse and businesslike. Catesby kept a stony poker face. Intelligence trading involved all the arts of haggling in a medina souk.

'How good's your Russian?' said Catesby.

'Not bad.'

Catesby tested him by asking him intimate questions in Russian about his mistress. Andreas's Russian was stumbling and schoolboyish, but the answers seemed convincing.

'Right,' said Catesby, 'what was the return address on the letter and the postmark on the envelope?'

Andreas gave the details and they matched up. Catesby was always suspicious that 'walk-in joe' intelligence might be fabricated at best – or a disinformation plant at worst. It was certainly not the latter. If the stuff was genuine, it was the last thing that Moscow would want the West to know about.

Catesby looked away and gave a bored sigh. It wasn't easy to keep up the act. He wanted the stuff badly. He wasn't sure what to do if Andreas didn't hand it over. During Catesby's initial training at Fort Monckton in the late forties they had all been taught how to break someone's neck, but none of the SIS recruits had taken the unarmed combat lessons seriously. The marine commando in charge had punished their flippancy with a long-distance run. Catesby now wished that he had paid more attention.

It was Andreas's turn to play souk trader. 'I can see that you're not particularly interested – I'd better be off.'

'I am interested.'

'Have you got the money?'

'I've got half of it – but there are strings attached.'

'What strings?'

Catesby looked closely at Andreas. 'In 1951 we ran an agent in Vienna who thought he was a gold mine – and expected a gold mine's profits. One day he said he could give us a full set of Soviet Army radio codes for fifty thousand US dollars. We paid up – and the codes were genuine and worth every penny. Fine. But the very next day our man turned up at GRU … you know them?'

'Soviet military intelligence.'

'That's right – and they've got lots of cash too. So our man, with a big Viennese smile, says to the Russian in charge, "I've got some important news for you – but it will cost you fifty thousand US dollars." The Russian general agreed because he knew this was a prize agent, and began to count out the cash. As the agent pocketed the money, he said, "I've just sold your top secret codes to the British." What do you think of that?'

'It sounded like a pretty stupid thing to do?'

Catesby smiled and shook his head. 'On the contrary. It was brilliant. The Russians were delighted because it meant they could use the compromised codes and radio frequencies to pump tons of false information our way.'

Andreas looked sceptical. 'How do you know he did this?'

'We know, because two days later our Viennese friend came back to us with a big shitty smile on his face and said, "I've got some *very* important news for you, but it will cost you fifty thousand US dollars."' Catesby smiled at Andreas. 'Wasn't our agent a clever lad?'

'Don't treat me like I'm stupid.'

Catesby looked at the ground and kicked a stone off the path.

'I think,' said Andreas, 'you've made your point.'

'No, I haven't.' Catesby grabbed the German by the lapel and pulled him close. 'You don't know what happened to our Viennese pal.'

Andreas stared at the trees for a few seconds; three blackbirds were huddled silhouettes on the bare branches of a birch. He finally whispered, 'Okay, what happened to him?'

'Nothing.' Catesby let go of Andreas's lapel and smiled. 'Nothing … that could be traced back to Her Majesty's representatives on the Allied High Commission. We used local talent: nothing written down, no names, no dates – just a sack full of used banknotes to pay them off. In fact, it was a pretty gruesome business.' Catesby paused. 'Have you ever been in a coal-fired power station?'

Andreas shook his head.

'Well, I hadn't been in a power station before that night either. It's all very efficient and logical. The coal is tipped on to conveyer belts which carry the coal to the furnaces. You can adjust the speed of any conveyer belt according to how much power you want to put out. In fact, you can lower the rate down to one centimetre per minute – so slow as to be almost imperceptible.' Catesby looked hard at Andreas. 'Except, of course, for the person lashed to a plank being fed into a furnace.'

The woodland around them was totally, eerily, still.

'Quiet, isn't it?' said Catesby. 'I thought about stopping them when they got out the bolt cutters – but I realised it was part of their procedure, part of the ritualised horror they use to keep other Vienna gangsters in awe and in line. In any case, they started by snipping off each toe beginning with the littlest … Do you know the nursery rhyme, "This little piggy went to market?"'

Andreas nodded.

'Well, they were singing it as they did the business … What's wrong?'

'Nothing.'

'Don't worry, Andreas, they stopped with the toes. They saved his other bits for the furnace.' Catesby cleared his throat. 'It was amazing how long it took him to lose consciousness – and then to die. Those guys are experts. Apparently, the gang are still at large – I suppose the cops don't want to tangle with them … And I've still got their number.'

The harsh rasping alarm call of a blue jay split the silence like a rusty saw.

Andreas looked up startled. 'What's that?'

'It's a jay, they can be noisy buggers. You're not a country person, are you?'

Andreas shook his head.

'They usually make that sound when they spot a hawk or a magpie. So don't worry, the warning wasn't meant for you. But … I have a warning for you.'

'What?'

'Don't ever, ever tell me a lie.' Catesby looked directly into Andreas's eyes. 'Tell me the truth. Have you passed on a copy of the letter to the East German Security Service?'

Andreas slowly nodded.

'That's bad. Have you passed it on to anyone else?' Catesby meant Washington, but didn't specify.

'No.' Andreas's face turned from chalk colour to grey.

Catesby tried not to laugh. Andreas was what the Americans called 'scared shitless'. Catesby had used the furnace story before and it never failed.

'I swear to you,' said Andreas, 'I'm not lying.'

'Don't worry, my friend, if you're straight with us we'll look after you.'

Andreas shifted nervously in the path looking at the ground.

It was good, thought Catesby, that Andreas realised the stakes and the sanctions. The Vienna double dipper may not have been slow roasted, but he hadn't got off scot-free. He had been shot, by Catesby personally, and deep-sixed in the Danube. The furnace story was a frightener tale that had been doing the rounds for some time. There were KGB versions, East End villain versions and Mafia versions. Catesby hoped it had never really happened.

In fact, Catesby hated violence. It was odd that both his adult jobs – soldier and spy – relied on violence. He justified his actions by rationalising that they prevented greater acts of violence. And now the greatest violence of all was hanging like an angry cloud over Britain and Europe – nuclear obliteration. Catesby didn't want his side to 'win': he wanted both sides to survive. And that was his biggest secret. A secret that some called treason.

'Let's take a walk,' said Catesby, 'I don't want anyone to see us standing here.' He touched the German's elbow. 'Come on, I'm not going to hurt you.'

They pushed their way through low-hanging pine branches. The ground sloped gently down towards the Müggelsee. The stillness was again shattered as a pair of jays swooped through the trees. Their warning cries were even more strident than before. It reminded Catesby how Suffolk gamekeepers can tell that poachers are about by watching for unexplained flights of woodpigeon or by listening for the bark of a cock pheasant.

Catesby suddenly stopped, took off his rucksack and removed a thermos flask. 'Would you like some coffee laced with *Weinbrand*?'

'Yes, please.'

While Andreas sipped the drink, Catesby unfastened the base of the flask by releasing a hidden latch and removed the rolls of bank notes that were hidden in the false bottom.

'Have you got the stuff?'

Catesby watched Andreas use a house key to unstitch the lining of his coat pocket. It was a feeble precaution, but better than nothing. Andreas reached deep into his coat. He finally fished out a film cartridge and handed it over.

'How do I know this is it?' Catesby hadn't expected to be given a film.

Andreas shrugged. 'If you don't think it's what I say it is, don't pay me.'

'Who has the original letter?'

'I didn't take it – I just photographed it.' Andreas smiled. 'I'm not brave enough to steal a letter like that. If Katya's husband had found out, he would have had me killed.'

Catesby turned over the film in his hand. Something else didn't add up. 'You just said you passed this stuff on to the DDR Security Service. How could you? It hasn't been developed and copied.'

Andreas smiled again. 'I photographed their copy on a separate roll of film.'

'Bad luck for you if they ask you to account for all the film they gave you.'

'I'll say I accidentally broke the cartridges while practising with the camera.'

He seemed to have all the answers, but Catesby didn't want to make an issue of it. Instead he pressed a wodge of banknotes into

Andreas's hands. 'We'll pay you the rest after we've had a look at the film.'

Andreas quickly stuffed them into his coat lining.

'Aren't you going to count them?'

'If you trust me about the film, I'll trust you about the money.'

'Exactly. And if your snaps of the letter are everything you claim, we'll give you a bonus.'

'Do you want me to break off with the Ministry for State Security?'

'No, they mustn't be suspicious. Keep on good terms – and keep passing them information. They'll know if you're holding back. But don't, my friend, tell them about this.' Catesby paused and smiled at Andreas. 'We'll know too.'

Andreas nodded. He didn't seem as frightened as he had before.

'Tell me more about Katya,' said Catesby.

'She's a very intelligent and a very wise woman.'

'Well educated?'

'She trained as a chemist, but prefers literature and languages. She's given me the complete works of Pushkin in Russian and tests me on them.'

'How good's her German?'

'Much better than my Russian.' Andreas smiled. 'And now she's learning Spanish.'

'Why?'

'I don't know.'

'Maybe she thinks Spaniards are better lovers.'

Catesby was surprised to see Andreas blush. He wondered if it was jealousy. He turned the screw. 'Has Katya any other lovers?'

'I don't think so.' Andreas paused. The question seemed to have touched a sore point. 'I'm sure she hasn't.'

'If she's unfaithful to her husband what makes you think she's going to be faithful to you?'

'Are you speaking from experience?'

Catesby smiled and looked coolly at Andreas. 'I'm not sure.'

The German finished the brandied coffee and handed the cup back. 'Don't play me for a fool. Who are you? I'm sure I've seen you before.'

'You're confusing me with someone else.'

'Maybe that's because you take so many different forms.'

'This is getting tedious.'

Andreas laughed and pointed a finger at Catesby. 'I know who you are. I remember.'

For a second Catesby was concerned that his cover was blown. He stared back. 'What's my name?'

'You're Mephistopheles and you want to buy my soul.'

'Wrong again. We don't buy souls. They're too expensive and they always turn rotten.' Catesby screwed the cup back on the thermos. 'But we might be able to give your mortal bits a new identity and resettle them in the West – if they proved valuable enough. Tell me more about Katya. We know she's a lot older than you, she's almost my age.'

'Not that old.'

'I look older because I've had a hard life, but I don't want to talk about that. I want to talk about Katya. What does she like a lover to do?'

'I think you should shut up.'

Catesby stopped. He realised that he was sailing on a bad tack. But ideally, he wanted to compile a complete and intimate file on Ekaterina Mikhailovna Alekseeva. Catesby knew that she and her husband weren't going to be stationed in Berlin forever. In fact, Lieutenant General Alekseev must be nearing the end of his tour. He realised that Andreas had just given an important clue. 'You said that Katya was taking Spanish lessons.'

Andreas nodded.

'What sort of Spanish? Castilian or Latin American?'

'I don't know.'

'See if you can find out.'

Knowing Alekseev's next assignment would be a little gem. Following the ebb and flow of key players was a vital part of the business. Where would the Russian turn up next? Buenos Aires, Madrid, Mexico City? It had to be somewhere important – not a backwater like Paramaribo or La Paz. And when the time came, Katya might want another lover. And how useful if that lover knew the ways to seduce her: where to touch and how to appeal. It was also important that the new lover learn how to blackmail her. It wasn't only documents that needed photographing. The camera was an essential bedroom accessory. Blackmail, as Catesby had long discovered, wasn't really such a cruel practice. It often gave the person blackmailed an excuse, even a moral justification, to do what they wanted to do anyway. Otherwise, it seldom worked.

'If you don't mind my saying,' said Catesby looking closely at Andreas, 'you seem awfully touchy about Katya. Have you fallen in love with her?'

'It began as a game – and then it became an obsession.' Andreas shrugged as if he had missed a train connection and there was nothing he could do about it. He clearly regarded his own character as a predetermined fate from which there was no escape.

'Don't you find it odd,' said Catesby, 'that you spy on her for money?'

Andreas blushed and shifted uncomfortably. 'It seems,' he said clearly groping for words, 'to intensify it.'

'You mean the sex – it makes it more exciting.'

'Yes, damn you.'

Catesby tried not to smile. He was amused by Andreas's prudery. He had once been like that. It was a young man's thing. 'You must,' said Catesby, 'keep your emotions under control. It's dangerous if you don't. You and I are pawns in this game – just like Katya. Her husband, I suppose, is a bishop or a rook. But none of us can move ourselves and we can never know when we're going to disappear as part of a gambit or tactical sacrifice. Katya must know this too and she would respect you for …'

'For what?'

'Combining love and realism. Just because we love someone doesn't mean that we don't use them.' Catesby paused. For a second he wondered if he was talking to himself or to Andreas. It didn't matter. We all need self-justifications; otherwise, the mirror image is unbearable to contemplate.

Andreas had his hands in his pockets and was looking at the ground. He seemed more relaxed, almost smiling. Catesby wanted to smile too. It was the warm glow of job satisfaction. It took years to become a good agent handler, a good interrogator. Threats, fear and torture only worked when you were looking for something simple, like the combination to a safe that could be verified immediately and on the spot. But such situations were very rare indeed. The best agent handlers became their agents' best friends: the fond sibling or soulmate that they had never had, but always longed for. And to do that best, the handler had to like his agent too. Catesby had begun, a little, to regard Andreas as a reincarnation of a dead infant brother. One who needed help with girl problems.

Andreas finally looked up and gave a sly smile. 'Katya isn't,' he said, 'a real blond.'

'And what else can you tell me about her?'

Andreas told everything in a flowing monologue of fondly remembered passion that included even the most fleeting of intimate details. He was clearly a young man in love. Nothing seemed sordid or pornographic as he recounted the various ways they made love. It seemed to Catesby that Katya was the more imaginative and experienced of the two. He began to envy Andreas with a certain bitterness.

'I have to go now,' said Catesby. He realised the *treff* had taken far too long and that Jutta would be concerned. He was about to make arrangements for further contacts when he heard a noise in the wood behind Andreas. Then he saw movement and someone emerging from the undergrowth. 'You shouldn't be here,' he snapped. For a brief second, he regretted the anger in his voice. Perhaps Jutta had come back because she was worried about his safety. But then he saw the gun.

The first two bullets hit Andreas in the face. His head jerked backwards and he crumpled. Andreas made no effort to move or to defend himself. Perhaps he recognised her – or perhaps he was paralysed with fear. Catesby saw the gun turn towards his own face. His only means of defence was the satchel with the thermos. He swung it at Jutta. She flinched and fired a shot wildly off target. Catesby then flung the satchel at her and started running between the closely planted conifers. He knew it wasn't easy hitting a moving target with a handgun. She fired two more shots. Catesby heard her stumble and swear. He kept running in a weaving crouch trying to plunge deeper and deeper into the undergrowth. She was coming after him, but couldn't aim and run at the same time. Each time she stopped to fire a shot, Catesby gained on her. Five minutes later he stopped and listened. The woods were now silent except for his own heavy breathing. He had flung himself into the thickest part of the wood, preferring cover as much as distance. His hands and face were heavily scratched by the thick weave of low branches that he had plunged through. There was no way that she could creep up on him without making a racket of snapping twigs.

Catesby decided that his cover was so good that it was safest to wait. Maybe she was listening and waiting for him to move. He looked at his watch; it would soon be getting dark. If she was going to find him, she had to make a move fairly quickly. As the minutes ticked away Catesby began to feel safer and safer. He wondered if she had given up the chase.

When he looked at his watch again half an hour had passed. Catesby decided to make a move. It was impossible to get out of the thicket without making noise, so he stopped every few yards and listened for answering sounds of stalking. There were none. After two more tentative moves, the grain of thought that had already been in Catesby's mind began to grow. He threw caution to the wind and began to move out of his prickly cover as quickly as possible. He finally came to a path which led in the direction of the lake. Catesby crouched beside it looking and listening for movement. Even the jays were silent. He was certain that she had given up the chase, if she had been chasing at all. Catesby knew that she had not intended to kill him. She had killed Andreas with cold competent professionalism. It was simply not credible that she had not been able to kill him as well. Catesby knew he wasn't part of the contract. She had been ordered to spare him. But why?

When Catesby reached the beach the opaque November sun was setting over the Müggelsee. For a second he wondered if Jutta was lying in ambush. He skirted wide of the concrete pavilion that had been built in the 1930s as part of the Strength through Joy sports movement. The pavilion's hygienic rows of showers, toilets and changing rooms, now clogged with layers of rotting leaves, were an ideal place to hide in waiting. Catesby sprinted past in a crouching run to the artificial white sand beach. An elderly man walking with two young children looked at him with curiosity. 'Why's he doing that, Grandpa?'

Catesby smiled. 'We're playing cowboys and Indians. Have you seen my little boy?'

'No,' said the old man, 'what's he look like?'

'He's ten,' Catesby made a hand gesture, 'about so high.'

'I hope you find him.'

'I'm sure he'll turn up.'

Catesby turned away and walked up the beach towards the setting sun. His cheeks were wet with tears. If only the fictional child were a real one. And if only he hadn't left a dead young man in the wood behind him. He hated violence and it always made him sick and depressed afterwards. He was in the wrong job. Catesby brushed away his tears and quickened his pace. He'd catch the S-Bahn train at Friedrichshagen and wanted to get there before dark.

It was a wet and cold Berlin night when Catesby got back to his office at Olympic Stadium. As always the adrenalin rush was being replaced by depression and tiredness. And the fact that there was so much still to do made him even more tired. He was tempted to have a beer and a bratwurst, but decided that strong black coffee and amphetamines were a better idea. He had started the pill popping – uppers and downers too – after Petra's death. It was one way of coping.

The first job was a cable to London. He went to the comm centre where he typed it directly on to the new DES encryption machine, a present from the Americans. He classified the cable UK Eyes Alpha and stated the barest facts.

Catesby needed to contact the BfV to let them know that Jutta was working for the other side. This was a more delicate business. He suspected that the organisation was even more penetrated by East German agents than he had hitherto supposed. It was obvious that the BfV officer who had chosen Jutta for the op was also one of Mischa's agents – and maybe the one above him too. Where did it stop?

On the other hand, was Jutta one of Mischa's gang after all? Berlin was a viper's nest full of spies. In any case, he needed to tell the BfV what had happened. They could form their own conclusions. Catesby decided to use the KY-3. It was an STU, a Secure Telephone Unit – another present from the Americans – and it used voice-scrambling technology. Catesby typed in the 'urgent priority' code and was soon put through to the senior duty officer. The conversation was mostly '*ja, ja, ja*' on the German side as if this sort of thing happened all the time. But despite the casual response, Catesby knew that a shit storm was going to erupt in the West German intelligence service.

Catesby signed the log so that the comm security officer would let him out of the centre. The door was blast-proof steel with massive bolts like a bank vault's. As the door wheezed open the security man said, 'Are you finished for the night, sir?'

'No, I've got to develop my holiday snaps.'

The stadium's lack of windows didn't make SIS Berlin Station a cosy place, but it did make it easy to set up a darkroom. Normally, there was a trusted and vetted technical grade who did the film and prints. But not this time. The nature of the intelligence service meant that on many occasions even the highest director grade had to spend tedious hours decoding a message, threading a tape recorder or printing a microfilm. The need for secrecy was a great leveller and no one could ever forget the basic skills needed to process raw material.

The most difficult bit is winding the tiny film strip onto the reel so that none of the surfaces touch – and doing it in utter darkness. Catesby enjoyed the delicacy of the task. It was like repairing something in a womb. The outside world no longer existed. Once the film was securely in the developing tank, Catesby turned on the light. This was the sorcerer's apprentice stage – developer, stop-bath, fixer and rinse. Catesby checked and rechecked the charts to make sure the temperatures and timings were correct.

The whole process took fifty minutes. When the timer pinged, Catesby poured the final rinse into the sink and unscrewed the lid of the processing tank. This was the moment of truth. Catesby carefully unwound the dripping film and held it up to the neon strip light. It had developed and the images were clearly documents, but were too small to read unless they were enlarged. He carried the film to the drying cabinet and hung it up, but hesitated before he turned on the heater. Ruining the film at this stage was the ultimate nightmare. Robert Capa's darkroom technician had done just that and destroyed nearly all of Capa's D-Day photos – after the photographer had nearly lost his life on Omaha Beach. No, thought Catesby, I'll be patient and wait for them to dry naturally.

As he waited Catesby began looking through the newspaper file. One of his staff prepared a daily news digest. It contained articles from public domain news sources in all the languages that Catesby could read. He regarded news reporting as a valuable intelligence source. Quite often the better sort of journalist uncovered something that the intelligence professionals had missed. But journalism, particularly from the big US syndicates and *Pravda/Isvestia*, was also valuable, perhaps more valuable, when the facts were wrong. *Why* were they wrong? *Who* was feeding the journalist disinformation? *Who* was pulling the ideological puppet strings? And *who* was going to benefit?

Catesby started with the economic section of *Isvestia*. It tested his vocabulary and had a certain surreal poetry:

The Krasnoyarsk Sibtyazmash Plant has made a metallurgical crane for Magnitogorsk. It has a hoisting capacity of 75 tons and an ingot stripping force of 250 tons.

He loved the heaviness of Russian names. He put aside 'News' and picked up 'Truth', *Pravda*. It was an important death, for the obituary was on the front page.

Chief Marshall of Strategic Missile Forces
Dies in Airplane Accident

Mitrofan Ivanovich Nedelin, Hero of the Soviet Union, perished yesterday in a ...

Catesby read the article twice, but found no clues other than terseness. He didn't find it odd that so little information was given about the actual crash or other fatalities. And neither would Russian readers. They were used to secrecy – and Nedelin may well have been on a visit or a mission that required secrecy. But there had been rumours.

The rumours originated from Berne, the Swiss capital. The city had always been a good listening post to pick up diplomatic indiscretions. Maybe it was the mountain air or Swiss neutrality, but people often blabbed in a way they would never dream of doing in Moscow or Washington. They seemed to think they were temporarily on a safe square and immune from surveillance. In any case, it started with a tale about a dead cosmonaut. The rumour was that the Russians had tried to surprise the world by launching a man into space – as a follow-up spectacular to the Sputnik dogs. But it didn't work. The capsule failed to separate from the rocket and consequently both capsule and cosmonaut disintegrated. Khrushchev, apparently, had been furious because he had planned to flaunt the achievement at the October Revolution parade. He had berated Nedelin for the failure – and poor Nedelin had slunk off and committed suicide. At least, that was the story doing the rounds.

Catesby sat back and tried to piece things together. A Russian man in space would certainly have upstaged the US presidential election which was due the very same day as the Bolshevik Revolution celebrations. It would have been a stunning propaganda coup that would have wiped the new US president off the front pages of the world press. No wonder Nedelin reached for his Makarov 9mm. It did add up – and air crashes were the usual Soviet cover story for suicides and other unnatural deaths.

Catesby put *Pravda* aside and started browsing the American papers. They were all full of the election which still seemed to be heading for a dead heat between Nixon and Kennedy. There was much discussion in the FO and SIS about which one would be less bad for Britain. Nixon was usually referred to as 'the shit' and Kennedy as 'the young warmonger'. Opinion seemed to prefer 'the shit' as the lesser of two evils and the easier to deceive. There was still bitterness about Kennedy's father, Joe, who as US Ambassador in London at the start of the war had relished the idea of a German victory. Son Jack was suspected of warmongering because he had campaigned on a totally fictional 'missile gap' between the USA and the Soviet Union. Catesby and his colleagues in the intelligence service knew perfectly well that the USA had ten times as many nuclear warheads as the Soviets. And there was also considerable doubt as to whether the Soviet Union had a single missile capable of reaching the USA. The grim fear in London was that a warmongering Kennedy presidency might panic the Russians into a pre-emptive strike against American bases in Britain – or that Britain would suffer retaliation for a pre-emptive US strike against the Soviet Union. Either way tens of millions of Britons would die. Personally, Catesby wanted to see the UK move towards neutrality – but it was an opinion he had to keep to himself.

The clock on the wall, like all the other clocks in the Berlin HQ, was run by battery – so that if war broke out and power lines were down they would still know what time it was. It was now half past two in the morning. What a lousy life. Catesby looked at the cut on his thumb; it was finally starting to heal. He had mistaken his thumb for an onion when he was tired and drunk and cooking a late-night meal in his bachelor flat. It was a lousy life. The only sound was the clock's second to second click. The second hand vibrated each time it moved and seemed to point at Catesby each time it reached the twelve. It was bad. It was the time of night he always thought of her when he lay awake. He was glad that no one could see him crying.

Catesby wiped his eyes and suddenly remembered why he was still there at three o'clock in the morning. The film. It must be dry by now. He went into the darkroom and turned on the red light so he could make prints. He took the film down – nicely dry – and threaded it on the enlarger spools. Work was good. His grief dissipated and the excitement of maybe discovering something filled its space. But he tried not to get his hopes up. Most of the stuff you gathered – and even paid good money for – was a waste of time. You had to pan through tons of silt before you found a nugget of gold.

The first frame was the beginning of the letter. He adjusted the magnifier so the Cyrillic letters came out in sharp focus. The person wrote in the clear script of someone used to doing technical work – like an architect or engineer:

Ground Control Station
Baikonur Cosmodrome
Kazakhstan

25 October 1960

My darling sweetest Katyusha …

Before he was even halfway through the letter, Catesby knew that he had panned gold. And he also knew he needed to fly back to England on the first available flight out of Templehof.

Catesby drove past the pub and parked the battered Austin A35 on rough ground behind the ridge of bulldozed shingle that stopped the North Sea from pouring in over the beach. The Suffolk coast was always at war. If it wasn't the Saxons or the Vikings, it was the sea itself – and the sea seemed likely to be the final winner. The autumnal tides were hungry and relentless and determined to have the Dingle Marshes that stretched like a vulnerable maiden between Walberswick and Dunwich. They had already had their way with Dunwich. In the thirteenth century the town had been one of the richest ports in England trading grain and wool for Russian fur, Flemish cloth and French wine. But the sea had finally swallowed everything leaving only the pub, a church and a few holiday cottages. In winter there was no one at all except for beach fishermen in oilskins long-lining cod. But Catesby loved the place. Suffolk was his home and he knew every river and forlorn muddy creek like the veins on the back of his hand. It was a secretive land that kept its mysteries to itself: a nocturnal land of poachers, smugglers – and spies.

Catesby took the letter out of his pocket and read it once more:

I wish you were here, my loving big sister, to wrap your arms around me and wipe my tears away – like you did when Papa and Volodya didn't come back in '45.

I want you to know, my darling Katya, that I am not badly hurt but that I still need you to chase away my nightmare. I feel like a child of three asking you to hold me again. When I close my eyes I can still feel your fingertips gently stroking my back to drive away Baba Yaga and all the other witches of the night. I felt safe because I knew that you were stronger than them.

What happened yesterday was worse than a nightmare, for when I opened my eyes it was still happening. I was very lucky – but I am still shaking with the dark exhilaration of escape and the shock of grief for those who did not escape. I owe my life to a technician who summoned me away from the launch pad to help solve a problem with the current distributor.

I was about forty metres away from the rocket when I heard the explosion. I turned around, but instead of fleeing I simply looked on. For a few seconds I was rooted to the ground by ghoulish fascination. I watched the orange fireball at the base of the rocket pulse outwards and swallow people and trucks. The heat burned my face and forehead, but I couldn't move for my eyes were fixed to a sight that was as magnetic as it was horrible.

The workers on the top level of the gantry were untouched, although everything below them, including the lower levels of the gantry, were consumed in flame. The poor men on the gantry looked like ants on the end of a burning branch in a bonfire. They knew they were doomed and started to run pointlessly back and forth. When the gantry was finally consumed, the men danced wildly like candle flames in the wind. Then dropped one by one into the fireball.

It was then that I realised that I was going to be next. A river of burning fuel was coming towards me. I began to run like I had never run before. The fuel had turned into a flood of fire as high as a tall man's knees. I looked behind and watched the burning flood lap across the tarmac and swallow my colleagues whole. The most awful moment was when their high-pitched screaming suddenly ceased. It was as if someone had lifted the arm on a phonograph record in the middle of an aria. At first I could not understand why the others were running so slowly, but then I saw their black galoshes. The enormous heat had melted the asphalt around the launch pad. My friends were screaming for help as they waded through a steaming black glue of freshly melted tar. Their clothes were on fire too. I watched helplessly as they fell into the sticky tar where they were engulfed by the spreading river of flames. Others managed to outrun the flames only to come up against the chain link fence where they were grilled like meat on a grate …

Catesby stopped reading and looked at his watch. It was time to meet Henry. He folded the letter, put it back in his pocket and got out of the car.

The cool sea breeze felt good on his face. He leaned against the car and looked around for his boss. Still no Henry. Finally, Catesby turned and tried to lock the Austin so he could go for a walk. After a while, he gave up trying. The door lock was too worn and loose for the key to turn. But it didn't matter; there was nothing important in the car. The important thing was on his person and he kept clutching his coat pocket to make sure it was still there. Catesby looked at the Austin. He had asked for the grottiest car in the pool and they had obliged. He felt a need to be inconspicuous and the last thing he wanted was a gleaming Humber Hawk that befitted his rank. The letter in his coat pocket had set the fires of paranoia raging. He touched it again to make sure that it was still there. He wished that he had written the translation on rice paper. If he got in trouble, that would make it easier to swallow. But the Webley.38 that heavily bulged his other coat pocket was intended to make that unnecessary. Catesby didn't like 'tooling up', but on this occasion he wasn't taking any chances. He was carrying a crown jewel.

Catesby climbed to the top of the shingle ridge and looked north towards Walberswick. It was getting dusk and the lighthouse across the river at Southwold had already started to blink – four flashes every ten seconds. Each light had its own code like an agent in place. Catesby searched the beach, but it was empty. He scrambled down the bank and started to walk in the opposite direction. Beneath the sand cliffs to the south there were still signs of life stirring in the twilight gloom. Two fishermen were unloading a broad-beamed beach boat; a boy of ten was throwing stones at the darkening sea.

But the dead, as often happened at Dunwich, outnumbered the living. The town hadn't stopped falling into the sea and never would until every brick and stone was gone. The recent tides had undermined the cliff face below the ancient churchyard. A jumble of thigh bones and ribcages were protruding from the sandy cliff below the green turf. It often happened after a storm, but this unearthing seemed exceptional. A figure in a black cassock was bent over something at the base of the cliff. As Catesby walked nearer he saw that the bent figure was gathering bones and putting them in a canvas sack.

'I've never seen so many bones here,' said Catesby.

The vicar answered without looking up, 'It's a plague pit.'

'What are you going to do?'

'I'm going to re-inter them in St. James churchyard – they should be safe, at least for the next few hundred years.'

Catesby smiled. His school friends had often cycled to Dunwich after a big north-easterly blow to gather bones. It was part of a

Suffolk childhood. He left the vicar to his work and continued up the beach towards Minsmere. Catesby was looking for his boss, the aptly named Henry Bone, but darkness was fast descending – and it was getting cold too. The wind had veered to the south-west and blew sand into his face. Dark clouds scudded across the sky and there was a spatter of rain. Catesby peered into the gloom and realised that the beach was empty. He turned around and walked back.

Catesby felt the emptiness grip him by both shoulders. The vicar had finished his gruesome chore; the fishermen had gone to the pub. As he walked past the cliff face of exposed bones Catesby felt something hit his shoulder. It was hard and solid like a stone. He looked down on the shingle. The object was white and round with flanges on the side. It was a lumbar vertebra. Catesby looked up to the top of the cliff. A figure in black was silhouetted against the less dark sky. It was his boss. Henry Bone normally lacked a sense of humour, but he must have found the joke irresistible.

Catesby nodded at Bone and both men walked in parallel until they converged on the level of the beach. When they met, Catesby reached out with the vertebra in his palm.

'Keep it,' said Bone.

'Thanks.'

'I assume, Catesby, this is important. I was enjoying a long weekend with friends – and I don't like playing the hush-hush drama card to disappear without explaining why.'

'I bet they love it – it makes them feel part of things.'

'You don't know them. In any case, why didn't you use the air bag? I was expecting a packet from an FO courier.' Bone was referring to the high-security diplomatic pouch that was flown to London each morning.

'I didn't want to take any chances – so I brought the docs myself.'

Bone looked closely at Catesby. 'Let's go further down the beach.'

Bone turned up his collar and put his hands in his pockets. The sound of their feet on the shingle seemed to echo the gentle sough of wave on shingle. Southwold Light kept blinking at them as if sending a Morse message. 'Have you heard anything from P3?' asked Catesby. In normal circumstances P3, Controller Eastern Area, would have been Catesby's line manager, but when Bone was swapped over to Director Europe/Sovbloc it was decided that Catesby (Head of E. Europe P) would report directly to Bone. It made sense because Catesby also ran Berlin Station – and when something happened in Berlin it needed to be treated urgently and go straight to director grade. But on this occasion, nothing had happened – in Berlin.

'According to P3,' said Bone, 'the general in charge of the Soviet Artillery Corps was killed in a plane crash.' Bone smiled. 'P3's encrypted Eyes Alpha cable arrived ten hours after I got the news from GCHQ – and one hour after I read General Nedelin's obituary in *The Times*. I think P3's retirement beckons.'

'Nedelin wasn't killed in a plane crash.' Catesby reached in his pocket and handed the translated letter to his boss. He suddenly felt a great sense of relief. The knowledge, and the responsibility that went with it, no longer rested on his shoulders alone. Catesby watched Bone squint to read the letter in the failing light. By the time he got to the end, Bone's face had drained of colour and his hands were shaking.

'Thank you for this.' Bone gripped the letter with both hands as if he were about to tear it to shreds.

Catesby looked on in silence.

'I assume,' said Bone, 'this document was photographed?'

Catesby nodded.

'Have you got the film negatives?'

Catesby handed him an envelope that contained the negatives and a print of the original Russian letter. It was a special 'burn' envelope that was permeated with a highly flammable substance. Bone folded the letter into the envelope and held it at arm's length. Catesby took a lighter from his pocket and ignited it. At the last moment, Bone pulled the envelope away and put it in his pocket. 'No, it's best I keep it.'

Catesby looked away from Bone and stared out to sea. The North Sea also kept its bleak mysteries – his own mysteries. Catesby's father was a dead Suffolk sailor; his mother, a Belgian. He knew his own identity was stranded halfway in that salty wilderness of quick fish and dead mariner. The sea was him: cold, grey and full of lost longing.

'You've gone all enigmatic again, Catesby.'

'Thanks for noticing.'

'I'd better get back to my kind and hospitable friends.' Bone tapped the pocket where he had put the letter and film. 'By the way, I'm going to classify this as Guard.'

'I always get told off when I try that one.'

Guard had been the highest security classification a British intelligence document could carry. It meant that the UK's closest ally, the United States, was denied access. But the use of Guard had been banned by the 1958 Mutual Defence Agreement with the USA.

'There's one exception,' said Bone. He looked directly at Catesby as if he were a prof prodding a dull student.

'When a secret is essential to the UK's national survival.'

Bone gave a bleak smile. It was his only smile. 'Have you revealed the contents of the letter to anyone else?'

Catesby shook his head.

'Was there a cut-out courier or dead drop?'

'No, the Romeo was a walk-in joe who contacted one of my officers?'

'What does your officer know?'

'He knows that Andreas was shagging Alekseev's missus. When I realised it might be something important I did the purchasing *treff* myself.'

Bone looked hard at Catesby. 'Had your Romeo been double dipping with the cousins?'

'Not yet, but he started out as an IM for Mischa's gang.'

'So the East Germans knew about the explosion all along – and they killed the Romeo for passing it on.'

Catesby frowned and looked out to sea. 'I know that our man passed on the stuff to the East Germans because he admitted it. They might have found out that he was double dipping with us. But I'm sure that's not why they killed him. Or if it was them.'

'In your cable you suggested that the gunman …'

'Gunwoman.'

'… let you escape on purpose. That seems unlikely.'

'You weren't there, Henry. Her shots were meant as frighteners not killers.'

'So Mischa wants us to know about the rocket disaster.'

Catesby shrugged.

'Of course he does, Mischa's no fool.' Bone almost whispered the words. 'He had to kill your Romeo to make sure he kept his mouth shut.'

'Could he be sending us a signal?'

Bone stared down at the shingle beach as if looking for a lost coin. 'I don't know. It would be very dangerous for him if he did.'

'So we ignore Mischa's message?'

'We don't ignore it, but we don't acknowledge it either.'

'Has it occurred to you, Henry, that the letter might be a plant?'

'No. It ties in with inconsistent reports of Nedelin's death that were monitored by GCHQ. It took Moscow more than a day to decide on a final version of how he actually died. And why would they want to make us think they're weaker than they are?'

'I don't know.'

Bone frowned; then looked out across the sea as if training his eyes on distant Russia. 'It's difficult enough keeping our own secrets from the Americans. And now someone wants us to help the Russians keep their secrets from Washington too.'

'What are you talking about, Henry?'

'Sorry, I was thinking out loud.'

'No, you weren't. You were testing me.'

'Perhaps, I was. But I'm looking for the answer too. It's not in the DDR's interest or in Russia's interest to broadcast Soviet weakness. So why has Mischa let us bag this gem?'

Catesby put his hands in his pockets and continued walking down the beach. The sifting sough of wave on shingle was like another voice. Some old dead Viking tongue you could almost make out, but too guttural for modern ears.

'Maybe I'm wrong about Mischa.'

'Or maybe,' said Catesby, 'he's giving us advance warning of Moscow's next move.'

'Their only move is the massive cover-up that they've already begun. Otherwise,' Bone paused and lowered his voice, 'some gung-ho American general may persuade his new president it's the last chance to thump the Sovs while they're down and out. It's very depressing.'

'Or Moscow could compensate by moving their medium-range missiles further west.'

'What?' Bone laughed. 'Sometimes, Catesby, I despair of your knowledge of weapons systems. Even if the Sovs moved their missiles up against the West German border, they wouldn't make it a quarter of the way across the Atlantic. Why are you smiling?'

'I wasn't thinking of East Germany – or anywhere in Europe.'

'Where then do you think the Russians are going to put their missiles?'

Catesby told him the name of the island.

Bone laughed. 'Don't be silly. See me back in London, I really must be going.'

Catesby watched Bone disappear into the gloom, then turned and walked along the beach alone and desolate. He had of late begun to envy Bone his social life. At first Catesby had imagined his boss as a miserable middle-aged bachelor who spent his weekends dusting his collection of eighteenth-century enamels and playing Tchaikovsky on the baby grand. But it wasn't like that at all: the weekends were more likely to be spent shooting, sailing or rock climbing. Henry Bone had a glittering, but discreet social life and a circle of even more discreet friends. And since the Wolfenden Report the need to be 'discreet' was no longer so pressing. Catesby sometimes wondered if Henry had an active love life, but he was reluctant to ask directly. In any case, Bone was a quintessential product of his mandarin English upbringing and past. Henry had at least once in his life suffered great emotional hurt, but never showed it or discussed it. Catesby admired his dignity.

Catesby continued crunching through the shingle as if summoned by Southwold Light. He wondered if he should carry on to Walberswick where the Blyth poured into the sea. There was a pub that would do simple suppers of fish and brown shrimp. Catesby knew the fishermen who propped up the bar, but the landlord was new. The fishermen always took the mickey out of his 'success'; they thought he worked in the Foreign Office and always called him 'Ambassador'.

Catesby stopped and listened to the night sounds. The North Sea sucking at the shingle; the communal piping of the oystercatchers from Dingle Marsh; his own breath. He wouldn't go on to Walberswick. He wasn't in the mood for jolly banter – and he could feel the tears coming. He counted the months. Twenty-three of them had now passed. Maybe there would have been a baby by now – and maybe another one on the way. The tears were really coming now. He looked out across the North Sea and tried to send his heart across the water and on to the cold Baltic to where he had last held her in his arms. He began to shout her name like a madman over and over again. Then he stopped and waited. But there was no reply. He turned to go back to where he had left the car. He needed to go back to London where he'd whisky himself to sleep and then spend a lonely Sunday in a nearly deserted Broadway Buildings reading cables and writing reports.

Catesby stopped and looked once more across the sea. The tears welled again like drops of molten iron. 'My job killed you,' he whispered, 'my job killed the only, the only … '

He wiped his eyes and continued walking, then stopped and reached for the gun in his pocket. But instead his fingers touched a folded piece of paper. Catesby remembered that he had saved a copy of the letter for himself. It was deceitful, he should have handed it over to Bone. Catesby took it out of his pocket and squinted at the words in the dying light.

… Those nearest the launch pad – including Marshall of Artillery Mitrofan Nedelin himself – were incinerated instantly.

I am more atheist than ever, but I will leave Babushka to believe in her old lies. There is no heaven or hell except what man creates. I don't know whether man can create heaven, but I know that he can create a hell beyond the imagination of any painter of medieval icons.

The fires continued to burn for more than two hours until well after dark. There was a full moon and the night was very cold. I was surprised at the way some of the bodies, naked and hairless, seemed to glow like phosphoresce in the moonlight. We had to scoop them up on long sheets of metal, otherwise they disintegrated like a fragile lace of ashen paper. There is nothing left of those nearest the rocket. Someone said the only remains of Marshall Nedelin are two molten keys. There are more than a hundred dead, perhaps 200, but most of the bodies will never be identified because there are no bodies to identify. I am sorry to have to tell you that Vasya, the young chemistry genius with the shy smile who turned beetroot red whenever a woman spoke to him, is among the missing. I know that you had a soft spot for Vasya – we all loved him. The fire at the centre was 3000 degrees.

This is a serious and tragic time for our Motherland. Most of our best scientists and rocket engineers are now dead. Mitrofasha ignored the safety rules because of haste. Nikita Sergeyevich had wanted the new rocket on display for the October Revolution parade. If the truth were known our country would spend 7 November in mourning instead of celebration.

I am sure that Zhenka already knows about this. It certainly would have been his job to brief the Ambassador. But perhaps he hasn't told you. When it comes to state security there are certain secrets a husband must keep from his wife – and, likewise, my sending this letter to you is one secret you must keep from Zhenka. And when you have read this letter you must destroy it. We have all been sworn to secrecy. Marshall Nedelin and all the others are going to be reported as having been killed in plane crashes. The truth must never be known.

Your devoted brother,
Arkasha

Catesby's eyes were now clear and dry again. He was back at work. He realised that he had been wrong to keep a copy of the letter. He tore it into tiny fragments and tossed them into the night wind which carried the particles into the North Sea. They dissolved like snowflakes as they touched the water.

It was quarter past seven and a very wet morning. Catesby had walked from his flat in Pimlico to Broadway Buildings in St James's. It was so early that the NDO, the Night Duty Officer, was still at his desk in the foyer. As Catesby put his dripping brolly in a rack with a dozen other brollies that were expertly rolled and dry – the taxi and car brigade – the NDO looked up. 'Mr Catesby.'

'Good morning, Captain Nowell.'

'Director Bone would like to see you.'

'Tell him I'd like a cup of tea.'

The NDO smiled at the impertinence and picked up an internal telephone.

Bone's office windows faced across to the headquarters of the London Underground. It was, playing on the double meaning, a somewhat apt view for a spy chief. It was also, considering Bone's dislike of modernist art and sculpture, a cruel irony to impose such a view on him. The Underground building was a feast of modernity. There were sculptures by Gill, Moore and Epstein. The sculpture that glared most directly at Bone's office was Epstein's *Morning* which featured a naked man, presumably the father, holding a child with an abnormally long penis.

Bone was standing behind his desk with his reading glasses sliding down his nose. He looked animated and was waving a piece of paper at Catesby. 'Have a look at this.'

Catesby took the document.

JOINT INTELLIGENCE COMMITTEE ASSESSMENT OF CURRENT SOVIET BALLISTIC MISSILE PROGRAMME

UK EYES BRAVO: STRAP 2 CAN/AUS/US EYES ONLY

LEDGER DISTRIBUTION:
FO - PUSD
CABINET OFFICE
ODA US EMBASSY
CANADIAN HIGH COMMISSION
AUSTRALIAN HIGH COMMISSION

1 NOVEMBER 1960

FROM: HENRY BONE, CBE; DIRECTOR FOR WEST EUROPE AND SOVIET BLOC, SECRET INTELLIGENCE SERVICE

There has been much speculation surrounding the recent death of Marshall Mitrofan Ivanovich Nedelin in an air crash. Marshall Nedelin was commander of the Strategic Rocket Forces development programme. Although Marshall Nedelin had neither a scientific nor an engineering background, his role was not merely symbolic. His primary function was to motivate and coordinate design teams. Nedelin's attempts, however, to pressure scientists into working in rigid military-style frameworks were often counterproductive. His methods inhibited ingenuity and creativity. Therefore, it would be wrong to regard Nedelin's death as a setback to the development of the R-16 and future Soviet ICBMs.

Our latest estimates suggest that the R-16 has a maximum range of 13,000 kilometres carrying a 'light' warhead of 3 megatons and a max range of 11,000 kilometres carrying a 'heavy' warhead of 6 megatons. We cannot definitively state whether or not the R-16 ICBM is currently operational. It would, however, be reckless to assume that it is not. The Western intelligence services have a poor record in predicting a timetable for Soviet military development. The successful test of a Soviet Atomic bomb in 1949 took place three years sooner than our most dire intelligence estimates.

THIS PAPER WAS DISCUSSED BY JIC AND APPROVED ON DATE.

As soon as Catesby finished reading, he stared past Henry Bone at the new paintings hanging behind his desk. There were three watercolours of what seemed to be exotic wildflowers. The execution was precise and detailed.

'What happened to the Poussin?'

'It was only on loan.'

'You're distancing yourself, aren't you?' Catesby knew perfectly well that the loan of the Poussin had been obtained through the good offices of an eminent art historian, who had once been an SIS agent. The ex-agent's name was no longer mentioned, even whispered, in Broadway Buildings.

'I suppose I am. One would be a fool not to. Would you like a cup of tea?'

'Yes, please.'

Catesby watched Bone go to a Regency sideboard to pour the Earl Grey from an Echinus Demotter tea service. The cups and saucers were delicate creatures with gold rims and spider's web patterns. Catesby was always terrified of chipping the china.

'When,' said Bone, handing Catesby his tea, 'you first had Earl Grey I had to stop you from putting milk in it. Please sit down.'

Catesby sank into an armchair and juggled the tea and his bowler hat on his knees. He had come such a long way, from the poverty of the backstreets of Lowestoft, and Bone always liked to remind him of it. The jibes were never malicious; they were more the praise of a schoolmaster reminding a favourite pupil of how well he was progressing. Catesby smiled at Bone, 'Where's my slice of lemon?'

'I haven't got any – very forgetful. What do you think?'

Catesby looked at the JIC paper.

'No, of the watercolours.'

'The craftsmanship is superb, but I'm not sure there is anything else. In other words, refreshingly unpretentious.'

'Well done. They're by Vishnu Prasad. He painted them for British naturalists in the nineteenth century who were recording the flora and fauna of India.'

'Government Art Collection?'

Bone nodded.

'Do you suppose,' said Catesby, 'that they will let you take them with you when you go to Wormwood Scrubs? Look awfully nice on your cell wall.'

'No, William, I'm not going to be arrested.'

'Are you sure? I can't imagine anything more serious than intentionally deceiving – lying actually – to JIC.'

'I wouldn't be the first.'

'But has anyone ever done it so bluntly?'

Bone paused as if lost in thought, 'Probably not – but the seriousness of the situation justifies the deceit.'

'Who else knows?'

Bone handed over a second document. 'I don't want you to think that I'm completely mad and reckless.'

Private and Confidential
TO BE OPENED AND READ ONLY BY THE ADDRESSEE

From: Office of the Director for West Europe and Soviet Bloc
Broadway Buildings
London

2 November 1960

To: The Rt. Hon. Harold Macmillan MP
10 Downing Street
London

Dear Prime Minister,

I am sure you read my JIC assessment with a large pinch of salt. You understand the UK's current predicament more than anyone. I discussed similar contingencies with you when you were Foreign Secretary in 1955. The current situation is even more dangerous. It would not be melodramatic to say that the existence of the United Kingdom is more at risk than ever before.

Much depends on the outcome of the American election. Neither result augurs well for our country, but I feel that a Kennedy presidency would be more dangerous. Much of Kennedy's election rhetoric has focused on the mythical 'missile gap'. Such irresponsible scaremongering could lead to unpredictable and disastrous outcomes. As you know, contrary to Kennedy's false claims, the United States has a strategic nuclear advantage over the Soviet Union of at least twenty to one. The Russians have no missiles that can reach the US mainland. As long as this American invulnerability exists, the position of the United Kingdom remains precarious because we, unlike our American allies, are not invulnerable to Soviet retaliatory or pre-emptive strikes. We are on the wrong end of 'the vulnerability gap'.

The worst contingency would be that the US military will persuade the incoming president to launch a 'preventative' attack against the Soviet Union. The awful reality is that such an attack would be perfectly logical in terms of narrow US national self-interest. The attack would eliminate once and for all a future Soviet threat and the United States itself would remain untouched. Unfortunately, our own country would be destroyed. The Soviet armoury of medium-range nuclear missiles is more capable than ever of the complete devastation of Britain and Western Europe even as a second strike. In the eyes of our main NATO partner, we would be a sacrificial pawn. There is, sadly for us, no faulting the cold logic of such a plan.

Our best assessments suggest that the 'vulnerability gap' will close within the next three to four years. By the mid-sixties, the Soviet Union will have achieved 'mutually assured destruction' parity with its American opponent. Until that happens, the survival of our island will be in the balance. Meanwhile, vis-à-vis the Americans, it is in our own national interest to exaggerate Soviet nuclear capability and to play down Soviet weakness.

I hope that you will have the time to meet me privately to discuss the situation in more depth.

Yours sincerely,
Henry Bone

Catesby handed the letter back to Bone. 'Has the PM agreed to meet you?'

'We already have. We had whiskies at Downing Street yesterday evening.'

'Was he angry at what you had done?'

'Not particularly, he was in a melancholy mood and quoted Homer at me.'

'In the original?'

'Of course – you didn't do Greek?'

Catesby shook his head. 'You'll have to translate.'

'I remember rendering the line in my own schooldays: *Men grow tired of sleep, love, singing and dancing sooner than war*.'

'Was he talking about himself?'

'Maybe a little. The PM is not a pacifist.'

'That's why he accepted the Thor missiles.'

'You hated that, didn't you, William?'

'Macmillan's worse than Eden and Churchill – at least they weren't American poodles.'

'The PM is a pragmatist – or likes to think he is.'

Catesby studied the dregs in his teacup – of finest china. He looked at his bowler hat, lightly blotched by raindrops. What had he become? Once again, he counted off the ideals he had grown up with: trade unionism, the solidarity of the working class, socialism – and the abolition of war. He remembered the 1930s when wages were cut and a baby next door died because the family didn't have the 2/6d to call out the doctor. The doctor would have come anyway, but they had too much pride – misplaced pride. The same sort of useless pride that made governments keep Britain's pointless nuclear bombs – and even invite the Yanks to bring theirs, like the Thors, on to British soil.

'You've gone all thoughtful, William.'

Catesby looked up. 'I'm going to resign.'

Bone slowly shook his head. 'No, you're not.'

'You think you can stop me?'

'Yes.' Bone's eyes glinted like a knife blade behind his glasses.

Catesby smiled bleakly and quoted what had become their shared mantra:

'*Under the spreading chestnut tree,*

I sold you and you sold me.'

'That's right, William, and nothing has changed. If you ever try to leave the service you will be stitched like no one has ever been stitched before – but, of course, as you descend that dark hole into chokey you can drag me after you. Would you like another cup of tea?'

Catesby's return to Berlin was marked by tedious and bad-tempered interviews at BfV HQ concerning the Jutta incident. The BfV, which was supposed to be West Germany's principal Security Service, had a terrible record of infiltration from the East. In 1954, the very Head – *Präsident* – of the BfV had fled to the DDR in the wake of a spy scandal that implicated fifty-four serving officers. Things didn't seem to have got much better. Catesby spent a lot of time talking in private to the new *Präsident*, Hubert Schrübbers, who was certainly not a DDR agent, but suspected everyone else in his agency. 'I have two officers,' said Schrübbers, 'who are blaming each other for assigning that woman to you. There are no incriminating documents, so I am going to have to suspend both.'

A day later Catesby received a cable from Bone summoning him back to London. But before he could leave, Catesby had to attend a BfV interrogation that turned into a screaming match as one of the officers under suspicion accused Catesby of being implicated. The summons back to London could not have come at a worse time; Catesby knew it would make the BfV think his own bosses had doubts about him. Before storming out, Catesby pointed his finger at his accuser and called him a piece of *Scheisse*. 'The only reason I'm going to London,' lied Catesby, 'is to get enough information to nail you to the shithouse wall.'

The real reason for his urgent recall to London turned out to be, in Catesby's eyes, utterly banal. It was a 'social' event – exactly the sort of thing he loathed. The US Ambassador, John Hay 'Jock' Whitney, had invited a load of Brits from FCO and SIS to spend election night at the embassy to listen to the voting results as they came in – a 'historic' event. Bone and Catesby were on the list of invitees and there was no way either could refuse to go. Since the US versus UK punch-up over Suez, the mood music in London was transatlantic reconciliation and friendship. Catesby hated it – especially the 1958 Mutual Defence Agreement. It meant that Britain had just pipped Alaska to become the forty-ninth state.

It was the first time Catesby had been to the new US Embassy. The Americans had moved to the opposite end of Grosvenor Square from the eighteenth-century townhouse they had passed on to the Canadians. The new embassy was brashly modern. A huge gilded bald eagle, the size of a bus, appeared to be swooping down from the roof with wings outspread. The eagle didn't fit in with the clean lines of the building: it was too ornate. The power symbol was more important than aesthetics.

As Catesby showed his invitation to a marine guard, he reminded himself of the rules: don't get drunk; don't insult anyone; don't get into a fight. It was nearly midnight, but the election results from the earliest states still hadn't come in.

The first two hours were dull, but not unpleasant. Catesby milled around through various function rooms, drinking non-alcoholic cocktails and nibbling proffered canapés. The grub was impressive. Catesby made a point of talking to Americans instead of Brits and of being polite – and didn't have his first alcoholic drink until it had gone two a.m. As he loosened up, he had a long chat with a history professor from Princeton who had been seconded to the State Department as an advisor. The professor was obviously cultured, but self-effacing. 'I really haven't travelled much beyond the library, so you could say I'm a bit of a provincial booby.' Catesby heard the echoes of ancient Rome. He realised that behind the veil of modesty and subtle charm was a confident and cosmopolitan scholar close to the Emperor's ear.

The election results were now streaming in. There were radios relaying the news located throughout the reception rooms where knots of people gathered. Kennedy was, as expected, sweeping most of the East Coast states. It was now after three o'clock and Catesby had found a comfortable armchair in a reading room full of print media. There were newspapers and magazines galore – including several in foreign languages. Catesby eschewed *Le Monde* for a copy of the *Los Angeles Times* printed on extra-thin paper for air transport. The front page reported that Clark Gable was recovering from a heart attack. He had just finished filming *The Misfits* with Marilyn Monroe. But it was an item on an inside page that caught Catesby's attention:

Atomic War Civil Defense Exercise

An experimental radiological shelter at Camp Parks, California, was occupied for a period of 48 hours by 99 men, women, and children. Ages of the participants ranged from about 3 months to 68 years. Family size ranged from single persons to a family of seven. Children of all ages appeared to adapt well to shelter conditions, but the importance of careful preparation, organization, and control of activities was demonstrated.

He remembered the ominous warning that he had heard from Bone years before: 'It is not enough for the Americans to survive the Cold War; they want to win it.'

Catesby folded the paper on his knees and closed his eyes. He soon drifted into a brief interlude of peaceful sleep – followed by the usual nightmare. The voices that swirled around him were Spanish, French and Dutch and full of urgency. The dream always ended the same way. The bolted oak door splintering, the clang of swords … and finally Catesby pathetically pleading, desperate to save his life, that he was a spy working for the Queen. They never believed him.

'Mr Catesby.' The voice was gentle American, almost a whisper. Catesby opened his eyes. The young man in front of him was handsome in a front office sort of way. 'I'm sorry to disturb you, sir, but the Ambassador has invited you to his residence.'

'How nice of him.' Catesby immediately wondered if he should have said 'His Excellency'. He never got protocol right.

'Would you like to come with me? There's a car waiting.'

There were several cars waiting – all black Cadillacs flying the Ambassador's flag. A chauffeur in livery held open a rear door. There were already three on the back seat. The very pretty wife of one of Macmillan's most promising ministers slid onto her husband's lap and patted the seat beside her. Catesby slid on to the seat and felt the wife's shins tightly nestle against his thighs. 'Hello,' she said offering a gloved hand, 'I'm Valerie.'

'I'm William,' said Catesby.

'D'you know Jack?' she said leaning on her husband.

'Of course, how are you doing, Jack?'

'Nice to see you again, William,' said the minister, also lying.

'Any idea what this is all about?' said Catesby.

'I believe,' said the minister, 'that Jock is going to give us a champagne breakfast.'

London was pre-dawn damp and empty as the cavalcade of limousines left Grosvenor Square and turned up Baker Street. The Ambassador's residence was at Winfield House, a neo-Georgian mansion set in twelve manicured acres of Regent's Park.

'Any idea who won the election?' said Catesby.

'Driver,' said the minister.

'Sir?'

'Could you turn on the radio and try to get a news station?'

As soon as the driver turned the knob, Catesby realised it was already tuned to the UK station of American Forces Network. The presenter's voice was clear and strong:

> *Senator Kennedy, aged 43, is a Harvard graduate and war hero. He will be the youngest elected president in US history and the first Roman Catholic. We are now going direct to Hyannis Port, Massachusetts, where President-elect Kennedy is giving his victory speech.*

There was a brief pause and some static. The transatlantic connection made Kennedy's voice fluttery and unearthly as if he were a creature from outer space.

> *I can assure you that every degree of mind and spirit that I possess will be devoted to the long-range interests of the United States and to the cause of freedom around the world.*

As the car purred through the gates of Winfield House, Kennedy was still talking. They would now prepare for a *'new administration and a new baby.'*

Although Winfield House, built in 1936, was fake Georgian, the hand-painted Chinese wallpaper was genuine eighteenth-century. It seemed to Catesby that Ambassador Whitney had gone to a lot of expense to create an ambience that was elegant without being vulgar. The breakfast itself was, however, a little over the top: poached eggs with Hollandaise, scrambled eggs with smoked salmon, eggs Benedict, Virginia ham, wafer-thin pancetta bacon, sausages various, hash browns, kippers, smoked haddock, bowls and bowls of fresh fruit, freshly squeezed orange juice clunking with ice cubes, American pancakes and waffles, every pastry imaginable including croissants and *pain au chocolat* that must have been flown over from Paris. The idea was that you served your first helping from a buffet. After that, champagne, coffee, tea and additional helpings were brought to you by servers – most seemed to be Filipino.

Catesby found himself at a table with three other Brits. The only one he recognised was Charles Hill, who enjoyed the splendidly ludicrous title of Chancellor of the Duchy of Lancaster – a sort of minister-without-portfolio job. Hill was, however, more famous as the 1940s 'radio doctor' who wrote the Ministry of Information recipe book, *Wise Eating in War Time*. As Hill tucked into a second serving of hash browns and bacon, he caught Catesby smiling at him and smiled back, 'Yes,' said Hill, 'it is a bit ironic – but you have my permission to tuck in.' With his black round spectacles, twinkling eyes and slight pudginess Hill looked exactly like the avuncular GP he was. Catesby strained to hear the conversation Hill was having with the other two. They seemed to be gossiping about a woman.

'Very pretty, very feminine,' said Hill, 'splendid ankles. And her main charm is that she does not look a career woman, but speaks with the clarity of a barrister. The best of the '57 intake.'

'Well she certainly seems to have enchanted you.'

The oldest of the three looked up from his eggs Benedict. 'What's her name, Charles?'

'Margaret Thatcher.'

A waiter came around and recharged their glasses with champagne. The most tipsy of Hill's companions proposed a toast, but Catesby was distracted by an American voice speaking softly at his side. 'Excuse me, Mr Catesby.'

'Yes.' Catesby detected something in the American's manner that explained the real reason he had been invited. It wasn't for reasons of protocol.

'Ambassador Whitney would be very pleased if you would have a word with him.'

Catesby nodded an apology at his table companions and followed a slim young American who exuded the relaxed assurance of his country's elite. It was an assurance that both charmed and annoyed – and Catesby knew he was going to experience it in bucketfuls when he met the Ambassador. Jock Whitney was a champion polo player, horse breeder, movie producer and war hero. He had so charmed the Queen and Duke of Edinburgh that they addressed each other by first names – an unprecedented relaxation of protocol.

The Ambassador's private study was more modest than the rest of Winfield House. It was comfortable and functional rather than grand and elegant. The furnishings were antiques, but not priceless ones. There were oil paintings of horses and photographs of Whitney's stepdaughters – and his polo team. As soon as Catesby was shown in, Whitney got up and warmly shook hands. 'Thank you for coming to see me.'

'Thank you for inviting me, Ambassador.'

'Please drop that nonsense, just call me Jock.'

The name triggered a memory in Catesby's mind – Jock for jockey. 'You nearly won the Grand National.'

Whitney gave a theatrical sigh. 'That was heartbreaking. Easter Hero twisted a plate and we were beaten by a nose. Are you fond of steeplechase?'

'Not particularly, I prefer football.'

'Soccer?'

'That's the one.'

'I've always been passionate about sport – but I'm only good at the ones us spoiled rich things can afford to play.'

Catesby was surprised by the frankness.

'May I offer you something to drink – brandy, coffee, tea, more champagne?'

'No, thanks.'

'I must confess ...' Whitney sounded genuinely embarrassed, 'that I have an ulterior motive for asking to see you.'

Catesby shrugged and put on a blank look.

'Betsey, my wife, is Kit Fournier's aunt. Kit was her favourite nephew. I only met him once. He seemed a very complex young man – and extremely witty and utterly likeable. I believe you knew him?'

The name Kit Fournier hit Catesby's ear like a pistol shot from close range. It was as if a complete stranger had casually said, 'You caught your wife flagrante and you buried her and the lover under the patio' – and it was all true. Catesby struggled to keep a straight face, for the Fournier file was one of London's most closely kept secrets.

'Yes, I knew Kit. We were both stationed in Bonn in the early fifties.'

'Were you doing similar jobs?'

Catesby looked directly at Whitney without blinking. 'I was in the consular section at the British Embassy.'

'I see.'

Catesby wondered how much further Whitney was going to push.

'Well, I'm having coffee,' said Whitney pushing a button on his desk intercom, 'I hope you will have some too.'

'Yes, please.'

Whitney placed the order. His voice, as ever, polite and non-magisterial. Catesby meanwhile began to put pieces together. The American elite were just as incestuous as the British – the same few families. He remembered that Betsey, Whitney's second wife, had been married to James Roosevelt, the president's son. The divorces and the revolving marriage beds didn't matter. They were still the same gang – and Kit was part of it too. If, thought Catesby, the Americans had got to Fournier first, there would have been a cover-up instead of a trial. The Brits did the gang a favour. A smiling Filipino entered with the coffee tray and shuffled out again wreathed in Whitney's warm thanks.

'Did you meet Kit when he was stationed in London?' Whitney was pouring the coffee.

'No, unfortunately.' Catesby knew that Whitney knew that he was lying again, but he had to go through the ritual.

'And they still haven't found a body?'

'No.' Truth was easy.

'Is there anything I can pass on to Betsey?' There was a note of faint pleading in Whitney's voice – oddly vulnerable in a man so rich.

'We can't assume that Kit is dead.'

'Thank you.'

Catesby immediately wondered if he had given too much away. But something in Whitney's manner suggested that he had an inkling of the truth. A word, perhaps, from a polo-playing Argentine who had contacts on offshore islands.

'What,' said Whitney changing the subject, 'do you think of Kennedy's election?'

Catesby shrugged.

'Of course, you can't say. You're supposed to be a diplomat.' Whitney paused. 'I hope you don't think my office is bugged.'

'I don't think it is. I'm sure you wouldn't tolerate it.'

'Not if I knew about it. In any case, William, since you are in no position to express an indiscreet opinion, allow me. I didn't want Nixon or Kennedy to win – and I'm sure that Eisenhower felt the same way. I love my country and I don't like the way it's going.' Whitney paused and stared hard at Catesby. 'But you don't like my country at all – or Americans.'

'I don't think that's a fair comment.'

'And it's unfair of me to task you with such a comment. And, of course, you can't be sure that this office isn't bugged.'

'It doesn't matter. I would say the same things regardless.'

'Well I'm going to continue with my indiscretions because there are messages I want to pass on before I leave this job.'

'But …'

'Please, William, the humble diplomat story is getting threadbare.'

Catesby sipped his coffee.

'I've chosen you,' continued Whitney, 'because in an odd sort of way our views coincide. I believe that my country has become increasingly enthralled to a group that could destroy us all.' Whitney paused. 'And it's not just my own family who are at risk. Nonetheless, my view is more commonly held by people of my … how can I say it?'

'Filthy-rich old money.'

'Thank you for being so succinct. In fact, we've got so much filthy lucre the stuff is an embarrassment. Our working weeks are spent giving away millions rather than accumulating them. I assure you that philanthropy is harder work than greed – the decisions are more complex.'

'Do you feel superior to the new rich?'

'Good heavens, no. The new rich aren't any different from our ancestors – completely amoral. But whereas our ancestors built railways, drilled oil wells, manufactured motor cars, exploited mines; the new rich have discovered something even more profitable – weapons. Not just old-fashioned guns and canon, but aircraft carriers, hydrogen bombs, ballistic missiles, submarines. They're not just greedy and amoral – they're dangerous and out of control.' Whitney looked closely at Catesby. 'Do you find my views eccentric?'

'A little unexpected perhaps.'

Whitney picked up a piece of paper from his desk. 'I'm going to read you a quote. See if you can guess the author. "Every gun that is made, every warship launched, every rocket fired, signifies in the final sense a theft from those who hunger and are not fed, those who are cold and are not clothed."'

Catesby shrugged. 'I don't know – sounds like someone on the very liberal left?'

The Ambassador smiled. 'President Dwight D. Eisenhower. It's going to be part of his speech when he leaves the White House. And Ike will conclude with,' Whitney read again: '"We must guard against the acquisition of unwarranted influence, whether sought or unsought, by the military-industrial complex."'

Catesby frowned. 'It's a pity he didn't follow that advice when he became president.'

'At least he's giving it now.' Whitney paused. 'You're a hard nut to crack. I'm trying to recruit you as an ally to a cause that you already believe in.'

'You don't know what I believe.'

'If that is so, then I've been misinformed.'

'Who informed you?'

'People who are … how should I say … your enemies.'

Catesby knew there was a long list, especially in the CIA. Two years previously, one had threatened his life and had to be physically restrained from throwing him back into the freezing Baltic. 'I'm giving you a list of contacts that someday you might find useful.' Whitney picked up a piece of notepaper from his desk and handed it over.

Catesby saw that it was typed for the sake of anonymity. There were three US telephone numbers with codenames.

'Don't mention my name if you ring them,' said Whitney, 'they will immediately hang up, for they know that real names are never used. But whatever happens, you must never forget that I am a deeply loyal American – and defender of our Constitution.'

Catesby stared at Whitney. The man was more old-school American than George Washington and Thomas Jefferson. He wondered what game he was playing at.

'I'm going to let you go now,' said Whitney, 'but I want to say one more thing, just one word.'

Catesby sensed the most important message of all was coming.

The Ambassador smiled bleakly and whispered, 'Cuba.'

Cuba. The word echoed ominously in the office before the machine clicked.

Bone then rewound the tape back to the beginning. They had already heard it twice. 'What in heaven's name, Catesby, possessed you to go to that party wired up?'

'Nothing much. The new gear seems light and easy to use. I wanted to give it a test run. I also thought I might catch a drunken American off guard.'

'But not the Ambassador?'

'He was cold sober.'

Bone looked at the tape recorder. 'There's almost enough there to blackmail him for a surreptitious contact with an intelligence officer from a foreign state, but I can't see what we would gain by it.'

'Maybe a hot tip for the Kentucky Derby?'

Bone frowned. 'Or maybe the contact was authorised by the outgoing administration?'

'Could be. A case of being demob happy and reckless.'

'It is worrying, however, that Whitney seems to have some info on Fournier. Maybe Fournier should have been killed instead of stashed.'

Catesby bit his lip to keep it shut. There was a ruthless side to Bone that troubled him more and more. There were times when Henry Bone behaved like a fugitive on the run who needed to eliminate anyone on his tail.

'I need a cup of tea,' said Bone, 'what about you?'

'I'd love one.' Catesby noticed that the Echinus Demotter china had been replaced by two chipped mugs. He watched Bone boil an electric kettle and wondered if his boss's stock had fallen in Central Stores.

'Milk and sugar?' said Bone. 'It's ordinary navvy's tea.'

'Milk.'

Bone handed Catesby a mug and opened an office drawer. 'Spot of brandy?'

'That'd be lovely.' Catesby sensed that Bone was going through a scruffy period. They usually occurred at times of change and uncertainty.

'I think,' said Bone, 'that you were right.'

'About what?'

'About Cuba. Things have started to slot into place.'

'But, Henry, it's not your area of responsibility.'

'Nonsense, I'm Euro/Sovbloc – and Cuba is now Sovbloc.'

Catesby sensed a wonderful demarcation punch-up in the offing. 'How's DP3 going to feel about you poaching on his patch?'

'It's already resolved and approved by C. I don't want the bother of running a big op. I've asked for only one officer in Havana, who will be directly responsible to me. DP3 was pleased as Punch that I didn't push to control the whole shebang.'

'Another bloodless Henry Bone coup.'

'How's your Spanish?'

'I can manage a menu.'

'Don't worry, Catesby, you're a good linguist and you've got a few months to learn. Meanwhile, I want you to tidy up in Berlin.'

'The BfV business has gone septic. The guilty bastard is trying to frame me.'

'That could be useful.'

Once again Catesby felt he was being dangled over a precipice. He looked blankly into space.

'It won't be like last time,' said Bone.

Catesby turned and stared at his boss without blinking. He wondered if Bone had any awareness of human pain – or was simply good at hiding it. 'I'm sure, Henry, it won't be.'

'But first, I want you to go to America to follow up one of Whitney's leads. And there's a perfect pretext for your visit.'

'I bet you want me to go under cover as a vacuum cleaner salesman – so I can clean up a reputation or two?'

'No, something much more credible – and necessary. I've managed to trace one of the phone numbers that Ambassador Whitney so indiscreetly provided. I was pleasantly surprised. It could be a way of making amends.'

'What have you done to my brother, you fucking bastard?'

Catesby was actually afraid that she was going to attack him, claw his eyes out. Her hair was disordered by rain and wind; her eyes were dilated and bloodshot. She had driven down to the Eastern Shore from New York as soon as she finished her shift at Bellevue Hospital.

'I've just had a patient die from multiple stab wounds – a beautiful sixteen-year-old Puerto Rican boy. God, how I wish it had been you instead. That boy had so much more right to life.'

'Caddie ...' A slight middle-aged man was whispering to the angry woman and trying to guide her away by putting his arm gently around her waist. The man was her and Kit Fournier's Uncle George. Catesby could see that George, despite being a retired Army officer, was one of life's gentle makers of peace.

'I'm okay, Uncle George. I'm sorry I created a scene.' Caddie had started to cry. The tears seemed to make her more composed. Meanwhile, George's wife Janet remained at the dinner table oblivious to the swirling drama and poured herself another drink.

Catesby was surprised at how quickly everything had unfolded. He had landed at Friendship Airport that very morning. His intention had been to take a taxi to Washington and book into a hotel under the false name he was using for the trip. But on impulse, he had phoned the first of Ambassador Whitney's secret numbers. It was the least secret of the three because it had been so easily traced by Bone's operatives. It seemed that Whitney had almost orchestrated the visit.

Catesby had fumbled putting a dime into the airport payphone slot. He found US coins small and slippery. He dialled the number and after ten long American rings, a man with a very gentle voice said, 'Yes.'

Catesby answered with the code words, 'Point Comfort Light.'

'Where are you?'

Catesby told him.

'I'll come and pick you up. We'd like you to stay here.'

'That's very kind of you. But,' Catesby lied, 'I'm already booked into a hotel and have hired a car.'

'What a pity. My wife and I were so looking forward to having you as our guest. We don't have many visitors. Can't you change things?'

The sincerity of the voice made Catesby agree. In any case, he knew that Fournier's uncle and aunt were the least likely people to do him harm. When George arrived to pick him up at the airport, it was already noon. Catesby had forgotten about American distances and regretted tasking a man of seventy with so long a drive. George's car was a 1940s grey Chevrolet – the most modest American car Catesby had ever seen. George was hatless wearing a tweed jacket – the very image of shabby gentility.

As they drove off, George ground the gears. 'Clutch going,' he said.

Catesby watched the countryside as they drove east towards the Chesapeake Bay Bridge. It reminded him of his native Suffolk, except for the endless parade of billboards and advertising hoardings.

'Your visit,' said George, 'wasn't completely unexpected.'

Catesby remembered Fournier saying that George had made his career in army intelligence. Although highly respected and influential, he had never got the general's stars he deserved. There was a hint that George had retired on a matter of principle.

'I'm not going to ask you,' said Catesby, 'how you knew about my visit.'

'Thank you, I didn't want to have to make something up just to be polite.'

'I suppose you want to know more about Kit?' Catesby was too tired for small talk.

'And so does Hilary, Kit's mother, my sister.'

'Is she going to be at yours?'

'No, she lives in France.'

Catesby also knew that George would want to know about something closer, more painful. He didn't want to leave it hanging in the air. He said the words as gently as he could, 'Jennifer was your daughter.'

George winced as if struck in the back by a sharp elbow.

Catesby suddenly realised that, thoughtlessly, he had used the past tense. He stared out the car window. 'I'm sorry.'

'You must be exhausted. Have a snooze if you like. I often doze off in cars.' George laughed. 'Usually when I'm driving.'

Catesby closed his eyes to leave George alone with his grief. The details of the Kit-Jennifer affair were not very pretty. Kit Fournier had been tortured by a lifelong passion for his cousin. It destroyed him. And gave the British Secret Intelligence Service their biggest coup of the decade. Catesby sank into his seat. The upholstery was softer and the engine rhythm of the old American car was far more soporific than a British banger. He was soon asleep.

When Catesby woke up they were on a straight road with fields on one side and thick woods on the other. The only signs of houses were grey metal mailboxes on posts.

'How was your nap?' said George.

'Good. Much farming here?'

'Cattle, pigs, corn, some tobacco. Around here they call it sotweed. I refuse to grow it – it ruins the soil.'

'Have I missed the bridge?'

'That was long ago.'

The countryside reminded Catesby of the Norfolk Broads. It was as if he hadn't come so far after all.

'As the crow flies,' said George, 'we're only a couple miles away, but because of all the meandering creeks we've got another ten miles by road.'

The house, white clapboard built in the 1780s, was just as idyllic and isolated as Kit Fournier had described it. There was a paddock studded with mature chestnut and oak that sloped lazily down to a deepwater creek with a jetty and a moored sailboat. The banks of the 'creek', a river in Catesby's terms, were thickly wooded with no sign of human habitation. It was, he thought, just as virgin as when Captain Smith discovered Pocahontas – and sotweed. Catesby wondered if Kit Fournier had fallen as much in love with the place as he had Jennifer.

Catesby was given the bedroom of Jennifer's oldest brother, Peter, who had been killed in Southeast Asia in '45 – a month after the war was over. It was a confused and regrettable incident that Kit blamed on the British. And now there was even more to blame the Brits for. As Catesby unpacked his things he was struck by the utter quiet and isolation of the farm. If someone wanted to kill him, this was the ideal place. No one would hear his screams and, if they had enough anchor chain, no one would find his body.

Dinner began with oysters washed down with Chesapeake Bay Bloody Marys. The oysters were from George's own bed in the creek. Catesby helped dredge them up using an enormous pair of tongs that were ten feet long. The main course was ham, fried tomatoes and potato salad. Everything came from the farm or the creek. 'If you come in summer,' said George, 'you will have the Chesapeake's *pièce de resistance*: the blue-tipped crab. The crab is the essence of Maryland: be it, soft-shelled fried, steamed, soup or crab cake.'

George's praise of the crab reminded Catesby of a story that Kit had told him about a drowned tramp who was pulled out of the bay with two dozen plump crabs clinging to his body. Kit had related the story when he was drunk and tired. They had just had a big argument about a German double agent that Kit had helped kill. 'When it comes down to it,' Kit had said, 'we're just meat.'

Catesby liked George and Janet, although she said little. Her life was a constant *stabat mater*. She had lost both her sons and now a daughter. Janet used drink to dull the pain and no one blamed her.

It was a wonderful meal, but the drink was completely out of sync. George was drinking his own homemade cider, Catesby had a dusty bottle of 1935 Spanish rosé and Janet was tossing back bourbon. George joked about the rosé. He said it was a present from a friend who had fought in the International Brigade and that it was time to 'drink the evidence' before the House Un-American Activities Committee turned up. Catesby understood why Kit had fallen in love.

They had finished eating when the door opened. It was a stormy night with rain and hail pattering against the windows and no one had heard the car. As soon as Caddie realised who Catesby was she started screaming.

Things eventually turned calmer. George had taken Catesby and Caddie to a small sitting room on the end of the house. Janet remained in the dining room drinking alone. The sitting room was untidy and much lived in. There was an open fire warming a dog that looked like a Labrador with tightly permed hair. George said, 'Hello Max,' and bent over to give the dog a scratch and a pat. Max groaned with pleasure.

'Is he a Labrador cross?' said Catesby.

George looked pained. 'No, Max is a Chesapeake Bay Retriever. I suppose they are related if you go back a long way.'

Catesby sat in an armchair closest to the fire enjoying the fug of seasoned oak and damp dog. Caddie and George were on a chintz sofa facing him. Catesby was aware that Caddie was staring at him. Her eyes were neither friendly nor hostile, but clinical – as if Catesby were a recently admitted psychiatric patient and she was considering medication. The silence was growing oppressive.

'I suppose,' said George in a voice that suddenly had a harder edge, 'that we have to cut a deal.'

Catesby looked at the dog. Max had one eye open and was staring back. Catesby thought it best to deal with the most painful issue first. 'Shall we begin with Jennifer?'

George nodded, his eyes crossed with pain. Caddie took his hand in both of hers.

'I never saw her body, but don't take that as forlorn hope. I'm certain that she is dead.'

'What happened?' George's voice was barely a whisper.

Catesby stared into the fire. He didn't want to lie, but he wasn't authorised to tell the whole truth. 'She was shot, along with her husband, late at night on an English beach while awaiting an exfiltration rendezvous with a Soviet fishing trawler.' No lies, but sanitised.

'Who killed them?'

Catesby didn't answer. He just stared into the fire.

Caddie was on her feet and shouting again. 'You did.'

Catesby faced her. 'No, I didn't – and I didn't authorise it either.'

'But you were there?' George's voice was calm and perceptive.

'Yes, I was – as a hostage.'

The other two looked perplexed. 'What?' said Caddie.

Catesby grimaced with frustration. The truth of the matter was more bizarre and less credible than any lie he could concoct. Sometimes you lied because the lie was more believable. 'Jennifer and her husband had kidnapped me. Their controller wanted them to bring me to Russia with them.' Catesby paused; then raised his voice. 'At least that was what I was told, but maybe I was just a dupe in a larger, more complicated plan.'

'And,' said George, 'Jennifer was killed in a gun battle?'

Catesby looked away and didn't answer. The whole truth was too hard, too ugly.

Caddie intervened, 'Why won't you …'

'I think,' said George, 'we know enough.'

'She was a beautiful woman,' said Catesby.

Maybe it was just a trick of the firelight, but Caddie seemed to frown sharply at the remark.

'And,' said George, 'it is completely certain that Jennifer was working for the Russians?'

'Absolutely certain.'

'In a way,' said George, 'I'm not altogether surprised.' He looked at his niece for confirmation. Caddie shrugged. 'Jennifer,' continued George, 'was incredibly idealistic from an early age. When she was seven she invited Negro children to come to our house.'

'Did they?'

'Oh yes, and we received them with open arms. We're not prejudiced. But then Jennifer, unknown to us, started giving her clothes away to Negro girls.' George paused. 'I don't think our poor daughter understood. One day a group of the girls' parents turned up and returned all of Jennifer's frocks. She didn't understand how she had hurt their pride. Her young Negro friends never came again.'

Catesby reflected on his own country's upper classes. They would never have made that mistake.

'She became even more difficult as a teenager. Jennifer seemed to turn her anger against her own family.' George looked at Catesby. 'Some of our ancestors, I must confess, did own slaves. Personally, I am ashamed of the fact, but I pleaded to her that we were not responsible for their sins. But Jennifer thought we were responsible for those wrongs. She wanted us to sell the farm and give the money to the NAACP. Maybe she was right. Once she said to me that our family, our very country, was under a curse because we had stolen the land from one people and enriched it by the slave labour of another.' George looked into the fire. 'It's difficult to deny those facts. And, somehow, Jennifer decided that becoming a Russian spy was the best way to put things right.'

As the final pieces of the Jennifer mystery slotted into place, Catesby felt guilt as well as longing.

Caddie had put her arm around her uncle, but was still looking at Catesby. 'Can we,' she said, 'talk about my brother?'

This, Catesby knew, was the beginning of the real bargaining. The confirmation and details of Jennifer's death, in isolation, were dealing chips of little value. He decided to put his opening card on the table. 'Your brother is still alive.'

'And safe?'

'Very safe.' Catesby smiled. Fournier was a crown jewel. 'Safer than any of us.'

'Where is he?'

'In a safe place.'

'You're starting to annoy me – intensely.' Caddie's eyes were smouldering.

'Caddie,' said George.

'Sorry.'

'I'm sorry,' said Catesby, 'if I sounded flippant.'

Caddie smiled for the first time. 'We're one sorry bunch too.'

'In a way, we rescued your brother. The choices facing him were a life in Moscow or in one of your prisons.'

'I assume,' said George, 'that you can't tell us where he is?'

'I can't do that or I'll end up in one of our prisons.'

'I apologise,' said George, 'for haggling like a souk trader, but what's on offer?'

'I've already handed over quite a bit, more than authorised. I'm sure a letter to your congressman or a telephone call to a journalist could create a nasty diplomatic incident and get me sacked.'

'Is that all that's on offer?'

'No.'

'But,' said George, 'you want to know what I'm giving you in return.'

'Crudely, yes.'

'First of all, it will be nothing that would embarrass the United States government or compromise the activities – the legal and authorised activities – of our intelligence agencies.'

Catesby thought that 'legal and authorised' was an interesting caveat, but wanted to remain unimpressed. 'I'm not sure that's enough to justify my agreeing to deal about Kit.'

George looked at Catesby with hard gimlet eyes. He wasn't as soft as his voice. 'What I can give is – how should I say – a series of perspectives on various aspects of current military and intelligence thinking.'

'Merely thoughts?'

'No.'

'And documents?' said Catesby

George turned slightly pale. 'And documents.'

'And what do we get?' said Caddie. 'Do we get my brother back?'

'No, but you get immediate access to him via letters – letters which, of course, will be censored.'

'Not much.'

'Take it or leave it. There's also the possibility of a future telephone link, once again supervised. And also, but not anytime soon, Kit's eventual release.'

George intervened. 'Think how much this will mean to your mother.'

'It's not my decision, Uncle George, you're the one who has to stick your neck out.'

'Don't worry, Caddie, I'm not going to end up in Leavenworth. In fact, they might give me a medal. I say we do it.'

'Fine, let's do it then.' Caddie sounded less than enthusiastic. 'I suppose I'd better go see how Aunt Janet is getting on. Would either of you like a drink?'

George gave his niece a reproving look. As she left the room, he turned to Catesby. 'She can be very acerbic, but there's a loving side too.'

'She's a lot different from Kit.'

'Caddie thinks she's the strongest of the three – the other sibling is a playwright.'

'Are you still in the intelligence loop?' Catesby wanted to get back to business.

'Unofficially. I was on Ike's staff during the war. He used to call me in from time to time for a chat. But I doubt if Kennedy will do the same – new generation, clean broom sweep.'

'Who do you know who's still in power?'

'The Joint Chiefs of Staff – all of them. I know Allen Dulles, but don't get on with him – and quite a few other CIA types including Angleton, Bissell and a somewhat loony one called E. Howard Hunt. But most importantly, I have a network of covert contacts. I can't give you their names, but they pass things on to me because they know I'll protect their identity.'

Catesby nodded. George was the sort of informal and trusted channel that kept governments from going off the rails.

'In the past, I sometimes passed on news of covert operations to Eisenhower. More often than not, Ike was surprised to find that they even existed and angry that he was kept in the dark. But for the last year or so I've been frozen out.' George looked closely at Catesby. 'I consider myself a sort of watchdog, but I feel I've lost my bark as well as my bite.'

'What's the most important thing that you've got to tell me?'

'That the ruling classes in this country are at war with themselves.'

'That's not an unusual state of affairs.'

'I agree, but what's happening in Washington has never been more dangerous for the rest of the world.' George stopped and smiled at Catesby. 'Don't I sound like a portentous ass? You must find us Americans awfully self-dramatising.'

'Only when you don't admit it.'

'Touché. I have, by the way, done a bit of acting. So I will continue.'

'Please.'

'At bottom, Eisenhower is a civilised man, but he lost control. Maybe it would have been better if he had died after his heart attack in '55 – or not run the next year.' George got up and gestured to a watercolour over the fireplace. 'That's a skipjack dredging oysters. For conservation reasons they're only allowed to dredge under sail.' George lifted the painting from its hook and handed it to Catesby. He then worked the combination of the wall safe. The thick steel door squeaked open and George reached inside to remove a paper bundle bound by black ribbon, then looked at Catesby. 'You wanted documents?'

Catesby nodded.

George closed the safe and re-hung the picture. They sat together on the sofa. 'The first thing we should look at is the latest SIOP.' George undid the ribbon and rolled out the first document. It was headed TOP SECRET SPECIAL HANDLING NOFORN. The acronym meant 'no foreign nationals' were allowed to see it. 'I'm not, by the way, just trying to buy access to my nephew. This is information that our British allies should know about. I'm not being a traitor.'

Catesby felt sorry for George. The American needed to reassure himself that he wasn't betraying his country. Catesby knew the feeling well.

'Are you familiar with SIOP?' said George.

Catesby nodded. It meant Single Integrated Operational Plan. It was the combined nuclear war plan for the US Air Force and Navy. It comprised a list of targets and the weapons to be used to eliminate them. There was nothing more secret.

'As you can see,' said George pointing to the document, 'these are the minutes of a recent Joint Chiefs of Staff meeting. It's pretty easy to see which individuals are the patients and which ones are the mental health professionals.'

Catesby's eye fell on an exchange between Albert Wohlstetter, a RAND strategist, and General Powers, Commanding Officer of the Strategic Air Command.

```
WOHLSTETTER: The counterforce strategy requires
SAC to restrain itself from hitting Russian cities
at the beginning of hostilities.

POWER: Restraint? Why are you so concerned with
saving their lives? The whole idea is to kill the
bastards. At the end of the war if there are two
Americans and one Russian left alive, we win!
```

Catesby looked up. 'Surely, Power was being ironic?'

George shook his head. 'Our four star generals are never ironic. Politicians need to accept their words at face value.'

Catesby recollected a drunken conversation he had once had with a US military attaché. 'Someone once told me that LeMay, even LeMay, thinks that Power is mentally unstable and sadistic.'

'That's correct – and could be the very reason LeMay appointed Power to command SAC. If the person commanding those bombers isn't crazy, who's going to believe we would ever use them? Would you like a drink?'

'Yes, please.'

While George went to fetch the whisky, Catesby leafed through the document. It was clear that SIOP called for a massive global attack deploying the entire US nuclear arsenal of 3,200 warheads. He was bleakly pleased that UK intelligence had accurately estimated the size of the US arsenal. But what UK intelligence hadn't apprised was the inflexibility of the US nuclear war plan.

George came back with a half-empty bottle of bourbon and two tumblers.

'Your SIOP is all or nothing,' whispered Catesby.

George nodded as he poured the drinks. 'The worst thing is that countries that are not even involved in the coming war are going to get hit. Look at the target list. Every single East European bloc country is there. It doesn't matter how much their people may object to Soviet rule: the brave Hungarians, the Poles and even the poor Latvians. They all get incinerated. And non-European countries too: China, North Korea, North Vietnam – and now,' George lowered his voice, 'Cuba.'

Catesby held up the document and smiled bleakly. 'This reminds me of what we used to say in the war.'

'Go on.'

'When the Germans open fire, the British duck. When the British open fire, the Germans duck. But ...'

'But when the Americans open fire, everyone ducks. I've heard that one before.'

'Sorry.'

'You don't,' said George, 'hold our military in high esteem.'

'I shouldn't judge.'

'We're not all bad – some of us are even on the side of the good angels. Do you know David Shoup?'

Catesby shook his head

'David is the Marine Corps Commandant. He's the only one of the Joint Chiefs who's stood up to General Power. May I?' George took the JCS minutes. 'Listen to what David had to say, he was very angry: "Any plan, General Power, any plan that kills millions of innocent Chinese, when their country isn't even in the war, is not a good plan. It's not the American way."'

Catesby noted how Shoup used 'American' as a synonym for 'moral'. That, in a way, was scary too.

George was smiling. 'I must say, Power's reply was a real gem.'

'What did he say?'

'"We can't leave out the Chinese targets, General Shoup, that would really screw up the plan."'

'The plan, of course,' said Catesby, 'is not just a military one. The intention is to completely exterminate communism as if it were an infectious disease. It doesn't matter how many civilians die in the process.'

'There is an evangelical side to many Americans. It is worrying.'

'Do you think this situation will continue under Kennedy?'

'I hope not, but it could get worse.'

'There's going to be a battle for Kennedy's ear.'

'Or another part of his anatomy – to put them in a vise. I am not sure that our new president realises how ruthless and devious his senior generals can be. These are men with enormous egos who think they are gods. And Kennedy certainly has his own weaknesses. He might want to prove he's just as tough as them.'

Catesby remembered how valuable the bits of gossip that Fournier enjoyed relating had turned out to be. It was clear that SIS needed more gossip and seedy secrets to build up a profile on the new president.

George looked closely at Catesby. 'The first crisis is already brewing and about to boil over. Kennedy wants to knock off Castro and invade Cuba.'

'He hasn't been in the White House five minutes.'

'New presidents tend to hit the ground running. Two days after the inauguration Lemnitzer turned up in the Oval Office with this.' George passed over another document. Beneath the security classification was the title OPERATION ZAPATA. 'By the way, do you know Lyman Lemnitzer?'

'I met him in Germany just after the war. I didn't like him. Whenever we tried to send a load of Nazi war criminals to Nuremberg, Lemnitzer's gang sent them to South America.'

George smiled wanly. 'Lyman Lemnitzer is now Chairman of the Joint Chiefs of Staff.' He sipped his bourbon. 'The most powerful military man in the United States.'

'Do you like him?'

'I hate him, strong words I know. But I didn't hate Lyman to begin with, I thought he was charming and intelligent – he was always smooth and smartly turned out. He looked the part. We were both on Eisenhower's staff. I outranked Lemnitzer, but he outmanoeuvred me – and then outranked me too. He's a dangerous man because he doesn't look like the monster he is. He's long been an advocate of a surprise nuclear attack on the Soviet Union.' George finished his bourbon. 'But now that the Russians have their own intercontinental ballistic missiles to hit back, no US president would ever sanction it.'

Catesby felt a chill run down his spine. The truth was otherwise. The words he had memorised from the letter danced before his eyes like the flames on the Baikonur launch pad: *This is a serious and tragic time for our Motherland. Most of our best scientists and rocket engineers are now dead.* The importance of that secret made him nauseous. Catesby needed to change the subject. 'Tell me more,' he said, 'about Cuba.'

'It's a tempting operation for the new president. It would prove that his tough words on communism are not just rhetoric. The plan is for an invasion by anti-Castro exiles which will spark off a popular uprising. But it won't work. I spent a lot of my career in Latin America. Gringo is not a compliment. Most of the people don't like us. Why? In my lifetime we have overthrown or undermined forty Latin American governments.'

'Then why can't you get rid of Castro?'

'I meant we can't get rid of him by a popular uprising. That's poppycock dreamed up by idiots in the CIA who believe their own propaganda. The only way we can get rid of Castro is by invading Cuba with a hundred thousand American soldiers. It would be a bloody mess even if it did work. It would spark off riots in Latin America and give Khrushchev an excuse to take Berlin. If Kennedy has a brain, he'll keep the military out of this stupid invasion thing.'

Catesby started leafing through the ZAPATA document. The plans looked vainglorious and doomed.

'And when it fails,' said George, 'things are going to turn nasty. Look at the AMLASH section – those are proposed plans to assassinate Castro ...'

The word AMLASH made Catesby sit up. It was also the codename of one of the telephone contacts that Jock Whitney had passed on. Catesby turned his attention back to George.

'... and I've heard that Lemnitzer is cooking up an agent provocateur scheme called NORTHWOODS. Stupid man.'

'You mean false flag ops?'

'That's right. Lemnitzer has this theory that we can stage a series of terrorist attacks on US soil and blame them on Castro. The idea is that the American people will be so angry it will be politically impossible not to invade Cuba. That's what happened when the *Maine* blew up in Havana harbour in 1898.'

'You sank her on purpose?'

George shrugged his shoulders. 'Who knows? But it gave us an excuse to invade Cuba – and grab the Philippines from Spain at the same time.'

'What,' said Catesby, 'would you do if you were Head of British Intelligence?'

George's watery blue eyes looked unbearably sad as well as frank. 'I'd dig a very deep bomb shelter – or emigrate with all my loved ones to Australia. I don't think that you fellows have a chance. Your island is in the wrong place at the wrong time.'

'Thanks.' Catesby smiled. 'I'll tell him that.'

'I'm going to bed. I'm a silly old man who talks too much.'

Catesby sat alone for a while in the sitting room watching the fire turn into ash and embers – and tried not to think of London doing the same. There were sounds of cutlery coming from the kitchen. He turned out the light and went to help.

Caddie was standing over the kitchen sink with her back towards Catesby. There was a radio tuned to a classical music station playing Copland's 'Appalachian Spring.'

'Shall I do the drying up?' said Catesby.

'No, I'll do it. I know where things go, to put them away. You can finish the washing.'

Catesby slipped on the washing-up gloves that Caddie had just slipped off. He was oddly content. There was something calming about shared domestic chores.

'I'm not sorry,' said Caddie, 'that I called you a fucking bastard. But I am sorry I made Uncle George feel uncomfortable by yelling at you.'

Catesby began to scour a saucepan with a Brillo pad. He felt Caddie's eyes studying him in profile.

'You're a bit common, aren't you?' she said.

Catesby laughed. 'Well spotted. I'm glad I don't come across all lah-di-dah.'

'So what are you then?'

'I come from a fishing port called Lowestoft, but there's also ship building and canning factories. You'd probably find it a bit rough, but I like it.'

'Was your family poor?'

'Very – why are you asking these questions? I'm supposed to be a fucking bastard.'

'I'm wondering how someone like you ended up with the job you have now? Sometimes you sound educated.'

Catesby shrugged. 'I don't like being interrogated about my background.'

'But I bet you interrogate lots of other people?'

'I suppose I do. It's part of my job.'

'That's why you're a fucking bastard.'

'Even if that is true, there's a lot you don't know about me.'

'It sounds like you want to justify your actions, your life.'

'No, I don't.'

'Good. All justification is weakness.'

'Are you as hard as you sound?'

'No.'

'By the way,' said Catesby, 'if you want to write a letter to Kit, I'll take it back to London with me – but it will be a while before he gets it.'

'I will write to him – and I suppose you'll read it.'

'I won't,' Catesby smiled, 'it's not my job.'

Caddie nodded at the pan. 'You might want to leave that to soak.'

'I don't like leaving a job unfinished – I suppose you would diagnose me as an obsessive.'

'I gave up psychiatry because I like working with my hands.'

'So do I.' Catesby continued scrubbing for a few minutes in silence. 'There, it's clean. Can I ask you something?'

'Go on.'

'What did you think of your cousin Jennifer?'

'I hated the bitch.'

'Because she had designs on your brother?'

'Jennifer had designs on everyone. Her ego required men to lust after her – she thought she was *la belle dame sans merci*. But in the end, she was just a cheap slut. In fact,' Caddie laughed, 'she would probably have even got off with you.' Caddie looked closely at Catesby. 'Would you have liked that?'

'Maybe I would have.'

Catesby caught the expression out of the corner of his eye. For a second Caddie's face seemed contorted with pain as if he had slapped her. Her jealousy seemed almost tangible, but she tried to brave it into a joke. 'And I hope she would have given you a case of the clap.'

'I'm sure you're a much nicer person.'

'So am I, but I'm not as pretty.'

'Are you fishing for compliments?'

'Don't make fun of me – too many people have done that.'

Catesby noticed that she was gripping the tea towel so tightly her knuckles were white. 'Sorry,' he said.

'Don't say sorry if you don't mean it.'

'I do mean it.' Catesby looked closely at her. She was tall and gawky, but also pretty in a way that was more appreciated in England than the USA.

'Well I'm sorry I've been so ratty. I'm very tired.'

Catesby put his arms around her. She was still for a second; then put her arms loosely around his neck. Her eyes were bright and damp.

George was frying eggs and grilling bacon when Catesby came into the kitchen the next morning. There was a welcome homeliness of condensation, bacon fat and coffee smells. Caddie, still in a dressing gown, was sitting at the table finishing a letter to her brother. For a second, Catesby was happy. But he quickly remembered that his life was elsewhere and otherwise. Caddie knew it too. It was why they hadn't made love. But they had gently kissed and held each other for a long time without saying a word.

Catesby pitched in with the breakfast by toasting bread. 'I'm an expert,' he said.

'Then you ought to stay longer,' said George, 'we need experts.'

'I wish I could, but I've got to be in Washington this afternoon.'

'One of us will give you a lift,' said George looking at Caddie.

'Thanks, but someone's picking me up.'

Caddie stared at him for a second, then finished her letter and sealed it in an envelope. 'Do I need to address it?'

Catesby shook his head. 'But it will get to him, I promise.'

It was a one-eyed, one-horned flyin' purple people eater
One-eyed, one-horned flyin' purple people eater
One-eyed, one-horned flyin' ...

'Bob?'
'Yes, William?'

I said Mr. Purple People Eater, what's your line
He said it's eatin' purple people and it sure is fine ...

'Would you mind turning the radio down, or maybe even off?'

Bob switched off the car radio. 'There's a story behind that song.'

Bob Neville had arrived just before noon to give Catesby a lift to Washington. He was driving his POV, privately owned vehicle. As an intelligence officer, he didn't like travelling around in an embassy pool car with CD number plates.

'Thanks, that's better,' said Catesby. 'What an awful song.'

'Oh, I rather like it. And it's caused quite a stir on Capitol Hill. A Republican congressman wants to get it banned.'

'On aesthetic grounds?'

'No, on political grounds. He reckons the Purple People Eater is a subliminal metaphor for socialism and the song is corrupting America's youth.'

Catesby smiled wanly. 'Bob?'

'Yes.'

'What sort of car is this?'

'It's a 1955 Pontiac Star Chief. What do you think of the rocket pod fins?'

'Do they shoot real rockets?'

'No.'

'Then why did you buy it?'

'I wanted to go native – and the car was cheap. I got it at a police auction.'

'It's the ugliest thing I've ever seen.'

'Ah, William, then you obviously haven't seen the 1958 Oldsmobile Eighty-eight. Its sheer vulgarity leaves you half blind and gasping for immediate repatriation.'

'Has it occurred to you that your American colleagues might think you're taking the mickey?'

'It doesn't make any difference. They don't trust me anyway.'

Bob Neville's specific job was liaising with the CIA and other US intelligence agencies. It wasn't an easy job. One of Neville's predecessors in the post, Kim Philby, had been declared persona non-grata by the Americans and sent back to the UK. In Britain the jury was still out on Philby, but not in Washington.

'Tarred with the same brush?'

'Not me personally, but there's still a lot of prejudice against SIS. And please, William, keep a low profile with whatever you're doing.'

'Haven't you been briefed?'

'No.'

Catesby was surprised that Neville wasn't in the loop. Once again, it made him feel lonely – like a puppet whose strings had been cut. In some ways being cut free was worse than being manipulated. He suspected it was another of Henry Bone's methods. It was called 'plausible deniability' – the Judas option. But why?

'If you haven't been briefed, Bob, how did you know where to find me?'

'The Head of Station was informed of your itinerary. I volunteered to pick you up so I could ask you about Aston Villa.'

'They're going through a bad patch.'

'So I gather.'

Catesby liked Neville. They had trained together in SOE and been parachuted into France in '43, but in different sectors. At first Catesby assumed that Neville was a posh kid from Eton, but then discovered that he was a fellow grammar schoolboy from East Anglia with a gift for languages.

'Bob, I met this girl who said I was common.'

'But you're not.'

'But I am.'

'Then that makes two of us.'

Bob, thought Catesby, always said the right thing. He had all the social skills that meant that he could get on without being constantly targeted as a troublemaker. Catesby knew that Bob's politics and social background were not far from his own. In many ways, Bob was the better spy. He could be as smooth and silky as Philby, but there was, of course, no question concerning his loyalty.

'Where am I taking you?' said Bob.

'You mean you don't know?'

'Well, I suppose,' said Bob, 'that we might try the Lord Calvert Hotel to see if anyone has booked you in.'

'I thought you weren't in the loop.'

'I just know your itinerary – and that Henry wants me to look after you.'

They were going over the Chesapeake Bay Bridge. The view was that of a wide misty estuary bounded by low wooded countryside woven with meandering creeks. There was one ship, an unladen freighter high in the water, thumping its way between a narrow buoyed channel up to Baltimore.

'Remind you of home?' said Catesby.

'A corrupted version – it looks like an East Anglia re-cast with too much money, over-rich food and racial prejudice. The beauty of the countryside is too lush, too obvious. It's overdone.'

'Not like a shingle beach on a winter's day.'

'Exactly.'

Catesby wasn't sure he completely agreed. There seemed to be two Americas at war with each other. But the better one, the one that wrote poetry, composed music and longed for social justice, was losing. Money was the poison that spoiled the dream and defaced the landscape. American money didn't create a national health service, but enormous phallic cars with rocket fins.

'What else,' said Catesby, 'has Henry asked you to do?' He wasn't sure that Neville was being completely open about how much he knew.

'He asked me to trace three telephone numbers – but you obviously found Calvert, aka Uncle Georgy, without my help.'

'Did Henry tell you how he found the numbers?'

'Absolutely not – "No need to know, old boy." And Bone never tells me anything even when there is.'

Catesby wondered if Neville was merely pretending not to know that the numbers came from the US Ambassador. The game was tedious, but he had to keep playing it. 'Someone gave them to me and I passed them up to Henry.'

'Actually, I thought so. In any case, it was easy linking the first number to Fournier's uncle. It was a rural Maryland exchange on the Eastern Shore, almost like getting the map grid coordinates. The second one is in Washington – that was a lot more difficult. But the third one is impossible to pin down. It looks like it's a secret exchange of some sort. Banks, private eyes and governments use them for confidential stuff. Very expensive.'

'Did the FBI help you?'

'You must be joking. No, I used a private detective agency that specialises in adultery.'

'Not good security. These people can be a bit leaky.'

'You think the FBI would have been a better idea? Did you want to end up on Hoover's desk the next morning?'

'Point taken. What about the DC number?'

Neville smiled. 'Delicious, absolutely delicious. The number traced back to a flat on N Street SW, 308 to be exact. I decided to put it under surveillance, checking for comings and goings around rush-hour times. Absolutely nothing. Whoever lives there doesn't do normal office hours. So I decided to have a saunter past during my lunch hour – and there she was. And very nicely turned out considering how early it was: bouffant hair, pancake makeup. Well, I was the only eyeball, no mobile backup, so I thought I would lose her as soon as she got in a car or taxi. But, would you Adam and Eve it? She started walking – and I saw why.'

'She had a dog.'

'Well done – and what a dog. It was white, small and fluffy. I'd never seen anything like it before. So I decided it was a good excuse to start a conversation.'

'And the English accent helps.'

'Yeah, it means you're respectable, not a weirdo or a mugger – how little they know. In any case, I started with, "Excuse me for intruding, but I was wondering what sort of dog that is. It's not a breed I know." And she says, on cue, as if she had just met a Martian, "Are you from England?"' Neville said it in a deep southern accent.

'Did she really talk like that?'

'Even more so. But here's the bit you're not going to believe.'

'Go on, I'm gullible.'

'The dog.'

'What about the dog?'

'It was a cockapoo.'

'A what?'

'A cockapoo – a cross between a cocker spaniel and a poodle.'

Catesby smiled. 'I'm sure C will be amused – he loves dogs.'

'She was friendly, without being flirty.'

'The cockapoo?'

'Don't be silly. She was quite a nice girl actually. I had the impression that she enjoyed having a conversation with a man that didn't require her to be flirty. She asked about me and I said that I worked in the hotel trade. And then she said, "I work in a hotel too."'

'I'm not completely surprised.'

'Don't be awful, William. I was starting to feel sorry for her. She was very pretty and very vulnerable – I didn't want to ask more.'

'You always were nice.'

'But I still said, "Which hotel?" She nodded in the direction of the new Senate Office Building. "You must know it, the Carroll Arms." "Superb location," I said.'

'And where is this hotel?'

'Directly across the street from the Senate Office Building.'

'Convenient.'

'Very. But things got even better. I could see that she was proud of her position, of being as it were an insider. I sensed that she even wanted to brag a little. I could see that she was afraid that I was about to go my separate way. Suddenly she said, "I don't work directly for the hotel. I'm a hostess at the Quorum Club." Of course, I made a big deal of it – about how exclusive it was and how the Quorum was at the heart of things. She was glowing when we parted.'

'Unlike you, Bob, I'm not a DC insider. Tell me more about this place.'

'The Quorum Club is the US Senate's private knocking shop. But it's not as sordid as you might think. It's all very polite – even the wives of the senators have lunch there. They do the best steak sandwiches in Washington. Kennedy still goes there even though he's president. You could, William, be on the verge of priceless intelligence treasure. But be careful, very careful.'

'Thanks.' Catesby stared out the car window. As they approached Washington, the scenery was more and more spoiled by advertising hoardings, motels and service stations.

'By the way,' said Neville, 'I'm not going to be here much longer. I've been so ineffective as liaison officer with our Anglophobe counterparts that C has promoted me.'

'Congratulations. Where are you going?'

'Cuba. I'm going to be Chief of Station in Havana.'

Catesby walked the streets of Washington in the rain. He was too paranoid to dial the phone number from the hotel. He went from phone box to phone box with the water dripping from his trilby. At least he looked like a spy. Each time he rang the number there was no answer. As Catesby emerged again into the rain he noticed that he was on M Street. Washington wasn't an organic town like London that had grown up around villages and greens as the centuries progressed. It was a severe grid of planned streets and funereal monuments bathed in unnatural light. The place scared Catesby, but he continued walking south towards the river. He looked at his watch. It was nearly midnight. He was going to try once more. The phone box reeked of stale tobacco, but they did in London too. He put a slippery dime in the slot and dialled the number. This time there wasn't a ring, but a busy signal. He hung up, waited five minutes and then dialled again. This time it was ringing and still no one answered. But someone was there.

It was only a short walk. Catesby knew there was no other way. He found 308. He tried to find a way to the back door. There was a gate, but it was padlocked from the other side and too high to climb. It was late to be calling, gone midnight, but the lights were still on. He pressed the doorbell and heard a 'ding dong, dong ding' from within. And a dog growling. He finally heard the sound of feet and a door chain unlatching.

The woman looked like the one Neville had described, except her hair was down and cold cream had replaced the pancake makeup. She was wearing a light blue negligee and holding the cockapoo in her arms. The dog was still growling. She stroked its head and whispered, 'Ruhe Schatz.' Then looked up at Catesby, 'Haben Sie das Geld?'

Catesby answered in German, 'How much money do you want?'

'Two thousand dollars.'

'I'll bring it tomorrow.' Catesby hadn't a clue what he was buying. It was obvious that she was mistaking him for somebody else, but Catesby knew instinctively that he had to pretend to be that person.

'But don't come here,' she said.

Catesby looked over her shoulder. The flat was done out with silk draperies and lavender carpets. The walls were hung with prints of animals, country scenes and eighteenth-century women on swings. 'Have you lived here long?' he said. He wanted to keep her talking so he could place her accent.

'That doesn't matter,' she said. There was a definite hint of Saxony. She was from East Germany.

'Where should we meet?'

'I'll see you at Martin's Tavern. It's in Georgetown. Be there about eight.'

Georgetown was the most prestigious part of Washington. The Kennedys had lived there before they moved to the White House. Martin's was the sort of place that Americans thought was cosy and old world. It wasn't that bad, thought Catesby. It had bare wooden floors and lots of dark wood and subdued lighting. But despite its old world pretentions, Martin's was still unmistakably American rather than the Irish pub it pretended to emulate. There were tables in the centre where you could eat in full view of everyone else, but there were also intimate booths where you could hide yourself away. Catesby thought it best to wait for his date in one of those. The waiter came over to take his order.

'I'd like a brandy,' said Catesby.

'Fine Champagne cognac?'

Catesby envisioned his expenses claim. 'No, just an ordinary one.'

The young woman arrived at the same time as the brandy. She ordered a daiquiri in the Southern accent that Neville had mimicked. She was once again a fragrant honey pie from Tennessee or Alabama. Catesby wondered if she was laying it on too thick. Her hair was done up in bouffant and she was wearing a double-breasted navy dress with pearls. Her style slightly reflected the tastes of the new First Lady, but, like the accent, it was overdone.

'You know,' she said, 'I am absolutely ravenous. I could eat a horse.'

'I bet you could,' said Catesby.

The waiter came over with the menus.

'We'll order now,' she said, 'I'll start with the shrimp cocktail and then I'll have the Delmonico steak with French fries.'

Catesby decided to go down the American route too and ordered Caesar salad and Oysters Rockefeller, but opted for a bottle of Chablis to wash it all down.

'Do you know something?' she said.

'Not much.'

'This booth,' she whispered, 'this is the very booth where President John F. Kennedy proposed to Jackie.'

Catesby wondered why she was continuing to act out her cover story. Maybe she wanted to practise the accent – or maybe she was schizophrenic and didn't realise she was playing a role. The starters arrived and she attacked the shrimp cocktail like a starved wolf.

'What,' she said, dabbing the pink sauce from her lip, 'shall I call you?'

Catesby smiled, 'Wilhelm?'

Her eyes flashed like swords and her face turned to stone.

'What shall I call you?' said Catesby.

'Norma.'

Catesby poured himself a glass of Chablis. 'Would you like red wine with your steak?'

'No, thank you, ice-water will be fine.'

'Have some of this for now,' said Catesby proffering the Chablis.

'Just a tiny tad.'

Catesby filled her glass.

Her face softened and she smiled. 'I think, my good sir, that you are trying to get me tiddly so you can compromise me.'

Catesby lifted his glass, '*Have some Madeira, m'dear*

You really have nothing to fear …'

'Is that an English song?'

'Yes.'

'It sounds really kind of quaint.'

'*I'm not trying to tempt you, that wouldn't be right*

You shouldn't drink spirits at this time of night …'

Catesby stopped singing. He could see that she was bored. But for a second, he had wanted to 'tempt' her. She sparkled with erotic electricity. But when he looked more closely, he saw only the vacancy of calculation and it left him cold. The main courses arrived and they ate in silence.

When the waiter came to take their plates away, she took out her compact and studied herself in the mirror checking that all was still in place. Maybe, thought Catesby, she had another date. Meanwhile, he took a fat envelope out of his pocket and placed it on the table.

She finished adjusting her lipstick, mewed and put her compact away. 'I've got the prints from the modelling agency,' she said in a voice loud enough to attract stares.

Catesby looked around furtively. It was all a bit too public.

'Here they are.' She handed Catesby a brown eight-by-ten envelope. Meanwhile she quickly scooped the other envelope into her handbag.

'Taxi?' said Catesby.

'I don't need one,' her voice had lost most of its Deep South honey, 'my lift is already here.'

Through the window condensation Catesby could make out the outlines of a black Lincoln Continental that was purring by the kerb. His dinner companion didn't even make eye contact as she slid out of the booth. The waiter came over. Catesby listened to the departing staccato beat of her heels as he paid the bill.

When Catesby first got into the taxi, he told the driver to take him to his hotel. He then settled into the back seat to see what had just cost the British taxpayer two thousand dollars plus the cost of a slap-up meal. All the photos were black and white, but of outstandingly good quality. They left nothing out. Norma wasn't the only girl in the photos, but was certainly the most imaginative. Overall, the new president seemed to be enjoying himself, but there were photos where there was clearly pain on Kennedy's face. It certainly didn't look like the pain of Roman Catholic guilt, but rather the grinding aches related to the president's chronic back problems. Kennedy seemed to prefer to have sex done to him while he was lying flat on his back. In two photos the president looked very odd indeed because he was still wearing his canvas back brace with tightly laced metal stays. The British taxpayer had got a real bargain for a change.

Catesby slipped the photos back into the envelope and decided it was best that he not go back to his hotel.

'Driver.'

'Yes.'

'Can you take me to the British Embassy instead?'

The embassy was located on the section of Massachusetts Avenue known as Embassy Row. Catesby had to explain to the taxi driver not to drop him at the Ambassador's residence itself, a grand building with columns that looked like something out of *Gone with the*

Wind, known as the Great House. What Catesby wanted was the large modern building entered from Observatory Circle where the actual business of being a major foreign mission was carried out. Some visiting Brits said the new office building looked like a giant public lavatory, but Catesby preferred it to the airs and graces of the Great House.

The Night Duty Officer was a young Second Secretary with a public school accent. He looked at Catesby's identity card with bemusement, 'Oh, you're one of those. How can I help?' His eyes soundly grew round and bright. 'Do you need a gun?'

'No, just a diplomatic bag.'

Catesby followed the Second Secretary to the mailroom where he resealed the photo envelope, tagged it UK EYES ALPHA/Delicate Source Attn: SIS/Dir/EU/SOV and popped it in the bag labelled 'priority air'. It meant that it would go on the next flight and then straight to Henry Bone via Royal Corps of Signals motorcycle courier. Catesby breathed a sigh of relief.

'Would you like a lift?' said the Second Secretary.

'No, I think a taxi would be more discreet.'

'You're not officially here.' The young man seemed to be one who enjoyed drama.

'Speaking about diplomatic bags,' said Catesby, 'is it true about the cigars?'

The Second Secretary winked and nodded.

'I'll keep it hush,' said Catesby. The news confirmed the rumour that the new British Ambassador supplied Kennedy with Havana cigars smuggled out of Cuba via the UK diplomatic bag. The young diplomat was obviously accommodating. Later, Catesby wondered if he ought to have taken up the gun offer.

The Lord Calvert Hotel had over 400 rooms. It had a gym, an indoor swimming pool, a restaurant and various bars. Most of its guests were expense-account lobbyists who flocked from all over the USA to pitch for government contracts. The Lord Calvert also had a large number of foreign visitors. Embassies used the hotel as overflow accommodation and officials from international organisations were regulars too. Catesby was certain that the FBI, and even less friendly Security Services, kept the hotel under surveillance. He was annoyed that someone, probably the British Embassy accommodation officer, had booked him in – even if it was under an assumed name, Timothy Manton. He ought to have found his own place. Bad security.

When Catesby got to his room he was glad that no one else was in the corridor to watch him. He began by listening with his ear to the door for five minutes. No noise, but he still had to be careful. He put the key in and turned it. When he felt the door unlock, Catesby pushed it open hard and then flattened himself against the wall. He was sure he had heard a sound: someone rustling in the room. Or maybe it was his overactive imagination.

Catesby remained flattened against the wall and started to plan his actions if someone was in the room. The training manual solution for 'room clearing' involved four armed operatives. You always went in with your gun pointed at the floor, never straight ahead. If you ran into someone in the dark you didn't want them to push your pistol away. Even if they grabbed you, you could shoot them in the foot or leg. But room clearing wasn't an option: the only option was to find an escape route. But maybe, after all, the room was empty. He remembered that he had left a window open. The noise might have been a curtain fluttering. This is, thought Catesby, really going to be embarrassing if someone comes out of the lift and sees me like this. Just then the lift door opened.

A man with spectacles waddled out of the lift. He was wearing an enormous paper hat that said: *Nebraska Meat Convention*. There was also a motif of cartoon pigs holding hands. The man staggered over to Catesby. He was trying to read the number on his room key and said, 'Is this the fifth floor?'

Catesby put his finger to his lips and said, 'Shhh.'

The man squinted and looked at Catesby. 'Are you all right? Why are you standing like that?'

'We're playing a game,' Catesby whispered.

'What kind of game?'

'Something like peek-a-boo. If they see me first, I lose.'

The man read the room number on the door nearest and said, '506. I'm just down there at 516.' His voice was slurred and very drunk. He leaned down to Catesby and said, 'Shhh.' And began to tiptoe up the corridor.

Catesby grabbed at the man's sleeve, but it was too late to stop him. The man got as far as the open door, but instead of continuing down the corridor he looked into Catesby's room. The drunk was smiling. He made a gun with fist, thumb and forefinger and pointed it at someone in the room. 'Peek-a-boo, I see you.'

A real gun answered back. Catesby watched the blood and tissue spray across the corridor from the man's head in the mini-second before he tumbled backwards. The *Nebraska Meat Convention* party hat, detached from its owner, fluttered forlornly in midair, but Catesby was already ducking and weaving towards the stairs.

The next bullet popped over Catesby's shoulder and holed the reinforced glass of the service stairwell in front of him. He didn't turn to make sure, but Catesby could tell by the pistol's muffled dull bark that it had been fitted with a silencer. Someone had organised a very professional hit. The next bullet hit the metal frame of the stairwell door as Catesby barged through it. A sliver of metal, shorn off by the bullet, must have cut the back of his right hand. There was no pain and Catesby wondered why blood was dripping down his fingers.

Catesby slipped on the top stair and ended up sliding down to the next level on his back. The stairwell was dimly lit by low wattage emergency lights. The assassin was now through the door and fired another shot wildly and un-aimed. He then wasted a precious few seconds looking for a light switch. He found it and switched it on. The stairwell was lit as bright as a stadium for a night match. Catesby turned and for the first time glimpsed his assailant. He was a large man in a dark suit. The harsh light made his black hair shine like wet coal. His face was dark, but the features more Mediterranean than Latin. Catesby was up and running before the gunman got a bead on him. He was now two flights ahead.

There were four more shots before Catesby reached the ground floor. They pinged and ricocheted down the stairwell like coins thrown down a well. Catesby could see the stairs continued down into a basement where there were washing machines and driers, but he didn't want to be trapped like a rat. He pushed on a door that he hoped would lead to the reception area. It was locked. The stair-pounding footsteps were getting closer. Catesby raised his foot and kicked with all his strength against the lower glass panel. It was hard safety glass and barely cracked with the first two kicks, but finally shattered with the third. As he bent down to crawl through the hole, a bullet went through the glass panel above.

There was a corridor in front of him with trolleys packed with glasses, cutlery, china and folded tablecloths. Catesby started running for the twin swinging doors at the end of the corridor. The two porthole windows in the doors signalled life itself. He heard his assassin crawling through the shattered door panel. There was another dull bark and a tray of champagne flutes exploded into flying shards. A second later Catesby was through the doors and into a restaurant where a few late diners lingered over brandy, coffee and mints. He kept running, but the only person behind him was a waiter calling, 'Sir, sir, sir …' Catesby wondered if the waiter thought he was trying to leave without paying the bill.

The restaurant was separated from the reception area by two wide glass doors. Catesby could see that reception was much busier than the restaurant. He stopped running and looked behind him. There was no one following him other than the waiter. Catesby raised his wounded hand. 'I've cut myself. Don't worry, it's not bad.'

'See John at reception, sir. He has a first-aid kit.'

Catesby walked calmly over to the reception desk hiding his bleeding hand in his pocket. He didn't want a bandage, he wanted a taxi.

The taxi driver was a black man who looked to be in his sixties, if not older. Catesby settled in the back seat putting pressure on his hand to stop the bleeding. 'Have you got some tissues?'

'I've got everything, sir.' He passed back a box of Kleenex. 'What happened to you?'

'I cut my hand on a broken glass.'

'Here, let me have a look.'

Catesby held out his hand to the driver who switched on the interior light. 'Let me put some iodine on it and then I'll wrap it up with a bit of bandage.'

Catesby watched the driver get out a first-aid kit and administer to his wound. 'You certainly have everything.'

'You need it in this town. Washington may be the nation's capital, but it is one bad-ass rough place. There you go, all done and no stitches.'

'Thanks.'

'Now that you're patched, where I can I take you?'

Catesby was about to say the British Embassy, but suddenly a self-preservation instinct stopped his tongue. The embassy was too obvious – he didn't want to get ambushed and he didn't want the kind taxi driver to get hurt. 'I don't know.'

'That's all right, sir, take your time and have a think.'

'Thanks. You know any all-night jazz clubs?'

'Several, what kind of jazz you like?'

'Miles Davis, Charlie Mingus, John Coltrane – and I wish Charlie Parker could be reincarnated.'

'I know where you're coming from. And where do you come from?'

'Lowestoft.'

'Is it a cool place?'

'It can be very cool.'

'Well the coolest place I can take you is the Blue Door on U Street. You might like it there. They got a white dude who plays tenor sax most nights. He's almost one of the brothers.'

Catesby leaned forward. He couldn't believe his luck. 'This sax player, what's his name?'

'Otis something. At least they call him Otis.'

'Let's go.'

On reflection, thought Catesby, it wasn't that surprising that Otis would end up in Washington. It's where Otis used to work when he wasn't abroad as a diplomat. The first time Catesby met him was in a jazz club in Bremen in 1947. He later found out they were both part of the Denazification Commission – and both angry at the way the CIA was covertly wrecking their work by whisking off war criminals.

Otis was too honest and outspoken. He eventually fell victim to the McCarthy witch-hunts and was sacked without a pension.

The Blue Door was packed and sweaty. As Catesby slid in at the back, the quintet was in the middle of Thelonius Monk's 'Well, You Needn't'. The pianist, an old black man with a wispy grey beard, was singing the lyrics:

It's over now, it's over now
You've had your fun, so take a bow
You oughta know, you lost the glow, the beat is slow …

When the piece was over, Catesby made his way to the bar and ordered a shot of Four Roses bourbon. He noticed that he and Otis weren't the only white people in the club. There was a handsome young couple at a table near him. They were speaking French. He wondered if they were from the embassy.

As Catesby sipped his drink, he studied Otis on the stage. He was blowing into his sax mouthpiece and getting ready for the next piece. He hadn't changed at all since the Bremen days. Otis looked like a man of fifty at the time and he still looked a man of fifty even though he was fourteen years older. His black hair looked like it had been lacquered to his head and hadn't a streak of grey.

The next two numbers, 'Benji's Bounce' and 'Stanley the Steamer', had long tenor sax solos and the club went completely silent as Otis did his stuff. Catesby envied the complete concentration. There was nothing else, absolutely nothing else, in Otis's world other than the music. When the last piece finished, the group were supposed to have a break, but there was so much cheering and clapping they encored 'Moose the Mooch'. Finally, the lights came on. The musicians put down their instruments and wiped the sweat from their faces. Drinks were passed to the quintet as they left the stage. Otis made his way to a table where an elegant black woman was sitting. She stood up to give Otis a kiss. She was absolutely stunning and six inches taller than Otis.

As Otis glanced around acknowledging his admirers he spotted his old friend. He shouted, 'Hey Catesby, let me get you a drink,' and started to walk over to the bar. Catesby noted his limp had got worse.

'I've already got one.'

'Come over here then.'

Otis gave him a big bear hug with lots of back thumping, then turned to his companion, 'Clarissa, I want you to meet Catesby. He's a big cheese in the British Diplomatic Corps, but won't admit it.'

Catesby took Clarissa's proffered hand. It was like meeting the Queen of the Nile. She was one of those women who could have been any age between thirty-five and fifty-five. She was effortlessly beautiful and her dignity filled the space around her like a magic spell.

'What brings you to Washington?' said Otis.

'The new Ambassador wants me to vacuum the staircase and change the oil in his Rolls.'

'Is that how you hurt your hand?'

'Yeah.'

'Hmm,' Otis lowered his voice. 'You look kinda tired. What have you been up to really? But maybe you can't tell me.'

Catesby smiled wanly and put a hand on Otis's forearm. 'My masters in London would like to know what's going on in Jack Kennedy's brain.'

'That's easy: "Where, how, when and with whom am I going to get laid next?" Can't you guys think up any difficult questions?'

'Like what?'

'How much are the Kennedys in hock to the Mafia?'

It had already occurred to Catesby that the gunman in the hotel had been a mob hit man. Security services don't like to leave fingerprints, so they subcontract the dirty jobs to the underworld.

'What,' said Otis, 'did you guys think of the election?'

'It was close.'

'Of course it was close. Joe Kennedy is one stingy son-of-a-bitch. There was no way he was going to buy his son a landslide.' Otis paused. 'I can tell from your gently mocking smile that you think I'm bullshitting you.'

'It seems astonishing.'

'Okay, here are the facts. Let's say the Catholic Church in Boston collects a million bucks in the collection baskets on a particular Sunday. Joe Kennedy then goes to the Cardinal and says, "I need some spare rhino, Your Eminence, how about I write you a cheque for one million *and* fifty thousand bucks." No way is the Cardinal going to do his diocese out of an extra fifty thou, so he takes the cheque. And Joe, of course, isn't going to be out of pocket either because he claims the money as a charitable donation and gets tax relief. It's called *la lavenderia Vaticana*, the Vatican laundry. In any case, Joe now has lots of untraceable mazuma to splash around for his son's campaign. That's how they squared West Virginia in the primaries.'

'What about the national election?'

'Kennedy needed the area around Chicago, my hometown, or he was dead meat.' Otis smiled. 'But I don't want to say too much. My best-paid gigs are in Chicago, at the Villa Venice – it's owned by Momo.'

'Who's Momo?'

'Christ, Catesby, don't you know anything? Momo Giancana. He's the Chicago outfit boss.' Otis lowered his voice. 'Momo sewed up Cook County for Kennedy in the election. Some ballot boxes were stuffed, others were emptied. I think Giancana overdid it. Kennedy won by 300,000 votes. It was a goddamn ridiculous majority.'

'Are you a friend of Giancana?'

'Everybody's a friend of Momo – and now Jack Kennedy has to be a friend of Momo too. Listen, the big question of Kennedy's presidency is whether or not he's going to renege on Giancana's favour. And, at the moment, Momo has done all the giving – for chrissake, Kennedy's even sharing two of Giancana's girlfriends.' Otis started laughing. 'Hey, listen.'

'Go on.'

'Last time I was at Villa Venice, I overheard one of the girls talking about Kennedy. Priceless.'

'What'd she say?'

'She said it was the best thirty seconds of her life.' Otis turned to his girlfriend. 'Sorry, Clarissa, you must find all this boys' talk tedious.'

'I wasn't even listening.' Clarissa had put on a pair of glasses and was reading a novel in the dull light.

'I still can't understand what a beautiful intelligent woman like you is doing with me.'

Clarissa looked down at Catesby over her glasses and said. 'Otis is needlessly self-deprecating.' Then went back to her novel.

Catesby caught a glimpse of the title. It was *Mill on the Floss*. He looked back at Otis. 'Your life has changed.'

'Yeah, Gladys divorced me after I got the sack. She liked having a diplomat for a husband, even one that found playing the sax more interesting than promoting the abomination known as US foreign policy. She liked the social life and wanted to take up golf.'

'How did you get sacked? Is it true that you pissed in the punch bowl at the Ambassador's garden party?'

'Nah, that never happened. No, I got demoted after London and sent to Paris where I was a cookie pusher in the office of the labor attaché.' Cookie pusher was US diplomat slang for junior officers who carried around trays of snacks at parties. 'But I still had the big mouth of a senior grade – and that was my downfall.'

'And you always wanted a Paris posting.'

'True. But I was only in Paris a little while before they sent me to Marseille. I like the city – they call it France's Chicago – but I didn't like my job. I need another drink. You too?'

Catesby nodded. A bottle of bourbon mysteriously appeared and a waiter recharged their glasses.

'When I got to Marseille I found out that I was no longer working for the labor attaché, but for the CIA Head of Station. At the time there was a big dispute over who controlled the dock workers unions. As you know, the Marseille unions used to be communist. The only rivals to communist control of the port were the Corsican Mafia. You can see where this is going?'

Catesby nodded.

'Basically, my job was paying mobsters to intimidate trade unions – which turned my stomach. Meanwhile, my CIA boss was providing the gangsters with weapons – which I thought was pretty damned stupid. And I said so: verbally and in writing. I pointed out that the CIA dimwit didn't realise he was financing and setting up an international heroin network as the price for getting rid of a communist union leader or two. But I was wrong – he and his bosses were completely aware of it. At least, that's what I was told when they dragged me back to Washington for a disciplinary hearing.'

'Just for that?'

'Oh no, there was more to it. I was accused of having leaked confidential information about the Marseille operation to a journalist. It wasn't true, I was stitched. It's a standard way of getting rid of troublemakers. The CIA has cages full of stool pigeons – especially journalist stoolies. Not enough evidence to send you to jail, but enough to get you sacked.'

Catesby wondered how long before the practice arrived in Britain.

'Well, Catesby, since they can't sack me again, I'm going to tell you a few secrets.'

'Why?'

'I've got my reasons. Have you heard of the French Connection?'

Catesby shook his head.

'It used to work like this: Saigon, Marseille, Havana, Miami. But now that Castro has broken the link, the Mafia and Corsicans are baying for his blood. They want Cuba back and they want it now. I don't think you Brits realise how important Cuba was to the mob – it was their crown jewel. It had it all: casinos, cocaine, heroin, gambling, sex. And no cops or FBI to ruin the party.' Otis smiled. 'Do you understand now?'

Catesby nodded.

'That's why Momo Giancana helped put Jack Kennedy in the White House and lets him bed his best girls.'

'When's payback begin?'

'This coming April in a place called Bahia de Cochinos.'

'Why are you telling me this?'

'Because, Catesby, you've got a little bit of influence and the more people in the loop who know the truth the better. I don't want this thing to work for two reasons. One is personal. The bastard who got me sacked is one of the honchos running the operation. The other is idealistic. I don't want US foreign policy to be determined by a bunch of gangsters. It's bad enough already.'

'I'm worried about you, Otis.'

'Yeah, I ought to be worried about me too. At least they do it quick. One slug in the back of the head, then six more in a circle around the mouth. It means you talked too much.'

'Well maybe you'd better stop talking now.'

'No, Catesby, there's one more thing you ought to know. The French Connection isn't just a smuggling route. It's a person too. Some people call him *le vrai Monsieur*, but his real name is Amleto Battisti y Lora. He's Coriscan, but was born in Uruguay. He doesn't look like a gangster: no tie pin and a ring on only one finger, and not his pinkie. You could take him anywhere. Very smooth, very dangerous – and he lost a lot of dough in Havana. He owned a luxury hotel, a casino – and even his own bank. If you meet Amleto someday, give him my regards.'

'I think I've already met him.'

Otis lowered his voice. 'I've heard he's in town.'

Something else began to nag at the back of Catesby's mind. 'There's a French couple over there by the door. Are they from the embassy?'

Otis shook his head. 'They're friends of Amleto.'

The next day Catesby made one phone call. He dialled the number from a booth at the airport while waiting for his flight back to England. It was the last of the three numbers that Ambassador Whitney had given him. He let it ring for a long time, then hung up and dialled again. This time someone picked up the phone, but didn't say a word – just listened and waited. Catesby felt a chill run down his spine. He finally said the codeword, AMLASH.

Whoever was on the other end decided to let Catesby wait. The words finally came two minutes later. The language was clear and ultra-refined French. For a second, Catesby wondered whether he had been connected to the French Ambassador's private line. But the words were not diplomatic. 'You are playing a very dangerous game, my friend. In North Africa, people like you are often left for the buzzards while still alive with their hands wired behind their backs. They look so droll as they lie choking on the hot sand with their severed penises and testicles shoved down their throats. It is extraordinary how many hours it takes for them to die.'

'Is that all you have to say?'

'No, you may have your uses, but you have no way of knowing in which way. Or of whom you may be serving.'

The line went dead and Catesby hung up.

The weather in London was unseasonably mild, but windy and wet. 'The daffodils,' said Henry, 'were very early this year. Do you know there wasn't a frost in all of February? Would you like another cup of tea?'

'Yes, please.' Catesby noticed that the chipped mugs had been replaced by a Burleigh Ware Willow Pattern tea service. He knew this because he had looked at the bottom of his saucer.

'I saw you peeping,' said Henry as he poured the Lapsang Souchong, another innovation. 'Burleigh, I can assure you, is by no means my first choice. Originally, Central Stores tried to fob me off with some ghastly Spode.'

'I'm surprised you didn't resign.'

'I'm sure,' said Bone, 'it wasn't an intended slight.'

Catesby, however, wasn't so sure. He reckoned that you could chart Henry's status in SIS by analysing his current and past tea services. It was a version of the way Kremlinologists charted the rises and falls of Soviet officials by noting the rearranging of chairs and positions on the reviewing stand for parades. Likewise, the Echinus Demotter tea service had been Henry's high-water mark; the chipped mugs, the lowest of his spring tides.

Bone lifted a folder on his desk. 'I've read your report. It was informative – and might even have an impact on policy.'

'What did you think of the photos?'

'They didn't make me squirm if that's what you're implying. The interesting thing wasn't what the president was doing, but who he was doing it with – especially one of the ladies in particular.'

'You mean the East German posing as a bargain basement Scarlett O'Hara?'

Bone gave an affirmative nod. 'And how do you suppose Ambassador Whitney got to know about this young lady?'

'Easily. The wealthy elite have their own intelligence networks, just like they do here. Whitney certainly would have known several members of the Quorum Club.'

'What were Whitney's motives for passing on her phone number?'

'The old money guys don't like Kennedy. In fact, they don't like anyone outside their own circle who threatens their power base.'

'Your analysis, Catesby, is flawless.'

'Thank you.'

'But Whitney isn't an important player. He may have passed on a few gems, but he doesn't know why they're valuable. It's like the priceless paintings they have on their walls. They haven't a clue.'

Catesby smiled. Bone's loathing of the American upper classes was an ingrained reflex.

Bone, having dismissed Whitney and his ilk, continued in a different vein. 'Have your lads in Berlin found anything linking her to Mischa?'

'Not yet. Personally, I think she's a freelance opportunist – not even an IM or one of his sleeper agents. Oddly, she seemed to think I was working for Mischa. I'm sure of it. Otherwise why she did come to the door speaking German?'

'I've been puzzling over that myself.' Henry poured himself another cup of tea and walked over to the rain-beaded window. He stared across the road at the dull grey of the London Underground office building. 'They're ashamed of us. That's why they put us in this ugly hole. No view, never a ray of sunlight. By the way, I forgot to tell you something.'

Catesby shifted uneasily. It was never a matter of forgetting: it was always a matter of withholding – often pointlessly. It was an annoying habit of Bone's. He always had to think he was in control and the drip feed of information was one way of asserting his power. But this time Bone continued to stare out the window as if in a trance.

'What's wrong, Henry?'

'I'm afraid things are getting out of control.'

'And you don't like that.'

'You sound angry, William.'

'I am. What was this gem you were going to tell me?'

'The woman who passed you the Kennedy photos has been arrested and deported.'

For the first few seconds Catesby wasn't alarmed by the news, but then the implications began to gallop into his brain like riderless horses after a cavalry charge. Catesby knew that US intelligence services had been out to get him for years. The people interrogating 'Norma' would certainly have shown her his photograph – and she would have said, 'That's him.'

'It's obvious,' said Bone, 'why there wasn't a criminal trial.'

'Don't try to skirt around the subject, Henry. What about me? Someone's dropped me in the shit.' Catesby looked closely at Bone. 'And you might even know who it is.'

'Don't make accusations, Catesby.'

'I'm not going to hang for you, Henry. I know a set-up when I see one. Someone told the girl that I had been sent by East German intelligence to pick up the snaps. So she talks to me – and the bloody dog – in her native lingo. And then hands over the photos at cheapo East bloc rates.' Catesby looked at Bone and shook his head. 'Oh my God. You did this to save money, didn't you?'

Bone shrugged, then said, 'There have been budget problems.'

'What an incredibly stupid thing to do.'

Bone laughed. 'I was teasing. I'd never do something like that. You are gullible.'

'Right,' said Catesby, still furious. He wanted to grab Bone by his silk tie and smack him in the gob, but decided words were better. 'You're a duplicitous bastard.'

'I'm not a bastard – and I deplore name-calling. It shows a lack of grace and self-control.'

'Back to the case, who grassed up the German girl?'

'She wasn't grassed. Hoover had her under investigation for some time. His survival strategy as FBI director is to have so much dirt on every president and top politician that no one would dare sack him. But this particular scandal sheet was sweetened by the woman's East German connections. That's why Bobby Kennedy got her out of the country as quickly as possible. And most likely with a regular payoff to keep her mouth shut.'

What a wheeze, thought Catesby, you appoint your kid brother Attorney General, your country's top lawman, so he can cover up the excesses of your sex life.

'You're looking thoughtful, William. Something wrong?'

'Yes, and you know what's wrong. That woman was interrogated by Hoover's gang and also by Bobby Kennedy – probably in person – before she got booted out. She's now fingered me, and probably poor Neville too, as an East German agent. And when that stuff comes flying back across the Atlantic I'm going to find myself in the centre of a shit storm.'

'But ...'

'No, Henry, I haven't finished talking. Why have you done this?'

'There is a reason, if you would give me a chance to explain …'

'You always have a reason – oiled by layers of self-justification. But here are my terms. First, I want a minuted meeting with C and the Chairman of JIC in which all this is disclosed and the minutes become part of the JIC archive. Secondly, I want Angleton to know the facts as well.'

'Not a good idea, Catesby. Angleton is going more and more bonkers – he still thinks Kim Philby is a Soviet agent.'

James Jesus Angleton was CIA Chief of Counterintelligence. He had started alarm bells ringing on Philby in 1951. Under pressure from the Americans, Philby was removed from his job as liaison between SIS and CIA and expelled from the USA. The fact that Philby had never been prosecuted was a running sore between the two intelligence services.

'There are two problems, Henry. One is that I don't want to go to prison because of pressure from Washington.'

'That isn't going to happen. You've got the support of C – and others in high places.'

Catesby nodded. It was Bone's way of saying that he could bring down others with him. It wasn't a sentimental trade.

'The other problem,' said Catesby, 'is that I don't want to die. My life may be miserable and lonely, but every time I get shot at I realise how much I want to stay alive. I'm not sure it was the cousins who tried to get me hit in Washington, but they seem the prime candidates.'

'Or it could have been the Mafia acting on its own.'

'That's the problem. Where is the borderline between the Mafia and CIA? In any case, I can't see how I can do my job in Berlin constantly waiting for a knife in the back, a bullet in the head or a poisoned bratwurst. And how can I function with zero trust from my Yank counterparts?'

'You're not going to be in Berlin much longer.'

'Is that definite?'

Bone nodded. 'How are your Spanish lessons going?'

'Fine, it's a lovely language – and Pablo Neruda's poems are full of chat-up lines.'

'I'm sure you won't need them.'

'We'll see.'

'But I'm sure you'll like Cuba.' Bone paused and took off his reading glasses. 'Now, William, concerning the conditions you set out: I'm willing to go as far as briefing C, but I don't want JIC informed.'

'I still want to get Angleton off my back.'

'That would be a mistake. He's so paranoid he'd think that we were protecting you to hide the truth.' Bone looked closely at Catesby. 'Besides it would be a wasted opportunity.'

Catesby closed his eyes. Bone's voice was like a pick hammer chipping away at his brain.

'There are two factors. One is that there's someone in the FBI passing on stuff to Moscow. Hoover huffily denies it, Angleton says it's true. But the more Angleton rants, the more he undermines his case. Hoover claims the double agent is one of Angleton's boys – and bins all the security violation reports that come across his desk concerning his own agent.' Bone paused and smiled.

'What do you think, Henry?'

'Both of them are right. And since much of the information the two double agents are passing on to Moscow is identical, each of their bosses can blame the other agency for the security breach. And, of course, if one of them finally gets nailed, the other guilty one will be exonerated and continue to operate.'

'How do you know this?'

'We get the stuff from HERO, but Angleton thinks that HERO is a fake double trying to discredit his own man. HERO, by the way, also has some interesting theories about Cuba. Once again, Angleton regards it as a disinformation ploy.' HERO was the codename for a KGB colonel who was passing on intelligence to London. There was a heated debate about whether HERO was a genuine double or a plant.

Catesby stared at the wall. Was it really a wall? And who was Henry Bone?

'Are you still there?' said Bone.

'Barely. How do I fit in?'

'It would be very interesting if the FBI mole passes on the details of … What was her pseudonym?'

'Norma.'

'… of Norma's interrogation to Moscow Central. If Shelepin sees your name as one of Mischa's agents, he's not going to be pleased to learn that Mischa isn't sharing stuff with Moscow. It's happened before and caused bad blood. Maybe it will be real blood this time.'

Catesby suddenly felt very tired. 'Sure, Henry, sure.' One of SIS's aims was to spread suspicion and distrust between East bloc intelligence agencies. Mischa Wolf, as Head of East German Foreign Intelligence, was the East bloc's most successful spy chief. Getting Wolf discredited in Moscow would be a great coup for the West.

'The ideal situation, William, would be for you to get approached by the Russians to find out what you were doing for Mischa.'

'That's why you sent me to pick up those photos from Norma?'

Bone smiled wanly.

'You want to use me as a dangled double?' It was an espionage ploy whereby a loyal agent pretends to be willing to work for the other side. It was a means of passing on disinformation – as some suspected HERO was doing.

'You've always been the ideal candidate.'

'We tried it before, Henry, and someone was killed – someone I cared a great deal about.' Catesby looked away and realised that he could no longer say her name.

'That was sad, but you're still under a cloud of suspicion – at least as far as the Americans are concerned. Which is perfect cover. You're our best ploy since Philby.'

Catesby was on his feet. 'Don't compare me to Kim Philby. I'm not a traitor.'

'And neither is Kim.'

'Oh, shut up. You know he is.'

Catesby sat back down, still fuming. The Philby issue was a festering sore. They had argued about it before. The suspicion of treachery in the ranks did as much damage to an intelligence service as the treachery itself. It was poison.

'Have you calmed down, William?'

'Just explain what you want me to do.'

'I want you to tidy up things in Berlin before you go to Cuba.'

'That's definite?'

'Yes, but not a permanent posting.' Bone polished his glasses and looked across his desk. 'Don't you see, William, how we're trying to use you?'

'Please explain.'

'We need to portray you as someone who is loathed by the

Americans, the quintessential duplicitous British lefty – which to a certain extent is what you are by nature.'

'I'm not like you, Henry, I'm not duplicitous.'

'I said to a certain extent. In any case, we want to present you as someone whom the Sovs think they can trust, who understands their situation.'

'I am not going to be used as a dangled double and fake defector – we've already tried that.'

'I never said we were. Try listening instead of jumping to conclusions.'

'And, Henry, you can try to explain things more directly for a change.'

'Fair point, I'll try. We're entering an incredibly dangerous international situation. Both sides now need back-channel diplomats just as much as they need spies. The problem is that such diplomats need to foster a close rapport with the opposition that some may regard as treasonous – that's the risk you'll be taking.'

Catesby knew that at a certain level nothing was straightforward: everything became grey and ambiguous. If governments never compromised their loudly stated principles – often secretly – there would be few treaties and a lot of war. But when did compromise become betrayal?

'And, by the way,' said Bone, 'our man in Havana has confirmed that Yevgeny Ivanovich Alekseev is now KGB *rezident* and that his wife is with him.'

Catesby often wondered how Alekseev's wife, Katya, had taken the death of her lover. Whether she had pined or simply found a new man.

'You know,' said Bone, 'that there's a very tragic story concerning Alekseev?'

'I'm not sure that having an unfaithful wife qualifies as tragedy.'

'She loves him, but that love can never be fulfilled.'

Catesby was surprised. He had never heard Bone talk of 'love', except dismissively.

'Alekseev was very badly wounded in the last days of the war.'

'Katya doesn't seem very lucky with her men.'

'You're becoming awfully hardboiled, Catesby.'

'This isn't a job for sentimentalists.'

Bone shook his head and looked away. 'Maybe it should be.'

The visit to the US Officers Club at Harnack House was Gerald's idea. He reckoned it was the classiest club the Americans had in Berlin. It was located in Dahlem, a leafy part of the city with lots of parks and tennis courts. Harnack House was a large white building with red roof tiles punctuated by dormer windows where you expected to see *Hausfraus* hanging *Fetterbetts* out to air. Before and during the war it had been used for high-level science conferences. Harnack House was where in 1942 the Reich's top scientists decided against pursuing an A bomb programme.

'You've got to meet these guys,' said Gerald, 'I think you'll find them an education in transatlantic culture.' He was referring to the US officers from the 7771st Document Center and the 7782nd Special Troops Battalion. They were Gerald's colleagues in searching Soviet Army training areas for the letters, supply chits and pages of field manuals. The ones that Soviet soldiers used as toilet paper.

'You find them strange?' said Catesby.

'Completely barking.'

At first Catesby thought the young lieutenants were drunk on alcohol, but then he realised they were drunk on being Americans in a foreign country. One of the most expansive was a tall lanky officer with parachutist wings and a ranger tab. His name was Redhorn and he spoke with an extreme Deep South accent of long diphthong vowels. The softness of his voice made it all the more sinister. 'Eisenhower,' said Redhorn, 'was a pussy wimp. He gave up in Korea and then he let the communists take over in Laos. I know, I been there and seen it.'

'And you think,' said Catesby, 'that Kennedy's going to be different?'

'Goddamn fucking A. And the first thing we're going to do is burn off Castro's beard and hang up the *hijo de puta* by his *pelotas*.'

The other lieutenants began to call out Spanish phrases too: 'Hey Fidel, tell your sister to *chupa mi pila*.' 'What does it taste like Che, *la concha de tu madre*?'

Catesby suspected that the officers had been on a language training course – with an interesting line of vocabulary – and were showing off. He didn't think it boded well for Cuba – or for the rest of Latin America. Meanwhile, Gerald handed him a beer. 'It's free,' he said.

'Who's paying?'

Gerald nodded towards Redhorn. 'He says Limeys are too poor to pay their own way.'

'Then why don't the Americans write off the war loans?' A constant moan of Catesby's generation was that defeated Germany was rebuilt with the Marshall Plan while Britain's economy was hobbled with the repayment of the US loans.

Redhorn sat down next to Catesby and looked at him as if he were from a different planet. 'Where you from?'

'Lowestoft.'

'What's that? Never heard of it.'

'It's a town in the east of England.'

'No,' said Redhorn, 'I meant what's your job?'

Catesby knew that in the context his threadbare diplomat cover was going to sound more ridiculous than usual. 'I'm the Berlin rep of the Cultural Attaché.'

'No, shit.' Redhorn's eyes sparkled. He turned to another American officer. 'Hey Donnie, this dude's a culture man.' Then back to Catesby, 'Come on, educate us, recite some Limey poetry.'

'I don't like being taunted.' Catesby was tempted to take a swing at the American, but realised that Redhorn was wearing glasses. Without the voice and uniform Redhorn could have passed for an academic. It occurred to Catesby that a lot of the bravado was an act.

Donnie suddenly joined in, 'He's telling you a load of bullshit, Red, he's Gerald's honcho.'

'You've been telling fibs,' said Redhorn.

'You're getting on my nerves,' said Catesby. He wouldn't have minded a fight. The banal mockery was grating. But before they could square up, someone else had joined the group. There was a sudden silence as if the headmaster had just entered an unruly classroom. The newcomer wore the two-star insignia of an American major general.

'I want every American officer to stand to attention.' The general had a full glass of beer in his hand. He looked at each of the lieutenants who had chins and tummies tucked in and shoulders thrust back in the rictus of parade ground correctness. Then he pointed at Catesby. 'I assume that you are drinking with that man because you do not know who he is. He may not wear a hammer and sickle on his lapel, but he certainly wears those emblems of oppression on his heart. That man is an enemy of the United States of America and everything our beloved country under God stands for. Beware of enemies posing as allies.'

The general than raised his glass of beer. For a second Catesby thought that, incongruously, he was about to be toasted. But instead, the general emptied his drink on the floor. The other officers followed his example. The general then turned smartly on his heel and marched out of the club with the others in step behind him.

'Well,' said Gerald, 'I've never seen you empty a pub so quickly.'

'But I'm still here.' The voice sounded drunk and came from the shadows in a far corner. A chair scraped and a figure carrying a glass clinking with ice came towards them. 'May I join you?'

'There's plenty of room,' said Catesby, 'please do.'

'Hi, my name's Paul.'

'I'm the anti-Christ,' said Catesby extending a hand, 'careful you don't burn yourself.'

'Nice to meet you, Anti, I've heard so much about you.' Paul was wearing the gold oak leaves of a US army major on his shoulders and the twisted snakes caduceus of the medical corps on his lapels. His tie was loose. Otherwise, he sounded more crumpled than he looked.

'I hope you don't get in trouble for not following the others.'

Paul raised his glass. 'No way am I going to throw away good Scotch. In any case, that asshole won't be here much longer.'

'Who is he?' said Gerald.

'You mean you haven't met him before?'

Catesby had, but kept mum.

'That was Edwin Walker. I don't how he gets away with it. Walker's been handing out right-wing pamphlets from the John Birch Society – and even tells his soldiers how to vote. There's a rumour that Washington is going to transfer him to somewhere in the Pacific where he'll be less of an embarrassment.'

'He seems to have quite a following,' said Catesby.

Paul squinted and looked thoughtful. 'That is worrying, very worrying. But Walker only survived because he had a protector in a very high place.'

'Who was that?'

Paul smiled and whispered, 'Lyman Lemnitzer, Chairman of the Joint Chiefs of Staff.'

Catesby smiled bleakly. Another ball cannoned across the green baize of his mind and clicked neatly into its pocket. Bone was never wrong. Catesby had all the right enemies in all the right places – and Moscow would know it too. He was the perfect dangled double.

'I suppose,' said Paul downing the rest of his drink, 'I'd better get some shut-eye, I've got a VD clinic in the morning.'

Gerald watched him leave and said, 'There are good Americans.'

'Just like there used to be good Germans in the thirties – and look what happened to them.'

'If you don't mind my saying so, sir, you can be a little ray of sunshine.'

'Thanks,' said Catesby.

'Uno, dos, tres, cuatro, Cuba sí, Yanquis no, Cuba sí, Yanquis no.' The chanting of the Pioneers flowed through the open windows of the British Embassy as they marched down Avenida Séptimo. The Pioneers were boys and girls of twelve or thirteen. They wore red berets, red neckerchiefs and white shirts.

The military attaché was standing in front of a map of Cuba with a pointer in his hand aimed at the airfield nearest the embassy. 'The nearest bombs will, I expect, fall here at St. Tony's.' He indicated a Havana suburb called San Antonio de los Baños which was about eight miles south of the embassy. 'Yes, Ambassador?'

'Don't you suppose, Tommie, there's a chance that they may have a pop at some of the ministries in Havana in the chance of bagging Fidel or Raúl or Che?'

'Their chances of getting a senior member of the government with an air strike are next to zero. In any case, the Brigade have at most only sixteen operational B-26s. They need to concentrate everything on neutralising Castro's air force. Otherwise, the invasion will be a certain failure.'

'Uno, dos, tres, cuatro, Cuba sí, Yanquis no, Cuba sí, Yanquis no.' The Pioneers were now marching up Calle 34. *'Fidel, seguro, a los Yanquis dale duro.'* Fidel, unyielding, hit those Yankees hard.

The Head of Trade looked up from her notepad. 'Do you think all that chanting and marching by is on purpose, because we're British?'

The Head of Chancery smiled benignly. 'They're doing it to all the embassies.'

The Ambassador looked at Neville, the new SIS Station Head. 'Anything to add, Bob? Are we still expecting D-Day on the 17th?'

'Yes, Ambassador, their security is truly appalling. It's certain that the Cuban exile brigade has been heavily infiltrated by DGI.' Neville was referring to *Dirección General de Inteligencia*, Castro's spies.

Catesby looked around the table at his colleagues. It was the first time he had been assigned to an embassy where he liked everyone. The Ambassador, Herbert Marchant, was rock solid and had a sense of humour. Neville was an old SIS chum. Mickey Blakeney, Head of

Chancery, was one of the warmest and most civilised diplomats the FO had ever produced. He had an endearing obsession with water towers and sketched and photographed them wherever he went. There wasn't a backstabber in sight. At least, thought Catesby, if the worst case did come true – as seemed increasingly likely – he would be vaporised among friends.

Catesby loved the lizards. He liked lying in bed and watching them race across the ceiling. They were light green, three to four inches long and had a top speed of about 400 miles per hour. The Cubans called them *chipojos*.

It had just gone six in the morning. It was already light and Catesby was lying on his back in bed staring at a *chipojo* poised for a sprint. He suspected that the lizard was going to launch himself at a mosquito that was straddling a crack in the ceiling plaster. But the *chipojo* was one very badly informed lizard. He didn't know what was going to happen and waited too long. The mosquito disappeared in a cloud of plaster dust as the ceiling crack suddenly yawned into an inch-wide gap. The first bombs had begun to fall. The ceiling shook. The lizard's head twitched as if he were confused. He finally did a pirouette and disappeared down the nearest wall.

Catesby decided it was time to get up. The bomb explosions were now joined by the clatter of heavy-calibre anti-aircraft guns. He put on his dressing gown and opened the shutters of the French windows that led on to the balcony. It was a beautiful clear morning. The sun was just rising over the *Castillo de los Tres Reyes Magos del Morro,* a magnificent sixteenth-century fortress at the entrance to Havana Bay built to ward off pirates. Catesby felt a wan sense of irony as he looked at the fortress. The British had finally taken it during a war with Spain in the eighteenth century and then lost half their garrison to yellow fever.

Catesby caught a glimpse of an attacking B-26 as it circled for another bombing run. It was now apparent that the military attaché had been mistaken when he predicted the nearest attack would be at 'St. Tony's' eight miles to the south. The bombs sounded like they were landing less than a mile away. It must, Catesby thought, be the airfield at Ciudad Libertad. It was in military jargon, D-minus-2. The actual landing with troops was still forty-eight hours away.

Despite the walls shaking each time a 500-pound bomb exploded, it didn't seem a particularly ferocious air attack. Catesby wasn't sure there were more than two bombers involved – and then there was one. He watched the stricken plane as it glided over the city. The silence was eerie. One engine was on fire and the propeller on the other wing was slowly turning by force of wind rather than engine. It was fascinating to watch in a ghoulish sort of way. The plane was flying lower and lower as if it were aiming at the old Morro Castle. Catesby mouthed a plea: 'Please, please don't crash in the city.' A moment later the plane seemed to elevate, like a hawk soaring on a thermal, before plunging into the harbour entrance. It was as if the old castle had seen off another pirate.

'Well,' said the Ambassador, 'that was a bit exciting.'

'And I'm sure it's going to happen again this evening,' said the military attaché, 'and the next day too.'

The morning briefing was two hours later than normal so that staff had time to decode cables and make evaluations. The most interesting cable that Catesby dealt with hadn't come from Washington or London, but from the SIS man in Nicaragua.

'What have you got to tell us, William?'

Catesby looked at the Ambassador. He wasn't supposed to brief colleagues who hadn't been security cleared.

'If you can tell us.'

Catesby made a snap decision to declassify. It would soon be common knowledge in any case. 'As you know, today's air strikes originated from a secret base in Puerto Cabezas.' He looked around at surprised expressions. 'Well, you know now. Our man in Managua has confirmed reports that only eight of the seventeen B-26 bombers available to the rebels took off.'

'Maintenance problems?' said the military attaché.

'No,' said Catesby, 'pilot problems. There were never enough trained Cuban exile pilots to fly all seventeen planes.' Catesby paused. He was starting to skate on limited-access security ice.

The Ambassador smiled and said, 'The other nine planes were supposed to be flown by American pilots, but it looks like Kennedy got cold feet at the last moment.'

'Thank you, sir,' said Catesby.

Mickey Blakeney joined in. 'It means, essentially, that Kennedy is signalling that there will be no US military support for the invasion.

I'm not a military expert, but it seems then that this operation is doomed to fail.'

The military attaché looked perplexed. 'Surely then, the invasion ought to be cancelled.'

'There's too much momentum,' said Catesby, 'and the green light is flashing. I bet it's still going to happen.'

'Unless Castro's air force is destroyed,' said the attaché, 'the invasion fleet will be sunk and any soldiers that get ashore will be slaughtered on the beaches.'

It seemed, thought Catesby, a sound prediction. It wasn't a military operation: it was a ritualised dance of death.

'Round two,' said Mickey, 'will be the blame game.'

The Ambassador was twirling his reading glasses and looking off into space. 'We could,' he said, 'be witnessing the beginning of the end of Jack Kennedy.'

The events of the next few days rolled out with dreary predictability. The SIS man in Nicaragua later told Catesby that he was in Puerto Cabeza the night that the 1,511 men of the Assault Brigade boarded the ships that would take them to the Bay of Pigs. The Nicaraguan dictator, Generalissimo Luis Anastasio Somoza, was on hand to see them off. Somoza was in a white military uniform clanking with medals and carrying a Thompson submachine gun. He waved the Thompson above his head and shouted to the men as they embarked, 'Bring me some hairs from Fidel's beard!'

Three days after the invasion 114 of the 1,511 invasion force had been killed and 1,179 captured. A handful of survivors had escaped by sea. It hadn't been a good week for Western prestige. On 12 April, cosmonaut Yuri Gagarin had orbited the earth as the first man in space. On the following Wednesday the ragged remnants of an American-sponsored invasion force were being hunted down in a Cuban swamp. The coincidence left Catesby feeling uneasy. A humiliated superpower can be a dangerous superpower.

The first time Catesby saw Fidel Castro in person was a week later. Members of the diplomatic corps and the press had been invited to see the Bay of Pigs prisoners at the Havana Sports Palace. Catesby thought the men had been scrubbed up for the occasion. They were all wearing clean white T-shirts, military trousers and shined boots.

They then had to listen to a speech by Fidel Castro that lasted from midnight to three thirty a.m. in which they were berated as criminals and pawns of US imperialism. Catesby was impressed by Castro's utter self-confidence and energy. At the end of the speech he told the prisoners that they all deserved to be shot, but he wasn't going to shoot them. Castro reminded the prisoners that Fulgencio Batista's regime, the one he overthrew, had murdered 20,000 Cubans in its seven-year rule – and that even Kennedy admitted that. Catesby later checked the facts. Castro was right.

The next day Catesby had a lie-in. He lay naked and exposed in bed, for the stultifying and humid heat made even a covering sheet too clammy. The ceiling lizard was back and staring down at him with disdain. He knew it was time to get up, but first he checked the inside of his brain to see if the rum *mojitos* had left the machinery intact. He opened one eye and closed the other, then vice versa. No serious damage.

After El Supremo's speech to the prisoners, a group of diplos and journos had ended up in O'Reilly's Bar in Calle O'Reilly. The bar and the street were named after Alejandro O'Reilly, one of the 'Wild Geese' who left Ireland to fight in foreign Catholic armies against the British. It was in fact O'Reilly, by then a Spanish general, who received Havana back from the British at the end of the Seven Years War. But the history imp still had strange twists to play out. O'Reilly decided that Havana had fallen because there wasn't a strong enough fort guarding the harbour entrance. He directed the construction of *Fortaleza San Carlos de la Cabaña.* Two centuries later another man of Irish descent, Ernesto Guevara Lynch, commanded *La Cabaña* fortress.

Catesby drew the curtains and felt the warmth of the mid-morning sun on his body. His bedroom window looked over a flat cityscape of red roofs punctuated by embassy flags fluttering in the sea breeze: the nearest was the red flag of Turkey with its crescent moon and a star in the centre. In fact, he had got a lift back from O'Reilly's with a Turkish diplomat whose name, Mustapha Something Rude, was a constant source of amusement to Brits with immature senses of humour.

Catesby looked north beyond the roofs and neat grids of tree-lined streets to the sea which was a gleaming line of silver. The embassy quarter, because of its sea front, was called Miramar Playa.

And, like the embassy quarters of other cities, Miramar was where the rich lived too – or had lived until the revolution. The millionaires may have gone, but their mansions and walled gardens were still there. Many of the grand houses were not only vulgar, but spectacularly so. These were not the mansions of Florentine dukes, but of gangsters and casino owners. Mercifully, thought Catesby, the onset of dilapidation gave the houses a shabby dignity they had lacked in their prime. Aren't I, thought Catesby, turning into a snob?

The British Embassy itself wasn't too bad. It was a white villa with red roof tiles built in the Spanish colonial style. Its baroque ornamentation, as if anticipating a British tenancy, had kept itself understated. There was a lodge by the gate where Francisco, an ancient Afro-Cuban, greeted visitors and played the guitar. He also looked after a great-grandson who, as Catesby arrived, was polishing the plaque on the entrance gate: *Embajada de Inglaterra*. The plaque worried Catesby. He wondered who was representing *Esocia*, *Gales* and *Irlanda del Norte*.

'Good morning, Señor William.'

'Good morning, *compay*.' Catesby was never sure that he was saying the right thing. He noticed that most Cubans called each other *compay*. It was Cuban for *compañero*, comrade, but without political connotations. The problem with revolutions was knowing what to call people.

'You're late this morning,' said Francisco.

'I was out late last night.'

'And too many *mojitos* and too many *mamitas*.'

'Just the *mojitos*.'

Francisco smiled and waved Catesby away.

Catesby's desk was in a corner of Bob Neville's office. It wasn't an ideal situation, but they didn't seem to have any secrets that the other wasn't supposed to know. Cuba was the only country in the world where the briefs of the two spies overlapped. Neville was a Western Hemisphere man and Catesby was Europe East. The area of overlap was Cuba's relationship with the Soviet Union and other East bloc countries.

'How did you get back?' said Bob.

'Mustapha Kunt gave me a lift.'

'Useful contact. He's a Russian specialist, you know. Was stationed in Moscow all through the war. Meet anyone else interesting?'

'No. Where's the best place to meet Russians?'

'Embassy parties. They don't go to bars much.'

'You know, by the way, that Alekseev is now officially the *rezident*?'

'On the diplomatic list?'

Neville nodded. The Soviets openly listed their head spy as the *rezident*, the diplomat in charge of intelligence gathering. The Brits and other countries used cover aliases.

'Did his wife come with him?'

'Yes. Her name, I believe, is Katya – a very enigmatic woman.'

'Why do you say she's enigmatic?'

'I saw her at a party at the Venezuelan Embassy. She just clung to her husband as if she were a little girl.'

'What colour's her hair?'

'Deepest black.' Neville smiled, 'I am sure, William, that you have more to tell me about Katya.'

'In time.'

The door opened a crack and someone whispered, 'Can I come in?'

'Is it Katya?' said Neville.

'No, it's me.'

'Come in, Debra.'

Debra was a petite woman in her late thirties who ran the Trade Section.

'Where,' said Neville, 'did you go last night?' Debra had been part of the British group at Castro's speech to the prisoners.

'I got chatted up – and I thought I'd better tell you about it?'

'I'm not surprised, you're gorgeous. Who's your latest admirer?'

'The Minister of Industries.'

Neville was suddenly attentive. 'Are you serious? What did he say?'

'He said he wanted to talk to me about buses.'

'That's a very odd chat-up line.'

'He loves our buses and is considering buying them. He's particularly fond of the Routemaster.' Debra was referring to the iconic red double-decker buses of London.

'Is that all he wanted?'

'No, he asked me to listen to him recite some poetry in English. He wanted to know if his accent was all right.'

'Love poetry, I bet.'

'No,' said Debra, 'it was Kipling's *If*.'

Neville started laughing and turned to Catesby. 'Well, if we ever want to learn anything about the art of seduction I suppose we'd better take lessons from Che Guevara.'

'Actually,' said Debra, 'he was utterly charming. He has a beautiful smile and I was rather taken with him.'

Neville looked at Catesby. '*If* isn't such a bad poem, William, especially for blokes in our trade: *If you can trust yourself when all men doubt you / But make allowance for their doubting too*.'

Catesby opened a file on his desk – it was an SIS 'biographical and personality report' on Guevara – and made a few notes.

Neville looked back at Debra. 'Have you got another date?'

'Yes, he wants me to come to his office.'

'Buses?'

'Of course.'

'I think, Debra, you'd better take William as chaperone.'

'Are you sure,' said Catesby, 'it wouldn't be a better idea to have Mickey go instead? After the invasion shambles, Che might want to send a political message for us to pass on to Washington – and Mickey has the status to receive it.'

'That's the problem. As Head of Chancery he's got too much status. Che has to be careful not to go over Fidel's head by making foreign policy statements to senior diplomats.' Neville paused. 'You forget, William, that our role as spies is changing. We're not just spooks, we're back-channel diplomats, the ideal conduits for passing on info that can be denied later.'

There was something in Neville's words that Catesby found troubling. The echo of Bone was too exact to be coincidence. Once again, Catesby felt he was being manipulated by forces unknown.

La Cabaña is an extremely impressive and, despite its being a fortification, beautiful piece of architecture. The smooth stone of the walls is beige-pink and reflects sensually in the sunlight. O'Reilly, thought Catesby, really knew how to build forts. He and Debra were escorted to Che's office along a parapet lined with a battery of huge eighteenth-century canon that pointed across the harbour entrance.

'It's a bit,' said Debra, 'like being in a film. I wouldn't be surprised if Errol Flynn swashbuckled up the wall with a dagger between his teeth.'

'I would. He died two years ago.'

'You're such a ray of sunshine, Catesby.'

The revolutionary militiaman, who had met them at the entrance gate, led them down a stone staircase to a massive oak door. He hammered the door with a massive iron knocker until someone shouted, '*¡pase pase por favor!*'

Che's office was sombre and austere like a cell in a monastery. The walls were panelled with dark wood, the floor was black and white marble tiles set out in a chessboard pattern. There were bookshelves piled with document files as well as novels and volumes of poetry. The only incongruity was a golf putter and a rolled-up carpet leaning against a wall.

Debra introduced Catesby as 'an official from the Department of Trade who was on secondment to the Foreign Office'. Che listened to Catesby's cover story with impish bemusement. He didn't believe a word and couldn't be bothered to pretend otherwise. Guevara was, however, genuinely interested in the Routemaster buses. They spent a half an hour discussing possible trade deals. Then, as she and Catesby had agreed beforehand, Debra looked at her watch and gasped.

'I am terribly sorry, Commandante Guevara, but I've got to go now. But William can stay. Thank you for seeing us. Please don't think I'm rude.'

Catesby watched in admiration as Debra turned on the departure charm giving Che a hug and *besos gordos* on both cheeks. He, in turn, was radiant.

As soon as Debra was gone, Che said, 'She misses her boys awfully.'

Catesby knew that Debra had two sons at a boarding school for military and Foreign Office dependants. He thought they were in the sixth form. Debra often talked about them, but Catesby didn't seem to pick up all her worries. Yet Che, after less than an hour with Debra, knew every detail: names, birthdays, ailments, the sports her sons played and the subjects they found easy or difficult. Catesby understood the secret of Che's charisma. People loved him, because he loved them.

'How are your daughters?' said Catesby trying to copy Che's interest in others.

Che smiled. 'Aleida took her very first steps yesterday. The elder, Hildita, spends most of her time with her mother, but now that they're both in Havana, at least I can see more of her.' Che folded his arms and looked reflective. 'Not long after Hildita was born I took her in my arms and said, "My dear daughter, my little Mao, you don't know what a difficult world you're going to have to live in. When you grow up, this whole continent, and maybe the whole world, will be fighting against the great enemy, Yankee imperialism. You too will have to fight."'

'How old is she now?'

'Five.'

'Now that she can understand your words, why don't you tell her the same thing?'

'No.' Che smiled. 'I don't want to upset her, to spoil her innocent childhood.' He paused. 'Maybe that is a weakness. Or maybe when I said those words I was talking to myself – or trying to impress my wife.'

Catesby was disarmed by the honesty and the self-criticism.

Che got up and went over to the window where he looked out over the harbour. 'It was stupid for the Americans to break off diplomatic relations. It means they have to ask other countries to use their embassies to do their spying for them.'

'They haven't,' said Catesby, 'asked us. Maybe you ought to check with the Canadians.'

'That was a very unfriendly remark to make about a close ally.'

'You've spoken freely to me, so I'm speaking freely to you.'

'Maybe,' said Che with his impish smile, 'the Canadians have been saying the same about you.'

The wonderful thing about espionage and foreign affairs, thought Catesby, wasn't what enemies do to each other, but the way allies stab each other in the back. 'Put a tail on this guy.' Catesby gave the name of a junior Canadian diplomat. 'And ask to see his sketchbook.' It was, he knew, a malicious thing to do. But Catesby's job was gaining the confidence of Che Guevara, not improving ties between Ottawa and London.

Che looked closely at Catesby. 'But you pass things on to Washington too.'

'Only if it is in the British national interest. We're not the poodles that Washington would like us to be.'

Che sat back down in his chair, which like the desk, was a dark colonial heirloom with elaborately carved ornamentation. Catesby felt that he was negotiating with a pirate who had been plundering the Spanish Main. 'I have,' said Che, 'a message for you to pass on to Washington. But if you don't want to carry it, perhaps your Canadian friend will.'

'I am sure we can do it.'

'First of all, I want to convey my thanks to President Kennedy for the Bay of Pigs. Before the invasion, the revolution was shaky. Now it is stronger than ever.' Che laughed. 'Kennedy chose to back the most incompetent band of criminals imaginable. Their defeat was the first great victory of the people of Latin America over US imperialism. Are you writing this down?'

'If you like.' Catesby took a pad out of his folder.

'The Bay of Pigs fiasco has allowed us to consolidate our power. Before the invasion, there was a small chance of reconciliation with Washington. Now there is none. The Kennedy administration has transformed our little aggrieved country to an equal with the USA. Likewise, the invasion has shown there is no alternative to following a communist agenda.'

Catesby sensed a pause. 'Is that all?'

'No.' Che pointed to the notepad. 'And I don't want you to write down what I'm going to say next. I want your mind – and the minds of those you share it with – to see not only the words, but the images too.'

Catesby put his pen down and looked at Che. At first there had been something pleasantly boyish about him, but now a cloud seemed to darken his face.

'We are now going to build stronger ties with the Soviet Union.' Che lowered his voice and spoke slowly. The words were calm, but deliberate. Che continued to speak for fifteen minutes as he carefully outlined every stage of what was going to happen. His voice never ceased to be calm and reasonable despite the enormity of the consequences. Catesby wasn't surprised. It all had a certain inevitability. But actually hearing the words had a finality that made him shiver.

'Is there no other way?' said Catesby.

Che slowly shook his head. 'Since imperialists blackmail humanity by threatening it with war, the wise reaction is not to fear war.' He looked at Catesby. 'What do you think?'

Catesby smiled. 'I'm more easily blackmailed than you.'

'Fear is a cultural trait. It is taught to us. You can unlearn it.' Che began to cough. He covered his mouth with a handkerchief and mumbled, 'Sorry.'

'Are you all right?'

Che was wheezing and seemed to be struggling for breath. He closed his eyes and took short shallow even breaths.

'Can I get you some water?'

Che put his hand up and continued taking short breaths. He opened his eyes, 'I'll be okay. Just give me a few seconds.'

'Let me know if I can help.'

Che nodded thanks as he struggled to breathe.

Catesby had read about Che's asthma attacks in various reports. He knew that he would now have to update the reports by confirming that he had personally witnessed one – and also describe the symptoms. It's what spies are supposed to do. But Catesby didn't want to do it. The man in front of him, with all his faun-like beauty, was also a vulnerable human being. He reminded Catesby of the girl in *The Rite of Spring* who is danced to death to appease the gods.

Che began to breathe more deeply. 'I'm better now.'

'Good.'

'But before you go, I have a present that I want you to give to President Kennedy.' Che got up and went to an untidy bookshelf where he found a box. 'I understand that Kennedy likes cigars. These are special hand-rolled ones. Perhaps you can send them to Washington in a diplomatic bag – I believe some far inferior cigars have already gone that way. There's a note from me too. Can you check the English?'

Catesby looked at a white card headed *Gobierno de la República de Cuba* with the national flag. Che had written underneath: *Dear President Kennedy, The Revolution is inevitable and unstoppable, but while you are waiting I hope you enjoy these cigars. Che.*

'The English is fine. Would you like to add anything?'

'What would you suggest?'

Catesby scribbled a few words on a notepad. 'Try that.'

Che read the note and smiled. He then copied Catesby's message to the card: *PS I bet you can't get Marilyn Monroe to sing at your birthday party.*

Catesby had never seen her before, but he knew it was her. Her hair was indeed deepest black, but that was no rare thing at the Brazilian Embassy in Havana. She wasn't alone. But there was something about her that was perfectly self-contained, as if she were enclosed by an invisible bell jar. Katya was wearing a simple white dress and holding between her hands a *caipirinha*, the Brazilian national cocktail, as if it were a bouquet rather than something to drink. The lime and ice in the *caipirinha* complemented her dress.

Katya's husband, KGB Lieutenant General Yevgeny Ivanovich Alekseev, was standing behind her talking to Che Guevara. Che was eating an impossibly large cream cake. He looked ravenous. There were only puddings and sweets to eat. It was a rather late reception, as many were in Havana, and too late for savouries. But it was still a big event. The reception was celebrating the visit of Brazil's newly elected president, Jânio da Silva Quadros, to Havana. Jânio was talking to Fidel and the British Ambassador was talking to the Brazilian Ambassador, but no one was talking to Catesby. He always felt awkward at these things. He wondered if he should find another spy for a chat. Just then he caught Katya looking at him. It was a very odd look. Catesby nodded back. She seemed to frown; then turned her eyes away.

'I say, William, it's a jolly good job we didn't wear evening dress with sashes and medals.' It was Mickey Blakeney, Head of Chancery.

'We would have looked complete tits,' said Catesby. There had been a brief debate at the embassy on dress code – and lounge suits won. The top Cubans, as usual, were wearing green battledress. And Che, in fact, looked even more scruffy than usual.

'The new Brazilian guy,' said Mickey, 'is a bit of a lefty which is why he's decided to get closer to Fidel and Moscow. Washington must be having a fit.'

'They think Cuba is turning contagious and only they can stop it.'

'That appears to be the mood music. Let's hope it doesn't turn into the last act of *Die Götterdämmerung*.' Mickey smiled. 'Have you noticed, by the way, the uncanny resemblance between Richard Wagner and John Wayne? They could be twins. Must circulate, see you later.'

Catesby looked at his watch. It was nearly midnight. Havana was like that. No one ever seemed to sleep. He sensed someone at his elbow. Then there was a voice speaking German.

'Good evening, Herr Catesby, would you like a little kiss?' The German was a dapper young man in a light grey suit.

'Have you brushed your teeth?'

'I don't mean that sort of kiss. I mean one of these.' The man held out a serving plate with what looked like tiny cupcakes. 'They're called *beijinho* – which I believe translates as *kleine Küsse*.'

'Thank you.' Catesby took one of the cakes and ate it. 'Lots of coconut. I'm not fond of coconut.'

'Neither am I. Have you tried mother-in-law's eye, *olho de sogra*?'

'No.'

'It's a sweet wrapped in dried plum. I prefer them.'

'Do you speak Portuguese?' said Catesby.

'A little.'

'But I bet your Portuguese isn't as good as your Russian?'

The German smiled blandly without answering.

Germans were a problem in Cuba. They could be either brand. The West Germans were fully represented with an embassy. But the East Germans, formerly completely unrepresented, had signed a trade deal with the revolutionary government and now had a 'commercial mission' in Havana. It seemed likely that the East German presence was going to grow and the 'Wessies' might clear off entirely.

'That's a nice suit,' said Catesby, 'did you get it from the HO?' The HO, *Handelsorganisation*, provided East Germany's official state shops. A lot of people found HO clothes frumpy, but Catesby rather liked them – and the suit did look very HO. Perhaps they were dressing down to fit in with the Cubans.

'You are obviously teasing me because you want to know if I represent the BRD or the DDR.'

'It could make a difference.' Catesby nodded towards Katya. 'Do you owe her an apology?'

'I don't know what you're talking about.' The German studied Catesby with hooded eyes. 'Maybe you owe her an apology.'

Catesby noticed that General Alekseev was staring in their direction. Things were getting complicated. Catesby nodded a greeting at Alekseev. The Russian raised his glass. Even more complicated. Catesby turned to the German, 'Do you know the general and his wife?'

'Manchester United,' said the German, 'aren't doing very well this season.'

'No, they look headed for a middle-table finish.'

'I suppose Busby's trying to rebuild with younger players.'

Catesby smiled. 'Would you like us to get you some tickets for Old Trafford?'

The German suddenly switched to English and put on a pastiche posh accent. 'That would be jolly spiffing good, old sport.'

Catesby laughed. 'We'd better not get you those Man U tickets after all.'

'Isn't my English good enough?' They were both speaking German again.

'It's not, how should I say, nuanced enough.'

The German looked deflated, but it wasn't because he couldn't speak Mancunian English. 'It's a pity we can't spend the rest of the evening talking about football. I never know when I'm getting things right.'

Catesby looked at his fellow spy. He probably wasn't much over thirty, if that. He could tell from the accent that he was a Berliner. He'd probably been fourteen or fifteen at the end. Catesby wondered if he had been one of those boy soldiers in uniforms three sizes too big lugging anti-tank grenades through the ruins and crying for their mothers. War is shit – especially if you have to fight for the wrong side.

'You want to tell me something,' whispered Catesby.

The German gave the instructions clearly and concisely. It was also important that Catesby went there alone.

Yo soy un hombre sincero
De donde crecen las palmas ...

Even though it was two in the morning the sound of music and people singing still percolated through the narrow streets that smelled of mildew and cooking.

Yo soy ... an honest man
From where the palm trees grow
Before dying I want
To share these poems of my soul ...

You heard the song everywhere. It wasn't just a Cuban song. It was the song of all the Americas from the Rio Grande to Tierra del Fuego.

Guantanamera
Guajira Guantanamera ...

It starts as a love song. A *guajira* is a young peasant woman, but *guajira* also means a song – the woman and the song become one. And the lyric becomes a love song of both place and person – for *Guantanamera* identifies the place, the province, of the *guajira*. As she tends her fields, she is not only a *guajira*, but a *Guantanamera* – the place itself.

The cobbles of *Calle San Ignacio* glistened in the light warm rain as Catesby made his way through *Habana Vieja* to the rendezvous. Most of the houses had narrow balconies with iron railings overhanging the footpaths. In the sunlight of day the balconies would be festooned with washing. From an alleyway there was the sound of a drummer pounding out a rumba beat. An Afro-Cuban woman emerged from a doorway in front of him. A white dress clung tight to hips that seemed to syncopate effortlessly to the drum rhythm. She was a *guajira* too, part of the sensual mystery that surrounded him. Catesby wondered if, despite his pale skin and ways, he could enter that dark warmth and drown himself in the night. The woman in front of him rapped gently on a door and softly called a name. The door opened and she was gone – leaving behind a smell of sweet musk and sweat.

Catesby crossed Calle O'Reilly. It had stopped raining and he could hear voices from the upstairs bar and the clink of *mojitos* being poured. He could tell from the smells that he wasn't far from the harbour. The tang of salt water and oily smoke began to permeate, and the inscrutable night noises of a working port – bumps, shouts and clangs – echoed over the water. Someone emerged from the shadows and stopped him. It was an old man wearing a tattered straw hat. He leaned towards Catesby and said, *'Oye chico, tú sabes ...'*

Catesby never found out what he was supposed to know, *saber*, for the old man lurched back into the night. A chill of cold sweat ran down his spine. Maybe the old chap was warning him of something, had spotted something dangerous lurking. Catesby turned around and said, *'Qué, compay?'* But no one answered. The old man was gone.

In daytime *La Plaza de la Catedral* would have been pulsing with human life, but in the moonless night it seemed to have reverted to the swamp from which it had been drained. Three sides of the square were bordered by arched colonnades. Catesby imagined alligators and giant lizards lurking in the shadows. Set back behind the colonnades were majestic eighteenth-century houses where rich merchants had once counted their gold doubloons after going to Mass and communion.

Catesby kept to the middle of the square, well away from the dark colonnades, as he made his way to the Cathedral of San Cristóbal. His footsteps echoed so loudly that he half-expected the ghost of a Spanish don with a pointed beard to throw open a shutter and order him arrested.

The silhouette of San Cristóbal loomed menacing against the night sky. Catesby felt like Childe Roland going to the Dark Tower to meet his fate – but here were two dark towers, one oddly smaller than the other. The incongruity of the architecture seemed to throw everything else out of balance too. The sense of unreality became even more eerie when Catesby remembered that he was in the centre of a capital which had just witnessed a Marxist revolution based on dialectical materialism. The old gods and the old voodoo spirits seemed to creep back in the dark watches of the night.

The heavy oak door groaned as Catesby pushed it open. The inside of the cathedral was as dark as a tomb except for the faint flicker of devotional candles on one side of the altar. He had been told to go to a pew beneath a painting of *La Asunción de la Virgen*. But it was too dark to see anything – and so spooky that he wouldn't have been surprised to see the Blessed Virgin turn up in person to warn of the coming apocalypse.

Catesby decided he needed one of the candles to navigate. His footsteps squeaked and echoed as he made his way across the marble floor. What a racket. But when he got to the candles he realised that he had no need to go further. In the faint light he could see the oil painting of the Virgin, swathed in her iconic lapis lazuli gown, about to be elevated beyond the clouds. Now he had to find the other woman.

Catesby heard her breathing before he saw her. He turned around and looked at the pews. She was four rows back, at the very limit of the candlelight. She was wearing a mantilla, a gesture of religious respect that you wouldn't normally expect from the wife of a KGB general. Maybe, thought Catesby, she wanted to make amends for her adultery. That's what the Spanish priests who built this place would have wanted.

Catesby retraced his steps down the aisle and slipped into the pew to sit next to her. He folded his hands and stared at the oil painting. The image of the Virgin hovered into sight and out of sight again as the candles flickered and sputtered. It was like watching a very old film.

'Did you kill Andreas?' Katya said the words without looking up.

'No.'

'Please don't lie to me.'

'I didn't kill him – nor did I order him killed either. I wanted to keep him alive because …'

'Because of his relationship with me.'

'I suppose you could say that.'

'Andreas was such an innocent. He was like a child.'

'The innocent never last long in our business.' Catesby could name a dozen other innocents. At the top of the list was Guy Burgess. His drinking, his wholesale sexual indiscretion, his outrageous sense of humour and even his spying were always the japes of a clever sixth former. Perhaps, thought Catesby, this was what had made Guy so much more likeable than the grey grown-ups around him.

'What,' said Katya, 'did Andreas give you?'

'Very little.'

'I know you can't tell me. But I can't imagine what he could have found to pass on.'

Catesby noticed a change in her voice. The last sentence sounded scripted. 'Are you close to your husband?'

'Yes.' Her voice was normal again. 'How can you even ask such a question?'

When he was younger, when he was less aware of the complexities of the human heart, Catesby would have laughed at her reply as blatant hypocrisy. Instead he said softly, 'I'm not here to judge you – I'm here to answer your questions.'

'I want to know what happened.'

'So do I,' said Catesby. 'Did your husband know about your affair?'

Katya looked at Catesby for the first time. Her eyes flickered in the candlelight like coals from behind the lace of her mantilla. 'Yes.'

'Have you been married long?'

'Why do you want to know?'

'Because I want to understand – and I can't put together the pieces to answer your questions, if I don't know more.'

The Russian woman stirred uncomfortably on the pew. After a minute she breathed deeply and began. 'Our wedding was also my nineteenth birthday, the 3rd of January, 1945. It was a beautiful sunny day and so cold. Zhenka was on leave, a tiny break before the Vistula offensive.' She paused and looked at the candles. 'Unfortunately our wedding turned into a funeral, my twin brother was reported killed the same day. But things like that happened all the time – so you just kept living. Her voice dropped to a faint whisper, 'Volodya, Volodya.' Katya then smiled bleakly, 'But you don't want to hear this stuff.'

'You've suffered a lot of pain – and none of it's your fault.'

Katya looked away. 'You can't say that. You don't know anything about me.'

'Except for what Andreas told me.'

'What did he tell you?'

'Intimate things, that only a lover could know.' Catesby paused. 'Why did you dye your hair blond?'

'I was sick of being me – I deceived others, so why not deceive myself.'

'Are you deceiving anyone by meeting me here?'

'We haven't much time. You said you didn't kill Andreas, but I think you were with him when he died.'

Catesby could see that Katya had been briefed to ask questions. He wondered whether it was by her husband or Mischa – or both. He decided to give straight answers. 'Yes, I was with him.'

'What happened?'

'He was shot – by a woman. But I suppose you know that already?'

Katya didn't answer.

'I assumed,' continued Catesby, 'that the woman was working for East German intelligence.'

'Mischa Wolf says that isn't true.'

'Maybe Mischa is lying.'

'Maybe you're lying.'

'This is pointless,' said Catesby, 'we could go in circles like this for ever.'

'My husband is certain that Mischa is telling the truth.'

Catesby smiled. 'If your husband thinks that the *Ministerium für*

Staatssicherheit keeps no secrets from the KGB, then he must believe in Baba Yaga and her magic broomstick too.'

Katya shivered slightly, as if the reference to the arch-witch of Russian folklore had given her a moment's fright.

'There's a part of you that still believes in spirits,' said Catesby, 'that's why you're wearing a head-covering in this church.'

'No, not really. But the worst thing about the war was not being allowed to mourn.' Katya laughed. 'How do you mourn twenty-six million of your fellow citizens? But that loss, as the years go by, creates a respect for the spiritual. But don't think for a second ...' she laughed again and suddenly removed the mantilla from her head, '... that I'm a believer.'

Catesby looked at her and watched her eyes flash like a cat about to leap. Her glossy black hair flowed free and sparkled in the candlelight. Catesby suddenly understood how Andreas had ended up nailed to a rosy rack of longing. Ekaterina Mikhailovna Alekseeva wasn't beautiful – she was magnificent.

'Stop staring at me. I don't like it when men stare at me.'

'Why do you think they stare at you?'

'Because ...' Katya fidgeted and turned away.

'Yes, I was staring at you – and I'm sorry that it made you uncomfortable. I hope you don't think ...'

Katya laughed. 'You don't want me to think what? That you desire me?'

'Does it matter?'

'No, it doesn't matter. I don't want another man. My husband satisfies me.'

Catesby sat staring in silence at the Virgin Mary as candlelight flickered across her stone face.

'Are you surprised?' said Katya.

'Why should I be surprised? Your intimate relations with your husband are none of my business.'

'Then you're not a very good spy.'

'I still get paid – that's more than you can say for Andreas.'

'You're disgusting. You have no respect.'

'I'm sorry. I shouldn't have said that about Andreas.' Catesby paused. 'You know that he loved you.'

'He told you that?'

'Yes, it was almost the last thing he said. Did you love him?'

'I'm not sure.' Katya looked away. 'You have heard about my husband?'

'There are rumours that he was badly wounded in the Battle of Berlin.'

'Do you know how badly?'

Catesby shrugged. He didn't want to say the words.

'My husband lost his manhood. He was emasculated.'

'It must be awful for both of you.'

Katya gave a sad half-smile that softened her face. 'It's worse for him. At first, we never talked about it, but still pretended we were a normal couple except for that. But we were a normal couple. We lived together, we shared a bed, we talked – and talked, but always about other things. Did you know that Zhenka sings?'

Catesby shook his head.

'He has a lovely voice. He could have been in the Red Army choir.' Katya smiled more broadly. 'One evening, after a little vodka, he was singing Katyusha – a favourite of his, because of my name of course: *Pust on zemliu berezhet rodnuiu / A liubov Katyusha sberezhet.*'

She looked at Catesby. 'You know Russian, don't you?'

He nodded.

'How would you say those lines?'

'Let him preserve the Motherland / Same as Katyusha preserves their love.'

'Of course,' said Katya, 'those words, after what happened to poor Zhenka, are unbearably sad. I started crying, like I am now, and he put his arms around me. And do you know what my wonderful husband said?'

Catesby shook his head.

'He said, with such a big smile, "At least, my darling Katyusha, at least, I can now do all the high notes."' Katya wiped her tears away. 'And it was good that he made that little joke. It broke the ice that had formed between us.'

'And could he do the high notes?'

Katya gave Catesby a playful slap on his hand. 'Zhenka would like you. You have the same sense of humour – and no, he still can't do the high notes.'

'Was Andreas your first lover?'

'No.' Katya looked away as if ashamed. 'It took me a while to explain things to Zhenka.'

'What things?'

'That you don't need a penis to satisfy a woman.'

Catesby looked over the sputtering candles at the Blessed Virgin being drawn up into heaven. Then back to Katya, a real woman. 'How did your husband feel about you having affairs?'

'I don't know. What he tells me and what he feels inside may not be the same.'

Catesby looked into the black void behind Katya. What, he thought, does it mean to be a man? How much of your life did you actually spend with an erection? You don't need one to write a poem, compose a symphony or enjoy a fine bottle of wine. You don't need one to take a life. But you do need one to create a life.

'What are you thinking about?' said Katya.

'I don't know.' Catesby looked at her again. 'Do you still think I killed Andreas?'

'No.'

'What did Mischa tell you?'

'He says it may have been you, but he doesn't think so. Neither Mischa nor my husband fully understands what happened. I know they're not lying.'

'Why?'

'If they were lying, they would make up a more interesting story than simply, "We don't know."'

Catesby smiled. Katya had obviously not spent much time in Bow Street Magistrates Court. 'And that was the end of that?'

'No. My husband asked Mischa about the woman who was with you.'

'How did they know there was a woman?'

Katya smiled. 'Mischa knows everything that goes on in the West German Security Services.'

Catesby wasn't surprised. 'So what about the woman?'

'Mischa swore to Zhenka that she was no longer in Germany – either Germany.'

'Are you supposed to be telling me this?'

Katya smiled. 'Of course.'

'And they don't know where she is?'

'No, but they said it may have something to do with someone called Galen. Have you heard the name?'

'Only in reference to the ancient Greek physician. Why do they want me to know these things?'

'They said that you would ask that.'

'And what are you supposed to say?'

'That it is in the shared interest of all our countries.'

'That's diplomat speak for telling the other side they have to give in.' Catesby gave a weary smile. 'It's like preaching about peace.'

'You sound hard and cynical.'

'That's a false impression. I'm neither.'

'Is that really true?'

'Yes.'

She leaned forward and kissed him lightly on the lips. 'I must be going now.'

Catesby slid out of the pew so that she could leave. He stood up and watched her disappear, like an extinguished taper, into the cathedral blackness. He waited until he heard the heavy door open and shut before he followed.

When he left the cathedral, there were two red lights shining low in the square and the oily whiff of a Trabant two-stroke engine. As the car set off into the night, the headlamps of a second car swept across the square and followed it. In the reflected light, Catesby caught a brief glimpse of the five-pointed red star mounted on gold hammer and sickle that emblazoned the bonnet of the GAZ M21 Volga.

PART TWO

Bremen. December, 1961

Domsheide was the tram stop in front of Bremen Cathedral. It was half past six in the morning and the cobblestones of the Marktplatz glistened under the freezing drizzle. A man wearing a black seaman's watch cap and a pea jacket walked bent against the cold to the tram stop with a canvas bag over his shoulder. His codename in Moscow and East Germany was the Russian word for harlequin, Arlekin.

The man had a black goatee and shiny brown eyes: he was obviously an *Auslander*, a foreigner. The other person at the tram stop was a large, thickset, middle-aged man wearing a Prinz-Heinrich-Mütze, a peaked dark wool cap, and a grey belted raincoat. He had the slightly arrogant air of a *Beamte*, a government official of rank. The newcomer huddled his shoulders and blew on the bare knuckles of the hand clutching the bag. '*Sehr kalt*,' he said.

'*Natürlich*, it is winter.'

The pea-jacketed newcomer whispered the rest of the identification scenario as if the words were a secret spell, '*Und frisch weht der Wind*.' The words were from a love duet in *Tristan und Isolde*. The liaison that had arranged the meeting must have chosen them as a joke. But Arlekin feared that other words of the duet contained a clue to his identity.

The man in the Mütze covered his mouth with a gloved hand, an inbred precaution against surveillance cameras and lip readers. 'I'm your controller for your time in Bremen – for a while afterwards you'll be on your own. Is that okay?'

Arlekin nodded, even though he was annoyed that the plan had been altered from a plane journey with false passports – and then to a rail journey, which was also cancelled. There must have been security breaches.

'The important thing is that you don't speak to anyone. Not a word, not even if they speak to you. Understand?'

'Yes.' Arlekin hid a purely personal annoyance. He wasn't used to being spoken to like that.

'Good. But for now we stay together. Follow me off the tram at Gröpelingen – it's the last stop. Stay close behind me when I go through the dockyard gate so you don't get lost in the crowd. Have you got a gun?'

'No.'

'Neither have I – I don't like guns. If anything goes wrong, we head for the sewers. Cops don't like sewers. But don't worry, nothing will go wrong.'

A few seconds later Arlekin watched a pair of lamps appear out of the gloom as the Linie 2 tram snaked off Bismarckstrasse and hissed across the Marktplatz. The drizzle distorted the approaching lights into prickly blurs. The two men boarded through the middle door and franked their tickets in the stamping machine. Arlekin chose a seat two rows behind his controller and stared blankly out the window. The hard dark towers of the Dom, the cathedral, stabbed into the soft dark of the sky. A statue of Roland, sword at shoulder, stood like a clueless anachronism in the square – as if wondering what his Europe had become.

The passengers who began to fill the tram were mostly Turkish *Gästarbeiter*, guest workers, cheap labour imported to fuel the West German 'economic miracle'. The guest workers all looked sullen, tired and fed up – or maybe they just didn't like the cold gloom of the North. The tram suddenly lurched to a halt where there was no stop. A man in a dark uniform boarded: the ticket inspector. The Turks stirred uncomfortably. The tram lurched off again and Herr Inspektor made his way down the aisle. Occasionally, he frowned at a ticket and demanded identity papers. He then copied details on to his clipboard before handing out a *Geldstrafe*, an instant fine. All the Turks had tickets, but many of them covered the ticket with a thin coating of Vaseline so that the ink from the franking machine could later be wiped away and the unfranked ticket used again. The inspector was on to this trick and disgusted by those who used it – there was a word for them, but it was no longer acceptable to use it – not since '45. There was, finally, a Turk with a Vaseline-covered ticket who objected to being fined and refused to show his identity card. The inspector shouted at him, but the *Gästarbeiter* still refused to comply. The inspector then began to hit the Turk about the head and shoulders with his palm and the back of his hand. It seemed that the situation was going to end only with more violence or a police arrest. Suddenly, a voice spoke in the clear refined German of the *Beamte* class. 'For God's sake, stop hitting the man – it's undignified.' It was the controller. Arlekin swore under his breath. Why was he getting involved at a time like this? The inspector, however, immediately stopped striking the Turk and looked away; he was used to obeying that sort of voice.

The controller then turned to the Turk. 'Listen, son, you're being a bit silly. Your ticket hasn't been properly stamped. Give the inspector your identity card and accept the fine summons – and that's the end of it.' The Turk did as he was told and the inspector quietly carried out his duty. The tram official then turned to Arlekin who was already offering his ticket. The inspector thought that Arlekin with his goatee and foreign clothing was an odd fish, but merely glanced at his ticket. He didn't want another run-in with that *Beamte* type. The inspector pressed the stop request bell and hopped off into the gloom.

The tram was packed to overflowing by the time it reached Gröpelingen, but then quickly emptied into the damp dark of the waterfront. Arlekin lifted the duffel bag on to his shoulder. He and the controller were the last to leave the carriage. The roadway was a chaos of workers on foot and bicycle crushing through the gates of the AG Weser shipyard. The bicycle lamps weaved through the dark like fireflies with bells. They played a strange minimalist music: bell followed by voice; '*Vorsicht!*', 'Watch out!' or '*Pass man auf!*', the more egalitarian 'Watch out, thou!' The shipyard entrance was picketed by two men in leather jackets handing out leaflets condemning the 1956 law that banned the KPD, the *Kommunistiche Partei Deutschland* … a revolutionary party of the working class that was heir to the anti-fascist struggle and endeavoured for an anti-fascist and democratic rebirth after liberation from Hitler's fascism.

Suddenly, the two men turned up their collars and disappeared into the swirling throng of workers. A second later the white peaked caps of two *Polizei* appeared. The KPD was '*polizeilich verboten*', 'policely forbidden.' Arlekin smiled to himself and wondered if German was the only language that made an adverb out of 'police'?

Arlekin had to walk quickly to follow his companion. The controller didn't head directly for the dock gates, but stopped at a lighted kiosk that sold newspapers and sundries. He bought two miniatures of schnapps then took Arlekin to the shadows at the back of the kiosk. 'Here,' he said as he offered the schnapps, 'drink this.' The strong liquor tasted fine and tingling warm in the damp cold. The controller then opened the other miniature and splashed it over Arlekin's goatee and jacket. 'You're an absolute disgrace, my friend. Let's go.'

Arlekin, burdened with his bag, struggled to keep up as the controller marched through the dock gates with long sure strides. The tall German, in his expensive mackintosh and Mütze, looked like he owned the shipyard.

Most of the workers forked off to the right, towards the locker rooms to change into overalls. The Germans wore dark blue overalls; the Turkish *Gästarbeiter*, light brown. The foremen wore white helmets and quartered the huge yard on bicycles. But none of them seemed to take note of the two men who strode past the huge slabs of hull sections waiting to be welded into a 300,000 ton tanker, then beyond the engineering offices with blueprints pinned to easels and racks of T squares and triangles, and finally past the blue lights of the *Feuerwehr*, the dock fire brigade. The skyline was etched with cranes and the masts of ships, but there seemed few people in the dark corner heaped with piles of hawsers and rusting chains. The air smelled of tar and oil. The controller suddenly took Arlekin by the elbow and led him to where the cobbles ended and where there was the only dark void of the River Weser below. Arlekin suddenly pulled back sharply from the edge; for a second he thought he was about to be hurled into the river. 'Don't worry,' whispered the controller, 'they're down there.'

It was low water and the pilot cutter was almost hidden in the shadow of the harbour wall. The controller leaned over the wall and shouted, '*Grenzpolizei*.' Border Police.

An annoyed voice answered from below. 'What do you want?'

'I've got a package for you to take to the *Lech*.'

'Why don't you use the *Bundespost*?' A crewman laughed.

'Because it won't fit through the letter box.'

The controller began to climb down the cold iron ladder rungs set into the harbour wall. Arlekin tied his duffel bag around his shoulder and followed down the damp slippery rungs. The pilot cutter was painted rescue orange and the big diesel engines were ticking over on low revs. It was a small boat, but built for rough seas. The last of the ebbing tide swirled around the hull with its own cargo of boxes, bottles and dead rats. The controller stepped through a gap in the guard rail on to the side deck of the cutter. A voice from inside the wheelhouse whispered to someone down below. 'Do you know this new policeman? I've never seen him before.'

Someone hidden in the shadows of the lower deck laughed. 'Maybe old Kurt got drunk and fell in the river.'

Then someone else said, 'Shhh.' And there was a tense silence.

Arlekin grasped his duffel bag firmly and looked at the swirling water. Finally, the skipper of the pilot cutter stuck his head out of the wheelhouse to confront his visitors. The skipper's upper lip was badly distorted – as if he had a cleft palate that had been poorly repaired. The damage thickened his speech. 'The *Lech* is on the other side of the river – in the Neustädter Hafen. You should know that – that's where all the ships from the East have to go.' The skipper paused and looked hard at the fake border policeman. 'We ferry pilots around the harbour, not just anyone.' The skipper looked at Arlekin. 'Is that the package you want me to deliver? He looks like a gypsy.'

'He's a Pole.' The controller picked up Arlekin's left arm and rolled back the coat sleeve. The hand and arm were bandaged. 'He burnt his arm on a steam valve – and had to go to the St Jürgenstrasse Hospital. When they let him go, he got too drunk to find his way back to his ship.' Arlekin stared expressionlessly into space. He tried hard to act out his cover story as a drunken sailor with learning difficulties. It was good to learn humility, to feel what it was to be powerless.

'I think,' continued the controller, 'he's a bit stupid – or maybe touched. In any case, he doesn't speak any German – the only thing he could say to the police when they picked him up was *Polski marynarz*, Polish sailor.'

The skipper turned to whisper something to the pilot, a self-assured looking man – an aristocrat of the sea who wore his peaked *Käpitanmütze* at a rakish angle and smoked a pipe. The pilot looked at his watch and said, 'It's getting late – we don't want to miss the last of the ebb.' Arlekin stared at the back of the skipper's neck and realised the deformed lip had nothing to do with cleft palate: there was a huge ugly wound where the machine-gun bullet that smashed his face had made its exit. They were all scarred by that heritage: it must never happen again.

Two tugboats were making their way across the river, the tide forcing them sideways. The skipper looked up at the controller. 'Your Pole really should go through customs. I've never done this before – and I don't want to do it now.'

The controller reached into the breast pocket of his coat and began to flourish what seemed to be identity documents. 'I'll clear it with customs, don't worry.'

The skipper shook his head and waved away the document wallet. 'You really ought to have gone around to the Neustädter Hafen – and embarked him properly through the *Zollbeamte*. They have to count all these birds off and then on again.'

'There's no sense in talking about what we should have done, we're here now and there isn't time to put it right.'

Everyone knew there were no bridges near the docks. A trip to Neustädter Hafen would have meant a lengthy drive back to the centre of Bremen and then down the opposite bank of the Weser. And by then the Polish ship would have long departed.

The controller lowered his voice and got confidential with the skipper. 'Look, I don't want to get stuck with this fellow – something's not right with him. If he misses that ship, it means we'll have to keep him in a police cell – and maybe get psychiatric help too. And the Polish consul is already away for Christmas, so it could be a long wait for repatriation. The simple thing is just to put him on that ship – and that's the end of it.'

'Make up your mind, Willy.' The pilot was speaking. 'We really must get going or we'll miss the lock at Brunsbüttel.' He gestured with his pipe to the *Lech*. 'That old girl can only do ten knots.'

The skipper waved a hand in front of his face as if brushing away responsibility, then gestured to Arlekin. 'Come aboard – it's back East with you where you belong.'

By the time it was light, they were abeam of the *Roter Sand* lighthouse. Arlekin had just finished a breakfast of rye bread and Twaróg, a sort of curd cheese. There was also a flask of black tea. Arlekin still felt a sense of pique. He knew that the Bremen controller had treated him with less dignity than was necessary. It was as if it was a matter of personal score-settling. It worried him and he wondered how much the controller knew.

Arlekin poured the last of the tea and went over to a porthole to look at the bleak seascape of dawn mist. *Roter Sand* lighthouse was a stately structure from the Bismarck era with two mock Gothic turrets, the larger one housing a light that flashed three times every four seconds. They were in the *Deutsche Bucht*, known in the British Shipping Forecast as German Bight. It was a treacherous sea area scored with sandbanks by the outflows of the rivers Ems, Weser and Elbe. Arlekin regarded the sandy brown water and imagined Saxon longships taking the tide on their way to harry the east coast of England as the Romans withdrew – and then carrying settlers across the North Sea to replace the Romans.

He sipped the tea and looked westwards trying to make out the island of Wangerooge, but the mist was too thick. Wangerooge was one of the islands that Erskine Childers had written about in *The Riddle of the Sands*. Arlekin peered hard through the porthole, but there was only swirling mist. Erskine Childers was more of a riddle than the shifting sands he had written about. Childers had been a man of complex loyalties – and even more complex disloyalties. His life had ended in front of a firing squad – the day after he had made his sixteen-year-old son vow to shake hands with each of the executioners. Arlekin wondered what it would be like to face a firing squad. The French were the only Western power that still used them. And the OAS generals and officers who attempted the putsch against de Gaulle were going to face them soon.

The pilot disembarked from the *Lech* when they reached the Baltic end of the Kiel Canal. As they lay alongside dock, Arlekin stretched out on a narrow steel bunk and pulled a blanket over his head. If anyone looked through the porthole they would see only an empty dark cabin, or at best a sick crewman curled up in bed. As Arlekin lay with his forehead against the steel bulkhead, he heard shouting in German, and then loud footsteps on the deck. These were real border police. Were they going to search the ship? There was more shouting and another voice speaking German, but in an accent that didn't sound German. Arlekin wondered if it was the ship's skipper. Whoever it was, he was laughing. Maybe that was a good sign – or good acting. Then silence. After what seemed like an hour, Arlekin looked at his watch – only ten minutes had passed. Then the worst thing happened. Hatches were being opened and closed: loud echoing, clanging noises. They seemed to be progressing from one end of the ship to the other. Each time a hatch clanged shut heavy running footsteps echoed around the ship. There also seemed to be a lot of people going up and down ladders. The most frightening noise was the unbearable racket of someone beating a hammer on what seemed to be an empty cistern. It was as if the hammer wielder was trying to flush a stowaway out of his hiding place.

Arlekin lay facing the cold steel of the bulkhead next to the bunk. He started planning what he would have to do. If he pretended to be mentally ill they might leave him alone. He tried to recollect the faces and gestures of the patients he had seen in a mental hospital. He especially remembered the lobotomised woman who took an hour to put on a sock – all the while rocking back and forth. And then, when she finally got the sock on, she pulled it off again and started screaming. If the searchers came into the cabin, that's what he would do. He would pretend to be her. But he knew he couldn't do it. It would be disrespectful to use her like that. Arlekin had loved the woman. He still loved her. He lay motionless as his tears dampened the thin mattress beneath his face.

It all ended as mysteriously as it had begun. The border police must have left the ship. Arlekin could hear the engines starting up and the slapping sounds of hawsers against the hull as they cast off. He waited ten minutes before getting up and looking out the porthole. There was no land: the view was seaward across the broad waters of the Baltic. Arlekin had just begun to breathe easy when he heard a knocking at the cabin door. He remembered that he wasn't to talk to anyone so he ignored the knocking. He waited for the person to go, but could hear shuffling and breathing on the other side of the door. The knocking began again in earnest. He assumed it must be someone coming to take away the breakfast dishes so he opened the door.

The visitor looked like an ordinary Polish seaman. He was dressed in khaki overalls with a soiled red bandana around his neck and a greasy rag hanging from one pocket. He smiled broadly and put a finger to his lips. Arlekin wasn't sure what was happening. He wanted to tell his visitor to go away; he was sure the crew had been warned not to fraternise and not to ask questions. He shook his head and gestured for the other to leave. But the man in overalls just kept smiling and gestured for him to follow. Arlekin knew the reason for his enforced silence – lest a single word or accent give away his nationality or identity. He didn't know how to deal with the visitor. He considered pushing him away and slamming the door, but the visitor's face was too kind and innocent for such a rude response. The seaman gestured again with a friendly summoning hand. Against his better judgement, Arlekin followed.

The corridor was narrow and dimly lit by low wattage bare bulbs. At the end was a hatch that opened to a steep stairwell that descended precipitously through the two lower decks. At the bottom of the stairs there was another bulkhead hatch which vibrated like a drum head to the loud thumping noise it contained. The seaman opened the hatch. He was smiling broadly as he turned to descend a ladder. Arlekin followed. The noise was much louder, but not deafening – pleasant, in fact. At the bottom of the ladder there was a workbench that faced a large panel full of gauges. The ranks of gauges were separated by a brass clock with roman numerals and a huge wheel of cast iron. The engine room was dry and warm like a Mediterranean beach in summer and smelt of hot oil. The man in overalls made a sweeping gesture as if to embrace the room and then pointed to himself with pride: he was the chief engineer.

The engineer picked up a pair of wire-framed reading spectacles from the workbench and put them on. The glasses, precarious and uneven on the tip of his nose, suddenly transformed him from worker to intellectual. The lens magnified his eyes and made him seem even kindlier and more knowing. The engineer took his guest by the elbow and led him to the very heart of the ship; the great pounding dark goddess that drove all her tons through the waters at a stately ten knots. And she was beautiful.

Arlekin stood for a moment in awe. The piston rods were radiant and sleek limbs in the half light. They looked like three dancers as they stroked in perfect syncopation to an endless minimalist music. Arlekin knew something about ships and he knew that he was in the presence of a triple expansion steam engine: a beautiful, but rare survivor into the marine diesel age of 1961. Her dance was graceful and slow as she turned the crankshaft at a mere sixty revolutions a minute – the pulse rate of a woman asleep and dreamless. He was almost hypnotised by the slow pendulum movement. He wanted to sleep too.

Suddenly, the engineer was tugging again at his elbow. There was something else he had to show him. The urgency suggested that this was the important thing, the very reason for the engine room tour. Arlekin was taken to inspect a large brass plaque, a data plate that was bolted on to the aft end of the engine assembly. The engineer took a clean rag from his pocket and gave the data plate an unnecessary buff, for it already gleamed, then stood back like a curator revealing the museum's prize exhibit. The embossed letters read:

SWAN HUNTER
NEWCASTLE, ENGLAND
1934

Arlekin was abashed, but kept a straight face and didn't even shrug his shoulders as if to say 'so what'. It was amusing, but it was also unfortunate. His job was to remain an anonymous piece of baggage on the way there and on the way back. Any speculation about who he was and why he was there could have serious consequences. Arlekin looked blankly at the engineer and jerked his head upwards to indicate he wanted to go back. He was worried. The behaviour of the engineer suggested bad security. Or it may have been part of the plan.

Arlekin spent the rest of the voyage lying on his bunk – and trying not to worry. He knew that what he was doing was a terrible risk, but not taking that risk could be even more terrible. He had changed a lot since he was a young man. Winning was no longer all. Winning could mean that everyone loses. The problem was that not everyone understood what was at stake. And people still used out of date words like appeasement and patriotism – and treason. And what was honour? A pointless duel where you shoot each other's children, until someone has the sense to shout, 'Enough!' But these were inner thoughts he had to keep to himself

The thump of the steam engine suddenly changed pace and a shudder went through the ship. They seemed to be stopping. Arlekin got up and looked out the porthole. It was dusk, but he could still make out a flat coastline without any lights. The engine then clunked back into gear and the coastline came closer. He could soon discern a line of sandy beach and a clump of driftwood. As they approached the narrow entrance there was a flashing red light on the end of a breakwater – and then, as unexpected as grace, a windmill as white and ancient as a ghost. Both banks of the waterway were bound by dark woods. A few minutes later, the woods were replaced by the cranes of Świnoujście Harbour scoring the sky.

Świnoujście was the outer harbour. The main harbour, Szczecin, was further inland on the other side of the Oder/Szczecin Lagoon. Both harbours had been German before 1945 – and known as Swinemünde and Stettin. When the borders changed, the former German residents had to shift thirty miles to the east, to the new Deutsche Demokratische Republik. And in turn, the newly christened harbours were repopulated with Poles who had been displaced from the parts of western Poland which had been annexed by the Soviet Union. Arlekin knew it was pointless to care too much about these things. There were far worse fates than packing bags and learning new languages. Peace was more important than just and fair solutions for all. But so was power.

The plans were not completely clear. But the important thing for now was complete secrecy. One option had been for Arlekin to leave the ship at Szczecin. But apparently Mischa wasn't happy about that one. The Szczecin option meant that the UB, the Polish Intelligence Service, would be responsible for taking him to the DDR border and turning him over to minders from Mischa's own East German State Security Ministry. It occurred to Arlekin that Mischa had abandoned the Szczecin option because he didn't trust UB security. When Arlekin's clandestine visit had been negotiated, Mischa's intermediary had bluntly asked if Polish intelligence had been penetrated by the Western allies. Arlekin gave the usual safe answer. He said he didn't know.

The *Lech* proceeded slowly past the Świnoujście cranes and docks as if waiting for instructions. For a while the navigation lights of a smaller craft motored abeam of the *Lech* as if lining up for a rendezvous, but then gave up the game and disappeared into the dark. The lights and cranes of Świnoujście then faded away and it was as if the ship had dropped into an underworld. Arlekin strained his eyes to make out something, to get a bearing, but there was only blackness. Finally, there was a green marker light that illuminated the end of a retaining wall. It looked like they had reached the end of a canal. A moment later there was a break in the clouds. A brief burst of moonlight revealed a broad lagoon of open water so vast that you couldn't see land. The ship continued at a slower pace than ever before; cloud extinguished the moon and a gust of wind pelted the porthole with icy rain. They appeared to have stopped.

The ship seemed suspended in a netherworld where time had

stopped. The stasis was suddenly broken by a roar of engines coming from the west that grew louder and louder. Arlekin put his face against the porthole and strained to see what was happening. He finally managed to make out a line of white wake cutting across the black waters of the lagoon. A second later a searchlight from the bridge of the *Lech* began to sweep across the waters until it found a black high-speed boat heading in their direction. The boat, still tracked by the searchlight, yawed sharply as it hove alongside the hull of the *Lech*. A voice from the boat shouted something in German, and then another voice shouted even more loudly in Russian – and the searchlight was quickly extinguished. There was then a clunky sound as a boarding ladder was lowered over the side.

Two minutes later Arlekin heard the sound of heavy boots approaching in the corridor outside his cabin. They stopped outside his door, and there was a pause as someone cleared his throat. Arlekin waited, but no knock came. For the first time, he was frightened: none of this was part of the plan. Just as he was about to call out, the door flew open. It was a tall man dressed in dripping black oilskins and sea boots. His face was masked by a dark scarf that only revealed his eyes. The man gestured and Arlekin followed.

There were no crew about as the pair made their way to the upper decks. For a second Arlekin wondered if the Poles had been imprisoned in a hold or forced to walk the plank. The emptiness was eerie. He followed the tall man in oilskins along the deck to the boarding ladder. The ship was in complete blackout mode; even the navigation lights had been extinguished. The man gestured for him to go first. As Arlekin stepped over the ship's side onto the ladder, he had a sense of déjà-vu. It was a repetition of going over the harbour wall the day before in Bremen. His fear dissipated. Boarding strange boats in the night rekindled the mysterious allure of childhood adventures.

The craft at the bottom of the ladder was a steel-hulled military assault boat powered by two enormous outboards. There were two crew, also dressed in black oilskins with their faces hidden. They cast off without a word and the boat was soon planing at thirty knots an hour across the lagoon. It was bitterly cold, but Arlekin found himself enjoying the fast boat ride in the utter blackness. The only illumination was the compass dial. Forty minutes later, the helmsman cut the speed and pointed the boat to the south. For the first time since leaving the *Lech*, Arlekin was able to see coastline: the silhouettes of trees and the roofs of houses and barns. The helmsman cut the speed to walking pace. Someone was signalling with a light from the end of a jetty.

The crew made fast and the man who had fetched him nimbly mounted a rickety wooden ladder. Arlekin followed. The air was quiet, less cold than before and smelt of farm manure. They were now alone again; the crew had remained behind in the boat. Arlekin's companion walked off the end of the jetty and up on to a turf dyke that protected the farmland from flooding. He stopped and turned at the top of the dyke. The boat crew had revved up the engines and were casting off. The tall man, his face still hidden, gave them a large wave of thanks and they were gone. Arlekin turned around to look for the person who had guided them in with the light, but saw he had set off in the boat with the others. Arlekin suddenly realised that the two of them were alone in a sleepy rural landscape that looked like a Dutch painting. His doubt and anxiety disappeared: he felt in safe hands. As Arlekin climbed the dyke wall, the other man unwound the scarf from his face and spoke to him for the first time. 'Welcome to the German Democratic Republic. My name is Markus Wolf, but everyone calls me Mischa.'

Arlekin looked closely at Wolf. He was as others described him. There were no photos, so Arlekin tried to take a mental one. Wolf was angular, languid, patrician. He had the bearing of a lean, tough, intelligent aristocrat: the sort of noble Roman who served the state as well as he used it.

'There were,' said Arlekin, 'several last-minute changes of plan that I found worrying.'

'I never take unnecessary risks,' said Wolf in a tone that was firm and polite. 'I use all the same precautions when I visit the West. Last-minute changes often decrease rather than increase risk of exposure.'

There was a logic to altering plans, but Arlekin still felt uneasy. 'How many people know that the plans were changed?'

'Fewer than knew about the original. We put out a secret notice to say that the visit was cancelled. And no one knows your identity other than myself and, of course, the most important person, the reason for your visit. Three of his deputies will meet you tomorrow, but for them it will be a surprise.'

'Who were the men in the speedboat?'

'They're not even in the Ministry. They're *Grenzpolizei See*, Maritime Border Police. They think it was just another interception and boarding exercise – we've put them through several.'

'And what about the Poles on the ship? One of them was awfully nosey.'

'Don't worry about them. It was still much safer than a train or coming by air.'

The use of the word 'still' seemed a caveat, but Arlekin was finished quibbling. It had, however, been necessary. He could see that Mischa was also a man used to getting his own way and not being queried.

'Did they give you something to eat?' said Mischa.

'Only breakfast.'

'Then you must be hungry – we should get going.'

They walked along a track to where a black Wartburg 311 was hidden in a barn. 'We've got a long drive,' said Wolf as he slid behind the wheel.

'Is the conference still planned for Kartzitz?' Arlekin was referring to an isolated manor house on the remote Isle of Rügen.

'Don't worry. Security there is absolute. That's why we use it.' Wolf started the engine. 'The car is safe too. It's only got seven moving parts.'

'All of the others are going to be Russians?'

'Yes – except maybe for one more.'

'Can they be trusted?'

'Absolutely. There are no people more secretive than Russians – it's not a question of character, it's a question of history.'

'Sure.'

'You sound doubtful.'

Arlekin frowned.

Mischa looked at him hard. 'You don't know Russia. But I do.'

'Of course I don't. You grew up there.'

'What you must understand is that Russia has tragedies with seasonal regularity,' Mischa paused, 'and sometimes their attempt to deal with a tragedy leads them to precipitate an even greater tragedy.'

'Other people do it too.'

'But this time what began as a Russian tragedy could destroy us all. What happened last year at Baikonur Cosmodrome has set off a chain reaction that has shaken the Kremlin more than any event since the war.' Mischa paused. 'There has been a fundamental change in policy.'

'Is he really going to do it?'

'Ask him tomorrow.'

It was late morning when the quiet stillness of Kartzitz was broken by the sound of a helicopter. Arlekin had changed into a lounge suit and was alone in the kitchen drinking coffee at a large table. The files he had brought with him in the duffel bag were open next to him. It was all part of the deal, all part of the peace process. Arlekin had now removed his fake goatee, contact lenses and washed the black dye out of his hair.

The door opened and Mischa came in. 'Our guests haven't arrived yet. The helicopter that just landed is bringing the security fellows from the Ninth Directorate. They're going to sweep the conference room for listening devices and cameras – and also deal with some personal protection issues. I hope you haven't got a gun.'

Arlekin shook his head.

'Good. I'll tell them I've frisked you myself so none of the Ninth Directorate goons have to see you.'

'Thanks.' Arlekin wanted to stay as invisible as possible and the thought of being searched by a Ninth Directorate attack dog wasn't a good idea. The fact that the Ninth was on hand proved that the visitors from the Kremlin were by no means small fry. In time of war, it was the job of the Ninth Directorate to shoot deserters – and to sacrifice their own lives too. In time of peace, they were the Kremlin's Praetorian Guard. They provided personal security for the Communist Party leadership, as well as for Soviet nuclear weapons and the Kremlin's secret communication systems and archives. The Ninth were the guardians of 'the supreme power of the State'. No Soviet leader could survive without them.

'By the way,' said Mischa, 'I must apologise.'

Arlekin instinctively tensed. 'For what?'

'One more person is going to join us. He arrived late last night.'

Arlekin remembered that Mischa had mentioned the previous night that an additional person might be attending. He wished that he had queried it then. 'Who is he?'

'I can't tell you.'

'Then maybe we should cancel the meeting.'

'There's too much at stake.'

Arlekin's eyes flashed. 'Don't push me too far.'

'If you like, I can inform our guest that he is not welcome. But I can assure you that having him here is in your own interest.'

Arlekin stared hard at Mischa. 'Let him stay. But no more surprises.'

After Mischa left the room, Arlekin heard the noises of heavy boots as the security men turned over various parts of the house. At one point he heard them at the door, as if they were about to come in. But Mischa's voice intervened in fluent Russian and convinced them it was unnecessary.

Fifteen minutes later there was the sound of another helicopter. It sounded much noisier than the one that had brought the security men. Then a third helicopter joined the racket. The windows and crockery rattled as if a poltergeist had been let loose. There was then a silent interval, which was soon broken by the scream of a pair of MiG fighters passing low overhead. As their noise subsided, the staccato beat of a final helicopter began to reverberate. It was the boss.

The escort fighters reminded Arlekin that the Kremlin was a dangerous place. Soviet politics was a blood sport. The players were brave men who knew there was no safety net beneath the high wire they danced on.

When Wolf returned a half an hour later he was wearing a well-cut lounge suit. Mischa looked more like the chairman of a merchant bank than a communist spy chief. Arlekin followed him into a room with a long table of polished dark wood. The size of the table left little room for more furniture. The curtains were drawn and the lights in the crystal chandelier were turned on. 'This,' said Mischa, 'used to be the dining room – not large enough for a banquet. Come sit by me. And remember,' he whispered, 'that we are all taking risks – I'm not sure that any of us is going to die in bed.'

Arlekin could only think of one word, but he dared not say it. It was the most precious thing in the world. It was a word more precious even than love or liberty, for without it, neither could survive. He closed his eyes and listened to the sound of Russian voices on the other side of the door.

The first to enter was a man with very black hair and a pitted complexion. Mischa embraced him and addressed him by his diminutive 'Andriushka'. The Russian looked at Arlekin with disdain and shook hands with cold formality before launching into a rant. Andriushka spoke English well because he had once been Ambassador in Washington.

'The Soviet Union is surrounded by a deadly Western nuclear arsenal. There are American missiles on her very borders in Turkey. And yet, the Western press and politicians keep pumping lies about the Soviet threat so their capitalist friends in the arms industry can make even more money.' Andriushka looked closely at Arlekin. 'But you, in your position, know the truth – you are privileged to peep behind the curtain of lies.'

Arlekin smiled bleakly and nodded for the former Ambassador to go on – which he did.

'The Soviet Union has been forced into a corner by aggressive Western actions. And if you corner an animal and keep taunting it, there comes a point when it will show its claws and attack. As long as the West, or I should say America, has the power to destroy the Soviet Union with one blow, the situation will remain critically dangerous. There is a line of thought among my colleagues that says: "They are poised to kill us; our only hope of survival is to strike first. What can, after all, be worse than what we have already suffered?" You can't fault their logic. You must see that the only way to a secure peace is for both sides to have some form of parity. The Soviet Union must be able to defend itself against the threat of attack.'

Andriushka finished just as the door opened and the other two Russians entered. At first, they looked like a comedy double act: one tall and lean, the other short and thickset. Vladimir Yefimovich Semichastny, the new Head of KGB, was the tall one and had an uncanny resemblance to Graham Greene. The resemblance was ironic for Semichastny made life very difficult for novelists in the Soviet Union. Despite his appearance, he was a crude man. Semichastny greeted Mischa with neither hug nor handshake, but a formal polite nod – like a prize fighter or chess master sizing up an opponent. Surprisingly, he showed no interest at all in Arlekin.

The short Russian wasn't as dumpy as the newsreel clips suggested. His real-life version was much more graceful and firmly toned. He glowed with the ruddy health of a self-assured peasant. He gave a bear hug to Mischa as he entered the room, the top of his head only coming up to Wolf's shoulder. He then shook hands with Arlekin, but used his free hand to playfully slap Arlekin's cheek. The Russian was laughing and had small uneven teeth. His hands were hard workers' hands and the slaps hurt.

As Wolf poured black tea and handed around a tray of hazelnut biscuits, the small but solid Soviet leader stared hard at Arlekin with playful eyes that gleamed like damp pebbles and said something in Russian. Andriushka translated the words, 'If you live among wolves, you have to act like a wolf.'

Arlekin then asked the question, the most important question in the world.

The Russian's eyes continued to sparkle, but his face was no longer laughing. He began to vigorously nod affirmation even before Andriushka had finished translating. Then he said the word with unambiguous finality, '*Da*.'

It was then that Arlekin noticed that there was a sixth man in the room. He hadn't heard or seen him enter. The sixth man was an almost ghostly presence. It was as if he had been there all the time.

'If he had stayed in Cuba and become part of the revolution, he would never have committed suicide.' Che was talking about Ernest Hemingway who had killed himself the previous summer.

'We'll never know,' said Catesby. He had mixed feelings about Hemingway's writing – and mixed feelings about Finca Vigia, the writer's former home on the outskirts of Havana. The Finca had recently been bequeathed to the Cuban government by Hemingway's widow. The Ministry of Culture had invited the usual load of diplos and hacks to a reception to honour the dead author as 'a friend of Cuba'.

'What do you think of the house?' said Che.

'It's airy and light, but rather a lot of dead animal heads hanging around – and I don't know about the tombstones for dogs.'

'To be honest,' whispered Che, 'I prefer Faulkner.'

'Another drunk.'

'Ah,' said Che, 'it's that ...'

'I know what you're going to say.'

'What?'

'Writers in capitalist societies are driven to alcohol, drugs and suicide because they can't resolve their internal conflicts.'

Che nodded and smiled. 'William, you will tell me if I'm ever being a bore?'

'Oddly enough, you never are.' It was true. Che was always aware of the people he was speaking to. He was never lost in an oblivious cocoon of self. And the self-deprecating joke was always close to his lips.

Neville was hovering nearby. He clinked the ice in his daiquiri to signal his presence. They were drinking daiquiris in honour of Papa Hemingway who had virtually invented the Cuban version of the cocktail. Presumably, thought Catesby, to resolve his internal conflicts.

'I say,' said Neville to Guevara, 'is it true that Ava Gardner used to swim naked in this pool?'

'I don't know.' Che looked at the thick layer of green slime and leaves in the bottom of the empty pool. 'I would rather swim in the sea – even when we have hurricanes.'

Catesby remembered his first Cuban hurricane and his first experience of car surfing. He was walking hunched against the wind and driving rain towards the sea for no other reason than he wanted to see the fury of the waves. As a boy in Lowestoft he had often done the same. It was late afternoon and the streets were deserted. Sensible Cubans were battened up in their houses. Suddenly and from nowhere a blue and white Chevrolet Belair pulled up alongside him. The windows were so dripping he couldn't see who was inside until the driver wound down his window a fraction. It was Che. 'Get in William, you'll love this.'

Someone pushed open the back door and Catesby tumbled into a warm fug of perfume and cigar smoke. He found himself sitting next to Katya who was wearing a black skirt and a beige blouse. Her husband was in the front passenger seat holding a camera. Spies with cameras always made Catesby anxious, but he quickly realised that General Alekseev was only interested in snapping the hurricane.

Catesby leaned forward to Che. 'Where are we going?'

'Car surfing.'

It was impossible to actually see where they were going. The wipers were powerless against deluge rain whipped by hundred miles per hour winds. It seemed, however, that they were heading towards the harbour entrance. Che kerbed the car several times as he swerved to avoid fallen trees. The conditions were awful, but it was also apparent that Che was a terrible driver – and the Chevrolet seemed a very flimsy and tinny car to be facing such a tempest. Catesby leaned forward and tapped Alekseev's shoulder. 'I wish we were in one of your sturdy Volgas.'

Alekseev smiled and winked. 'No, no, we must be in this car. It's a *Che* Vrolet.'

Katya groaned. 'Oh, Zhenka, you've made that joke several times already.'

'But,' said Catesby, 'I've never heard it before and I think it's very witty.'

Alekseev smiled gratitude.

Catesby kept looking through the awash windscreen to get his bearings. He could just about make out the grey turrets of San

Salvador de la Punta, the sixteenth-century fortress that guarded the western approaches to Havana Harbour.

What happened next was one of the most extraordinary experiences of Catesby's life. Directly in front of the car was a seawall and accompanying roadway called the Malecón. It stretched along the Gulf of Mexico for five miles until it reached the Rio Almendares which separated Vedado and its derelict casinos from Miramar. In clement weather, the Malecón was where Havana's young gathered to talk and sing and flirt. There were always drums, guitars and rumba dancing. But now the Malecón was a white hell of boiling surf and crashing waves. Catesby watched not just spray but thick dark curtains of water rise forty feet after impacting the seawall – and then collapse on the road like the brick wall of a bombed building. Meanwhile, Che was gunning the car engine.

Catesby leaned forward. 'You're not going to do it, are you?'

Che raised his fist in salute and shouted, '*Hasta la victoria siempre*!'

As the car hit the first crashing wave Catesby felt it lurch violently to one side. The wheels on the seaward side were lifted clear of the road surface and it seemed certain that they were going to flip over. Catesby felt Katya pluck at his sleeve with her left hand. The wave retreated and the car landed back on all fours with a thump. The roof of the Chevrolet flexed inwards as tons of water thundered down on it, but then popped back again as Che pressed the accelerator to the floor to power through the next breaking wave.

There were times when the car really did *surf*, floating free of the road for two, three or four seconds, before the wheels found the concrete again like the paws of a leaping cat. But the most abiding impression was of white pulsating walls of foam and spray that covered the car in rough caresses. Catesby felt Katya thrown against him as the Chevrolet was broadsided by a bull-headed wave. Her hand was on his thigh. Meanwhile Alekseev was snapping photos of giant claw-like waves that reminded him of Hokusai's print.

The car continued to power through seemingly impossible walls of green water only to emerge in boiling white foam on the other side. Che continued to floor the accelerator and to shout *Hasta la victoria siempre*. Alekseev continued to aim his camera at a chaos of warm sea so unlike the waters of his native land. Katya moved her hand from Catesby's thigh and put it between his legs where he was already throbbing with longing. It was the beginning.

Havana was Catesby's happiest assignment. The embassy was a cheerful relaxed place where everyone had started calling the Ambassador by his first name because he asked them to. The informality wouldn't have been appropriate in Paris or Tokyo. 'But,' said Herbert, 'this is Havana.'

Catesby and Neville had also gone native to the extent of growing beards and not always wearing ties. Herbert didn't seem to mind, but hoped they might shave them off if someone, like the PUS for example, popped over from London. But there would be plenty of warning. The US embargo meant that Cuba was no longer easy to get to from the UK.

It was odd that everything was so relaxed, for everyone knew that a crisis was looming. No one yet knew what form the crisis would take, but it was definitely going to happen. Catesby was certain that it would come from America. He couldn't imagine that Kennedy would ever accept the humiliation of the Bay of the Pigs – or that his generals would allow him to accept it. Every morning, after saying *buenos días* to the ceiling lizard, Catesby drew his window curtains expecting to see the US fleet looming in the offing. He knew, from the intelligence he had been cabling back to London, that there was no way the Cuban militias, no matter how brave, could defeat a full-scale US invasion. Unless? There was another option – and he didn't know whether the Cubans should fear it or welcome it.

But in a way, Catesby didn't care as much as he should. Because, in a way, he was happy. The affair wasn't everything he wanted it to be because she only wanted to satisfy him – and did so. Which is fine, he supposed, for a lot of men, but Catesby found pleasure in giving pleasure – especially when he was so fond of the other person. Maybe, he hoped, Katya would change and stop pushing him away when he tried to satisfy her. He knew the psychology of it. That part of her only belonged to her husband. It was her way of remaining faithful. He had to find a way to stop loving her. There were, after all, a lot of men on the island who envied his luck.

But despite his lack of complete happiness with the affair, Catesby was still deeply disheartened when he decoded Henry Bone's latest cable. The fact that the message was so urgent it had to be cabled rather then sent by the air bag was a bad sign.

```
Return to London immediately for temp duty. Crisis
involving CIA counter-intell. Angleton throwing
things out of pram and headed for London. Not
about you personally, as far as I can tell.
Something naughty has happened on your old patch,
allegedly. Paranoia rules. C, PM, JIC aware.
```

The latest addition to the embassy car pool was a powder-blue Ford Fairlane that Neville had found in a backstreet garage. He paid twice what it was worth to one of the few Cubans who thought the revolution was *mierda* and Castro a *culo grande*. The suspension on the car was shot and the bottom scraped every time you drove over a pothole. The Ford, in fact, resembled the corrupt Batista government the garage owner preferred. But at least the Ford had the advantage of Cuban number plates rather than the conspicuous *corps diplomatique* CD. It meant that Neville and Catesby could move about with some degree of anonymity. It helped for meeting Katya too.

The Soviet Embassy was in the leafiest and most exclusive quarter of Vedado. The Russians had taken over the neo-colonial mansion of a rum and sugar magnate whose family had lived there for two hundred years. The old-money rum tycoon preferred Fidel, whom he considered a man of some learning and cultivation, to the casino crooks and pimps who had ruled Vedado since the thirties. But he didn't much like the disruption of the revolution and was content enough to relocate to Uruguay – where he could plot in splendid isolation.

The Russians had done little to disturb the old-world ambience of the mansion, except to build bomb shelters. The high black iron railings that surrounded the compound were still covered in golden chalice vines with their goblet-sized yellow flowers. The porticos and balconies were heavy with wisteria and morning glory. The gardens were a barely contained tropical forest of palm and almond trees. Above the lush riot of vegetation Catesby could see Katya's bedroom balcony. It was maddening in the night. The flower perfumes of evening confused the senses and each shadow suggested a place to embrace.

The rendezvous signal, a vase of *mariposa* silhouetted against the soft light of the bedroom window, was in place. Catesby checked the time and continued past the embassy. He then drove in an evasive way, tracking back on himself and checking the mirror, to make sure he hadn't grown a tail.

The pickup point, the Hospital Maternidad Obrera, had been chosen by Katya. The maternity hospital was the least likely place in Havana to meet Soviet personnel. Katya, her face hidden by a mantilla, was waiting near the entrance cradling an empty blanket. As soon as Catesby pulled up, she hopped in the car and threw 'baby' in the back seat.

'Was it difficult to get away?' said Catesby.

'Not at all. Zhenka is very busy. He's been called back to Moscow.' Katya sounded breathless. There was something in her manner that seemed on edge.

'Is something wrong?'

'I don't know. Zhenka has been in a terrible mood – and everyone at the embassy seems very nervous.'

'Was he called back suddenly?'

'Yes. You usually don't ask me about these things.' Katya's voice had a sharp edge. There was an unspoken agreement that intelligence and spying were to have nothing to do with their relationship.

'I'm not prying,' said Catesby. 'I promise you that. But it's just that I've been called back to London too.'

Katya grabbed his arm hard. 'Permanently?'

'No, thank goodness.'

She still clung to his arm. 'Will you be away long?'

'I hope not.'

'Is it not unfortunate to lose one's husband and one's lover the same day?' Katya let out a long sad breath. 'I'm not a lucky woman.'

'You haven't lost us – unless Baba Yaga makes the planes crash into each other.'

'Don't make jokes like that, William.'

'Sorry.'

Something like that had, however, happened to a woman Catesby knew during the war. Her lover, an American pilot, blew up over Suffolk the same day her infantry officer British husband was killed in Italy. The American's name was Joseph Kennedy, Jr., Jack's older brother.

'This does frighten me,' said Katya. 'It seems too much of a coincidence that both you and Zhenka are called back at the same time.'

'I'm sure it's nothing more than a coincidence.' But he wasn't sure. A dangerous symmetry was taking shape.

Catesby was driving towards a beach on the outskirts of Miramar. The suburb gradually became less and less prosperous. All along the road were posters asking for volunteers to become *alfabetizadores*, literacy tutors. There were also posters featuring wizened workers and peasants with battered straw hats. The captions proclaimed: *We shall read! We shall conquer*! The campaign, initiated and directed by Che, was a fabulous success. In one year, illiteracy, which was forty per cent in many rural areas, had been reduced to four per cent and was still falling. It wasn't a story that was well known on the churchy Main Streets of the USA. Maybe, thought Catesby, those white picket fence ghettos, needed their own 'battle against ignorance'.

Catesby parked between two weather-beaten coconut trees. It wasn't a pretty beach, which may have been why it was so empty and lonely. The most beautiful beach in the region was at Varadero, sixty miles from Havana. The embassy once had a party there. It was a blissful day of snorkelling, Pimm's and beach cricket. He longed to take Katya there for a midnight swim, but it was too far. Instead, they embraced for a long time without saying a thing. Then the ritual unfolded. Catesby blind with longing, but wanting something else too.

Afterwards, they walked along the beach. The sea was serene, as if the hurricane season had left it spent and flaccid. Katya broke the silence which was weighing awkward. 'There's something I've never told you.'

'Are you sure you want to?'

'Yes.' Katya looked closely at Catesby. 'I would never see you again if I thought that you were using me to spy on my husband. But maybe you already knew that?'

'I realise that. And I would never, never do it.'

Katya smiled. 'Then you're not a very good spy.'

'You told me that the first time we met.'

'Would you betray your country for me?'

Catesby didn't answer. He wondered if Katya was playing the coquette.

She smiled again. 'A good spy would have said yes – and then used me to pass false information to Moscow.'

'You obviously know how we do things in the trade. It's not surprising.'

'Yes,' she lowered her voice, 'and that's why I was aware of what Andreas was trying to do.'

'But he loved you.'

'I think so, but he also loved money.' Katya's eyes flashed. 'I hated it when he tried to use me to spy on Zhenka. Hated it.' She smiled. 'We had an awful argument when I found the camera. I made sure he never brought it again. Each time he visited, I stripped him and went through every stitch of his clothing. I made sure he was only seeing me for love.'

Something big and loud dropped in Catesby's brain. It sounded like a steel girder landing in an empty ship's hold. Andreas hadn't told him the whole truth.

'But something awful happened.' Katya had placed a hand on her mouth as if trying to stop the words. Her face had turned pale. 'One day he stole one of my letters. I didn't realise it at first, but it must have been him.'

Catesby turned away. He didn't want her to see the deceit lines on his face. 'Was it an important letter?'

'The most important letter.'

Catesby didn't pry further. He didn't need to. He'd already read it.

Henry Bone looked at Catesby with a wry half-smile. 'Are you going through a D.H. Lawrence phase?'

'Okay, I'll shave it off. I've come straight from the airport and haven't had time.'

'Well, it does suit you. But at the moment a more conventional appearance might be preferable – particularly when we meet the Americans.'

'Your annoyingly urgent cable suggested that the cousins are having a fit about something. Any chance of a cup of tea?'

'Will ordinary workmen's tea suffice?'

'Of course, I am an ordinary workman.'

'Please don't start singing the *Internationale*, Catesby, it's too early in the morning.'

'I can sing in it Spanish, if you like?'

'No, not even in Spanish. There's still a bag of Lapsang Souchong left.'

'Ordinary char will be fine.' Catesby was a bit shocked to see that Bone was making 'bag' tea. He also noted that the barely satisfactory Burleigh service had been replaced by vile-looking cracked mugs. One mug had a handle missing. He had never known Bone to fall so low in the tea service league table. He must be in danger of relegation.

'Help yourself to milk.'

'So what's the situation with the Americans?'

Bone sighed. He looked tired and annoyed, as if he had been asked to explain something tedious for the tenth time.

'Okay,' said Catesby, 'don't tell me.'

'No, you've got to know. It's almost as serious as it is ridiculous. The Americans, especially Angleton and his goggle-eyed acolytes, are now in the land of the Great British Conspiracy. They think that Albion, at her most perfidious, has just stabbed Washington in the back.'

'Pity it isn't true.'

Bone looked at Catesby with one eye. 'For the foreseeable future can you learn to be perfidious and keep those views private?'

'Sure.'

'The Americans claim to have received numerous intelligence reports, all supposedly confirmed and corroborated, that a high-level meeting took place in either Poland or East Germany between a high-ranking British politician or UK government official and the Soviet leadership. The Americans, of course, don't know – or won't say – what this meeting was about. They prefer letting the pot of wild speculation boil over. Is Britain planning to leave Nato and join the Warsaw Pact? Is the Queen, wearing hammer-and-sickle earrings and a Red Army tunic, about to announce the Sovietisation of the United Kingdom? The Americans love this sort of thing. It somehow justifies their self-righteous xenophobia.'

'Are C and the PM in the know?'

'Very much so. On the surface at least, Macmillan is very blasé about it. He shouldn't be.'

'Oh?'

'I like your wide-eyed curiosity, Catesby. You haven't been in England for some time. While you've been swanning about on your Caribbean idyll, there's been a time bomb ticking away beneath the government – which is why this secret meeting nonsense comes at a most awkward time.' Bone paused. 'You love scandal, don't you?'

'I don't really. You're confusing me with Kit Fournier.' Catesby remembered the crude way Kit used to refer to scandals as 'cum stains on cassocks'. The expression probably said a lot about his strict Catholic upbringing.

'Well,' said Bone, 'I have to tell you in any case. It isn't just tittle-tattle. It's a crisis that's going to bring down Macmillan's government. I suspect that the Americans already know about it – at least Kennedy does. I suspect the secret meeting in East Germany nonsense is something the CIA is concocting to discredit a future Labour government as Moscow stooges.'

'They've interfered this way before, Henry. It's outrageous.' Catesby was referring to the CCF, the Congress for Cultural Freedom. The CCF was a CIA front organisation that tarred left-wing Labour MPs as 'undercover communists'.

Bone smiled. 'I certainly know which buttons to press to get you going. Meanwhile, let's get back to the other business.' Bone picked up an A4 size envelope and passed it over.

Catesby pulled out the photographs. The undressed cabinet

minister was the one with whom he had shared a lift to the Ambassador's residence on US election night. He hadn't seen the girl before.

'What do you think?' said Bone.

'She's very pretty and sensuous – in the way young women from my social class often are. Your toff friends don't know what joys they're missing.' Catesby gestured at the photo. 'He looks embarrassed, as if he can hear the camera clicking. She looks bored.'

'There are more photos.'

Catesby shook two more out of the envelope – than sat up as if he had been stung. 'Good god, I don't believe it.'

'You recognise him?'

'It's Ivanov.' Catesby laughed. 'They weren't a threesome, were they?'

'No, fortunately, but the fallout could be just as bad.'

'Is this still going on?'

Bone shook his head. 'Five told Brook, Brook told the PM and the PM told the minister to stop slumming it.'

'I resent the last comment.'

'You have, Catesby, got very tetchy since we sent you to Cuba. Fine, the woman's social class is not a factor – nor is an extra-marital affair. After all, the PM's wife is still having an affair with Boothby, who, interestingly, shares his affections with Ronnie Kray. And the PM, as you know, has a close relationship with Eileen O'Casey. Meanwhile, the Leader of the Opposition is enjoying a long-standing affair with the wife of a former SIS colleague – the one who writes those Bond books. In fact, Catesby, the ruling class's attitude to sex and sexuality is a refreshingly open and liberal one that the rest of the country would do well to emulate.'

'Except,' said Catesby holding up the photo of Ivanov in his birthday suit, 'you don't share a mistress with the Soviet military attaché?'

'It's never a good idea. I was there, by the way.'

'In the bedroom?'

'Don't be silly. No, I was at Cliveden when, apparently, the affairs got going. Billy Astor invited some of my friends and they dragged me along. It was a splendidly warm weekend, the warmest of the summer, so the action centred around the pool. The young woman must not have packed her swimming costume – not that it mattered. The garden sculpture was also resplendent with female nudes.' Bone sighed. 'You know, it was a little vulgar – especially the topiary.

Catesby, in the unlikely event you ever own a stately home, avoid topiary at all costs. It's the sign of a parvenu.'

'Thanks. I'll keep that in mind.'

'In any case, what with the lovely sun, the still heat and the splendour of Cliveden, there was a sense that anyone could get away with anything. It was only natural that the minister and the Soviet military attaché should have a swimming competition. It was very close. I'm not sure who won – but it must have been our lad for he got to have the girl first.'

'Did you behave yourself, Henry?'

'Impeccably. In fact, I had a quiet word with Five about what went on, on the following Monday. Which is odd.'

'What's odd?'

'That it took Hollis so long to get on to the Cabinet Secretary about what happened. Hollis has to watch his back. There are some unsavoury characters in Five who are out to get him. In any case, you'll see for yourself. We're all having a big powwow about this secret summit that allegedly happened someplace in East Germany. Utter paranoid nonsense.'

'Who's going to be there?'

'Hollis, a pair of his poisonous underlings, Dick White, Chairman of the JIC, myself – yourself, of course, since you're still officially Head E.Eur.P – Angleton and at least one other American. You must understand, this meeting is meant to be a sop to Washington.'

There was, thought Catesby, something in Bone's demeanour that was a little too glib and assured. He finished his tea and looked at the chipped and cracked enamel of the mug. Henry was going through a rough patch and trying not to show it.

After a UK-USA intelligence agency stand-off over venue, it was decided to have the meeting at the Dorchester Hotel in Park Lane. At first, the Americans tried to bounce their Brit counterparts into coming to Grosvenor Square. The Brits then suggested Leconfield House, MI5's anonymous HQ in Mayfair. In the end, the Dorchester was agreed as neutral ground. The Americans were happy because it's just around the corner from the US Embassy.

The conference room was far from the Dorchester's grandest – that one looks like the main ballroom in the Versailles Palace. The room the Americans had chosen was no-nonsense and modern. There was a light oak table that sat twelve people and windows that would have looked out over Hyde Park if the curtains hadn't been drawn.

James Jesus Angleton, CIA Head of Counterintell, began the shouting. He pointed at Catesby as if he had just spotted a dead toad in a pot of Chantilly cream. 'What's he doing here?'

Dick White smiled blandly. 'William is our man in Berlin. The places under discussion fall within his areas of responsibility.'

Angleton turned to a florid-faced assistant sitting next to him and whispered something. The assistant, who had fingers like little pink sausages, began to write things down in a lined yellow foolscap notebook that Americans call a 'legal pad'. Meanwhile Angleton finished one cigarette and lit another. He then poured a slug of Jim Beam bourbon into a crystal tumbler. The Catesby problem already seemed in the past.

Roger Hollis, head of Five, appeared to be chairing the meeting. 'I'd like to thank Jim,' Hollis nodded to Angleton, 'for inviting us here tonight to brief us on FEDORA.'

'Excuse me,' said Bone, 'we don't even know who or what …'

Angleton glared at Bone before speaking. 'FEDORA is a high-ranking Soviet agent who defected to us at the end of last year. It's taken us until now to establish his bona fides, which is why we've waited until today to have this meeting.'

Catesby kept staring at Angleton trying to peel off the layers.

Some thought the American was mad, clinically paranoid-schizo. Even if he was mad, Angleton had been clever enough to distance himself from the Cuban fiasco. The most dangerous combination, as Catesby well knew, was someone who was mad, but who was also extremely intelligent and cunning at the same time. He was sure that Angleton fitted that category.

'The FEDORA debriefings,' continued Angleton, 'have alarmed us as much as they would yourselves if we could give you all the details. But I can't give you all the details – particularly the ones referring to your own politicians and your own intelligence agencies.'

All the British seemed to reel back in their chairs as if slapped in the face. Hollis looked particularly pained. Catesby began to say something, but Bone gestured for him to shut up.

'I know,' said Angleton smiling for the first time. The American was so thin and the skin around his face so tight that Catesby expected to hear flesh tear as Angleton's lips contorted into a cadaverous smile. 'I know, you must be thinking that this is one hell of a way to treat your closest ally. But I'm going to make no apologies. If it's any consolation, I am certain that my own agency has been penetrated at the highest level by a Soviet agent. And the United Kingdom is not the only Western European country with leading politicians who are puppets of Moscow.'

Catesby sensed that the mood among the Brits was embarrassed bemusement, that polite awkward silence before someone tells madam she needs to readjust her clothing. But in this case madam's tits were hanging out and she didn't care.

'I know what you must be thinking,' said Angleton looking around the table. 'You're thinking I'm just another goddamned reds-under-the-bed paranoid Yank – and that you British, so much more sophisticated and knowledgeable than we naïve Americans, have to listen with polite condescension. I can see your hidden contemptuous smiles. But you forget that I've lived among you. I went to one of your most elite public schools and learned the spy trade in London.' Angleton nodded at Dick White. 'In fact Dick was one of my mentors – and Kim Philby was another.'

None of the British rose to the bait. They all sat stony-faced and silent with hands calmly folded.

Angleton shattered the awkwardness with a laugh that sounded like gravel being thrown against a window. 'Where's Kim this evening? Oh, pardon me, I forgot. Kim is your man in Beirut, isn't he? He's working under cover, of course – as a journalist. But we all know that Kim Philby still gets a generous stipend from Her Majesty's coffers for intelligence services rendered – or not.' Angleton paused. 'Maybe, my friends, you are the naïve ones.'

'Thank you for those thoughts, Mr Angleton.' The comment came from an unexpected source. The speaker was one of the MI5 men who had accompanied Hollis. Catesby called them Ferret and Fox because that's what they looked like. They had both entered Five via technical services. Both flaunted the fact they were practical men who had trained as engineers. They felt contempt for Oxbridge-educated mandarins who couldn't tell the difference between a megacycle and a bicycle.

'I hope, Jim,' Dick White was wearing his conciliatory voice, 'that you haven't misconstrued our silence as scepticism.'

Angleton exhaled a cloud of cigarette smoke and swigged another slug of bourbon. 'Truth always looks complicated at first, especially when you're dealing with defectors. But the joy of one like FEDORA is that practically all of the pieces fit together – and the ones that don't fit are easily recognisable as poor memory or human error.'

Catesby doodled on the Dorchester Hotel headed notepad: *Authenticity = Imperfection > So intentional errors in disinfo = best fake gems > as any fool knows*. Bone glanced at the pad and gave an imperceptible nod. Catesby was convinced that one of the reasons Philby got away with it was because of his stutter. That imperfection of speech made him sound innocent – a genuine master of deception would never be word perfect.

'We have,' continued Angleton, 'debriefed FEDORA for over a thousand hours. Several pieces of intelligence have emerged that are vital to the security interests of the United Kingdom. The most important intelligence revelation is that a very senior and influential member of the British establishment met covertly with the Soviet leadership at the end of 1961. This, gentlemen, is not speculation, but verified fact. I am sure we know the identity of the person involved, but this information is case sensitive for political as well as intelligence reasons. It is not our intention to interfere in Britain's domestic politics.'

Catesby stifled a smile and an inclination to say 'Since when?'

Hollis, however, was bolder. 'Is this person a politician, a peer, a royal, soldier, civil servant?'

'I can't say, Roger, I really can't. I would strongly suggest, however, that you launch your own investigation to find this person as a matter of urgency.'

Dick White pitched in. 'How much help are you going to give us, Jim?'

'Not much, but we will point you in the right general direction. I think it is vitally important the British themselves arrive at the same conclusion – preferably without our help.'

'It would look bad, wouldn't it?' said Catesby.

'What would look bad?' said Angleton.

'I don't think the British press or people would be very happy if one of our senior politicians were seen to be slandered as a commie spy by the CIA. There would be a backlash, which wouldn't be in US interests.'

Angleton glared at Catesby. The thickness of the lenses in his spectacles made his eyelashes look like writhing tarantulas. 'First of all, I didn't say that he is a politician. Secondly, I never implied he is a Soviet spy. Perhaps you have insights of your own into this matter? And finally, the intelligence that we have isn't "slander". It's hard factual evidence.'

'I think,' said White to Angleton, 'what William is trying to say is that he completely agrees with you. He agrees, as do all of us, that it is absolutely essential that the investigation be British led and conducted.' White looked at Catesby. 'Isn't that so, William?'

Catesby smiled wanly and nodded. At the same time he noticed that Angleton's assistant was staring at him in an odd, almost seductive, way.

'It is likely,' said Hollis, 'that this investigation is going to involve ourselves primarily since the person under suspicion appears to be a British national living in Britain. We will, of course, have to liaise with our SIS colleagues for investigating outside the UK. Fair enough?'

Everyone nodded except for the two Americans – and Ferret and Fox. Catesby thought it odd they weren't at least making a show of supporting their boss in public. Very odd. It suddenly occurred to Catesby that Ferret and Fox were siding with the Americans at every turn.

'It would be extremely useful,' continued Hollis looking at Angleton, 'if you could give us a timescale. The actual day, if possible, or at least week that the meeting took place?'

Angleton lit another cigarette. He paused thoughtfully in his veil of smoke, then said, 'No.'

'Well actually,' said Hollis, 'a time frame would allow us to quickly eliminate suspects by checking their diaries. It would save a lot of time and effort.'

Angleton went stony-faced.

'That may be so, Roger,' the fox-faced underling spoke for the first time, 'but it would also give a warning to the guilty one – or ones – that we have sufficient detailed information to nail them. They might do a runner, like Burgess and Maclean.'

'Nonsense,' said Hollis. He sounded exasperated. 'We're obviously not going to make the date known,' he paused, 'to anyone not sitting around this table.'

'I don't think, sir,' it was now Ferret's turn, 'you fully appreciate what our colleague is saying. If Jim Angleton were to tell us the exact dates, at this very meeting, it is highly likely that the person who made that trip would find out how much we know.'

There was a long stunned silence, not even broken by a cough or shifting chair. Finally, Catesby looked across the table at the American and said, 'Would you like me to leave the room?'

'No, William.' It was Dick White. 'If there was any doubt about you, you wouldn't be here.'

'But someone has doubts about someone sitting around this table,' continued Catesby, 'and those doubts have just been voiced. May I suggest, sir, that all of us except yourself and Sir Roger leave the room. If Mr Angleton feels that he cannot reveal the date involved to Head of SIS and Head of MI5, then there is no ...'

'William,' said Henry Bone, 'I think that you've said enough.'

'Fine.'

Hollis and White exchanged pained glances. Then Hollis spoke. 'I feel that there are a lot of tensions being aired tonight – and that it is very unfair to put Jim under so much undue pressure.'

Angleton meanwhile was making his way through the bourbon bottle at a rate of knots. He almost flaunted his alcoholism. But the Russians, Catesby knew, were just as bad. What a situation, as bleakly comic as tragic. Most of the world's nuclear arsenals were poised in the trembling hands of two opposing gangs of dipsos. It made closing hour in a mangy Glasgow pub look like a haven of peace, reason and tranquillity.

Angleton peered first at Hollis, then at White, before saying, 'Have either of you distinguished gentlemen read Sun Tzu?'

Hollis shook his head. White smiled blandly.

'Well, you should.' Angleton now did sound a little drunk. 'Sun Tzu was a sixth-century BC military strategist. He once wrote, "Of all the senior officers close to the commander none is more intimate with him than the secret agent of the enemy. Of all matters concerning the security of the State, none is more critical than those relating to secret operations."'

The embarrassment among the Brits was now palpable. The accusations of treason in high places were starting to grate. Even Angleton must have realised that he was making an ass of himself. His manner became less portentous as he said, 'Before we close the meeting, I'd like to introduce you to Jennings Galen.'

The name gave Catesby a jolt, but he kept a straight face. Katya had asked about Galen in Havana. He looked closely at the American for the first time. Galen beamed back shyly through rimless glasses. He looked, thought Catesby, like a bank clerk with a secret vice.

'I'm flying back to Washington tomorrow,' continued Angleton in a slightly slurred voice, 'but I'm leaving Jennings behind as my deputy. He'll have diplomatic status and be working out of the Chief of Station's office in the embassy. Jennings' role will be to assist you in the investigation, but also to carry out his own enquiries – under, of course, the appropriate international protocols.'

In other words, thought Catesby, Jennings was going to be a spy operating under diplomatic immunity. He scribbled *surveil?* on his pad. Bone glanced and gave a slight nod. Catesby doodled a seagull over the word.

The Americans gathered their papers and were the first to leave. There were no little clumps of chatterers as is usual after most meetings. Everyone slunk away in silence without even making eye contact. It was difficult to tell the cats from the pigeons.

Catesby and Bone loitered in the hotel lobby while Dick White asked the doorman to fetch the Humber Hawk from wherever he had parked it. Out of the corner of his eye Catesby caught sight of the two Americans talking to the two junior MI5 officers, Fox and Ferret, near the lift doors.

'Don't look behind you,' whispered Bone.

Catesby stood still and looked at Bone instead. He listened to the sounds behind him: lift doors opening, a shuffle of feet followed by a bell pinging – and the velvet wheeze of lift doors closing.

'Good,' said Bone, 'they've gone up.'

Meanwhile, White was gesturing them to the car.

'Nice of you to give us a lift,' said Bone.

Catesby sat in the back and used the opportunity to look closely at Dick White. In the service the SIS boss was known simply as C. He was, thought Catesby, certainly a smooth suave dog. Someone had once described White as David Niven without the moustache. It was true. C was the ultimate Englishman – and, as such, he was the only person who had ever been honoured to head both MI5 and the Secret Intelligence Service. Hollis must have found White a difficult act to follow. It was obvious that Hollis lacked the cunning and firmness to deal with poisonous and dangerous underlings such as Fox and Ferret.

'What did you make of all that?' said White. The lights of London flickered across his face making him look even more like his cinema familiar.

Bone laughed. 'Angleton didn't give us the date of the meeting because he doesn't know it himself or because the meeting never took place. There was a lot of bluff going on.'

'The Americans,' said White, 'have done a good job of keeping FEDORA for themselves. It looks like they deceived us into thinking that BUTTERFLY was the big defector they were bragging about.'

Catesby stared out the car window and tried to subdue the loss and sense of pain the BUTTERFLY operation had caused him. It was the only time he had taken satisfaction, if not joy, in killing someone.

'What do you think, William?' said White.

'I don't think they were playing a deception game with BUTTERFLY. I've heard that FEDORA was a walk-in joe who turned up completely unexpected at the US Embassy in Stockholm.'

'From whom did you hear that?' said White.

'From my man in Säpo.'

Bone suddenly stiffened. 'I think Säpo are too fond of playing games.' Säpo, or *Säkerhetspolisen*, were the Swedish secret police.

'In any case,' said Catesby ignoring Bone's scepticism, 'walk-in joes usually begin by telling the truth to convince their new masters of their bona fides. Once they've got that, they start to embellish the truth with exaggeration. As soon as they see their interrogators have taken the bait, they start slipping in the lies. They test the water with harmless little porkies at first, but these soon grow into venomous lies that can destroy careers.' Defectors, Catesby knew from experience, were masters at recognising the divisions in a Security Service and setting officers at each others' throats. That's why fake defectors could be lethal. But Catesby's spy intuition told him that FEDORA was genuine, a genuine troublemaker with his own agenda of attention-seeking mischief.

White turned the Humber on to the roundabout dominated by the Queen Victoria Memorial. Beneath Victoria, who was seated on her throne, there were three figures at the base of the statue. Charity faced the palace, the Angel of Justice looked over Green Park, but the Angel of Truth peered directly and sternly towards SIS Headquarters.

'By the way, William,' said White over his shoulder, 'you did a brilliant job at taking Angleton down a peg or two. There was no one else who could have done it without creating a diplomatic incident.'

The reel to reel tape machine was set up on Bone's desk. They had already heard the recording once and now Bone was re-winding it.

'Does C know about this?' said Catesby.

'No, it would put him in an embarrassing position if he did. So it's best to spare him.'

'It could put you in jail if Five found out about this.' SIS were strictly forbidden to undertake surveillance or any other espionage activity on UK soil. Bugging Angleton's hotel room in the Dorchester was a blatant violation of SIS's remit.

'Don't be silly. I would only get disciplined, sacked at worst.' Bone put on his headphones and gestured for Catesby to do the same. 'Listen to this bit again.'

It was Angleton speaking. *'Frankly, the intelligence FEDORA provided about OMEGA was a shocking revelation ...'*

Bone switched off the machine and looked at Catesby. 'Who is OMEGA?'

'It's their codename for the Sov Director of OT. It's the technical services and research branch of KGB First Directorate – the invisible ink and exploding cigars boffins. Let's hear more of Angleton.'

'... the emphasis is now on developing poisons that mirror natural

causes of death to use as assassination weapons. Which isn't to say that the KGB has given up on shooters and ice picks. But most important is the policy change from the top. Until recently, the KGB only ordered foreign assassinations on Soviet dissidents and defectors living in exile – like those Ukrainian nationalists they hit in '59. Which, by the way, is one of the reasons we know FEDORA is genuine – otherwise, he wouldn't have known about the cyanide gas pistol used.'

Bone halted the tape again. 'Are you impressed?'

'Not much. As you know, Henry, I'm never impressed by anything. Just because intelligence is new doesn't mean it's a surprise. Of course, they're working on poisons that don't leave a trace – so are we. Look at VX.'

'But it looks like they're doing a better job. The problem with VX is that it doesn't mimic a heart attack or something else. You've still got to furnish a likely cause of death.'

'Got someone in mind, Henry?'

Bone smiled wanly. 'Let's hear more.' He forwarded the tape.

'... his KGB codename is WAXWING. He developed close friendships with Molotov and Mikoyan during frequent visits to the Soviet Union when he was a cabinet minister. FEDORA managed to bring with him transcripts of some of his more revealing private conversations with the two. Have a look.' There was the sound of papers shuffling.

Ferret's voice came in. *'We've had our own file on him since 1945. Do you know he once played a game of cricket on the banks of the Moskva River? When he was batting the KGB man at square leg dropped a catch that would have had him out for a duck. We now know why.'* Sound of laughter.

'Or maybe,' said Catesby, 'the KGB bloke was a rotten fielder. He was probably drunk and it's not exactly their national sport. This is the sort of evidence we used to use to burn witches.'

The tape continued with Angleton's voice: *'... we are very concerned, especially in light of the FEDORA debriefings, about this particular politician. As I am sure you must be as well?'* Sounds of assent. *'In fact, FEDORA has given us proof that WAXWING is a Soviet agent.'*

'But not,' it was Fox's voice, *'but not proof that could be presented in court without compromising intelligence operations?'*

Angleton laughing. *'That's always the case, isn't it? Which is why we often have to use other means ...'*

Catesby thumped the table. 'You see what this unspeakable filth is trying to do, don't you?'

'Shh, listen.'

'*... we should take FEDORA's warnings seriously that the KGB is willing and capable of assassinating Western political leaders in order to replace them with their own agents.*'

Ferret came in again. '*So you're saying that WAXWING may have visited East Germany last year to get his orders straight from the Kremlin leadership?*'

'*We don't know,*' said Angleton, '*I'm not even sure it was WAXWING himself. It could have been one of his secret cabal – it could have been a deputy. But certainly someone of high rank. And I'm not sure it had anything to do with the running of a future pro-Soviet government. I think the meeting was about something much more serious and immediate.*'

'*Why,*' said Fox, '*haven't you passed on this information to Hollis?*'

'*I think you know the reason why?*'

Bone stopped the tape. 'What do you think?'

'I don't know – I'm not his doctor.'

'Angleton isn't as mad as you think. He's playing to an audience who have more malice than brains.'

'He's also playing on our pro-Yank anti-Yank divide.' Catesby knew that millions of his fellow Britons adored America. It was an admiration that also reached deep into the Security Services. The pro-Americans were the ones who feared that Britain had become too 'socialist' – and that something needed to be done to stop the rot. How far would they go?

Bone had gone mysteriously silent – as if mentally ticking off a list of names.

'In any case,' said Catesby, 'Angleton has always been a master at getting ourselves and Five at each other's throats – and now he's trying to get Five to tear itself apart too.'

'And after that,' said Bone, 'he'll get Five to undermine any future government that isn't to Washington's liking.'

Catesby stared at the worn and frayed Indian carpet on the office floor. He felt just as tired and threadbare. 'I agree with what you're saying, Henry, but Angleton's claims about a looming assassination are pure fantasy.'

'Why?'

'Angleton seems to be inferring that the KGB is planning to assassinate Hugh Gaitskell so that WAXWING, obviously Harold Wilson, becomes their man in Downing Street. Utter nonsense.'

'You think it sounds far-fetched?'

'First of all,' said Catesby, 'if Gaitskell fell under the Number 19, the next leader of the Labour Party would be George Brown, provided his liver held out, and not Wilson – and the Russians loathe Brown even more than Gaitskell. In fact, the Sovs would prefer the Tories to either of them.'

'You seem to think that truth and logic matter to those Angleton is trying to influence.'

'Good point, Henry.'

'Twists and turns, William, twists and turns.' Bone put his hands behind his head and leaned back in his chair. 'Meanwhile everything is linked to Cuba – even Berlin and the Thor missile sites in East Anglia. Can't you see?'

'Of course I can.' In fact, Catesby didn't see the links at all. But he did know that Bone's gnomic utterances were almost always based on withheld secrets that would, when Henry judged the time right, be revealed.

'Tea?'

'I'd love one, Henry.' Catesby watched Bone go the sideboard. The chipped mugs that looked like refugees from a building site were still there, but there was a red wooden box with Chinese ideograms.

As Bone spooned the loose leaf tea into the pot, he said, 'I got this brew from a shop in Wardour Street. The tea's distinctive smoky flavour comes from it being dried over burning pine.'

'What's the Cuba connection?'

Bone beamed. 'I don't always enjoy trumping the glib jibes that probably passed for wit in your grammar school sixth form, but I will on this occasion. Here is the Cuban China connection. "I will force the enemy to take our strength for weakness, and our weakness for strength, and thus will turn his strength into weakness."'

'Sun Tzu?'

'Correct. Sun Tzu wasn't only a general – he was also a renowned tea merchant.'

'You just made that up.'

'Perhaps I did. In any case, enough banter. Have a look at this.'

Catesby opened the folder. It was a thin file that had just been started. The opening page gave the security classification and title:

```
BIOGRAPHICAL AND PERSONALITY REPORT
Jennings Galen, CIA Intelligence Officer
```

'We need,' said Bone pouring the tea, 'to flesh this folder out quite a bit. Both Neville and his successor in DC think there is, how should I say, quite a bit of flesh involved – and not just Galen's own.'

Catesby suddenly realised that his first impression of Galen, as 'a bank clerk with a secret vice', may have been a correct one.

'So, William, you're going to have to do some travelling and visit an old friend – that master of gossip and indiscretion.'

The airport north of Punta Arenas wasn't the end of the world, but it wasn't far away from the end. It had taken Catesby eight hours to get there on a scheduled flight from Santiago.

The next part of the journey would have been dangerous even if the pilot had been sober. But Catesby didn't blame Ramos for being drunk. He had had a hard life and was clearly bored with living in exile in the middle of nowhere. Born in Barcelona at the end of the nineteenth century, Ramos had discovered South America as a courier pilot for Aeroposta in the twenties and early thirties when he flew with Saint-Exupéry. He returned to his native Spain to fly an obsolete Potez 540 against Franco's Fascists and was badly wounded. Catesby was in awe of the wizened old pilot as he guided the tiny Cessna 170 into the mist of the South Atlantic. Ramos was also the ideal pilot for such a mission. He had absolutely no curiosity in Catesby or what he was doing.

There were no airfields on the islands. But on previous flights Ramos had found a flattish pasture near the settlement which served as a landing place. As he went into the landing glide Ramos spoke for the first time. 'What's the difference between a live pilot and a dead pilot?'

'I don't know,' said Catesby.

'A live pilot can tell the difference between a field of boulders and a flock of sheep.'

Fortunately, there were neither boulders nor sheep on the make-shift landing field.

'Thanks for the whisky – and the letters. And it's even good to see you again.' Kit Fournier continued speaking as he opened the front of the cooker and put in a peat block. 'They cut this stuff as a sort of spring ritual at the beginning of October. The peat cutting is a big event, even bigger than Christmas. The idea is that the peat ought to be dry enough to burn when winter comes – July's the worst month. But it's never really warm and never dry for more than two days in a row. Since it's a bit chilly this evening we'll have lamb stew. Tomorrow we can catch some fresh trout. Have you ever had *truite au bleu*?'

Catesby shook his head.

'You have to do it with live trout. You knock them out and gut them seconds before you put them in a court bouillon. Of course, the poor fish are still twitching when you throw them in the boiling liquid. They quickly turn a remarkable blue and you serve them with Hollandaise.' Fournier paused and stared at Catesby. 'And that's what you bastards have done to me.'

'I'm sorry, Kit.'

'Don't worry. I would have done the same to you. Have some wine. It's carmenère. I buy wine off a Chilean jigger, a squid boat, that calls in at Port Howard a few times a year. Look,' Fournier went over to a crude bookshelf made of breeze blocks and planks. 'The captain of the jigger brings me books too.' He picked some volumes off the top shelf and caressed them with his eyes. 'Neruda, Mistral, Quiroga, Borges, Asturias …' He looked at Catesby and waved the books at him. 'These books are my world …' Fournier's eyes were glistening with tears. He wept freely for a few seconds, then blew his nose and wiped his face on his sleeve. 'I hate it when anyone sees me like this. But I'm so fucking lonely.'

'I hope the letters are helping.'

'What was the deal?'

'If any of your family reveal that they're in contact with you, we stop the letters.'

'And mine are censored?'

'Of course.'

'My sister said she met you. What did you think of her?'

'I thought she was a nice woman.'

Fournier smiled. 'You must be the only one who thinks so. Caddie can be very acerbic. Don't you want to know what she thought of you?'

Catesby shrugged.

'She said that she thought you were a hard person who had been badly damaged.'

'Should I vomit in the sink or outside?'

'But she liked you – which is odd, because she usually prefers her own gender. Maybe she thought you were a bit of a girl.'

'But a hardened bitch of a girl.'

Fournier went over to the cooker and put chopped mushrooms in the stew. 'There are ninety-seven species of native coprophilous fungi in these islands, but the ones we're eating are cultivated. I don't want to kill you with a poison mushroom. They might stop the letters.'

'How's your cover story holding up?' Kit Fournier, who spoke Spanish as a first language, had been given a fake passport and papers purporting he was a Guatemalan naturalist who was making a study of the islands. He was supposed to cultivate eccentricity and a liking for his own company.

'To be frank, I don't think the locals give a flying fuck who I am. They call me "one-two-eight".'

'Why's that?'

'Because I brought the population of the island up to 128.'

'We did think the naturalist cover story would wear thin after a while. But listen, Kit, you've got to keep up the pretence or …'

'Or they'll deep six me?'

Catesby shrugged. 'I don't know. Their biggest worry is the thing leaking into the press.'

'They could send me to St Helena?'

'Sorry, Kit, you're no Napoleon – and besides, we have to keep St Helena ready for de Gaulle in case he gets too cosy with the Sovs. In any case, you haven't got too cosy with anyone. Have you?'

'The person concerned, along with her husband and boy, have just emigrated to Australia – so they should call me "one-two-five".'

'That's bad. Anyone else?'

'I occasionally get drunk with Ramos on his stopovers – but I assure you it's platonic. Did you know that one of the characters in Malraux's *L'espoir* is based on him?'

Catesby shook his head.

'But since Ramos is another comrade in dodgy exile he knows how to keep his mouth shut.' Fournier paused. 'The saddest thing, and most inspiring thing, was what Ramos said about Madrid when the Fascists were bombing the poorest quarters of the city to punish the workers. There was only one sound that rose above the exploding bombs and the screams of the wounded and the crackling of flames. That heroic sound was the defiant music of a blind beggar playing the *Internationale* on the violin. *Groupons nous*, William, *groupons nous pour la lute finale*.'

'You've finally become a believer?'

'Yes. It's funny, isn't it? I wasn't one at the time. I only wanted to go to Moscow so that I could be near Jennifer. It didn't matter if I had to share her with someone else – with the whole Politburo for that matter.' Fournier laughed. 'But now that she's gone, what she believed in has taken her place. But you haven't come 8,000 miles to hear my ideological views?'

'Not entirely.'

'Have you replaced my agent handler?'

'No. In any case, I'm sure they've squeezed you dry about most things by now.' Catesby raised his glass. 'Excellent wine, this.'

'Have some more.'

'Thanks. But, Kit, no matter how much we squeeze someone like you, there's always some juice we didn't realise we needed – or even existed. The amount of stuff a human brain can hold is impressive.'

'Not the fucking Kennedys again, *please*.'

'No, Kit, someone far less significant. The sort of creature you probably thought was less than the dust under your chariot wheels. Remember those halcyon days when it looked like your chariot was romping towards the National Security Council, or even to be Director of the CIA? What a star you were.'

'Catesby, old pal, can you cut out the bullshit and tell me who the fuck you want to know about?'

Catesby opened a file and passed it across the table. 'Remember him?'

Fournier looked at the file photo, then laughed and slapped his thigh. 'Sheeee … it! Is this sick puppy still in the agency?'

'You knew him well?'

'Jennings Galen was in my induction training cohort when I joined the Agency. He was lousy at all the physical stuff and nearly washed out. I'm not sure he ever completed parachute training. But Jennings was brilliant at other things: intelligence analysis, languages, deception techniques – and most of all, his ability to memorise. He was subject to a lot of bullying on the course, the sort that led one guy to suicide. But bullying didn't affect Jennings.'

'Why not?'

'Because his ego was elsewhere. He saw us for what we were – a bunch of jocks and East Coast preppy snobs. He didn't want to be one of us, that was his great strength.' Fournier smiled at Catesby. 'But this isn't what you want, is it, William? You don't want to know his strengths, you want to know Galen's weaknesses so you can frame the bastard.'

'Anything would be useful.'

'Well how about this? Jennings Galen is a sexual pervert – not, I know, a particularly unusual trait for those in our trade. Hoover was once quite shocked to discover that two of his prize agents had a penchant for bestiality.'

'But Jennings prefers humans?'

'So it would seem.' Fournier poured himself more wine. 'To get the full picture you ought to know that Jennings was born in a small shit-kicking town in Texas – the sort of place where the girls admire star quarterbacks and other clean-limbed heroes. Everything that Jennings was not. He knew he was never going to be able to compete. So, he developed a different persona – one that was silky, observant and mysterious.'

'What did he do?'

'He became a Roman Catholic. Don't laugh, William, this was a big deal in gringo Texas. He had been brought up as Southern Baptist – so going over to Rome was like ...'

'Like you going over to Moscow?'

'In some ways worse. But, thanks to you guys, I didn't get there. I ended up here instead. In any case, Jennings went Catholic in a serious way. I'm surprised he didn't become a priest.'

'Did it help him get laid?'

'I think so, I know so. When he finished his training, Jennings married a very pretty girl from Louisiana. She looked like a piece of candy floss. Everyone thought they were an odd couple. On the other hand, they both were sort of pink and fluffy.' Fournier lowered his voice. 'Meanwhile things were getting very strange indeed.'

'In what way?'

'Theologically. Jennings became a member of Opus Dei. You know about them?'

Catesby nodded wearily. Opus Dei had strongly supported Franco's Fascists in the Spanish Civil War – and their personal habits were even creepier than their political ones. Catesby had once been assigned to look after a Polish defector in a Berlin safe house who was Opus Dei. Every morning the Pole leapt out of bed and shouted '*Serviam!*', Latin for 'I serve'. The rest of the day was punctuated with rosaries and sudden outbursts of piety, but Catesby was spared the weirdest ritual. Maybe the Pole just didn't do it in front of others or maybe he didn't have the equipment.

'I suppose,' said Fournier, 'a psychiatrist could work it all out. Maybe Jennings felt he had to compensate for the recently acquired pleasures of the marriage bed – but I think there was more to it.'

'You're talking about flagellation?'

'It became one of his obsessions.'

'How,' said Catesby, 'do you know all this?'

'When Jennings arrived in Germany he made me his confidante. It was partly because we had been on the induction course together, but more so because he knew that I was a "fallen away Catholic" and wanted to bring me back to the Church.'

'So you could whip him?'

'I don't think so. Jennings whipped himself and also got his wife to do it. But her heart wasn't in it and she never hit him hard enough to give satisfaction. And, of course, he whipped her too – I suppose he saw her as some sort of Whore of Babylon who needed to be punished for loving him.'

'It's difficult to see where religion ends and the other stuff begins.'

'I agree absolutely, but I never told him that. Maybe Jennings already knew. In any case, the poor wife wasn't living up to his expectations – especially with her whip hand – and Jennings became a frequent user of prostitutes, even addicted to them you might say.'

'And he told you all this too?'

Fournier gave a wry smile. 'Well, some of it, but most of it I found out myself.'

'How and why?'

'I was asked to investigate Jennings by our Chief of Station. It wasn't a question of moral prudery – we're a lot more open-minded in those areas than you think. It was a question of where the hell was Jennings getting the money to pay for all those Fräuleins.'

'Why are you smiling?'

'Because, William, the answer is so wonderful. Absolutely priceless. Jennings spent most of his time in our Munich office – practically ran it in fact. Does the name Eugenio Pacelli ring a bell?'

'Vaguely.'

'Pacelli became better known as Pope Pius XII. His first big job was Apostolic Nuncio to Germany from 1920 to 1929. Pacelli was later notorious for his role in negotiating the *Reichskonkordat* between the Vatican and Nazi Germany. In any case, from 1920 to 1925 the future pope was based in Munich.'

Catesby smiled. 'And Jennings ended up in Munich – I see where this is heading.'

'Clever boy. Jennings took advantage of his Munich posting – together with the open-sesames of his Opus Dei membership – to do a job of dirt-digging that was close to genius.'

'Sex, money, war crimes?'

'Definitely the first two – and complicity in the last. I wish that I could tell you more, but I never actually got a chance to see all the files because Jennings had already sold them.'

'To whom?'

'To the Vatican, of course. Apparently, they have to shell out for this sort of stuff all the time.'

'Did you confront Jennings Galen about your findings?'

'Of course not, it wasn't my job. I packed up the stuff and sent it off to DC "eyes only" to Angleton. He had just been appointed Head of Counterintelligence.'

'What happened?'

'Absolutely nothing. The situation benefited everyone concerned. Jennings is no fool. He had already sent a copy of the incriminating Pacelli file to Angleton. And Angleton, of course, was delighted. The file meant that the CIA had loads of dirt to blackmail the Vatican into supplying false passports and other services. The Church is a much more important international player than people realise.'

'Did Jennings confess to Angleton about blackmailing the Vatican?'

'I don't think so. At least not at first, but when he did own up Angleton would have been even more pleased. Angleton knows that he has acquired one extremely loyal and devoted servant in the person of Jennings Galen. If Jennings ever fails to do his master's bidding, he'll end up in a federal penitentiary.'

'And how does the Vatican gain?'

'They can be damned sure that the incriminating horrors in the Pacelli file are well and truly buried. The CIA may have dirt on the Vatican, but the Church has its own cartload full of shit to throw at the CIA. At the moment they want to hush the Montini rumours – assuming the CIA can still squash a newspaper or two.'

'Who's Montini?'

'You mean you've never heard of Cardinal Montini?

'No.'

'Montini is pencilled in to be next pope after John XXIII. But, I suppose, by Vatican standards it's not much of a scandal. Montini used to have an actor boyfriend who dyed his hair red. Pacelli, to be fair, wasn't so much concerned about one of his cardinals having a boyfriend, it was the hair dye and the theatre connections. Standards, you know. Pacelli wasn't just a pope, he was also the snootiest of aristocrats.

Once again, Catesby realised that Fournier was a gossip columnist manqué, but one who needed steering back to the main business. 'Did Jennings remain in Opus Dei?'

'Very much so. From an outsider's point of view blackmailing the Church doesn't seem the sort of thing loyal Catholics do. But Opus Dei likes to keep the Vatican off balance.'

'And did his love life change?'

'It got even more sordid. I don't know whether or not Jennings knew that I had been investigating him, but he even got more pally with me. He started showing me pictures of his wife in various states of undress and positions. He had taken to giving her knock-out drugs. I think he preferred doing things to her when she was unconscious. He wanted me to join in.'

'And did you?'

'Of course not, what do you think I am?'

Catesby bit his tongue.

'No way was I going down that route. Instead, I reported it all to the Chief of Station, copied to Washington, but nothing ever came of it as far as I know.' Fournier paused. 'Oh, and one other thing, Jennings organised the ratline that Klaus Barbie used to get to Bolivia.'

Barbie, also known as the Butcher of Lyon, was a Gestapo officer that the CIA had helped escape in a programme know as PAPERCLIP. The rationale was that Barbie was too valuable as an intelligence asset to send to Nuremberg.

'You hated us for that. Didn't you, William?'

Catesby nodded.

'Well, I'll tell you something. I hated us for doing that too.' Fournier drained his wine glass. 'It was when I first began to turn.' Fournier laughed and refilled his glass. 'And probably the first step on the journey that brought me to this cold damp treeless island.'

'You have to look on the bright side, Kit.'

'Which is?'

'When's there's a nuclear war this will the safest place in the world.' Catesby smiled and helped himself to more wine. 'You are, Kit, our most valuable asset. We sent you here to protect you.'

'Thanks.'

'And, Kit, one more thing about Galen. You said he drinks a lot?'

'Not as much as Angleton, but a lot.'

'What does he drink?'

'Scotch.'

'On the rocks?'

'Always on the rocks. He's an American for chrissake – we even drink tea on the rocks.'

Henry Bone kept nodding approval as he read Catesby's report on the Fournier debriefing. He looked up at Catesby over the top of his reading glasses. 'This is great stuff, William. You always do an excellent job of establishing rapport with prisoners.'

'In this case it was genuine friendship.'

Bone nodded. 'That's what we have to keep teaching our younger officers. They have to convince every agent they're running that they are their best and only friend.'

The problem, Catesby realised, was that the people you had to deal with were often vile, gross, filthy and prone to repulsive habits they wanted to share with you personally. If you don't like the world's most depraved, then spying isn't the job for you. And yet, those who deserved friendship least were often the ones who needed it most. Catesby reckoned that Jennings Galen fell into that category – and Galen's neediness would be the path to his undoing.

'The information you brought back,' continued Bone, 'ties in neatly with what our new man in Washington has sent. Liaison, by the way, with our American counterparts is much improved. The Bay of Pigs has created such an atmosphere of blame in DC that senior CIA officers are queuing up to rubbish their colleagues to anyone – even us. Meanwhile, the FBI have got their knives out for all of the CIA. Which is probably how our man got this stuff on Galen.' Bone pushed a single page report across his desk. 'Have a look.'

Catesby glanced at the report and summarised: 'Marriage has split up, financial difficulties, heavy drinking, suspected suicide attempt, taking anti-depressants as well as amphetamines – I suppose he needs the uppers for the day job.' Catesby passed the page back. 'It sounds like Jennings Galen isn't the happiest rabbit in the warren.'

'It's a beautiful day. Let's go for a walk.'

The daffodils in St James's Park were in full bloom. Catesby and Bone followed the footpath that connected Birdcage Walk to the Mall via Blue Bridge which spanned the lake. The two men, with their suits, bowler hats and rolled umbrellas, looked like stereotypical

Whitehall civil servants. The look didn't come natural to Catesby. He had to be poured and moulded into the image. It had taken a few years, but now the point of his brolly tapped the footpath in the proper cadence – and his Oxford shoes shone impeccably whatever the weather and his regimental tie was knotted into a perfect four-in-hand.

They stopped briefly, as always, to admire the view of Horse Guards and Whitehall from the bridge. Then they continued on. It was a balmy spring day and the tulips and hyacinths were out early.

'"April,"' quoted Bone, '"is the cruellest month." At least Eliot got that bit right.'

'I thought you didn't like Eliot.'

'I don't. He tries too hard to be British and ends up looking like a cartoon parody. But April certainly is the cruellest month. There are statistics to prove it.'

'What are you on about, Henry?'

'More people commit suicide in April than any other month. It must be the utter contrast between the life and beauty bursting around them and their own miserable inner feelings.'

'Don't do it, Henry. We'll all miss you.' Catesby laughed. 'You've got so much to live for.'

'Once again, William, your attempt to be droll and ironic has fallen flat. And, actually, I do have a lot to live for. And, in any case, I wasn't reflecting on my own self-destruction.' Bone stopped and stared into the distance. 'But someone else's. And when you do these things you've got to get it right.'

'Sometimes it's easier just to kill the person and get rid of the body.'

'But not as complete – and it doesn't send a precise signal of doubt.'

'How can doubt be precise?'

'It is precise when the target you are aiming at is uncertainty itself. Sometimes confusion is better than disinformation. People don't act when they're confused.'

They left St James's and crossed the Mall to continue their stroll in Green Park. Catesby preferred the trees and shadows of Green Park to the almost tropical lushness of St James's. It was a calmer, a quieter place to talk of killing. You couldn't of course call it murder. As Max Weber pointed out, the one monopoly that the state keeps for itself is violence. The state alone can kill legally. Ultimately, it's what those uniforms and flags are all about.

'You've obviously decided,' said Catesby, 'that we need to get rid of Jennings Galen.'

'I can't see that there's an alternative. But we need to squeeze him first to see what else he knows.'

'If we squeeze him too hard it's not going to look like suicide.'

'We're not going to torture him, Catesby. In any case, the experts say it doesn't work, but what do they know? No, William, you're going to be his friend – a friend with very deep pockets.'

'Henry, you've left something out.'

'What?'

'You still haven't told me why we have to kill Galen.'

Bone smiled bleakly. 'What makes you think it's any of your business?'

'Fine, but let me have a guess. Galen really does know the identity of the bloke who stitched up some sort of deal with the Kremlin geezers – and you and your pals are running scared?'

'Your supposition is eloquently put, but not necessarily a correct one.'

'But Henry, supposing it is correct? Surely, Galen has already passed on the information to his boss in DC – so there's no point in killing him as a hush job.'

'Perhaps,' smiled Bone, 'Galen is a greedy bitch.'

Everyone calls it Brompton Oratory, but they shouldn't. Its proper name is the London Oratory Church of the Immaculate Heart of Mary. Which is quite a mouthful. And would only confuse a taxi driver. Which is why Catesby simply told Galen to meet him at Brompton Oratory.

Catesby was kneeling in the pew nearest the Lady Chapel. He had considered bringing a rosary so he could count off the beads as he pretended to mumble Hail Marys, but thought that would be laying it on too thick. So instead he just clasped his hands, bowed his head and recited the names of Ipswich Town football players: 'Blessed art thou Roy Bailey in goal and hallowed be thy name Ray Crawford …' Catesby paused. He heard a door open, then footsteps squeaking up the nave on the parquet floor. Catesby closed his eyes and mumbled the names of more conventional, though less useful, saints. The steps came closer and paused next to the pew.

The new visitor coughed softly. Catesby continued to pretend to be lost in prayer. The visitor clumsily slipped into the pew. Catesby opened his eyes and looked at Galen. 'Sorry, I was far away.'

'I understand,' said the American.

'It's peaceful here, isn't it?' As Catesby spoke the organ started to boom Couperin's *Sanctus*. 'Except when Father Emile gets going.'

'Is this your parish church?'

'Yes. It's rather magnificent, don't you think?' Catesby tried to drain his voice of irony. In actual fact, he found the flamboyant baroque of the Oratory unspeakably vulgar and overcooked.

Galen looked in awe at the altar and crossed himself. 'It is so beautiful.'

'You ought to come here to Mass.'

'I'd very much like that,' said Galen, 'we could take communion together.'

Catesby tried to hide his revulsion. The 'friendship' with Galen was the most nauseating duty he had ever undertaken – especially the feigned mutual interest in religion. The organist was now playing the toccata from Widor's *Wedding March*. Catesby wished that Henry Bone hadn't found his way into the organ loft. He feared Bone's sense of humour was going to give the game away.

'Have you,' said Galen, 'considered my offer to introduce you to Opus Dei? You would start as a supernumerary member.'

'I am not sure that I am worthy.'

'You are, my friend, you are.'

Catesby didn't know how much longer he could bear such oily sincerity. Fortunately, the friendship with Galen was turning more and more to espionage matters. The use of shared religious conviction, however, had been an excellent ploy. There was something about religion that created unquestioning trust and allegiance. School ties and being members of the same golf club created rivalry rather than loyalty. In Galen's mind, Catesby was a fellow Roman Catholic soldier. Other differences were irrelevant.

'Last time,' said Galen, 'you told me you wanted more verification about how I identified your English colleague. Don't think for a second that I doubted your trust in me. I know that you have to have proof to provide to other people. I've brought some things with me.' Galen slid an envelope across the pew.

'From the Swedish end?'

'That's right, a very reliable agent.'

Catesby slid the document and photos out of the envelope. He recognised the handwriting and the stilted English. Galen was using the same Säpo intelligence officer that Catesby used – another 'double dipper'.

'The first set of photos,' said Galen, 'were taken on the Sassnitz-Trelleborg ferry. The Swedish intelligence service always have an agent on the boat.'

The ferry, as Catesby well knew, was part of a boat-train that ran from Berlin to Trelleborg on the southern tip of Sweden via the Isle of Rügen port of Sassnitz. It was a convenient way of getting agents into and out of the East bloc. Consequently, it was under heavy surveillance. The train toilets were notorious as dead letter boxes.

'What do you think?' said Galen.

'The photos from the ferry are not high quality, but the person does bear a resemblance. But, I agree, it certainly is the Sassnitz boat-train.' It was one of the few boat-trains where the train actually goes on the boat. Catesby looked at the other photos. 'But this one is definitely him. Where were they taken?'

'In front of a hotel in Trelleborg.'

Catesby looked closely at the photos. There were only two of them. One of them was taken from behind the man. The Hotel Horizont and a Volvo taxi with Swedish number plates are clearly visible. Both photos were taken at night. The photo showing the man's face is set against a background of car and streetlight glare. He put the photos and covering letter in the envelope and handed them back to Galen.

'You've certainly nailed him,' said Catesby.

'Don't you want to keep them?'

Catesby smiled. 'I would love to, but I don't want to take them back to the office with that chap prowling around. And besides, I haven't got the money.'

'What about the letter?'

'My bosses want me to match up the handwriting to make sure it really is from Dr Tarasov.'

'That's fair enough, but I've already checked the handwriting against other documents – and it is his.'

'Perhaps,' said Catesby, 'the Sovs forced Tarasov to write a letter about an incident that never happened.' He hoped it wasn't too obvious that his doubts about authenticity were fake ones. Catesby didn't want to arouse Galen's suspicions. Nonetheless, he knew he had to ask all the sceptical questions that a fellow professional like Galen would expect.

'In any case, why would the Russians want to exaggerate their weakness and vulnerability by forging such a letter?'

Catesby shrugged. 'How much do you want?'

'Two hundred thousand US dollars.'

'Ouch.'

'But that includes the photos and documents identifying Arlekin.'

'Arlekin?'

'I should have told you. That's what the Russians and East Germans call your man who did the secret deal. It's Russian for Harlequin.'

'I know.'

'I forget, William, that you are a talented linguist.'

'How about *dona nobis pacem*?'

'Freedom is more important than peace, William. I'm sure you agree with that too.'

It's funny, thought Catesby, the people who spout that stuff about freedom usually haven't been in a war – especially if they're Americans.

'When you consider the issues involved,' said Galen, 'it's not really a lot of money. You're going to get rid of a traitor in your ranks – and you're going to make sure neither Washington nor anyone else ever gets to see Dr Tarasov's letter.'

Catesby knew that the last was an unenforceable promise. Galen had surely copied the letter and would be using the threat of passing on copies of the letter to ensure future payments. But it wasn't going to matter. Catesby looked at Galen out of the corner of his eye. He must have been bullied unmercifully at school. He would have disliked Galen a lot more if he wasn't going to have to kill him. Having to do that always made you feel sorry for them. It always made them human and vulnerable and even likeable in a way they wouldn't have been otherwise. At least that's what it was like for Catesby – except for once.

'And what,' said Galen, 'about the young lady?'

'She'll be there.'

'Where?'

'The place we're going to meet to do the deal – she'll arrive afterwards. But,' said Catesby smiling, 'it's just a grotty safe house so you might want to take her to a swish hotel. And, to be frank, you can't trust those colleagues of mine. I think they've put cameras in the bedroom ceiling.'

'Would you give me a copy of the film?' Galen suddenly blushed. 'That was a joke, William, just a joke.'

'I'm sure it was.' Catesby wrote something on a piece of paper. 'It's on Gladstone Street, near the Albert Arms. It's South London, not far from where Charlie Chaplin was born.'

'Chaplin's a communist, you know.'

'Maybe that's why he took the piss out of Hitler,' said Catesby aware that Galen wouldn't pick up the irony.

'That's the problem with people like Chaplin,' said Galen. 'They use being anti-Nazi or anti-fascist as cover for being pro-communist.'

Maybe, thought Catesby, killing Galen wouldn't be such a bad idea after all.

The advantage of the Gladstone Street house was that it had vehicle access to the rear. The back of the house overlooked a marshalling yard for British Rail freight. It was dark and bleak in the night drizzle. Catesby kept watch from the upstairs back bedroom with the light off. He was anxiously waiting for Bone who was supposed to nick Galen's Ford.

The bloody car was a pain. It was the one thing most likely to make the whole plan go tits up. Galen had an embassy pool car, but only used it for trips outside London. He kept the big Ford in a lockup garage near his rather grand house in Hampstead. It was going to be Bone's job to pick the lock on the garage, which should be pretty easy – and then, one hoped, start the car with a set of skeleton keys. If that didn't work, Bone would have to hotwire the car: battery, coil, starter solenoid. He had spent an hour practising at the motor pool in Vauxhall that SIS shared with Five.

And, even if all that went to plan, what about the car keys? It wouldn't be a problem if Galen had the keys with him. But what if he hadn't? The cops investigating the 'suicide' would want to know what happened to the keys. Why weren't they in the car or on Galen's person? They would, of course, do a fingertip search of the area around the body and not find them. Catesby and Bone had discussed the possibility of a 'black bag job', a break-in, on Galen's house. But it wasn't worth the risk. What if he kept the keys in a desk in his office? Little details, like those bleeding car keys, were what gave spies sleepless nights.

Catesby knew it was an American car as soon as he saw the wide powerful sweep of headlights against the chain link fence of the railway yard. The big Ford turned up the alleyway and stopped at the back gate where there was a coal bunker and an unused outdoors privy. Catesby went downstairs to unlock the back door and signalled the coast was clear.

Bone came into the house via a dank damp scullery. He was smiling and swinging something over his head. 'The keys,' said Bone, 'they were in the ignition. What luck.'

'Thanks for doing this, Henry. I know it's beneath your pay grade.'

'It was great fun. Besides, you needed be here waiting for Galen. No show yet?'

'Not a dicky bird.'

'Is the house wired up?'

'Definitely not,' said Catesby. 'We can't risk a breach of trust at this point.'

'You haven't lost the money, have you?'

'Stop worrying.' Losing one of SIS's currency stashes was a constant nightmare.

'I don't think,' said Bone, 'I should be in the house. I'll wait in the car.'

'Good idea.'

Catesby sat in the front room and waited. This time with the lights on. It was still cold so he struck a match to ignite a gas fire that was set into a black cast-iron Victorian fire surround. Safe houses were always grim soulless places for grim soulless people. The sitting room with its grey linoleum floor, tatty scatter rugs, peeling wallpaper and brown three-piece suite was as gruesome and desolate as the job Catesby was going to have to do. Could, he thought, anyone actually live in such a place? Of course not. To live wasn't the point. Not if he did his job. There were two glasses and a bottle of whisky on the Formica coffee table in front of the sofa. Catesby opened the bottle and poured himself a drink.

It was just gone eleven when Catesby heard the taxi pull up. It was drinking-up time at the Albert Arms and the landlord was bellowing, 'Hurry up please, it's time.' Another thing that Eliot got right in the poem. *Ta ta. Goonight. Goonight.*

Catesby listened to Galen paying the taxi driver. That was another problem. If the thing ended up in the press would the driver see it and go to the cops? No, he'd keep it from the police, but he would tell all his mates and passengers. *You know that Yank geezer that topped himself…*

Catesby continued to listen. Galen waited until the taxi was gone before he came to the door. Good professionalism. He could hear the American breathing and waiting at the door. He finally knocked lightly and Catesby let him in.

'How you doing?' Galen pumped Catesby's hand in his pink fist as if he were his best friend, only friend.

'I'm fine.'

'Now, William, I don't want you to be offended.' Galen took a heavy-looking bag off his shoulder and unzipped it. 'I trust you completely, but I don't know about the others. I just want to do a little anti-bug sweep before we go any further.' Galen put on a set of headphones and started waving what looked like a microphone around the room. He was very thorough and covered every nook and crevice. He finally smiled and took off the headphones. 'Clean as a whistle.' He patted the anti-surveillance device. 'Nothing gets past this baby.'

'Good. I'm actually very relieved that you did that. Some of my colleagues spend more time spying on us than they do the enemy.'

'But they have to. It's a pity they didn't do more of it when Burgess and Maclean were around.'

'We've learnt the lesson.'

'But maybe you haven't.' Galen passed over the envelope with the Arlekin photos and details. 'We had to find this fellow for you. What do you expect will happen to Mr Bone?'

'He'll be arrested and severely interrogated. We'll want to find out who else was involved. I agree it looks like he was acting on behalf of the Labour shadow minister you call WAXWING. If there is a trial, I hope it isn't in camera. I think this thing needs a public airing and full press coverage.'

Galen smiled. 'I totally agree – and so does Jim Angleton. But you didn't seem too happy about that prospect when we had that meeting in the Dorchester.'

'I suppose you could say that my public face isn't the same as my private one. Sometimes you have to perform for certain audiences.'

'Like Henry Bone.'

'Exactly.'

'Have you suspected Bone before?'

'Constantly, ever since I first started working for him. But he's a very powerful cunning man. You have to watch your step if you want to survive.'

'I know what you mean.'

I bet you do, thought Catesby.

'Have another look,' said Galen nodding at the envelope, 'at the case for the prosecution.'

There were a number of new documents. Most relating to the Labour politician that Angleton wanted to nail. There were also more affidavits claiming sightings of Bone in the Swedish port town. The hatchet job was impressive, but not watertight. Basically you can stitch anyone you want if you go to enough trouble. Truth was an oft-violated maiden. And the ones who violated her most were the rich and powerful.

'But this,' said Galen handing another envelope, 'is the jewel in the crown.'

Catesby slipped out the letter and read the Cyrillic script yet again, but for the first time on the paper and ink original.

> *My darling sweetest Katyusha ... The fires continued to burn for more than two hours until well after dark ... The fire at the centre was 3000 degrees ... This is a serious and tragic time for our Motherland. Most of our best scientists and rocket engineers are now dead ...*

'You realise, of course,' said Galen, 'why that letter is so important for Britain, for your country, William?'

Catesby nodded.

'If the Pentagon knew about this, if they knew how weak our Soviet enemies are in reality ...' Galen's eyes had grown intense and distorted behind the thick lenses of his glasses. 'The Joint Chiefs of Staff, William, are good men. They see it as their patriotic duty to eliminate the Russian threat before it grows into a monster that can strike the American homeland – even if it means disobeying orders from the White House.' Galen shrugged. 'Unfortunately, Britain would be destroyed by the Soviet Union's intermediate-range ballistic missiles. But our generals regard the sacrifice of our British ally as a price worth paying to eliminate communism once and for all.'

'But surely, you agree with the generals?'

'But I also need the money.' Galen laughed. 'In fact, this letter is so important to the United Kingdom that I ought to be asking a hell of a lot more for it.'

'But we're throwing in the girl for free.'

'What time does she get here?'

'Just after midnight.'

Catesby knew that the girl and the two hundred thousand were just the first tranches in Galen's blackmail plan. Galen wasn't stupid. He would later admit that he had kept copies of the letter – and that the UK treasury would have to keep coughing up to keep those copies safe. And, maybe someday, Galen would have a fit of patriotism. He would pass the letter on to the Pentagon and the bombs would rain down in any case. That's why they had to kill Galen now.

'What's the matter, William, you look very strange and far away?'

'I was just thinking about Andreas.'

'You mean Mrs Alekseeva's lover?'

'That's the one. Did you have Andreas killed?' Catesby meant it as a genuine question. It was a mystery that still hadn't been resolved.

Galen laughed. 'No, but we would have if someone else hadn't killed him first. We were afraid that he was going to give a copy of the letter to you guys. I'm sure he photographed it.'

Catesby was certain that Galen was telling the truth. There was no logical reason for him not to. 'Who do you think killed Andreas?'

'I think the East Germans did it because they found out Andreas was selling stuff to us. Or maybe you did it?'

'No,' Catesby smiled bleakly and lifted the letter, 'we would have wanted this first – and then we would have killed him. In any case,' Catesby opened the suitcase on the sofa next to him, 'would you like to count the money?'

'But I trust you, William.'

'Would you like a drink?' Catesby lifted the whisky bottle. 'To seal the deal so to speak?'

Galen gave a very nervous smile.

'Ahh, I thought you trusted me.' Catesby drained his glass, refilled it direct from the bottle and drank that too. 'No ill effects, at least not yet.'

'I would like a drink, thank you.'

Catesby poured the whisky into Galen's glass and watched the American sip it.

'This is very good Scotch.' Galen smiled. 'I can't taste the poison at all.'

'Good. It's a single malt from Islay. They say it has a smoky flavour because of the peat, but I'm no expert.'

The American swirled the whisky around and sniffed the rich aroma. 'I like it.'

Catesby smiled wanly as Galen finished his glass. *Come on you little bastard, don't you want it on the rocks?*

'I think I'll have another.' Galen helped himself to the whisky. 'You know Jim is completely right. The UK government is in mortal danger of being infiltrated by sleeper agents controlled by Moscow. You've got to get rid of them – especially WAXWING.'

'Who are the others?'

Galen recited a list of names that included the most humane and progressive voices in British politics. Basically, anyone who wasn't a dupe of Washington and big business was a traitor. It was the same picture the Vichy collaborators tried to paint in occupied France. The troublemakers were the Resistance. The patriots were the *collabos*.

Catesby watched the level of whisky in the bottle diminish. He didn't want to suggest 'rocks' for that might give the game away. Perhaps, thought Catesby, he could put ice in his own whisky and Galen would follow suit. One side of the ice tray had been filled with uncontaminated cubes just for such a ruse. It was on the left when you opened the freezer compartment.

Galen looked up as if he had read Catesby's mind. 'Would it,' he said, 'be sacrilege to put ice in this very excellent whisky?'

'Not at all. In fact, the people of Islay always drink their whisky with ice – when they have it. But I'm not sure we have any ice. I'll check in the fridge.'

A moment later Catesby came back bearing the aluminium ice-cube tray. 'We're in luck,' he said lifting it. It was just then that he slid on a scatter rug. The rugs moved like sleds on the smooth lino. He didn't fall down, but the ice tray did a few somersaults in midair before Catesby caught it.

'I didn't know you were a ballet dancer,' said Galen clapping.

But it wasn't funny. Catesby now couldn't tell which side of the tray was poisoned.

'Help yourself first,' said Galen.

Catesby popped a cube out of the tray and put it in his own whisky. He then popped two cubes from the opposite side and plopped them in Galen's glass.

'Cheers,' said Catesby raising the glass to his lips. He quickly sipped the whisky before the ice had a chance to melt and he tried not to grimace when the cube touched his upper lip. No more, he thought. If I got it wrong, I'll just strangle him. It's not worth it.

Galen continued to drink steadily. He began to seem a little drunk. The American eventually looked closely at Catesby. 'You don't seem to be drinking much, my friend.'

'I'm not really a whisky drinker.'

'But this is lovely stuff.' There was a note of suspicion in Galen's voice.

Catesby looked at his glass. The ice cube had nearly melted. He raised the glass and said, 'Cheers.' He then knocked it back in one.

'What's the matter?' said Galen a little slurred. 'You don't look very well.'

Catesby was holding his stomach. 'I think I'm going to be sick.' He took off running to the kitchen and put his head in the sink. The problem was that he wasn't being sick. Catesby thrust two fingers deep down his throat. He was desperate to vomit up the whisky, but nothing would come. He felt beads of sweat bursting on his brow. He tried again. Still no vomit. He looked around the kitchen for something to stick down his throat – or some chemical to make him vomit. It was then that he heard a muffled thump from the sitting room. Catesby's stomach suddenly settled. He had chosen a poison-free cube after all.

When Catesby got back to the room. Galen was sitting upright on the floor with his legs flayed out in front of him. His glasses had fallen off. Without the glasses his eyes looked soft and human. Galen had a Smith & Wesson .32 in his hand, but seemed too weary to point it. The American stared for a second into inner space then fell over flat. Catesby pulled on a pair of surgical gloves. The rule was no fingerprints. For a second he thought about checking for a pulse. But what was the point?

The London plane trees in Green Park still hadn't come into leaf, but seemed on the verge of unfolding. It was one of those spring days when wearing an overcoat makes you sweat, but taking it off makes you shiver. Catesby and Bone were sitting on opposite ends of the park bench as if they were strangers or a couple who had quarrelled.

'Why don't you just admit it, Henry, you're Arlekin?' As Catesby spoke, his eyes settled on a young woman in jeans and a thick turtleneck sitting cross-legged on the grass. She had a raincoat tucked beneath her and was sketching the trees. Bursting life drawing bursting life. 'And the real reason we killed Galen was to save you.'

'If it pleases you, Catesby, I'll confess all. I am Arlekin. It was I who travelled to the DDR to meet with the Soviet leadership. And I also admit that killing Galen was useful to my career.' Bone laughed bleakly. 'It might have been useful to everyone.'

'Don't be facetious.'

'Let's put it this way, William. If I'm not Arlekin, I am quite willing to take the rap for the person who is.'

'Now you're talking riddles.' Catesby laughed. 'But maybe you honestly don't know who you are or where you've been. Maybe you're totally mad.'

'It is an occupational illness. But an illness that I've escaped,' Bone paused, 'so far.'

There was a point for many, Catesby well knew, when the layers and layers of deception became too much. When every doubled agent was doubled back again; when every defector was a fake; when every coveted piece of intelligence was a crafted lie; when truth itself was so dressed in falsehood that you longed again for lies.

'I suppose,' said Catesby, 'that I ought to apologise to you.'

'For what?'

'For accusing you of having Galen killed to save your own skin?'

Bone looked at Catesby. 'My own skin is a very minor part of it. Don't you understand what's happened?'

Catesby shook his head.

'You were the one who predicted it. All those months ago on Dunwich Beach – and I laughed at you.'

'And that's what the meeting in the DDR was about?'

'Yes, in a nutshell.'

'What happened?'

'We were informed ...'

'Who do you mean by "we"?'

'"We" doesn't imply "I". And I'm not going to give you a guest list either. But let's put it this way. There was more than one, how shall I say it?' Bone looked closely at Catesby. 'More than one ally present.'

Catesby knew there was a reason why Bone was giving him a clue. And a reason why he wasn't saying more. Catesby's eyes returned to the young woman bent over her sketch pad drawing trees. She caught a strand of hair with her index finger and tucked it behind her ear. Catesby's heart was bursting – not with love or desire – but simply the overwhelming urge to protect.

'We were informed,' said Bone, 'that a decision had been made – and that there was nothing we could do to change that decision.' Bone looked straight ahead and explained what the decision entailed. His voice was a monotone like a tired barrister summing up. Each apocalyptic detail made Catesby's blood run colder. And yet he wasn't surprised. Death was always more predictable than life. When Bone had finished he looked at Catesby. His voice had turned almost cheery. They had passed from horror into the humour of the gallows. 'So what do you think of that?'

'I think the Americans ought to get used to it – just like we have.'

'But that's not going to happen. They think they're special – "one nation under God". The rest of the world can go hang.' Bone paused. His eyes fixed on an elderly couple walking arm in arm. Behind them the faded decorum of a Regency townhouse. 'Now you know why we had to kill Galen. If the American generals find out about the Russian rocket disaster at Baikonur, they'll know that the Soviet Union hasn't a single missile that can reach the USA. They'll want a pre-emptive strike to take out Moscow and the Soviet military.'

Catesby stared bleakly into nothingness until he saw an image of his own self as a ragged urchin running down to Lowestoft harbour to beg a few herring from a docking steam drifter. The fishermen always obliged because they were kind and knew what it was like to be poor.

'Of course,' continued Bone, 'a prudent president usually has the power to stop the generals. But not,' Bone shook his head with grim finality, 'but not when confronted with this new situation.' Bone waved his umbrella at the London cityscape. 'Look around, William, the new Hiroshima. The revenging bombs won't fall on Washington, they'll fall here.'

'But there's another option.' Catesby said what it was.

'If that happens, the result would be an even messier and prolonged world war with one stage of escalation inevitably leading to another.'

'Why?'

Bone gave him the facts in low measured words.

Catesby stared bleakly across the park, no longer seeing the young woman bent over her sketch pad, but only fires of conflagration leaping from radiated sinking ships to apocalypse Berlin and the funeral pyres of Warsaw, Paris, Prague, Rome and London.

'And that,' said Bone, 'is why you need to get back to Havana. We need the facts, the proof.'

It was the first time that Catesby had been to a *béisbol* game and Fidel Castro was pitching. Fidel's team were called *los Barbudos*, 'the bearded ones', and were playing an exhibition against *los Tigres*, one of Cuba's best professional teams. The game, like much else in Cuban life, was taking place at night. The lights of *Estadio Latinoamericano* flickered and popped as if they were a giant firework – every few seconds a bulb disintegrated into a tiny shower of glowing tungsten.

Catesby had been invited to the game by Lionel, the Canadian diplomat whom he had denounced to Che as an American spy. It was an awkward social situation. Catesby hardly knew the Canadian at all – and assumed the invite was because Lionel suspected him of being the grass. He half-expected that the Canadian was going to use the occasion to shout abuse at him and maybe even punch him in the nose. But, at least at first, Lionel seemed more interested in talking about baseball.

'Fidel,' said Lionel, 'has a damned good fastball. He keeps it tight in to the batter's wrists well away from the business end of the bat.'

'Like an inswinging yorker.'

'Exactly.' The Canadian smiled. 'I play cricket too, you know. But sadly it's been overtaken by baseball. Canada, unfortunately, has fallen too much under the influence of our giant neighbour to the south. But at least we still have the Queen on our banknotes.'

Catesby was taken aback. They weren't the words he expected from a Canadian who was spying for Washington. Maybe he had grassed the wrong bloke – or maybe Lionel was boxing clever. Meanwhile, the batter seemed to be finding Fidel's pitching difficult. He only managed to nick one of *el Líder Máximo's* fastballs, which flew harmlessly into the stands as a 'foul ball'. He missed the next one completely and was 'out'.

'Do you suppose,' said Catesby, 'that he missed it on purpose because he's batting against the boss?'

'Absolutely not. When he was a teenager Fidel was scouted by Major League teams. He could have been ...'

But before Lionel could complete the sentence, the next batter belted Castro's first pitch into the far stands for a 'home run'. It was obvious that *los Tigres* were not going to let themselves be rolled over in order to flatter their country's leader. The stands were also standing and cheering. But what impressed Catesby most was the way Castro himself joined in by doffing his cap and applauding the batter. It was, Catesby realised, not only good sportsmanship but good politics too.

'Well,' said Lionel, 'they are a top professional team.'

'Thanks for inviting me.' Catesby lowered his voice. 'But I'm sure you don't want to talk just about baseball.'

The Canadian shifted uneasily. 'No, I want to give you a warning.'

'Am I in danger?'

'I think so … at least of being PNG'd.' It was diplo slang for being declared Persona Non-Grata and thrown out by the host country.

'What makes you say that?'

'Because I think it's happened to me. I've been recalled to Ottawa.'

'Any idea why?'

'The Cubans think I've been spying for the Americans.'

'Why would they think that – assuming you haven't been?'

'Because the Americans would like us to – but Ottawa has resisted the pressure from Washington.'

'Why have you chosen to tell me? I'm only here on temporary duty.'

'Because someone in the British Embassy is spying for the Americans and I'm sure it's not you.'

Catesby tried not to smile. Lionel was playing a complex game. He was trying to get revenge by making Catesby paranoid and suspicious of his colleagues. Or was he playing a game? It was after all Neville who had told him that the Canadian was a surrogate spy for Washington. Was Neville trying to cover his own tracks? There was cheering from the crowd as *los Tigres* scored two more runs to take the lead.

'How,' said Catesby, 'can you be so sure?'

'I've been working closely with a woman out of the French Embassy named Sophie. She has the evidence. You will meet her.'

Catesby decided to call Lionel's bluff. 'You're a lying piece of shit.'

The Canadian looked startled for a second or two. He could have recovered his balance and continued the game, but instead he leaned close to Catesby and said, 'Fuck you.'

'Likewise.'

The Canadian made a fist and Catesby ducked. But when he looked up again, Lionel was gone.

In the end, *los Tigres* prevailed with a 5–3 win. The game ended with both teams hugging like long-lost brothers.

The baseball quickly turned into an impromptu concert as guitars, bongos, maracas and even double basses appeared out of nowhere. There were now as many women on the baseball diamond as men. A woman in a glittering sequin dress was standing on the pitcher's mound and swaying between players from both teams as she sang into a microphone. When the woman reached the final verse, she passed the microphone to a *los Tigres* player who huskily declared as much as sang:

Con los pobres de la tierra
With the poor people of the earth
I want to cast my lot ...

The stadium erupted with cheering and clapping. The woman then passed the microphone to another player who hugged her tight as he sang the final words:

Guantanamera,
guajira Guantanamera.
Guantanamera,
guajira Guantanamera.

It was after midnight when Catesby got back to the embassy. There had been an architectural change since he was last there. The embassy now had its own 'secure room': a room without windows and a thick metal door. The room had its own power supply and had been built by vetted staff from the UK. Things were heating up and it was the one place where embassy staff could talk freely. The morning briefings were now held in the secure room instead of the Ambassador's office. But this time Catesby and Neville were sitting alone under the fluorescent light.

'Our man in Moscow,' said Neville leaning back with his tie undone, 'managed to copy a very interesting conversation from one of Khrushchev's closest advisers.'

Catesby raised his eyebrows. Moscow was a notoriously difficult environment for Western intelligence officers. 'How did he manage that?'

'He picked it up via the best listening device anyone in Moscow has ever used – vodka. Forget your cunning electronic devices – just hang around with those guys when they're blotto. In this case, the advisor was trying to impress a pretty girl at a cocktail party in the Palace of Congresses while one of our girls was innocently lingering within earshot. Booze and young ladies, eh?'

'And other variations.'

'Quite. In any case,' Neville picked up the transcript and read: '"Kennedy is too young and too intellectual, not prepared well for decision-making in crisis situations. He is too intelligent and too weak."' Neville looked over his reading glasses. 'The Russians seem to agree with our notion of "too clever by half". The French, on the other hand, treat the phrase with contempt.'

'The contempt it deserves.'

'A debatable point.' Neville went back to the transcript. 'In any case, the adviser goes on to say: "Nikita Sergeyevich needs to take advantage of young Kennedy's indecisiveness and do something bold. He needs to ignore the generals, they are always too cautious."' Neville put the paper down. 'What do you think, William?'

'I think it was the booze talking.'

'You seem singularly unimpressed.'

Catesby smiled. He wasn't authorised to share the intelligence about the Russian missile deployment with Neville or anyone else. In one way, it was a good thing. It meant that Neville and others would continue to sniff around. If they came to the same conclusions separately, it would verify Bone's story. Being a spy was a bit like being a research scientist. Your theories need to be tested by peer review. Meanwhile, armies are invading and bombs are dropping.

Neville looked closely at Catesby. 'You have a close working relationship with Henry Bone. I don't have to tell you how dangerous that is. On the other hand, it gives you power and access that no other officer of our rank enjoys. Why do you do it, William? Is it because you like having instant access to C – and being only one ear away from the Prime Minister?'

'Because I can be trusted to the end.'

'Which end?'

'Very funny.'

'But why does Bone trust you – and not the rest of us?'

'Because he knows that I haven't anything left to lose.' Catesby smiled. 'And don't take that as self-pity. It's very exhilarating. It makes me free. That's why I loved jumping out of aeroplanes at night.'

'Have you ever told anyone this before?'

'No.'

'Thank you for telling me.' Neville picked up a sheaf of papers and walked over to a wall map of Cuba. 'While you were gone I managed to set up a little agent network in the countryside. By the way, I won't use anyone that's motivated by ideology – and never have. They shape their reports to suit their political agendas. I only use greedy peasants. But if they get rumbled by *Dirección de Inteligencia*, it's a no-return ticket to *La Cabaña* where your friend Dr Guevara will cure their greed with a bullet in the back of the head.'

Catesby shrugged. 'It's part of the game, but I always feel sorry for the families.'

'Then why do you do it, William?'

'Because it's part of my job.'

Neville was standing with his back to the map and staring at Catesby. 'The awful thing, William, is that I might be risking lives to find out things that you already know.'

'Then it might be an idea to tell those agents to stop reporting and destroy any evidence connecting them to you.'

'You don't have to shout.'

Catesby smiled. 'I thought these walls were soundproof. Sorry, Bob, just tell me what you've found out.'

Neville turned to the map and pointed to the west end of the island. 'There's a lot of heavy construction work going on here, at San Cristóbal and a lesser amount here, at Guanajay. The countryside around both places is a fertile region for sugar cane and tobacco. Which would explain,' Neville smiled wanly, 'the large influx of Soviet agriculture advisers and irrigation specialists into the area.' Neville pointed to an area east of Havana. 'There are three more places – Sagua la Grande, Remedios and Santa Clara – that are also attracting a lot of heavy traffic. There's a similar pattern concerning all the sites. At first there was an endless flow of lorries carrying cement, diggers, bulldozers and all manner of heavy construction plant. But more recently longer, even heavier loads, covered in tarpaulins. Well, I'm no fool – and neither are the local peasants. At first, I thought I had it sussed. Now what do you think?'

'Anti-aircraft defences. Surface-to-air missile sites, probably for S-75 Dvinas.'

'And the size of some of the lorry loads matched the dimensions of the S-75 exactly. But then I started getting reports of other loads that didn't fit in with the Dvina theory. All the movements took place at night – and the locals were not encouraged to look closely. But my chaps did. The low-loader lorries were carrying very long canvas-covered cylindrical objects. So long in fact, that it was impossible to manoeuvre the loads through the villages without backing up several times to try again. A number of walls and gable ends perished in the process. They didn't have that problem with the S-75 SAMs. These big ones aren't defensive missiles – and they must be single-stage monsters. Otherwise, they could have been disassembled in sections for easier transport. Do you agree?'

'I think, Bob, you know the answer.'

'The Sovs are deploying intermediate-range R-12s. You can't disguise them as anything else. You see those black beasts being paraded through Red Square every May Day.'

The R-12, Catesby well knew, was the first Soviet missile to be mass produced and deployed with thermonuclear warheads. It had oddly tiny tailfins, like the deformed-looking arms of a Tyrannosaurus Rex. But the R-12 was road transportable and propelled to its target by storable fuel. This meant that you could launch them from almost anywhere. It was the missile most likely to destroy London.

Neville pointed at the map. 'The Sagua la Grande site is the nearest to the United States – and a perfect fit. The maximum range of the R-12 is 1,292 miles. The distance between the missile site and Manhattan is 1,290 miles.'

The overhead fluorescent light began to flicker making Neville look like a character at the end of a cinema film reel. The light finally went out. Catesby turned on a desk lamp. They both looked more human in the softer light.

'Well,' said Neville, 'it looks like the Sovs have wiped out their strategic disadvantage in one bold move. It's a dangerous gambit, but the logic is faultless.' Neville stared at his colleague. 'You already knew this. Didn't you, William?'

Catesby nodded. 'But I didn't know the location of the sites.'

'Shall I cable the locations to London?'

'I wouldn't, but it's your decision. I'm not your boss.'

'But I value your advice. Why shouldn't I send them?'

'Because some dolt might pass them on to the Americans.'

'Why's that a bad thing?'

'Are you playing devil's advocate?'

'Yes.'

'Because this situation is going to turn into a crisis that could spin out of control – and full intelligence always makes crisis resolution more difficult. Governments are more likely to go for peace when confronted with uncertainty.'

'I'm impressed, William. Do you like playing God?'

Catesby smiled. 'Yes.'

'I see your point about keeping mum.' Neville slid the reports into a folder. 'I won't send these on. But the Americans would have to be pretty stupid not to notice something strange is going on.'

'What assets have they still got in Cuba?'

'First of all, a large number of anti-Castro Cubans with radio transmitters who are strung out through the countryside. The problem, of course, is that a lot of them have been doubled by *el Dirección* and are sending false information. CIA can't be sure which is which. But Washington's other source is quite an anomaly. Totally against the normal run of play.' Neville smiled like a card shark about to trump.

'Go on, surprise me.'

'The French. At first, I thought they were doing it just to show us up – and maybe annoy us too. But then I remembered their man in Washington – he simply adores the USA. It seems that he's running two of his own agents out of the French Embassy here. The lad, and the girl especially, are very active.'

Memories began to jostle for space in Catesby's brain. The first was the refined French voice that had answered the phone number secreted to him by the US Ambassador – and then threatened him with castration and death. There was also the young French couple in Otis's Washington jazz club. And finally, Lionel's reference to 'Sophie'.

'It seems,' said Neville, 'that our French colleagues enjoy the dubious glory of being heavily infiltrated by *both* Moscow and Washington. I think it's a rather splendid achievement.'

'I wouldn't be surprised if their Sov doubles swap stuff with their Yank doubles.'

'Of course they do.'

'At some point,' said Catesby, 'it becomes an art.'

'What?'

'Our game. It's like a complex musical composition full of tonal tricks and unexpected dissonance.'

'I think you need a drink, William.'

'French brandy?'

'Of course.'

'Cheers.' Catesby raised his glass, but decided not to tell Neville about the R-14s due to arrive at the end of the month. Those missiles had a range of 2,800 miles and were capable of hitting the rest of the continental United States.

'Would you mind wearing these blindfolds?' Che's voice was almost apologetic, but his face wore an impish smile. Catesby was sitting in the back of Alekseev's GAZ M21 Volga – and Alekseev was driving. He had, thought Catesby, returned from Moscow unscathed and still in post. The other passengers were a woman from the French Embassy who called herself Sophie and an Italian journalist. 'I don't need a blindfold,' said the Italian, 'I only have eyes for lovely Sophie.'

'Me too,' said Catesby as he tried to piece together the intentions behind Lionel's lies.

Sophie, wedged in the middle of the back seat between Catesby and the Italian, stirred nervously. Che threw up his arms in despair and looked at Alekseev.

'Okay,' said Catesby, 'we'll wear the blindfolds.' He put his on and the others followed. They were going to be given a tour of the SAM sites. The Russians and Cubans didn't mind showing off the new anti-aircraft missiles, but quite reasonably didn't want to reveal their exact locations.

'Haven't we met before?' said Catesby leaning towards the woman next to him.

'I can't remember. I don't think so.'

'But you look so familiar.'

'Have you taken your blindfold off?' The remark wasn't playful. The Frenchwoman's voice was stern and flat.

'No, of course not.' Catesby was sure that she had seen him at the jazz club in DC where Otis played, but she wanted to hide the fact. He wondered if her name was really Sophie. In any case, she looked older and more attractive than she had in the jazz club. She spoke French with an accent that was so suave and refined that it was almost irritating. The French Connection were thugs in silk underwear.

An hour later they were allowed to take their blindfolds off. The car, after a long bumpy ride on a rough track, was parked in a grove of palm trees. They were greeted by a group of Cubans in green battledress who looked more like professors than soldiers. There were also a handful of Russians lurking in the background, but not in uniform. All the Russians were serving military, however, disguised as civilians with open-necked shirts and badly fitting jeans. They could have passed for farmers from the American Midwest. The Sov soldiers were still operating under the threadbare cover of agricultural and irrigation advisers. Catesby began to notice a pattern of hierarchy. The soldiers wore checked shirts, the officers white shirts.

The six S-75 Dvina missiles were beautiful in their sleekness. It was difficult to believe they had anything to do with the frumpy Russian hayseeds in checked shirts. The missiles were thirty-five feet long, but as slender as a young girl's waist. Unlike the stumpy fins of the R-12s, the Dvina's fins were wide and graceful – almost like a ballet dancer's tutu. Were they beautiful, thought Catesby, because they were defensive weapons? As the visitors were shown around, their Cuban and Russian hosts kept repeating the word 'defensive' like a mantra. Catesby knew perfectly well that the visit was a whitewash exercise. The aim was to showcase the peaceful intentions of the Cuban government and their Soviet backers. Catesby could see that both Che and Alekseev were bored with having to go through the ritual. Everyone knew that something more sinister was lurking under the palm trees, but it wasn't yet the time to admit it.

Catesby walked around the missile battery shoulder to shoulder with Alekseev. He wondered if the Russian knew that he was his wife's lover.

Alekseev stopped to stroke one of the missiles. He ran his hand down its slender body. It was impossible for Catesby not to imagine him touching Katya with the same tender concern. Oddly, he felt a pang of jealousy.

'You know,' said Alekseev his hand still on the Dvina, 'that it was one of these that brought down the American U2 that was spying over Sverdlovsk.'

Catesby nodded. The 1960 incident had resulted in the capture of CIA pilot Gary Powers and soured improving relations between the two superpowers. Catesby wondered if intelligence agencies caused such incidents on purpose because a world in conflict meant better job prospects. Or maybe they just liked conflict because it was more exciting. His trade had more than its fair share of deviants and psychos.

'These missiles,' continued Alekseev, 'can strike higher than any aircraft can fly. I fear I am boring you.' Alekseev smiled. 'Because I am boring myself. Let's talk about something more interesting. Who is your favourite poet?'

Catesby looked at Alekseev and understood why Katya loved him. 'I like lots of poets, but you might know this one:

Let us drink, dearest friend
To my poor wasted youth.
Let us drink from grief – Where's the glass?
Our hearts at least will be lightened.'

'Do you really like Pushkin?' said Alekseev. 'Or is this an indirect way of saying you want a drink?'

'Both,' said Catesby.

'Follow me.'

There were trestle tables set up under canvas awnings strung between the roofs of the radar vans. The food and drink were as Russian as the missiles. There were trays of blini with caviar, pickled herring, beetroot, assorted gherkins and chilled vodka. The radar vans, which needed refrigeration to keep their electronics healthy, had probably helped keep the food fresh too.

Alekseev filled Catesby's glass. 'Do you think,' said the Russian nodding towards Sophie, 'that the Frenchwoman is pretty?'

It is an awkward question when asked by the husband of a woman with whom you are intimate. Especially if the husband knows about it. A 'yes' answer devalues the wife in comparison and makes the adultery more sordid. A 'no' confirms an intensity of commitment, for the lover has eyes for no other. Catesby looked closely at Sophie and decided to give an honest answer. 'She knows she's pretty and wants men to acknowledge it. I prefer women who are unselfconscious about their beauty and just accept it as natural to them.'

Catesby paused. He realised that he had just described Katya. 'And besides, Sophie has a hardness about her mouth that will turn spiteful when she ages.' Catesby looked at the Russian. 'Do you find her pretty?'

'Yes. I think she's very vulnerable – and that makes me want to protect her. Do you find it odd that I associate vulnerability with beauty?'

'No, I suppose it's bred into us. It's what makes us treasure babies and children and want to look after them. But that's not, Yevgeny Ivanovich, what makes me love a woman.' Catesby liked the Russian custom of addressing someone who is not family or close friend by full first name and patronymic. But he wondered if his statement about love had been too personal for formal small talk.

'Our paths, Mr Catesby, have crossed in so many places. In Berlin we were, how should I say? Counterparts?'

'You flatter me. I assure you, Yevgeny Ivanovich, that your rank far exceeded mine – and still does.'

'That's only because we are a larger organisation. We have to be. Do you like your job?'

'It's not a matter of liking it. It's a matter of having to do it.'

'I hope,' said Alekseev with a sparkle in his eye, 'that you enjoyed your leave.'

'Oh, I wasn't on leave. I was called back to London for consultations.' Honesty was just as much a tactic as lying. 'And I believe that you were in Moscow at the same time.'

The Russian smiled and raised his glass.

'Shall we drink a toast?' said Catesby.

'Of course.'

Catesby speared a piece of pickled herring and raised it high. 'You must understand, Yevgeny Ivanovich, that I'm from a fishing port called Lowestoft. To the herring!'

The drinking and toasting continued for the next two hours. The Italian journalist was lying on his back with his panama hat over his face. The Russian and Cuban soldiers were singing each other's songs after having finished off the food. And Sophie was sitting in a canvas chair next to Che and looking cross. Catesby could see it was time to go.

'The Frenchwoman doesn't look very happy,' said Alekseev.

'That's because ...' Catesby was aware that his voice was slurred, so he began again. 'That's because you haven't shown her your R-12 nuclear missiles.' Catesby meant it as a joke, but as soon as he saw Alekseev's face he realised he had made a mistake.

'She thinks we have brought nuclear weapons to Cuba.' Alekseev sounded completely sober. 'Did she tell you that?'

'No, it was just a joke.'

'What sort of joke.'

'You realise,' Catesby was surprised by how sober his own voice now sounded, 'that the R-12 story is a rumour that the Americans are passing around. I meant it as a joke.'

The Russian looked at Catesby with eyes that were more sad than surprised or angry. 'She shouldn't say things like that.'

'I told you, she didn't say it. I made the story up.' Catesby realised that, no matter how much he tried, he couldn't put the genie back in the bottle.

Everyone was quiet and subdued during the drive back to Havana. The Italian was dropped off first at his hotel in Miramar Playa. 'I am sure,' whispered Catesby now alone in the back with Sophie, 'that I saw you in Washington.'

'You might have.' She spoke with the icy politeness of a tired official. 'I was stationed there for a time.'

'Did you ever go to a jazz club called the Blue Door on U Street?'

The lines around her mouth, the ones Catesby didn't like, tightened like steel hawsers. She didn't like being caught out in a lie. She finally answered in a voice full of affected boredom. 'Yes, I might have been there once or twice.'

'Your boss in Washington gets on much better with the Americans than our guy.'

'Our Ambassador there is a very charming man.'

'I didn't mean the Ambassador.' Catesby looked at the back of Alekseev's head. He wondered if the Russian understood French and if he was eavesdropping. Che did understand French and spoke it very well, but he seemed to have fallen asleep. Not surprising since he often worked thirty-six hours or more without a break.

They were now near the British Embassy. The day had turned into a balmy humid evening. The rich scent of jasmine, the Cuban national flower, drifted in through the open car windows. The Cubans called it *la mariposa blanca*, the white butterfly. During the guerrilla war the flower became a secret code that symbolised a pure but rebellious nature that longed for independence. Catesby looked at Sophie and realised that she was not wild jasmine, but a cultivated and stylised lily. She belonged to the enigmatic eighteenth-century corridors and formal gardens of Robbe-Grillet's *L'année dernière à Marienbad.* And like the woman at Château Marienbad, she insists that they have never met.

As Alekseev turned the GAZ 21 into Calle 34, Catesby reached into his pocket for a card with his contact details and scribbled a note on it. He tried to press the card into Sophie's hands, but she pushed him away as if repelling an unwanted advance. Catesby then dropped the card on to her lap. She looked at it as if it were a scorpion that had fallen from the roof. Catesby whispered the words he had written on the card since she seemed in no mood to read them: 'Get in contact with me as soon as possible. It's professional, not personal – and absolutely vital.'

The car had now pulled up outside the British Embassy gates. Catesby got out on the driver's side. He closed the door and stepped back into the centre of the empty road. He looked at the dark silhouette of Alekseev behind the wheel – at least this coach driver wasn't a headless one. He then looked at Sophie alone in the back – and for the first time longed for her. He understood what Alekseev had meant by vulnerable.

The script unrolled with the inevitability of a Greek tragedy – except some of the characters had swapped parts. Neville's man at José Marti Airport had reported that Alekseev had left the country again. Presumably for emergency consultations in the Kremlin. Catesby welcomed the news for completely selfish reasons. Alekseev's absence would make it easier for him to see Katya. And the more he saw her, the more he wanted to see her. Catesby knew it was a weakness, perhaps even a pathetic weakness. He had always had contempt for intelligence officers who were compromised by honey trap entanglements. Of course Katya wasn't a honey trap. If anything he was using her more than she was using him. The thought cheered Catesby up – a bit. Spying was a lonely profession even when you were surrounded by other people. The loneliness was from having continually to wear a false face. Katya was an escape not just into passion, but into true emotions.

Catesby's flat was on the top floor of a neo-colonial house called *La Mansión Blanca*. The rest of the house was occupied by other embassy staff, including the military attaché and his family. Even though the place was crumbling and breeding lizards, it was the most opulent accommodation Catesby had ever enjoyed on a foreign posting. There was a balcony and a large garden with palm trees – and the susurrus of the sea in the near distance. There was no security other than a locked door on the ground floor entrance.

Catesby woke up when he realised that someone was trying to contact him with an ST One. It was the first and most reliable means of covert communication that Catesby had learned in SIS basic training. The ST One never let you down. The first stone rattled the wooden shutter of Catesby's bedroom window. The second pinged against the iron railing of the balcony. Catesby turned on the bedside light to let the person in the garden know that he was awake. He then turned off the light so that he wouldn't be silhouetted. Catesby put on his dressing gown and grabbed a gun from his bedside table. He opened the shutter and peered into the night without exposing himself. He flicked open the chamber of the revolver to make sure it was loaded. It was. He waited in the shadows listening to the sonar shrieks of diving bats. He could wait all night.

Finally, there was a voice. It was Katya speaking Russian. 'William, is that you?'

Catesby walked on to the balcony with the revolver in his hand. He didn't put it in his pocket because he didn't want to stain the dressing gown with gun oil. It was a silk gown that his sailor father had brought back from China in 1910. His only heirloom.

'I need to see you.' But Catesby couldn't see her. Katya was speaking from somewhere in the dark under the palm trees.

'I'll come down to let you in.'

Catesby went back into the house, the gun still heavy in his hand. He was about to put it back in its drawer. But he decided to take it with him in case Katya had been forced into luring him into a trap. The Havana air had been buzzing with intrigue for weeks.

He went down the stairs without turning on a light and opened the heavy oak door. Katya was standing there alone, her face hidden behind a black mantilla as if she had just come from a funeral. Catesby quickly let her in and closed the door behind them. When

Katya reached out to embrace him, she found the barrel of the gun protruding into the palm of her left hand.

'Is this for me?' she said. Her hand groped along the barrel as if she wanted to take the pistol.

'Be careful.' Catesby pulled the gun out of her reach.

'How did you know I needed a gun? Who told you?'

Her words confused Catesby. It was as if he were in a play and someone had given him a script with lines missing. 'Why,' he said improvising, 'do you need a gun?'

'I need to kill her.'

'Who?'

'Sophie Devereux.'

'Come upstairs.'

'I want to, but I haven't time.'

'But I need to get dressed.'

Katya followed him upstairs and then sat on the side of the bed as Catesby took off his dressing gown. He had started to stir and she noticed it. She leaned her head against his thigh as she caressed him. 'I love you,' she said.

Catesby bent down to kiss her. She had never said that before. 'Can you stay?' he said.

She embraced him tightly. 'No, but you don't have to come with me.'

Catesby began to dress. He didn't know what he was doing – or why he was doing it. He felt lost in an out-of-focus rosy dream where there were thorns and steep cliffs. He wondered if he would let her have his pistol, a British-manufactured Webley revolver. Any bullets recovered in an autopsy would point straight to the UK. On the other hand, everybody sanitised their wet-job guns by using foreign weapons – so a British bullet wouldn't prove a thing. Maybe the opposite. Bluff and double bluff. In any case, Catesby didn't want to help kill Sophie. He wanted to save her. But maybe there was a good reason why the Frenchwoman should be dead.

'How,' he said, 'do you know Sophie?'

'I met her at the Ministry of Culture where we attended courses on Latin American culture and language. We became friends and often had tea together. Zhenka suggested – the way he does – that I should get to know Sophie better. I told him that I wasn't going to spy on my friends for him. Then he told me why it was important that I did so. I was a little shocked. I could never do the things that she did. It made me see her differently.'

'And now you want to kill her?'

'I don't want to kill her, I have to kill her.'

'But why does it have to be you?'

'I want to save Zhenka. He was ordered to have her killed, but he wouldn't do it. He told me he couldn't bear to do it. That's why he was called back to Moscow.' Katya looked at Catesby. Her eyes were dark bottomless pools of pain.

'What's wrong?'

'It's something to do with what happened to him at the end of the war in Berlin.' Katya paused. 'My husband, my darling husband, said that it is wrong for any man to kill a woman because it was a woman who gave him birth. But he said it was even more obscene for a eunuch, who could not cast his seed into a woman, to take a woman's life. He shouted, "It's a sin against nature." Then poor Zhenka began to weep the most bitter tears I have ever seen. I put my arms around my sweet husband, but I could not comfort him.'

They sat still together on the side of the bed. Catesby watched a wall lizard stalking a spider. He held Katya's hands in his, but felt afraid – almost unworthy – to look at her.

'Will you help me?' she said. 'I don't want Zhenka punished for disobeying orders.' In Kremlin terms, 'punished' had unknown layers of nuance.

'What did Sophie do?'

'She found out important military secrets by sleeping with one of Fidel's ministers?'

'What happened to the minister?'

'He's already dead.'

'Then the Cubans may have already done Zhenka's job for him.'

Katya smiled bleakly and shook her head. 'You don't understand what happened. I didn't say that the minister was killed. He committed suicide. The Cubans still don't know why he did it. They may never find out. We need to find Sophie and kill her before she passes on the information.' Katya looked at Catesby with pleading eyes. 'It's the only way we can save Zhenka.'

Catesby opened the door of a small fridge in the corner of his room where he made ice cubes and kept the ingredients for his mojitos and daiquiris *modo de* Hemingway. He removed a hidden panel from the back of the chill compartment and took out a loaded hypodermic syringe.

'What's that?' said Katya. There was a chill in her voice as cold as the liquid in the syringe.

'Cleopatra's asp.'

'Do you want me to take it?'

'No,' Catesby slipped the syringe into the pocket of his beige linen jacket. The jacket was a hand-me-down from a rich friend at Cambridge. He loved the jacket, even though he didn't have the voice and the manners to go with it. But he deserved to wear it. For he was doing their dirty work so they could sleep safely and send their kids to Eton and drink Pimm's at garden parties.

'And the gun?' she said.

'Put it in your handbag in case we need it.'

'Do you trust me, William?'

'Why shouldn't I? You just said you loved me.'

As they drove to the Frenchwoman's flat Catesby made what Catholics call an examination of conscience. Was killing Sophie Devereux justified? Catesby's eyes followed the beams of the car's headlamps as they flowed along the broad tree-lined boulevards through Vedado and into Habana Vieja. It *was* justified because stopping the information about the missiles reaching Washington was in the UK's interest. The ensuing crisis would make London the Soviet military's prime target. Weighed against those millions of deaths, Sophie's life was expendable. Just as American generals saw Britain and Western Europe as expendable pawn sacrifices in the crusade to eliminate communism. But it didn't make killing a single person any less ugly and disturbing. It was tempting to use psychopaths to do these jobs, but psychos couldn't be trusted to keep their mouths shut. They were proud of the fact that they didn't mind inflicting pain on others. They thought it made them special and they liked to brag about it.

Catesby parked the car, a Humber with a *corps diplomatique* badge, on Paseo de Marti. There were lots of all-night bars around. It would give them an alibi for being in the neighbourhood. A late-night liaison with a diplomatic corps wife was a better plea to cop than murder. And too commonplace to even raise an eyebrow. Any bar would do, but Catesby wanted to flaunt it. They drank their daiquiris on the roof garden of the Hotel Saratoga, probably the most elegant hangout in Havana. They were sitting on a yellow sofa next to the swimming pool. The dome of the capitol, modelled on the Paris Pantheon, was silhouetted against the sky. Fairy lights reflected in the water of the pool. Catesby was tempted to ask Katya to do a few naked lengths as Ava Gardner had at Hemingway's place. It would be a big thing to ask, but not as big as asking him to kill another woman. He leaned over and kissed Katya on the lips. The sound of guitars, maracas and laughter drifted and faded on the midnight air.

They left the hotel and walked arm in arm across Prado Boulevard like a pair of adulterers who just didn't give a damn. Sophie's flat was on the top floor of the Hotel Inglaterra. It did seem a little odd that a French diplomat was lodging there. The Inglaterra was the oldest hotel in Cuba and big on faded elegance. The daiquiris had made Catesby lightheaded, but clearheaded at the same time. Plans and alibis were forming. '*We went to her flat to invite her for a drink, but no one answered the door.*' Or. '*The door was open and we found her slumped over.*' Doing things on the hop, like covering up a murder, seldom went to plan. But, when you had diplomatic immunity, they didn't need to.

They walked up the narrow white wooden staircase because the lifts were out of order. The stairs were uncarpeted and their footsteps seemed to rattle the very fabric of the hotel. Katya led the way down the corridor when they got to the top floor. The sound of her heels on the bare wood was as subtle as rifle shots. When she got to the dark oak door of Sophie's flat, Katya raised her fist to knock. But before her knuckles touched the wood, the door opened.

'Good evening,' said Che bowing graciously to Katya. He then looked over her shoulder at Catesby. 'We were expecting you, William. Please come in, both of you.'

The flat looked like a bomb had hit it. All the lights were glaring and all the furniture and possessions had been completed turned over. In addition to Che, there were six others in the room including two women. What looked at first like casual vandalism was, in fact, a thorough forensic examination. Catesby watched as one of the men unstitched a sofa cushion.

'You realise,' said Catesby, 'that what you are doing is in complete violation of the Vienna Convention on diplomatic immunity.'

Che looked bemused.

'You are not allowed, Dr Guevara, to enter the residence of a diplomat without his or her permission.'

'You are absolutely correct,' said Che, 'but Sophie Devereux is not, and never has been, on the list of accredited diplomats. I'm surprised you didn't know that.'

Catesby felt mildly ashamed. It would have been so simple, but he had never checked. Assumption, as Kit Fournier used to say in his direct American manner, is the mother of all fuck-ups. The fact that Sophie had been operating as an 'illegal' put a lot of things in perspective. Such as the fact that the French intelligence chief in Washington was running unauthorised operations on his own. And if Paris wasn't paying for them, who was?

'What did she do wrong?' said Catesby.

'I think you need to wash your hands. If the señora will excuse us,' Che bowed gallantly to Katya, 'I'll show Señor Catesby where the bathroom is.'

Katya nodded and Catesby followed Che to a marble-lined bathroom with a bidet and a huge cast-iron bath painted blue. Che closed the door and turned on the taps full blast to counter any hidden microphones.

'We've already found one bug,' said Che, 'so there might be others. Our big problem isn't foreigners, but Cubans spying for Washington who may be spying on Sophie.'

Catesby completely understood why Washington spied on their own agents. It was the tiresome logic of espionage. You had to be certain that the people working for you hadn't been turned.

'You asked,' said Che, 'what Sophie had done wrong. It was the worst thing.'

'Which is what?'

'She tried to kill Fidel. We're still trying to catch her and her accomplices.'

'Is that a secret?'

'No, but this is.' Che reached into his pocket, took out a card and read the note written on it. '"Get in contact with me as soon as possible. It's professional, not personal – and absolutely vital."' Che looked closely at Catesby. 'Look. It's your card and it's your handwriting.'

'I don't deny it.'

'You know how serious this is. You and your government could be implicated in a plot to assassinate the leader of our country. I don't think the international community would blame us for ignoring your diplomatic immunity. Why are you smiling?'

'Because Sophie did the job so well. She thinks on her feet. She's not only dropped me and my country in the shit, but she did it in style. She's a real professional. And that's why you'll never believe the truth.'

'And you think that's funny.'

'I tend to smile and laugh at the wrong time – it's a bad habit.' Catesby realised it wasn't funny at all and he needed to do something. Che was unarmed. He felt the hypodermic syringe in his pocket.

'Why,' said Che, 'did you give her the card?'

'You wouldn't believe me,' said Catesby edging his hand towards the syringe.

'Maybe I would believe you.' Che held up the card. 'No one else knows about this. I found it on Sophie's desk. Your card was lying completely in the open, as if she wanted us to find it. That made me suspicious.'

Catesby moved his hand away from the pocket with the syringe.

'The way she planted the card was too obvious,' continued Che. 'She wanted to get you and your country in trouble – to lay a false trail.' Che touched Catesby's lapel. 'Nice jacket, Irish linen?'

'Yes. Would you like one?'

'Maybe someday.' Che closed his hand on the lapel and pulled the jacket open. With his other hand he slipped the card into Catesby's lapel pocket. 'You keep that.'

'What size are you?'

'Forty, but I'm getting a bit fat.'

'We'll send you a straw boater and a bottle of Pimm's to go with it.'

Che gave a closed fist salute. '*Hasta la victoria siempre!*'

Catesby smiled and returned the salute.

'Come to see me tomorrow at *La Cabaña*.' Che reached to turn off the taps. 'It would be nice to talk without wasting so much water.'

The drive back was more relaxed than the drive there. Not having to kill was almost as much a reprieve as not being killed – almost. At first, Katya lay back in the passenger seat with her eyes closed and a look of blissful relief on her face. But after a few minutes her eyes were open and worried. She was still thinking of the consequences for her husband. 'What's happened to Sophie?' she said more to herself than Catesby.

'I think she's still alive. I'll find out more tomorrow.'

'I want peace for Zhenka,' said Katya staring out the passenger window. 'I want them to leave him alone.'

'Is Zhenka going to tell his bosses that he disobeyed orders by not killing Sophie?'

Katya smiled bleakly. 'Of course not, my husband is not stupid.'

'Does he know about us?'

Katya stared out the window.

They spent an entire night together for the first time. No words were spoken, but things would never be the same again. Catesby didn't realise it at the time, but one day he would. We don't control life; life controls us.

Che's office seemed narrower and more austere than it had before. The stained-oak ceiling beams slanted towards the outer wall giving the impression of a poet's garret. Guevara, framed by the dark woodwork behind him, looked like a figure in a seventeenth-century Spanish painting. There was, thought Catesby, a striking resemblance to the freed slave Juan de Pareja in the painting by Velásquez – a natural dignity and poise that neither chains nor death could contain.

Che was writing something. His pen moved quickly and fluently as if there was neither need nor time to pause for thought. He finally picked up the page and read: 'Cuba does not recognize the right of the United States, or of anyone else in the world, to determine the type of weapons Cuba may have within its borders.' He put the page down and looked at Catesby. 'What do you think?'

'There are people in Washington who would find that provocative.'

'It isn't a provocation. It is a statement of fact.'

Catesby shrugged. He wasn't there as Guevara's foreign policy adviser.

Che leaned back in his chair, an ornately carved Spanish colonial antique that would go for a bomb at Sotheby's. 'I suppose you want to know more about Sophie Devereux.'

'I thought that was why you invited me here.'

'Sophie Devereux was a killer.' Che paused and stared at Catesby. 'Have you ever killed anyone?'

'Yes.'

'And how did you feel?'

'Shaky, a bit sick inside. Even though it had to be done.'

Che nodded. 'During the guerrilla war we had a spy travelling with our column. He was betraying our positions to Batista's air force. He eventually confessed. He knew he had to die – we all knew he had to die. It was embarrassing – no one wanted to do it.' Che paused. 'So I ended the problem by giving him a shot with a .32 pistol through the right side of the brain. His eyes were open and looking straight into mine. I aimed at his forehead and the bullet exited through his right temporal lobe, just behind the ear. He gasped for a little while as the autonomic nervous system closed down – and then he was dead.'

The clinical description reminded Catesby that Che was a medical doctor.

'His name was Eutimio,' continued Che in a soft voice, 'he had knelt down before me, not to beg for his life, but that I look after his children – which I have. The sky darkened and a heavy thunderstorm broke just as I prepared to shoot him. The thunder claps were so loud that even those *compañeros* who were standing next to us did not hear the shot.' Che's voice lowered to a whisper. 'One has to grow hard but without ever losing tenderness.' His voice rose back to normal. 'But I digress, you want to know more about Sophie Devereux.'

'Yes.'

'Sophie is not one who kills out of duty or necessity. She kills for money – and more malevolently, for the thrill, the excitement.' Che looked at Catesby. 'Sophie is beautiful and bright, but not a woman who lives for anything beyond her own beauty and power. We, you and I, are different. We live for our ideals – and I am sure, that some of those ideals are ones we share.'

Catesby smiled. There was a side to Che that was silky, feminine and seductive. Some felt threatened by it. The image of Che's face, framed by its untidy black ringlets, affected the USA like a full moon affects a werewolf. It was an affront to the tidy conformity of shopping mall and church. Che's androgynous allure was even more dangerous. Desire was something dirty that you had to keep under cover at the Quorum Club.

Guevara offered a cigar that Catesby refused. Then lit one for himself. 'We think,' Che took a puff, 'that Sophie Devereux was the person who spread the poison on the inside of Fidel's wetsuit. Have you been to Cayo Coco?'

'No.'

'We must take you there sometime. It's part of a string of coral islands to the east of Havana – the perfect place for scuba-diving. The water is a brilliant turquoise and jade. Its only disadvantage is being too close to the Florida Keys.'

Catesby could see a pattern emerging.

'In any case,' continued Che, 'Fidel is no fool or he would no longer be alive. Whenever a beautiful woman sleeps with him he does not assume that she is only interested in his manly charms, considerable as they are. Fidel certainly would never eat or drink anything that such a woman had been near. But this woman was so beautiful that he also checked his clothes, his socks – and even his wetsuit. He noticed something inside the wetsuit that looked like fungus – and knew that it was poison.

'Well,' Che took two long puffs, 'Fidel was more amused than angry. He is very gallant in these matters and wanted another night of love with the guilty party. So, without Sophie knowing, he found another wetsuit and they both went off for a morning's diving. And it ended up being a very interesting morning indeed.

'Sophie suggested that they explore a coral reef that was a kilometre offshore. They motored out to it, just the two of them, in a small rubber dinghy. By now, Sophie must have been wondering when the wetsuit poison was going to have its effect. In any case, they landed the dinghy on a small island – about the size of this room – that Sophie had pointed out. I thought that Fidel was far too reckless, but he enjoys playing these games. There was another femme fatale who tried to poison him last year. She hid pills in her cold cream jar. When Fidel found the pills he handed her his pistol and said, "Here, shoot me." She didn't have the nerve, but Fidel would never have tried that game with Sophie. He knew instantly that she was much colder, much tougher-minded – a natural killer.

'In any case, they started diving on the coral reef – which is beautiful. Fidel was impressed that Sophie wasn't frightened by the sharks that came to investigate as they swam along the reef. Owing to the sharks there aren't many other fish, but the coral is an example of great natural beauty – so many pulsating colours. You ought to see it. In any case, Fidel's eyes were drawn to a huge conch that was stunningly beautiful – and a rarity too, for that species of conch is virtually unknown on the reefs of Cayo Coco. He gestured to Sophie that she should take it for a prize. She shook her head and pointed to Fidel, meaning it was his. She then swam away towards the surface. Sophie is a very swift swimmer and reached the dinghy well before Fidel. She pushed it back into the water, started the outboard and was motoring out to sea while Fidel was still ten metres away.

'Our security boys on Cayo Coco beach saw what was happening and were quickly in pursuit. And it was at that very moment that the Florida speed boats arrived. Great big steel ones with twin-mounted .50 calibre machine guns in their bows. They sprayed the tiny island with gunfire, but Fidel, for once, had done the sensible thing. He dived back into the water and kept well below the surface for the rest of the battle. Our boats were outgunned and far less fast than the gangsters. But they didn't get away completely. We called in the air force and one of the boats was sunk.'

'Was it the boat that picked up Sophie?'

Che shrugged. 'Who knows? By the way, we later discovered that the trophy conch was a bomb with an anti-disturbance device. It would have killed Fidel if he had touched it. Unfortunately, we had to blow it up in place. It would have been a lovely souvenir for the Museum of the Revolution.'

'What happened to Sophie's other lover?'

Che's face was a blank. 'What other lover?'

'The government minister who committed suicide.'

'I think you have been misinformed.'

Once again Catesby felt he was lost in a corridor of mirrors where the reflections were not so much false as distorted. He looked away, but felt Guevara's eyes boring into him.

'Who,' said Che, 'told you about this minister who killed himself?'

Catesby wasn't going to answer. He didn't want to implicate Katya even further. He changed the subject by gesturing to the handwritten page on Che's desk. 'In this statement you read to me, you said that only Cuba had the right to decide which weapons to keep within her borders. What weapons were you talking about?'

Che smiled. 'You must know. I revealed most of the plan last time you were here.'

'Are the nuclear missiles already operational?'

'You know that I can't tell you that.'

'If you don't want to get bombed and invaded by the United States, it might be a good idea to pretend they are operational.'

'The situation is difficult. We need to give a more precise definition of peaceful coexistence. Peaceful coexistence among nations does not mean coexistence between the exploiters and the exploited, between the oppressors and the oppressed.'

Catesby felt a chill run down his back. He agreed with Che's words, but not the likely consequences. You can't always have peace and fairness on the same plate.

'You look worried,' said Che.

'No, just thoughtful.'

'You need, William, to stop thinking of yourself as a spy.'

'What should I be then?'

'A back-channel diplomat. Someone who does not officially exist, but who can be trusted to convey messages between the powers.'

Catesby felt a certain unease. Che was echoing the advice that Henry Bone and Bob Neville had given months before. It was too much of a coincidence.

Che looked closely at Catesby. 'I believe you've heard of Aleksandr Semyonovich Feklisov?'

Catesby nodded. Feklisov was one of Russia's best spies. He was thought to have run the spy ring that passed on US atomic secrets to Moscow in the late forties.

'Aleksandr is now working in Washington under the name of Fomin. But a certain powerful American knows who he is and what he is doing – just as I know what you're doing. Maybe one day you will meet Aleksandr.'

'You seem to have forgotten that I do not work for you, Dr Guevara, I work for the British government.'

'I have never doubted that for one moment. I am not asking you to work for me. Nor am I asking you to be a mere messenger. I respect you – and feel that I can trust you, not only to convey my words, but also to interpret them accurately.'

Catesby understood the situation. The role of the back-channel diplomat wasn't to repeat the words, but to explain what they *really* meant.

'Feklisov tells us,' said Che, 'that the Americans have suspended U-2 flights over Cuba. He says the suspension is the result of an accidental U-2 flight over the Soviet Union for which the USA had to make a humiliating apology. And also because another U-2 was shot down over China. It shows that Kennedy is weak.'

Catesby looked out the window. It was still the hurricane season and the sky was overcast. 'Maybe,' he said, 'the Americans are not overflying Cuba because of the weather.'

Che puffed his cigar. 'You think so?'

Catesby was tempted to say *I know so*, but shrugged instead. He didn't want to give too much away. He knew that the flights had been re-authorised for nearly a week, but there hadn't been a hole in the cloud cover.

'If they do overfly,' said Che, 'we will shoot them down.'

'So you control the surface-to-air missiles and not the Russians?'

Che smiled. 'It depends on the weather.'

It depended, thought Catesby, on a lot of things. The most interesting aspect of international relations wasn't the conflict between enemies, but the conflicts between allies. You only had to go to an embassy cocktail party to see those conflicts in the flesh. It was easier for Western diplos to talk to the Russians than to talk to each other.

'There is,' said Che, 'a side to Cuba's defensive weapons that you should know about. It is important for Washington's future calculations – and hence to Britain's survival.'

'What about Cuba's survival?'

'In some ways we are less vulnerable than you. Washington doesn't want clouds of radioactive fallout drifting back over Florida. Our nearness to our enemy is an advantage that Britain doesn't have.'

Catesby suspected that he already knew the secret that Che was going to reveal. 'What is it, Dr Guevara, that you want to tell me?'

Che leaned forward and spoke in a quiet deliberate voice. 'These are the weapons we have in place and they are invulnerable ...'

Catesby listened to the discourse in numb silence. As soon as Guevara had finished, Catesby sensed it was time to go.

'Are you leaving?' said Che.

'I thought you were finished.'

'There's one other thing.'

Catesby found Che looking at him with an impish half smile. Something about the smile worried him. 'What is it?' said Catesby fidgeting.

'Are you good friends with General Alekseev and his wife?'

'I think that you've already come to your own conclusions.'

'Perhaps I have. It's wrong of me to tease you.' Che waved his cigar in a gesture of apology. 'You know, of course, that Yevgeny Ivanovich made ... how should I say it, the ultimate sacrifice in the Great Patriotic War?'

'I know.'

'And I think it wounded his mind too. Would you kill yourself if that happened to you?'

'I don't know. But I'd probably drink a lot – a lot more.'

'It's a pity. The Alekseevs had just married weeks before it happened. That meant that the other person was wounded as well.'

'I am aware of the circumstances – you don't need to tell me.' Catesby's voice was sharp and abrupt. 'And why is this any of your business?'

'It's my business because General Alekseev plays an important role in the relations between the Soviet Union and Cuba – and I want to imagine what it's like to be him.' Che closed his eyes and touched his forehead with two fingers as if his head were aching. He looked exhausted. He continued in a voice that was almost a whisper. 'Alekseev and I had a terrible argument. Maybe I was wrong.'

Catesby sat in silence and stared at Guevara.

Che opened his eyes. He looked even more tired and drained. 'It wouldn't have been so bad if it had only been Alekseev and myself alone, but there were other Russians present – including General Pliyev. I raised my voice and pointed my finger at Alekseev as if I were accusing him of being a traitor. Everyone started staring. If only ...'

'I'm confused. What did you say?'

'Haven't I told you?'

'No.'

'I said that, "We must never establish peaceful coexistence. We are in a struggle to the death between two systems and we must gain the ultimate victory – no matter what the cost in lives."'

'Did you mean it?'

'In a way, as rhetoric at least.'

'What happened next?'

'I don't know. I think there has been a big dispute between the Russians.'

'How do you know?'

'The Alekseevs have been recalled to Moscow. I just got the news an hour ago.'

Catesby struggled to hide his shock and pain. He knew that he would never see Katya again.

When Catesby got back to the embassy there was more bad news. Not about Russian missiles or double agents or a dire international crisis. Bad news about his family in Suffolk. His Uncle Jack and his cousin Bill, also named William Catesby, had drowned in a fishing accident while long lining for early cod. Catesby was devastated. Family was more important than job. It wouldn't be a long compassionate leave – only seventy-two hours including flights – but there was no way Catesby was going to miss the funeral.

Eternal Father, strong to save,
Whose arm hath bound the restless wave,
Who bidd'st the mighty ocean deep
Its own appointed limits keep ...

No one in the congregation at St Margaret's Church, or any Lowestoft church, needed a hymn sheet to remember those words. Catesby put his arm around Aunt Jean. She hadn't cried until then.

Oh, hear us when we cry to Thee,
For those in peril on the sea!

Jean had suffered the worst thing: the double loss. The worst nightmare of a fishing port woman. And yet, fishing hadn't been the primary job of her son and husband. Jack and Billy were shipyard workers by trade. The long lining was just something they did at weekends, like a lot of Suffolk men, for extra cash.

Billy's widow, Sally, was on Catesby's other side. Her face was stiff and hard. She was going to have to get used to bringing up four children on her own. Catesby knew there was nothing he could do to console Sally. She had always regarded Catesby and his sister with suspicion. Sally had left school at fourteen to work in the food-processing industry. Depending on the time of year, she gutted herring, plucked pheasants, filleted fish, dressed Cromer crabs or jointed chickens. Her hands were always rough and red. Part of Sally resented Catesby and his sister. It didn't seem fair that they were the only ones in the family to go to university and escape a harsh life of manual labour and poverty. And yet another part of Sally desperately wanted that different life for her children. But with Billy dead, the sixth form for the children, let alone university, was a vanished dream. The trawlers and the factories beckoned.

Catesby knew how Sally felt. He understood why she didn't like him. But he would never turn his back on her or those like her even if they turned their backs on him. And once again he prayed, as much as an atheist can pray, that he would never have to make the choice between betraying his class or his country. For he knew which one he would choose.

After the church service there was only family at the graveside. It was short and bitter. Uncle Jack had washed up at Kessingland and Billy at Pakefield. It was as if both had been riding the ebb tide to get as near to home as possible. Catesby wondered what had happened to their gold earrings. It was a tradition among Lowestoft fishermen. The gold earrings were meant to pay for their funerals if their bodies washed up.

Catesby had been in the same class at Roman Hill Primary as cousin Billy. They were as close as siblings until Catesby went on to Denes Grammar and Billy left school to become an apprentice fitter. Catesby always regarded his cousin as his 'what if' alter ego. Billy was blond, blue-eyed and tall. Catesby was dark and smaller, more like his Belgian mother than his English father. Billy was open and friendly; Catesby always a little reserved and shifty. They complemented each other and used their different styles to outwit opponents on the football field. But they had the same name. When Catesby and Billy went to the pub after Catesby's first term at Cambridge, Billy put his arm around his cousin and shouted: 'Don't forget. *I'm* the *real* William Catesby.' Catesby knew that Billy was right.

The wake was held at the Labour Club and after three pints Catesby found himself talking broad 'Lowes'toff' as if he had never left home. Both Billy and his father had been strong trade unionists and both had been shop stewards. Inevitably, the mourners linked arms and began singing. Catesby sensed that a number of eyes were on him to see if he knew the words by heart. He did.

The people's flag is deepest red,
It shrouded oft our martyred dead,
And ere their limbs grew stiff and cold,
Their hearts' blood dyed its ev'ry fold ...

'What exactly happened?'

'No one seems to know, Will. The coastguard and the police are still looking at records of shipping traffic in the area.'

Catesby was alone with his sister in the family home in Dene

Road. It was late at night and they were in the back sitting room. It was a large house that had once been home to a number of Belgian relatives on the run from either war or the law. It was where Catesby and his sister Frederieke, 'Freddie', had become fluent in Flemish, French – and Russian too from an aunt by marriage.

'The only thing I've heard,' said Catesby, 'is that it was a real October pea-souper with visibility down to less than the length of the boat.'

'I remember the day. It was foggy here too.'

'You know, Freddie, I've been out on that boat and it had a fog horn that ran off a gas bottle – and if that ran out there was an old frying pan they could hit with a spanner. And a radar reflector too. Why are you looking so thoughtful?'

'It just doesn't seem right.'

'Of course it isn't right. The shipping companies never own up if there aren't any survivors to point the finger.'

'Sally could use the money.'

'I'll have a chat with some of the other fishermen who were out on the day, but I'm flying back to Cuba the day after tomorrow. How's your new job?'

'At least it's not far to walk.' Freddie was teaching modern languages at Denes Grammar – about 400 yards away. 'But going back to teach at your old school makes you feel a failure.'

'You'll never be a failure, Freddie.'

Freddie had been a translator at GCHQ, but had lost her security clearance. It was the result of an ugly incident that had affected both their careers. Catesby had kept his job – even though he had lied to protect Freddie. It was one of the swords that Henry Bone kept dangling over Catesby's head.

'They say there's been "foreigners" around, but that could be anyone who isn't from Orford.'

Catesby was having a drink with old school friends John and Ange in the Jolly Sailor. John had rightly pointed out that in Suffolk 'foreign' began at about five miles away. In North Lowestoft, 'foreign' began south of the bridge. Cuba wasn't even in the same galaxy. And yet Cuba could toll the final end and obliteration of Suffolk. The county's airbases were frontline targets of the first resort.

'Apparently,' said Ange, 'they had American accents. They were probably from the airbase.'

'What did they want?' said Catesby.

'They wanted to hire a fishing boat – and the answer of course was no.'

Catesby had spent the day nosing around Orford and talking to fishermen. Several had been out to sea the day that Jack and Billy had disappeared. Visibility had been dreadful, but no one had noticed anything untoward. The chances of Sally getting compensation seemed nil.

'Sorry I can't stay longer,' said Catesby, 'but I'm heading back to London this evening. And then Heathrow in the morning.'

'Interesting new job?' said John.

'Not particularly, I'm second to the press attaché when I'm not drinking rum.'

'Sounds like jolly hard work the Foreign Office.'

'If you only knew.'

The most dangerous thing about driving the road from Orford to Woodbridge at night is leaping deer. They seem to panic when caught in a car's headlamps. Another hazard is a drunken countryman weaving his way home from the Butley Oyster.

On this occasion the countryman seemed to have fallen off his bicycle in the middle of the road. He was so sprawled across the road that Catesby was going to have to run over him to get past. He pushed his foot down on the accelerator, but covered the brake in case the countryman didn't roll or jump out of the way. Catesby's paranoia, not for the first time, was vindicated. The fake countryman jumped up and to the side with his pistol out. The first shot hit the back passenger window. The next one managed to take out a rear tyre. Catesby's car slewed off the road and two more shots hit the rear windscreen. Then the car stalled.

Catesby lay down across the passenger seat as if he had been hit. At the same time he removed his Browning 9mm automatic from where he carried it beneath the passenger seat. If the shooter had any sense he would fire a few rounds into the car to see if Catesby was faking it. He wondered if the Humber's bodywork would deflect the bullets. He continued waiting. There were footsteps on the road and then voices – voices as unmistakably American as a shot of rye whiskey.

'Hey, Joey, you think that guy's playing possum?'

'Let's make sure he's a dead possum.'

Two shots rang out, but the bullets didn't make it through the boot and back seat. There was then the sound of a single set of footsteps coming up alongside the car. Catesby reckoned the shooter was going to put a few rounds through the driver-side door. And British motorcar steel wouldn't stop those. Catesby reached for the passenger door handle and pushed. He landed on the damp grassy verge just as bullets ripped through the fabric of the front seats.

Catesby saw Joey appear from behind the car to get a clear shot, but Catesby fired first and hit him in the knee. Joey went down clutching at his injury and Catesby put a bullet through the top of his head. The other guy then fired two shots which passed through the driver-side door and ricocheted over Catesby's head. Then there was the sound of footsteps running down the road. The gunman had run out of ammunition.

Catesby was up and after him. Joey's pal wasn't a good runner. Catesby dropped him with a bullet through the thigh. He was now certain that the two gunmen had been responsible for the deaths of Jack and Billy. Catesby realised that his relatives had been killed to draw him into an ambush. He calmly walked up to the wounded gunman and put two bullets into his crotch. The gunman then grabbed his mutilated genitals and screamed so loudly that Catesby had to end the noise with a bullet in the temple.

Catesby checked his own pockets to make sure he had enough money for phone calls. He then went through the pockets of the gunmen to see what they had. Joey's pal was completely clean, except for a half-finished pack of Wrigley's Spearmint chewing gum. Maybe it was what Americans carried instead of passports.

He then had a look at Joey. His eyes were open and the whites reflected in the dark like little moons. Catesby decided it was a good idea to pull the bodies and the bicycle off the road and into the shadow of the wood beside it. When that was done he went through Joey's pockets. There was a huge wad of banknotes. Catesby transferred the money to his own pocket. He wondered if he should hand it in to SIS or pass it over to Sally. Catesby methodically went through the rest of the pockets. He was troubled that there weren't any car keys. Did it mean that someone had dropped them there and was soon going to return to pick them up? Or did it mean they had hidden the car and left the keys in the ignition? Catesby decided he'd better get a move on. He went through Joey's breast pockets. The only thing he found was a business card. It was too dark to read so Catesby put it in his own pocket.

Catesby tucked the Browning automatic in his waistband and started walking. The nearest phone box was outside the Butley Oyster, about a mile away. The loom of advancing headlamps would give him plenty of warning of approaching cars so he could disappear off the road. As he walked along Catesby made a mental list of the people who wanted to kill him and why. He suspected that revenge for the Galen hit was high on the list. A lot of people lurking in dark corners must have realised that Galen didn't kill himself. And Catesby also suspected that a lot of the same people reckoned, incorrectly, that he had grassed Sophie to the Cubans.

All the arrows eventually pointed back to the CIA, but it wasn't anything official or even intended. It was just the way they did things – especially since they had got involved in dirty tricks against Cuba. The CIA had got in bed with gangsters to keep their own hands clean. And once they made that compromise they lost control of what happened at the pointy end. Once you give a nod or wink to those guys you can't cancel. And more and more the CIA were finding they couldn't get their new partner out of their shared bed where he was farting and dropping cigarette ash all over the silk sheets.

The Butley phone box was the only light in the Suffolk night. The pub, run by two elderly spinster sisters, was dark and locked. The Oyster never had after-hours drinking sessions. The tractor drivers and the few remaining horsemen who ploughed with Suffolk Punches were well tucked up. Catesby leaned his forehead against the glass of the phone box and listened to the screech of hunting owls. He loved the place, but he wasn't sure the place cared.

The first number he dialled was the Night Duty Officer at Broadway Buildings. There was no need to speak in code. He couldn't imagine that a foreign power had tapped the Butley Oyster phone box. And so what if they had? Catesby explained all the necessary details to the NDO. The NDO would then alert MI5 and Special Branch. CIPS, the Classified Incident Planning Section, would go into action with clockwork precision. The bodies would be tidied up and the Suffolk Constabulary informed that the whole thing was a heavily D-noticed matter of national security. The Suffolk police had been involved in such matters before. They loved the hush-hush drama and the rare feeling that their provincial force was at the centre of things. In fact, a Suffolk police inspector would soon arrive to give him a lift to London.

When everything was arranged, Catesby hung up the phone. He was beginning to feel relieved and depressed at the same time. It was the psychological after-effect of the adrenalin rush of 'action'. Gradually the relief would turn into nervousness and the depression would grow deeper. Catesby remembered something. He reached into his jacket pocket for the card he had taken off Joey. He looked at it under the phone kiosk light: *Gold Coast Restaurant and Lounge, Biscayne Boulevard, Miami, Fla.* Catesby turned the card over. There was a phone number written in pencil: a number that was etched into his memory by bitter acid.

Catesby picked up the phone again and put a tuppence in the slot. He asked for the international operator, gave her the number and said he wanted to reverse the charges.

'Whom shall I say is calling, sir?'

Catesby remembered the codeword that Ambassador Whitney had given him two years ago, and that the only time he had dialled the number he had been threatened in elegant French. He prepared himself for a repeat conversation, but this time Catesby would be the one taunting. 'Say,' said Catesby changing the codeword into a name, 'it's Mr Amlash.'

Catesby listened as the operator handed over to an American counterpart. She called it a 'collect call', American for reversed charges. He listened to the long softer dial tones of the USA. The phone was finally answered. The operator spoke first, 'Would you accept a collect call from Mr Amlash dialling from Great Britain?'

The person answered 'yes' in a voice that was very American.

'You are now connected to your caller.'

'Hello,' said Catesby.

'Who is this?' The voice was not only American, but one of the most recognisable voices in the USA. Catesby didn't need to know more. He didn't need to crow his revenge. He simply returned the phone to its cradle without saying another word. The biggest missing piece from the jigsaw had just slotted into place.

Catesby's return to Cuba was delayed by an MI5 debrief about the events in the country lane. Sadly, you don't leave the Security Service with bodies to clear up and local constables to hush up without having to answer a few questions. But it went smoothly enough – and as soon as that was done and dusted he was summoned to 10 Downing Street.

Catesby had never met the Prime Minister before, but knew that he was smoother and more modern than his Edwardian persona suggested. Macmillan leaned across his desk to shake Catesby's hand. It was a limp handshake because the Prime Minister had suffered nerve damage as a result of a war wound. Macmillan's third and final wound was a bullet in the pelvis during the Battle of the Somme. He had spent a day lying in a slit trench waiting for stretcher bearers. Macmillan passed the time by reading Aeschylus in the original Greek. Catesby only knew the playwright in translation: *There are times when fear is good. It must keep its watchful place at the heart's controls.*

'You may never have to pass this message on,' the Prime Minister handed Catesby a piece of paper, 'but if you are authorised to do so, the offer will have the full backing of HM's government.'

Catesby read the document. The words were clear and unambiguous – and signalled what could be a stunning change in UK policy. Britain still had cards to play.

'Is there anything you don't understand?'

'No, Prime Minister.'

Macmillan reached across the desk with his damaged hand. 'I can't let you keep that.'

Catesby made the PM wait as he carefully re-read the handwritten words. He finally looked up and handed the paper back.

'Have you memorised it?'

Catesby repeated the message.

'Good.' The PM paused. 'Needless to say you must never reveal this offer to anyone – regardless of rank – other than the person to whom you pass it on.'

'Who is that person?'

'I don't know yet. That's for the other side to decide. When – and if – the time comes, the identity of their secret envoy should be apparent.'

'What if I get duped – and hand it to the wrong chap?'

Macmillan smiled. 'I'm sure you won't.'

Catesby stirred uneasily.

'We have to use someone like you, Mr Catesby, because this offer, however sincere and binding, cannot go through official channels. And remember, a man who trusts nobody is apt to be the kind of man nobody trusts. Bon voyage, Mr Catesby, and I hope that all will go well.'

Within the past week, unmistakable evidence has established the fact that a series of offensive missile sites is now in preparation on that imprisoned island. The purpose of these bases can be none other than to provide a nuclear strike capability against the Western Hemisphere.

There had been rumours throughout the day. In the evening all the embassy staff had been urgently summoned to the briefing room to listen to President Kennedy's televised speech. Catesby had known the facts beforehand, but the President's words still chilled his blood. Kennedy's use of the word 'imprisoned' was particularly worrying. Was it just rhetoric or a justification for an imminent invasion to 'free' Cuba? It looked bad.

Kennedy then listed the sites containing *medium range ballistic missiles capable of carrying a nuclear warhead for a distance of more than 1,000 nautical miles.* And *additional sites ... designed for intermediate-range ballistic missiles – capable of travelling more than twice as far – and thus capable of striking most of the major cities in the Western Hemisphere.*

Catesby looked around at the faces of his colleagues. They were ashen. The Ambassador and Neville, who were also privy to the top secret cables that had warned of the developments, were just as pale. For the one thing that none of them knew was what Washington was going to do next. Catesby and his security-cleared colleagues may have known about the missiles and the U-2 flights, but none of them knew what had been decided in Kennedy's Oval Office.

The next part of the speech troubled Catesby. Kennedy had begun to tell the American people that the missiles in Cuba were completely unnecessary.

... because I quote their government, 'the Soviet Union has so powerful rockets to carry these nuclear warheads that there is no need to search for sites for them beyond the boundaries of the Soviet Union.'

The key phrase was *I quote their government*. Kennedy's tone of voice was full of mockery. Catesby knew that Kennedy was implying that Moscow had lied about having those *so powerful rockets.* Catesby felt his blood turn cold despite the tropical heat. He suddenly realised that Kennedy and his generals knew that Soviet nuclear deterrence against the USA was a sham. Washington had found out about the launch-pad disaster that had killed Marshall Nedelin and wiped out the Soviet Union's rocket elite.

Kennedy's next words were the chilliest of all: *In that sense, missiles in Cuba add to an already clear and present danger.* The words were unambiguous. *Clear and present danger* was diplomatic speak meaning that war is imminent and justified.

The next part of the speech heightened the sense of crisis: *We will not prematurely or unnecessarily risk the costs of worldwide nuclear war … but neither will we shrink from that risk at any time it must be faced.* The embassy staff listened in stony silence. As trained diplomats, they understood every nuance. They knew that Kennedy's words carried dire implications.

As soon as Kennedy said *further action is required*, Catesby braced himself to hear the President declare that hostilities were about to commence. He expected to hear the bombs dropping any moment. But instead of bombs, he heard Kennedy say there would be *a strict quarantine on all offensive military equipment under shipment to Cuba … All ships of any kind bound for Cuba from whatever nation or port will, if found to contain cargoes of offensive weapons, be turned back.*

It didn't mean peace, far from it. Catesby looked at the military attaché who nodded. The quarantine option had been used before as a ploy to buy time before launching hostilities. What Kennedy really meant by 'quarantine' was that the US military needed a day or two to assemble forces for an attack.

The rest of Kennedy's speech seemed to confirm Catesby's worst fears. The President warned of … *a full retaliatory response upon the Soviet Union*. He went on to say that he had … *reinforced our base at Guantánamo, evacuated today the dependents of our personnel there, and ordered additional military units to be on a standby alert basis.* Catesby looked at Debra. Her eyes were wide open and unblinking like someone staring into an abyss. He began to hate Kennedy for doing that to her, to all of them. Catesby then looked at Mickey

Blakeney who had calmly written a note when Kennedy mentioned the Guantánamo 'dependents'.

Kennedy ended his speech with an attack on the Cuban leadership calling them *puppets and agents of an international conspiracy.* It was clear that Kennedy wasn't going to be happy until *the Cuban people have risen to throw out tyrants who destroyed their liberty.* Catesby smiled when he heard Kennedy refer to the time when the Cubans *will be truly free.* Free, in other words, for the Mafia and the casino owners to come back. Catesby remembered Otis's words about Cuba being the Mafia's crown jewel and how the mob would stop at nothing to get it back. At the time, Catesby had thought that Otis saying that the Mafia had got Kennedy elected so he could hand them back Cuba was far-fetched. Now he wasn't so sure.

As Kennedy wound up his speech ... *Thank you and good night,* the Ambassador reached up to turn off the television. 'I think,' he said, 'we've all had enough of that.'

Mickey Blakeney, referring to the notes on his pad, immediately spoke up. 'Considering the seriousness of the situation, Ambassador, should we not consider repatriating family members and non-essential staff to the UK?'

The Ambassador slowly shook his head and answered with a bleak smile that was full of weariness. 'What's the point, Mickey, we're safer in Havana than we would be in London. The Russian bombs on England will be more vicious than the American ones on Cuba – the Yanks don't want too much radioactive fallout blowing back over Florida.'

At that moment Debra broke down in tears as if a dam had just broken. Her weeping wasn't loud, but shook her whole body in deep convulsions. She had two boys home in London for half-term and her husband too – who had wrangled a last-minute leave from Malaya. Of course, the boys wouldn't have been any safer at Royal Hospital School. The East Anglian school, which took in boarders from military and diplomatic families, was located in a 'target rich' environment.

The region was also Catesby's own home and had always been Britain's most dangerous border, but never more so than now. East Anglia provided most of the bases for sixty US Thor nuclear missiles aimed at the Soviet Union. It didn't matter that the missiles were under the joint control of UK as well as US officers, they would still be prime targets in any confrontation between Washington and Moscow. In fact, there was a strong logic for the Soviet military to launch a pre-emptive strike against East Anglia if hostilities seemed imminent.

Catesby felt a lump in his throat. He had a vision of firestorms sweeping inland through the river valleys and incinerating each town in their wake: Lowestoft, Beccles, Bungay; Southwold, Blythburgh, Halesworth; Orford, Aldeburgh, Leiston; Felixstowe, Woodbridge, Ipswich. And all the sleepy villages and cornfields in between. Catesby wanted to gather them all up and hold them close to his chest. There was no mystery about why people died to protect their homes.

Catesby looked at the Ambassador. The poor man was absolutely mortified. Sir Herbert knew that he had said the wrong thing. He realised how tactless he had been and went over to put his arm around Debra.

'If London is going to be a funeral pyre,' she said, 'I want to be on it with Nick and the boys.'

'I'm sorry, Debra. It was thoughtless of me. If you want to go home, you can leave as soon as possible.'

She nodded and dabbed at her eyes. Then she got up and left the room. Catesby stared at Debra's empty chair. He felt almost ground into and through the floor by the weight of responsibility. He wished there was someone else he could shift it to.

The meeting was now over. The embassy staff filed out of the room in silence as if leaving a funeral service. The only two left behind were Catesby and the military attaché. The attaché was an RAF Wing Commander approaching retirement. Wing Co, as everyone called him, was a keen fisherman who spent endless hours at his fly tying vice weaving damsel nymphs, hoppers, brown zonkers, coachmen and dog nobblers. Fly fishing was just as much about deception as espionage.

'You look,' said Wing Co, 'as if you need an anti-malarial?'

Catesby nodded.

Wing Co opened his brown leather briefcase and fished out a hip-flask. 'Oh dear,' he said, 'I've only packed the snakebite medicine, I hope you don't mind. It's a single malt from Islay – a gillie friend gave it to me.'

Catesby smiled at the coincidence. It was the same whisky that he had fed Galen. 'It's lovely stuff. I've drunk it before.'

'Well have some more.'

Catesby accepted the flask and sipped. The Wing Co's whisky tasted even more mellow and rich. He swirled it around in his mouth as if it were a precious nectar and handed back the flask.

Wing Co then took a drink and closed his eyes to complete the act of comradely communion. They were brother officers on a darkling plain.

'Now if I were young Fidel,' said Wing Co, 'I would petition the Russkies to lend me a dozen or so Luna 2K6s. You've heard of them?'

'No,' Catesby lied. 'What are they?'

Wing Co raised an eyebrow. 'I'm surprised you don't know. Surprised indeed.'

'Are they some sort of missile?'

'Quite. The Luna 2K6 is a very handy bit of kit.'

'Does it make a big boom?' said Catesby.

'Rather – about two kilotons worth. Of course, that's less than a tenth of the bomb the Americans popped over Hiroshima, but all the more useful for battlefield use. In fact, if Rommel had had a half-dozen Lunas available to him at Normandy he would have obliterated the D-Day beachheads. A single Luna will immediately kill any soldier within a thousand yards of the blast – and destroy any tank within 500 yards. Any survivors would die of radiation in less than a fortnight. As I said, handy bit of kit.'

'So it wouldn't take many Lunas to defeat a US invasion of Cuba?'

'They wouldn't just defeat the Yanks, they would incinerate them on the beaches ...' – Wing Co buttoned up his briefcase – '... and their radiated ashes would blow away on the wind. We live, as our Chinese friends say, in interesting times. But I'm going to have a quiet evening listening to Elgar and attempting to tie Marabous and Greenwell's Glories – a deuced difficult fly to get right. Sleep well, Mr Catesby.'

Catesby listened to Wing Co's footsteps. He walked with a slight shuffle because of a bad crash-landing when his Hurricane was shot to pieces. Catesby liked Wing Co. Behind the old buffer façade was a kind man who hated war. He also suspected that Wing Co, who was no fool, knew more about the Luna 2K6s than he was letting on.

The midnight rendezvous was as inevitable as the conclusion of a Greek tragedy. Character and historical forces create unavoidable reckonings. Catesby somehow knew that the car would come up behind him on Avenida Séptima. He knew that it would slow to a walking pace beside him, with the Volga's big engine throaty on low revs and growling at him like a predatory cat. The rear door would open in silent welcome. Catesby would recognise the face in the shadows of the rear seat. The face would look older and sadder than ever before.

'You've come back,' said Catesby.

'So I have. Would you like to come for a ride?'

Catesby got in. He knew it would be the end.

'This is where the Marines will come ashore.' General Alekseev swept his arm towards a low flat stony beach. Catesby knew they were near Santa Cruz del Norte, twenty-five miles east of Havana, because he could see the tower of the big electric power station silhouetted against the night sky. The tower's red aircraft warning lights had been blacked out in anticipation of an invasion.

They then turned inland and walked a couple of hundred yards across rough scrubby ground. They were heading towards the main coast road. The shadows of large Soviet military trucks moved slowly without lights along the road. The road had been blocked to all non-military traffic. There were no more jeans and checked shirts. With war imminent, the Russians had changed into military uniforms for the first time since their deployment. In order to get through the checkpoints Catesby had to don a Soviet uniform as well. He was wearing the distinctive field grey camouflage of the KGB Ninth Directorate. His shoulder boards bore the three stars of a colonel. It didn't matter that his Russian was heavily accented. The Soviet Union comprised several nationalities – and no one was going to query the origins of a Ninth Directorate colonel. The only other person who knew Catesby was bogus was Viktor, Alekseev's driver. Viktor seemed to be completely trusted.

They continued walking towards a large clump of prickly brush. When they got to it, Alekseev drew back the camouflage netting that had been carefully arranged to disguise the profile of the tracked vehicle and the Luna 2K6 tactical nuclear missile that lay ready for elevation and launch upon the transporter. Catesby clambered up on to the tracked transporter and began taking photos of the Luna missile with the Fedka 3 camera that Alekseev had given him, 'a present'. He snapped the serial numbers in particular, for it was important that the evidence be complete and irrefutable.

When he was finished, Catesby jumped down and Alekseev replaced the camouflage netting. He had already snapped four other Luna 2K6s of the twelve that Alekseev claimed were deployed. But even more sinister were the FKR cruise missiles. No one had predicted, or even wildly guessed, that the FKRs would be present in Cuba. The missiles were fourteen kilotons, the same as the Hiroshima bomb, and would wipe out an approaching US fleet. Alekseev said that thirty-six had already been deployed – and several were aimed at the US Guantánamo base. Catesby had photographed ten of the FKRs earlier in the evening. They had been hidden in a palm grove near the port of Mariel. The missiles looked like small pilotless jet planes and were towed on launch trailers behind big GAZ 63 trucks. Viktor was normally one of the drivers.

'I hope you've got enough photos,' said Alekseev as they walked back to the car.

'More than enough.'

'I can't, of course, give you an underwater tour, but our submarines are equipped with nuclear torpedoes that could destroy an American carrier group – and the submarine commanders are authorised to fire them without authorisation from Moscow.'

'And what about Pliyev?' Catesby was referring to the commander of the 41,000 Soviet troops in Cuba.

'He's authorised to use the Lunas if there is a US landing.'

'It's become a nightmare.'

'I've heard,' said Alekseev, 'that Khrushchev realises that he made a mistake and wants to find a face-saving way out. He fears, however, that if he shows a lack of firmness, then the Americans will take it as weakness and attack.'

'That's exactly how wars start.'

Alekseev unbuttoned the top of his tunic. 'It's a very hot evening.'

Catesby looked out to sea. He was longing for a swim.

The vodka and the caviar were cold and crisp although the night was hot and clammy. Viktor had built a driftwood fire where he toasted brown bread for the caviar. Catesby was still in his Soviet colonel's uniform even though they had left the restricted military area. He tried to imagine what it would have been like to have been a comrade of Alekseev's that cold spring day in Berlin.

As if reading Catesby's thoughts Alekseev said, 'It was a *Panzerfaust*.' The weapon, literally 'armour-fist', was a German anti-tank weapon fired by a single soldier. 'The boy wasted it on me, instead of waiting for the following tank. He must have been so frightened. Have some vodka.'

'Thank you, Yevgeny Ivanovich.' Catesby held out his glass which was frosted from the ice chest.

'Why be so formal?' Alekseev's eyes sparkled in the firelight as he poured the drink. 'We are, in a way, friends. Please call me Zhenka.'

Catesby raised his glass, 'To you, Zhenka.'

Alekseev nodded and drank. 'And what is your preferred diminutive?'

'Will,' said Catesby, although the only person who called him Will was his sister. Even his mother called him Catesby.

Alekseev returned the toast, 'To you, Will.' And by that simple act of communion, an enemy spy entered an intimate family circle.

Catesby looked at the Russian. He knew that Alekseev, like himself, would never play his country false. If either disobeyed orders it was out of patriotism, not betrayal.

'The thing,' said Alekseev, 'that was odd about Berlin was that there were so many child soldiers. We seemed to be fighting whole battalions of twelve-year-old boys. We had seen fourteen-year-olds before, but in Berlin some of the soldiers were as young as ten. And the Germans said that we were barbarians for using adult women as pilots and snipers.'

Catesby looked closely at Alekseev. The tragedy of Europe was etched on the Russian's face. It was a tragedy that turned some into dumb oxen, others into escape artists and racketeers – and made a few even more monstrous and brutal than before. But for many, like Alekseev, it was a tragedy that deepened wells of compassion and wisdom – and fine-tuned their benign intelligence. Suffering didn't turn their hearts into stone, but made them more generous and warm.

'Of course,' said Alekseev, 'we still had to kill the German boys. They were, after all, armed enemy soldiers trying to kill us. But the one who rose from the rubble of the underground station was so small – he wasn't even as tall as the *Panzerfaust* that he lifted to his shoulder. He was so small that I made a mistake and paused. I don't think that he was more than ten – and a frail ten-year-old with spectacles. He seemed to have difficulty raising the heavy weapon to his shoulder – it caught his spectacles and they nearly slipped off. He needed help. I ought to have shot him then.'

Viktor brought more driftwood for the fire and stirred it.

'Thank you,' said Alekseev.

Viktor disappeared again into the shadows.

'Why didn't I pull the trigger? Was it an imprinted instinct? Something evolutionary that ensured our survival as a species – an instinct to preserve the young even to our own cost? Survival of the group is more important than survival of the individual.' Alekseev smiled. 'Nuclear missiles don't possess such obsolete sentiments. More vodka?'

Catesby nodded.

'In any case, evolutionary speculation aside, I had paused for whatever reason. The boy meanwhile wobbled, but finally managed to balance the *Panzerfaust* on his shoulder. At that moment, I pointed my gun at him and pulled the trigger. But it was too late. My little world had turned into fire and, literally, brimstone. The *Panzerfaust* exploded on the cobblestones in front of me.' Alekseev laughed. 'The doctors later told me I was lucky not to lose a leg. And, oddly, I still feel guilty about the boy. I'll never know what happened to him. Let's eat the caviar.'

Viktor emerged out of the shadows bearing plates with thin slices of toasted bread and heaped caviar.

'Never,' said Alekseev, 'eat caviar with a metal spoon – it transfers a metallic taste. These spoons are made from mother of pearl. I inherited them from my grandmother.'

They ate the meal in reflective silence. Viktor sat away from them and stared into the fire. The young man wasn't a professional soldier, but a conscript. Catesby wondered if Viktor would ever see his family or sweetheart again. He wondered if Viktor was conjuring his family's faces out of the flames.

Alekseev leaned towards Catesby and spoke in a whisper. 'Do you love Katya?'

'Yes.'

'I love her too and will never stop loving her.'

'Are you jealous?'

'I used to be. But there's no longer any point.'

'In some ways,' said Catesby, 'I wish that Katya was married to someone else.'

Alekseev laughed. 'I don't.'

'I mean someone that I didn't respect.'

'Someone you wouldn't have minded hurting – and humiliating.'

'That's right. I once had an affair with a woman. I was genuinely attracted to her, but I hated her husband. I enjoyed torturing him with jealousy and seeing him make a fool of himself in public.'

Alekseev stared hard at Catesby. 'But have you ever been jealous?'

'Yes, enormously.'

'Enough to kill someone.'

'I think so.'

'Then you will forgive me.'

'Are you going to kill me?'

'No.'

Catesby smiled. 'Thank you, Zhenka.'

'More vodka?'

'Yes, please.'

'It was wrong of me to ask forgiveness. It isn't yours to give. But I do want you to understand my feelings. I want you to understand the rage, the insanity perhaps, that led me to kill someone out of jealousy.'

Catesby knew that the last piece was about to fit in to the puzzle.

'The German woman who killed Andreas was working for me and under my orders. When Katya told me that Andreas had stolen the letter about the Baikonur disaster, it gave me the excuse for which I had been secretly longing.' Alekseev poured more vodka. 'I used the security breach as a justification to murder for jealousy. The genie was already out of the bottle – so, in a way, the killing was pointless. Andreas had already sold the letter to the Americans.'

'How did you feel afterwards?'

'Good at first, then empty. Perhaps I would do it again.'

'You're very honest.' Catesby paused. There was something else he wanted to know. 'Why did you let Andreas pass on a copy of the letter to me – before killing him?'

'Because it was useful to us that London knew of our dilemma. We've always looked upon Britain as a potential brake upon the impetuous Americans.'

'Because we have so much more to lose.'

'Precisely.'

The thing, thought Catesby, that made the Cold War so dangerous was that the Russians were playing chess and the Americans poker. The Russians deployed an elaborate defence with layers of deceit to protect their vital squares. The Americans responded with upping antes, calling bluffs and flexing muscles.

'Have you ever written poetry?'

Catesby smiled. 'None that was any good. And you?'

Alekseev shook his head. 'Perhaps it is better to love poetry than to write it. When I returned home after being wounded and patched I used to recite Mayakovsky to Katya:

I have no cause to wake or trouble you.
And, as they say, the incident is closed.
Love's boat has smashed ...'

Alekseev laughed. 'I am sure the poetry helped mend my feelings more than hers.'

'Maybe that's why poets write poems.'

'What an odd conversation to be having with an Englishman.'

Catesby thought of the Prime Minister lying in a shell hole with a bullet in his groin reading Aeschylus. Words were bandages.

'Thank you for listening to me.' Alekseev smiled bleakly and looked out to sea. 'But it's time to stop thinking of myself. Are you going to have time to take those photographs to Washington?'

'I think so. The Americans need at least seventy-two hours to get their forces in position.'

'And will you be able to see the person you mentioned?'

'I hope so.'

'If you have any difficulty, contact Aleksandr. He might be able to arrange it – he's operating under the name of Fomin.' Alekseev produced a card. 'Here are his contact details. His direct phone line and a password.'

Catesby pocketed the card. 'Are Aleksandr Fomin and Aleksandr Feklisov the same person?'

'Of course.'

It was just as Che had said. Feklisov had also run the atomic spy ring that stole secrets from Los Alamos. A memory from years past was nagging at a corner of Catesby's brain. 'Was,' he said, 'Feklisov at the London *rezidentura* in the fifties?'

'Yes, I thought you knew that.'

Another piece of the jigsaw slotted into place. Catesby now realised that it was Feklisov who had organised the sting that trapped Kit Fournier.

'You must trust Aleksandr,' said Alekseev.

Catesby smiled bleakly. 'Why?'

'Because he is a direct line to Khrushchev.'

'Does Aleksandr know what you've done?'

Alekseev paused, then said, 'Yes.'

'So both of you are disobeying orders and acting without authority.'

'Aleksandr won't get caught. There's no proof against him – and I want to keep him in the clear.'

'But what about you, Zhenka? I heard you had been ordered back to Moscow.'

Alekseev smiled. 'It was a rough interrogation. But they let me go.'

'Why?'

'I denounced Katya. She was flown back to Moscow yesterday. Our planes crossed in the sky.'

Catesby froze and stared at the Russian.

'Are you shocked?'

'Why didn't you protect her?'

'There was too much evidence against her. Her liaisons with enemy agents such as Andreas and yourself suggested treachery. I thought about telling them that I had instructed her to have the affairs as a means of penetrating your intelligence services. But they would have seen that as a lie – and it would have indicted us both.'

Catesby turned away and looked at the night sea. He thought once again of the question that had haunted him ever since he became an intelligence officer: *What is the greater crime? Betraying your country or betraying the person you love?* If, thought Catesby, you were really unfortunate, you ended up doing both. And it wasn't a matter of cowardice or weakness; it was just the way things were.

'You now think I'm a bad man?'

Catesby slowly shook his head.

'Moscow Central knows that one of us has been treacherous. I need to prove it's me. That's one of the reasons I invited you to take those pictures.'

'Is there another reason?'

Alekseev gave a weary smile. 'I don't want there to be a war, but maybe I'm just making things worse.'

Catesby nodded agreement. Alekseev was facing the dilemma of a chess master being asked to the poker table.

'The leadership in Moscow is split down the middle – and so are we in Cuba. One side believes that if the Americans find out about the Lunas and the FKR missiles, it will provoke them into an attack. But why should it? These weapons are short range and prove no danger to the American mainland.'

'But public opinion whipped up by the evangelist American right may not differentiate.'

'That's the argument. And there's also the problem of the American generals. They want war – maybe they haven't seen enough of it. And they will use any excuse to launch one.'

'And what does your side think?'

'We think that the Lunas and the FKRs are a deterrent that will prevent the Americans from invading Cuba. But they won't be a deterrent if Washington doesn't know about them and doesn't realise that the weapons are mobile, easy to conceal and impossible to neutralise with surgical airstrikes.' Alekseev looked at Catesby. 'You can, I am sure, explain that.'

'If they listen.'

'I don't believe that the Kennedy brothers are good men, but I do believe they are rational and intelligent. We have got to the point where the world will not be saved by goodwill, but by good pragmatic judgement.'

'It's still a gamble.'

'Is it not a gamble you want to take?'

'I never wanted to be in this position.'

'That's why it's best that it's someone like you. Will you do it?'

Catesby looked out on to the night sea as he had done thousands of times in Suffolk. There was no guidance. 'Yes,' he said, 'yes I will.'

'Let's go for a swim.'

As Alekseev stripped off, Catesby caught a glimpse of his naked body. The Russian's right leg was badly scarred and partly withered. There were huge suture marks over his lower abdomen as if he were a much-loved but badly stitched rag doll. And nothing below at all: more woman than eunuch. His penis urethra had been replaced by a pale catheter tube.

Alekseev went into the water first. The waves were gentle and lapping. The night was windless. Catesby waded in behind the Russian and cupped his genitals when the water was waist high. He felt so afraid, so naked and vulnerable – and then ashamed of his fear.

Catesby could see that Alekseev was a strong swimmer. He had to struggle to keep up. The Russian headed straight out to sea doing an even and graceful crawl. Despite his injuries he was a good athlete. They were getting further and further from land. The only light on the shore was the campfire which gradually faded into an intermittent glimmer like a distant star.

They had been swimming nearly half an hour. Catesby guessed they must be a mile from shore. All was utter blackness. The campfire had disappeared. Alekseev stopped and turned. 'Where are you, Will?'

'I'm here.'

'We've come such a long way. Do you want to turn back?'

'I think so.'

'I'm going to continue swimming.'

'I'll stay with you, Zhenka – until you're ready to turn back.'

The Russian laughed.

'I wish,' said Catesby also laughing, 'that we had a compass.'

'There'll be a moon later – just for you.'

'Thanks.'

'That poem I recited to you …'

'The one by Mayakovsky?'

'Yes, that one. It was the last thing that he wrote before he shot himself. Do you know how it ends?'

'No.'

'Behold what quiet settles on the world.
Night wraps the sky in tribute from the stars.
In hours like these, one rises to address
The ages, history, and all creation.'

'You've done just that.'

'Thank you, Will.'

'Let's turn back.'

'No.'

It was the answer Catesby had been expecting.

'Don't follow me – I'm going for a very long swim. But you must go back – you have work to do. And look,' the Russian pointed to the horizon, 'here comes your moon to guide you.'

A sliver of crescent rose above the eastern sea.

'Maybe,' said Catesby, 'you should follow it home to Katya.'

'What a good idea, Will.' Alekseev laughed again. 'Imagine the places I will see and the adventures I will have. A Russian Odysseus going home to his Penelope.'

'You're the only person she will ever love.'

The two men were treading water facing each other in the moon-silvered sea. 'But I hope,' said Alekseev in a quiet voice, 'she will love her child even more. Katya is pregnant with your baby.' The Russian looked at Catesby and quoted the lines in English:

'There's a divinity that shapes our ends

Rough-hew them how we will.'

Then back to Russian. 'I hope I didn't slaughter your beautiful language.'

'You would have been the best Hamlet ever – and an even better father.'

'I must go now.' The Russian reached out and embraced Catesby. He held him close for a few seconds and they both began to sink. He released him. They bobbed to the surface as if reborn. Alekseev turned away without saying another word and started swimming into the moon path.

Catesby treaded water and watched as Alekseev swam into the long night. And beyond the sea horizon the armies of the night were stirring. The steady pulse beat of the swimmer's arms and feet kneading the water became more and more faint. Catesby kept watching until the midnight swimmer had vanished in the moon path.

Catesby turned to swim back to shore, then looked once again out to sea. He called into the night:

'Good night sweet prince;

And flights of angels sing thee to thy rest.'

He waited, but there was only silence. He began his long swim back.

PART THREE

Now hear this: general quarters, general quarters. *All hands man their battle stations. This is not a drill!*

The *USS Beale* had scented its prey, pursued her and now had her cornered. The *Beale* was one of eleven destroyers in Task Force Randolf that were stalking Soviet submarines. The ship's call to battle was a deafening combination of sirens, klaxons and bells. Several sailors held their ears as they dashed along the decks to their stations.

The *Beale*'s weapons officer and skipper were staring at the green sonar screen which showed the depth and location of the target. The sonar operator was wearing earphones. 'She's so close, sir, you can hear the propellers and the engine clanking.'

The skipper spoke first. 'The biggest fear is that you got to make sure it's Ivan and not one of our own.'

'It's definitely an Ivan, sir.'

The skipper nodded and left the sonar station for the CIC, the Combat Information Center, to begin to plan for the attack.

The damage control officer was giving a briefing in Damage Control Central, a cabin in the middle of the ship hung with diagrams of the ship highlighting the locations of watertight doors and fire hose outlets. All the men were wearing lifejackets and grey helmets. They had their sleeves rolled down and buttoned and their trousers tucked into their socks. A few of the sailors had rosary beads draped around their necks.

One of the younger sailors looked particularly nervous and tried to hide his nervousness by making little jokes. His socks weren't long enough and his trousers kept popping out. 'Here,' said the damage control officer handing him a piece of string, 'tie them.'

'Why, sir, have we got to tuck our trousers in like that anyway?'

'Because when a ship gets hit and the explosions start a lot of guys get nervous – and they start pissing and shitting themselves. You don't want to be slipping and sliding on decks full of piss and shit when you're trying to fight fires and deal with dead and wounded.'

The skipper of the *Beale*, like the other ship commanders involved, was authorised to conduct anti-submarine operations without much interference from above. The highest priority was to avoid losing an American warship by lack of decisive action. The skipper turned to his weapons officer: 'Prepare practice depth charges for immediate launch.'

It was the ultimate Cold War game for a US destroyer commander: finding a Soviet sub and forcing her to surface. The procedure approved for the Cuba crisis was to drop four practice-depth charges as close to the Soviet submarine as possible. The depth charges produced a loud bang, but were supposed to be otherwise harmless. It was a signal for the Soviet sub to surface and identify herself. The US Embassy in Moscow had passed on the details of the procedure to the Kremlin, but the Soviet government had not yet passed the message on to their submarine commanders.

The mission of Major Anderson's U-2 flight was the photo-reconnaissance of six surface-to-air missile sites. It was essential that the US military have up-to-date intelligence on the Soviet air defence systems as a prerequisite to launching surgical airstrikes against the nuclear missile sites.

Major Anderson was on a very dangerous mission because the very S-75 Dvina anti-aircraft missiles he was photographing were the only weapons capable of shooting down U-2s at 70,000 feet. On the other hand, the S-75s could only be fired by Soviet personnel, who were more restrained than their Cuban colleagues manning the lower level anti-aircraft guns. It was a critical time and the Russians didn't want to escalate. The Soviet general in charge of the S-75 sites had been ordered to act with restraint, but the order did not anticipate that a U-2 would fly directly over a battery of nuclear-equipped FKR cruise missiles aimed at the US base at Guantánamo Bay. The tension was heightened by the fact that one of the missile transporters had overturned in a ditch during the previous night's deployment. The driver, young Viktor, had been killed. The general knew that the U-2 had photographed one of the most sensitive secrets in Cuba. He was one of those who, unlike Alekseev, believed that knowledge of the tactical nuclear weapons would provoke rather than deter the Americans. There wasn't time to get authorisation from Moscow, the U-2 would soon be on its way back to the USA and out of range. The general picked up the radio handset in his underground bunker and gave the order.

The news reached the White House cabinet room in the middle of a hot discussion. EXCOMM, the committee formed to deal with the crisis, was debating the President's proposal to swap the removal of US missiles in Turkey and Italy for the removal of Soviet missiles in Cuba. The hawks were against it. The Joint Chiefs wanted massive airstrikes against Cuba within thirty-six hours unless there was 'irrefutable evidence' that the Russian missiles had been dismantled.

The debate was interrupted when one of the Defense Secretary's aides passed him an urgent message. The secretary looked up at his colleagues. 'A U-2 has been shot down over Cuba and the pilot killed.'

'This is ominous,' said the secretary's deputy, 'those missiles are under sole Soviet control.'

The Defense Secretary looked drained. 'This signals a change in pattern. And why is Moscow changing the pattern? I simply don't know.'

One of the generals hammered his fist on the table. 'We've got to go in now and go in hard.'

The crew of the B-59, a Soviet Foxtrot class submarine, thought they were about to die. The practice-depth charges were exploding right next to the hull of the sub – one even bounced off the hull with a loud clang before detonating. It felt like they were trapped in a steel barrel that someone was hitting with a sledgehammer.

The B-59 was in a desperate situation. Her batteries were so low that she had been forced to switch to emergency lighting which left the submarine in a murky gloom. It was stifling hot, plus forty-five degrees Celsius, and the carbon dioxide level had become so dangerously high that crew had begun to pass out. Ironically, the most comfortable place in the submarine was next to the ten-kiloton nuclear-tipped torpedo in the forward section of the hull. It was the place furthest from the toxic fumes and heat of the engine room.

The captain of the submarine, Valentin Grigorievich Savitsky, had had enough. 'We're under attack,' he shouted. 'It is obvious that war has already started. Prepare the torpedo for firing. We're going to blast them now. It doesn't matter if we die, we will sink them all. We will not disgrace the Soviet Navy!'

Over the North Pole tragedy was turning into farce. Captain Charles W. Maultsby had got lost. The mission of his U-2 flight was to collect air samples to monitor Soviet nuclear tests. The U-2 had flown from Eilson Air Base in Alaska and, once the mission over the Pole was complete, the plane would return on the same track. There is, however, a serious problem with navigating over the North Pole. Compasses are useless. The needles gyrate wildly or point to the magnetic pole, totally confusing north with south. A pilot has to rely on the stars to plot his plane's position. But on this night it was impossible. Captain Maultsby could not distinguish the stars because of a spectacular display of the aurora borealis, the northern lights. The night sky had turned into a fireworks display of whirling cartwheels streaked with red, blue, pink and luminous green. It was as if nature was providing a preview of the looming nuclear apocalypse.

Captain Maultsby was a dapper man with a thin moustache who looked oddly British and bore a resemblance to Peter Sellars. He was one of the USAF's most capable and experienced pilots. This wasn't the first time that he had been in trouble. His F-80 Shooting Star fighter had been shot down over Korea and he taken prisoner. But this situation was even worse because of the complete disorientation. The northern lights eventually disappeared, but seemed to have left behind a vastly changed sky. It was as if the dancing lights had mischievously scrambled the position of the stars. Maultsby realised he was totally lost. No star was where it was supposed to be. This was because Captain Maultsby was flying forty-five degrees off course to the west and had entered Soviet air space.

Shortly after Soviet military radar spotted the intruding U-2, two squadrons of MiGs took off to deal with the American plane. As soon as US Strategic Air Command became aware that MiGs were pursuing Maultsby, F-102 fighter-interceptors were scrambled to protect the U-2. Maultsby meanwhile had finally made radio contact with Alaska and was being talked back to base. The U-2 was now out of fuel, losing height and gliding back to Alaska. It was a race against time. Maultsby needed to leave Soviet air space before the MiGs came within firing range. If not, the F-102s coming to his rescue were armed with nuclear-tipped Falcon air-to-air missiles which would completely vaporise the squadrons of pursuing MiGs.

When Catesby arrived at the British Embassy in Washington he was treated with far more deference than he was accustomed. He was met by the Ambassador, David Ormsby-Gore, and given a room in the residence that was usually reserved for visiting cabinet ministers.

Ormsby-Gore was patrician without being posh. When he spoke to Catesby there wasn't a hint of condescension in his voice. It was as if he and Catesby were members of the same club. Catesby had noticed that upper-class people were now more civil to him than when he had been an army officer during the war. He wondered if he had changed or if they had changed. Catesby now spoke with a classless accent and had adopted the manners of the embassy environments that were his usual workplaces. He tried to assure himself that it wasn't a matter of selling out, but of fitting in. And maybe the toffs had begun to realise that Britain was a different place and they had to alter their ways to fit in too. But for the moment, class differences no longer mattered. When the nuclear bombs rained down on Britain they wouldn't make a distinction between vowels, income or education.

'How was your trip?' said Ormsby-Gore.

'Tense. The Aeroméxico flight from José Martí to Mexico City was packed with fleeing diplomat families. Then Pan Am to here – that one was nearly empty.'

The Ambassador smiled grimly. 'No one wants to fly into a nuclear target. How are things in Cuba?'

'No sign of panic, at least not among the Cubans. There are still lovers strolling along the Malecón between the anti-aircraft guns, joking and chatting with the gun crews. Crowds gather at the harbour entrance to cheer any ships that manage to run the blockade. There don't seem to be any civil defence preparations. I suppose there's a whiff of carnival in the air.'

'Carnival indeed.' The Ambassador looked thoughtfully out of his study window. There was a view of manicured lawns and oak trees, almost like an English country estate. Ormsby-Gore finally spoke in a voice that was quiet, humble and completely unaffected. 'It would indeed be the ultimate *tragedy* if the history of the human race proved to be nothing more noble than the story of an ape playing with a box of matches on a petrol dump.'

'We need to stop that ape.'

'It might be too late. Have you heard the latest?

Catesby softly said, 'No.' He had been cocooned in airliners for most of the past twenty-four hours.

'A US plane has been shot down over Cuba. Consequently, the American Strategic Air Command has gone to DEFCON 2 – for the first time ever.'

Catesby felt his stomach lurch. DEFCON 2 was the alert level just short of war. It meant that B-52 bombers, fully loaded with nuclear bombs, had been dispersed to 'start line' locations and were ready to take off at fifteen minutes' notice. They would then join nearly 200 more B-52s which were already airborne in holding positions. It also meant that the Thor missiles in East Anglia were loaded, fuelled and ready to launch.

The Ambassador turned to Catesby with a world-weary smile. 'I shan't detain you longer. I am sure you have much to do.' He handed over a slip of paper. 'This cable arrived for you this morning from Downing Street. I deciphered it myself. Please don't tell me what it concerns.'

Catesby dialled the number from the embassy. The number he was ringing connected to one of the most secret and important phones in America. It was still the same number that Ambassador Winthrop had passed on two years before. Although the phone and its location changed, the number remained the same. Catesby later realised it was the Mongoose line, a telephone that connected low people to high places. He wondered if people washed their hands after touching it.

The voice that answered was American, but one that Catesby hadn't heard before. It was an educated voice that sounded stressed. As soon as Catesby said the codeword, AMLASH, the line went quiet as the person on the other end put a palm over the speaking end. A few seconds later, there was sound again and background voices – a familiar one saying, 'This could be important.' Then more distinctly into the phone, 'What's the latest?'

'I'm in Washington.'

'Who the fuck is this?'

'I'm William Catesby ringing from the British Embassy. I've just come from Cuba and I have very important information for you alone.'

There was a pause punctuated by the sound of breathing. It was as if the person on the other end was piecing together something important, but half-remembered. Then the voice came back sharp and direct, 'Meet me at Hickory Hill in one hour.'

The phone clicked dead before Catesby could reply.

The house was huge, but not colossal. Maybe eight or ten bedrooms. It was set well back from the road in a rambling garden with large mature trees. The architecture was traditional East Coast American: wooden clapboard painted white. Catesby guessed it dated from the middle of the nineteenth century. It was grand without being pretentious. The house had the relaxed simplicity of the American Dream.

A man in dark glasses carrying a clunky walkie-talkie showed Catesby where to park the embassy car. He then gestured for Catesby to follow and led him to a door at the back of the house. The man pushed the door open and said, 'Go through the kitchen to the back stairs. The office is on the second floor. Or what you guys call the "first floor".'

'You've been to England?'

'Yeah, during the war. Warm beer and easy lays.'

Catesby smiled and said, 'They must have been wearing utility knickers – one Yank and they're off.'

The American didn't laugh, just turned and walked away.

The kitchen was untidy with unwashed dishes. The house was completely silent. Eerily silent, for a family home lived in by seven children under the age of eleven. The door to the stairs was ajar. As Catesby mounted the steps the stairs creaked loudly under his feet in the empty house. He realised, with a chill, that wife and children had been evacuated to a safer place. But the spirits of the children were still there. The stairway walls were decorated with their paintings. There was a forest and hills landscape with birds, a flower-bedecked birthday cake homage 'to Kathleen', a bumblebee wearing a striped blue jumper.

At the top of the stairs Catesby heard a voice shout 'fuck' and slam down a phone. The door to the study was open. The same voice shouted, 'Come in.'

The man was slightly younger than Catesby, but his eyes looked far older. He looked like he hadn't slept for a week. His tie was undone and his feet were propped up on the desk as if wishing it were a bed. Catesby had personal issues with the man opposite. It seemed likely that this was the man who had ordered his own killing. And who was also indirectly responsible for the deaths of Catesby's uncle and cousin. But these were issues that had to be put aside. Robert Kennedy in turn stared hard at Catesby and said, 'Bill Harvey says you're a deceitful son-of-a-bitch who sucks Russian ass.'

'Harvey's a bitter and twisted drunk.'

The president's brother gave Catesby a look that seemed to convey a certain amount of agreement. Bill Harvey, while CIA Station Chief in Berlin, had tried to scapegoat Catesby and the Brits for everything that went wrong.

'What have you got to tell me?' The younger Kennedy's voice had a remarkably feminine quality which contradicted, and possibly explained, his tough-guy posturing.

'There are a large number of tactical nuclear weapons in Cuba that are scattered and hidden throughout the countryside.' Catesby handed Kennedy an envelope bulging with photos.

Bobby Kennedy seemed unexpectedly calm as he looked at the photos. He held up a photo of the FKR cruise missiles, the ones that looked like toy jet planes. 'What's this?'

Catesby explained.

'Shit, we didn't know they had those.'

'Did you know about the Lunas?' said Catesby.

Kennedy didn't answer the question, but looked closely at Catesby as if trying to peel off layers. 'Maybe Harvey's right. You're a Russian spy that's been blown and doubled back by London.'

'That's not true, but it wouldn't make those nuclear weapons any less real if it were.'

Kennedy nodded at the logic. 'How then did you get this intelligence?'

Catesby told him about Alekseev and added, 'Trust my judgement as an intelligence officer. There is no way that your planes can destroy these weapons in a pre-emptive strike. At least ninety per cent of the Lunas and FKRs will survive intact. Not only will the vast majority of an American invading force be incinerated on the beach, but the US Navy ships in the offing will also be vaporised.'

Bobby Kennedy stared thoughtfully at his desk. Catesby noticed a folder labelled TOP SECRET: OPERATION MONGOOSE.

'Is there anything else you want to know?' Catesby spoke in a voice that was a hoarse whisper. He had never been so tired.

'I've changed my mind about a lot of things in the past week. This isn't a football game where scoring touchdowns means you win.' Kennedy looked at the Mongoose folder. 'I want to do something for your uncle's family.'

'Did you order them killed so that you could get me?'

The president's brother slowly shook his head. 'No, but I ordered you killed. I have a liaison officer in the CIA who reports directly to me. Bill Harvey, for reasons you can well imagine, suggested to my liaison that we do a hit on you and make it look like it was the Cuban intelligence service. Two birds with one stone – we get rid of a pinko Brit and we sour relations between London and Havana. But the thugs we used for this didn't appreciate the London-Havana nuance. They seem to have lost their Cuba connections, so they lured you to England instead. I was appalled when I found out the details. I am ashamed that I let things get so out of control – but know that you can never forgive me.'

Catesby was surprised to hear one of the most powerful men in the world sound so contrite and self-critical. For the first time that week he felt that peace might have a chance.

Aleksandr Semyonovich Feklisov, aka Fomin and KGB Head of Station, was waiting for Catesby in front of the Cathedral at Rouen. Not the real one, but Monet's impressionist version in the National Gallery of Art on Constitution Avenue NW. Feklisov was wearing a black leather jacket and looked like an off-duty cop trying to soak up a bit of culture.

Catesby's shoes squeaked as he walked across the waxed parquet flooring. He recognised Feklisov, not only from the photo file, but also from embassy cocktail parties in early-fifties London. The Russian was dark, ironic and had a reputation as a survivor. He had spent the Great Patriotic War in New York where he worked out of the Soviet Consulate recruiting atomic and other spies with great success. Which probably explained, thought Catesby, why he was now operating under the Fomin alias.

Feklisov shook hands and said, 'This is where I recruited Jeffers

Cauldwell, who in turn recruited Kitson Fournier.'

Catesby wasn't certain that was exactly how it happened, but didn't want to have a debate about spilt milk. Nor did he care for the inference. 'But you're wasting your time, Aleksandr Semyonovich, if you think you can recruit me.'

'I did not mean to infer that. In any case, we are not meeting as spies but as back-channel intermediaries.'

'It's nearly closing time. Shall we go for a walk?'

Feklisov nodded. 'By the way, I got here early to have a look at the American collections. Many of them have been put in "temporary storage". What a pity that Winslow Homer should be saved for survivor posterity,' he gestured at the painting, 'but the Monets left to burn?'

The National Mall is lined by American elms and stretches for a mile. The massive 'grand avenue' of lawn and reflecting pools begins at the Capitol. Two-thirds the way along its length, the Washington Monument sticks up like a giant exclamation mark. The Mall finally terminates at another presidential memorial where 160 tons of marble Lincoln sits staring back at Congress.

'The Kremlin,' said Feklisov admiring the view from a park bench, 'is so much smaller than this, but so much older.'

'And so is Trafalgar Square.'

'Zhenka is a good man. Have you passed his message on to the Americans?'

'Yes.'

'Thank you for telling me. It makes me less worried, more hopeful.' Feklisov lowered his voice. 'There are other things going on, but I'm not sure it's enough to avoid war. Thank you for meeting me.'

'There's something else,' said Catesby in a rough, tired voice.

'Yes.'

Catesby swallowed hard. He had never had to convey a message like this before. He wanted to get each word correct. 'I have been authorised by the Prime Minister of the United Kingdom to give you the following message to pass on to First Secretary Khrushchev. If the Soviet Union removes all R-12 and R-14 nuclear missiles from Cuba, the United Kingdom will reciprocate by permanently removing all sixty Thor nuclear missiles now located on British soil.'

'What's the timescale?'

'The first Thor will be removed next month. No Thor will remain on British soil beyond the end of August next year.'

'You can't give me any of this in writing?'

'No,' smiled Catesby, 'we're not real people. We're back-channel shades gibbering and squeaking in the wind.'

Feklisov took Catesby's hand and squeezed it hard. 'I think this offer might be enough to stop midnight coming. We'll see.'

'You know that Zhenka is dead.'

'I'm not surprised.'

'Give my condolences to Katya,' said Catesby.

'I will, my friend.'

They got up to go their separate ways like ships passing in a narrow dangerous channel.

Lieutenant Commander Pavlov was not only in charge of the nuclear torpedo on the B-59, he slept beside the polished grey tube like a fond lover. When Captain Savitsky gave the order to prepare the torpedo for firing Pavlov felt two competing pangs of regret. One, he was going to be separated from a complex piece of machinery and advanced technology that he had looked after with obsessive care for many months. Two, he was almost certainly going to die and never see his homeland or his loved ones again. But Pavlov overcame those feelings and began the final preparation rituals. It was impossible not to think of the enormity of his actions and the lives that would be extinguished. Pavlov assumed that the world was already at war and that he had to carry out his duties as part of a greater scheme that he could not question. He unscrewed a cover to make a final check on the coils and electrical connections that connected detonator and warhead. When that was done, he completed the final task. Pavlov could not keep his hands from shaking as he removed the green 'safety connector plug' and replaced it with the red 'arming plug'.

The submarine's second in command, Vasili Alexandrovich Arkhipov, came from a peasant family and had made his way up the ranks through technical expertise and calm judgement. The previous year he had helped save a nuclear submarine with a coolant leak that resulted in the deaths of eight sailors and threatened to blow up the reactor. Arkhipov received a heavy dose of radiation, but helped devise a jury-rigged coolant system that saved the submarine. Arkhipov was now trying to save the world.

The authorisation of all three senior officers aboard was needed to launch the nuclear torpedo. The Political Officer, Ivan Semonovich Maslennikov, was in accord with Captain Savitsky that war had broken out. The submarine had been buffeted by four more explosions. Although the crew of the B-59 had no way of knowing, the explosions had been caused by hand grenades dropped by a destroyer that had joined the *Beale*. Both Savitsky and Maslennikov felt they were now bound by honour and duty to attack the US aircraft carrier leading the task group. 'We have no choice,' said Maslennikov, 'we need to defend Soviet forces from further attacks. This is war.'

'If,' said Arkhipov, 'the Americans were trying to sink us we would already be dead.'

'They're incompetent,' said Savitsky, 'and we've been taking evasive action.'

'They may be incompetent, but they are not trying to sink us. They have not dropped fully-armed depth charges. If we are not certain that a state of war exists, we cannot take the risk of starting a war that will kill tens of millions of our citizens. I refuse,' said Arkhipov, 'to give my authorisation to use that torpedo. If you ignore my refusal, you are both disobeying standing orders. In any case, it will soon be night. I suggest we surface under cover of darkness and radio Moscow for further instructions.'

Savitsky looked hard at Arkhipov. He then angrily picked up the internal telephone connecting the control centre to the torpedo room.

A hundred feet forward Pavlov lifted the clanging phone off its hook. He felt a shiver go down his spine as he heard the captain's voice bark out the crisp order. Pavlov wasn't sure that he had heard correctly, so he asked the captain to repeat the order for confirmation. Savitsky's voice sounded even more irritated than it had the first time. Pavlov replied, 'Order understood. I will carry out instruction immediately.'

Pavlov put the phone down and returned to the torpedo. His hands were completely calm as he removed the arming plug and replaced it with the safety connector plug. Tears were flowing down his cheeks as he stroked the torpedo tube. 'Not now my sweetest, maybe never.'

In the end, the B-59 was not able to have a quiet chat with Moscow. She surfaced on to a night sea surrounded by American ships that were shining search lights at her conning tower. One of the destroyers had a jazz band on deck playing loud amplified music. The idea was to show the Soviet submarine officers that war had not broken out. As the B-59 broke the surface, the band shifted from 'Boogie Woogie Bugle Boy' to 'Yankee Doodle Dandy'.

When Captain Savitsky appeared from the hatch he was greeted with 'When the Saints Go Marching In'. He ordered the sailors who followed him not to smile or make eye contact with the Americans. 'Behave with dignity,' he said, 'they are trying to humiliate us.'

A large group of American sailors were dancing on the jazz band ship's deck in time to the music. Others were throwing packages of cigarettes and Coca-Cola at the Soviet submariners. Most of the offerings fell into the sea, but the ones that landed on the submarine were ignored and left to the washing waves.

Captain Maultsby realised he was finally and definitely going in the right direction when he saw the faint red glow of nautical twilight on the eastern horizon. It was now some time since he had heard Russian folk music on his radio. There was just enough light to see the ground – and it was the snow-covered ground of Alaska and not Siberia. The MiGs had given up pursuit and the USAF F-102s sent to protect him were now guides showing him the way to a primitive airstrip just above the Arctic Circle. Ten minutes later Captain Maultsby had safely landed. He quickly climbed out of the U-2 cockpit, unzipped his flying suit and peed onto a bank of pure white snow.

It was 5 p.m. in Moscow and 9 a.m. in Washington on Sunday, 29 October 1962. The Russian radio announcer introduced the news by saying that he was about to read a letter written by Nikita Sergeyevich Khrushchev to John Fitzgerald Kennedy. Without hesitation or further explanation he read the letter:

> *In order to eliminate as rapidly as possible the conflict which endangers the cause of peace ... the Soviet Government, in addition to earlier instructions on the discontinuation of further work on weapons construction sites, has given a new order to dismantle the weapons you described as offensive – and to crate and return them to the Soviet Union.*

On 29 November 1962, exactly one month after General Pliyev had begun dismantling the Soviet R-12 sites in Cuba, the commanding officer of RAF Breighton in the East Riding of Yorkshire was ordered to stand down his three Thor IRBMs. The nuclear missiles were codenamed Lion's Roar, Beach Buggy and Foreign Travel. The most difficult part of the immobilisation process is draining the fuel. Rockets are essentially fuel canisters. In its ready-to-launch state, a Thor weighed 110,000 pounds – of which 98,500 pounds was rocket fuel. An RAF Wing Commander and the RAF Regiment Squadron Leader in charge of security looked on from a distance as the white-suited technicians began to drain the highly volatile liquid oxygen from Beach Buggy into storage tanks.

'I wonder what this nonsense is all about,' said the squadron leader.

The Wing Co shrugged. 'I think they're going to be redeployed somewhere else. Ours is not to question why.'

—

'Can I give you some advice, William?'

Catesby shrugged.

'Never ever tell anyone about the Thor business. Not even a wink or a raised eyebrow. If a leak is traced back to you, you are going to be hung, drawn and quartered – or simply shot as was your Gunpowder Plot ancestor.'

'Did ours make a difference? The rumour mill says that Khrushchev agreed to remove the missiles from Cuba in exchange for Kennedy taking his missiles out of Turkey and Italy.'

'Look at the maths. There are thirty Jupiter missiles in Turkey and fifteen in Italy – all of which are obsolete and scheduled for decommissioning. There are sixty Thors in England with larger payloads. We were the dog that didn't bark in the night. We broke the deadlock.'

'I wish you could hear yourself, Henry.'

'Why?'

'The whole business is so infinitely childish, infantile. It belongs to the playground world of conkers, Chinese burns, bulldog and blind man's bluff.'

'But infinitely dangerous.'

The two men were sitting on a bench in Green Park. It was a bleak December day. They were wearing bowler hats and city suits. They had not yet become anachronisms and London had not yet begun to swing. But the old order was cracking. Catesby was both shocked and amused to find that his sister was living in a commune in the south of France devoted to the study of Eastern philosophy – and the practice of free love.

'How,' said Bone, 'were things in Cuba when you got back?'

'Fidel and Che pretend to be incensed that the Sovs have backed down. But I'm sure that was for public display. Privately, I suspect they are relieved.'

'And, if you don't mind my referring to the childish world you so much despise, what about the tactical and cruise nukes?'

'I am sure, Henry, they are still well hidden in Cuba – and will be for years to come. That's the real reason why the Kennedys have given a non-invasion pledge.'

'I think, William, you deserve some leave.'

Catesby smiled. He liked the idea of paying his sister a visit at the commune. He wondered if he would have to wear a white robe and practise meditation. But what he really wanted was a personal visit to Moscow, but he knew that would never be permitted by either side.

EPILOGUES

Dallas. 22 November 1963

They wanted to blame it on Havana. That's why the fall guy, Lee Harvey Oswald, was told to become a member of the Fair Play for Cuba Committee and to make a big show of handing out pro-Castro leaflets. The truth was otherwise. The gang still wanted Cuba back and that was one of the reasons Kennedy had to die.

Moscow. 14 October 1964

The plotting had begun months before. It wasn't just agricultural failures; it was the lingering humiliation of what they called 'the Caribbean Crisis'. The plotter in chief said as much when he suggested the coup to Head of KGB, Vladimir Yefimovich Semichastny.

'I'm worried,' said the plotter on the day, 'if Nikita Sergeyevich finds out about this, he'll have us all shot.'

'Don't worry. Everything is in place.'

'What if he phones for help?'

'He no longer has a phone that works. I've taken control of the whole communication system.'

In the end Khrushchev went quietly and no one was shot. That evening, he wanted to be alone and there were tears in his eyes. Of all things he was proudest of having denounced Stalin and created a new era. 'The fear is gone. That's my contribution. I won't put up a fight.'

Algiers. 1965

Algiers, Algeria

24 February 1965

Dear Carlos,
I have just spoken at the Afro-Asian Conference. The enclosed article, 'The Cuban Revolution Today', includes many of the ideas I expressed. I hope you will publish it in March.

At the risk of seeming ridiculous, let me say that the true revolutionary is guided by a great feeling of love. It is impossible to think of a genuine revolutionary lacking this quality.

Che

From somewhere in the world

4 April 1967

Dear Compañeros,
I cannot be with you at the Tricontinental Conference. But I have included a speech that I would like to be read on my behalf. Remember one thing:

To die under the flag of Vietnam, of Venezuela, of Guatemala, of Laos, of Guinea, of Colombia, of Bolivia, of Brazil – to name only a few scenes of today's armed struggle – would be equally glorious and desirable for an American, an Asian, an African, even a European.

Che

La Higuera, Bolivia. 8–9 October 1967

The prisoner wasn't behaving himself. Despite being shot in the leg, he managed to kick one officer against a wall when the officer tried to confiscate his pipe as a souvenir. Later, a Rear Admiral arrived by helicopter to have a look at their prize prey. The prisoner was lying on his back on a table in the one room of the village school. He was smoking the pipe that he had managed to retain and staring at the ceiling. The Rear Admiral bent over to look in the prisoner's face to see if it was really him. Che removed his pipe and smiled at the visitor. He then spat in the Rear Admiral's face.

Che's first visitor the next morning was the schoolteacher. He had asked to see her. At first, twenty-two-year-old Julia Cortez was frightened by the sight of a man with his clothes in rags and his long unkempt hair caked with mud and blood. She then saw that he was 'nice looking' and had soft gentle eyes. But Julia Cortez could not bear to look in those eyes because his glance was so piercing, but yet so serene.

'How,' said Che, 'can you teach *campesino* children in a schoolhouse in such poor condition? You have so few books – and yet your government officials drive new Mercedes cars and live in villas.'

The young teacher could no sooner speak to him than look in his intense unblinking eyes.

Che gestured at the crumbling schoolroom. 'The injustice of this poverty is what we are fighting against.'

At noon more visitors began to arrive. There was a pinch-faced man who spoke Spanish with a German accent, whom everyone referred to as Señor Altmann – except for an American officer who insisted on calling him 'Herr Barbie', which seemed to annoy Altmann.

Just before one o'clock the final order was received from the Bolivian president. Che was to be executed. Colonel Arnaldo Saucedo

Parada, an intelligence officer, came into the schoolroom to tell Che that he was going to die.

Che stared at the ceiling for a long moment. When he spoke it was in a calm voice. 'I knew you were going to shoot me – I should never have been taken alive. Tell Fidel that this failure does not mean the end of the revolution, that it will triumph elsewhere. Tell Aleida to forget this, to remarry and be happy, and to keep the children studying. Ask the soldiers to aim well.'

Santa Monica Bluffs. June, 1968

Catesby had been invited to California to help out with a book. The author was very busy because he was running for President of the United States, but the editor was trying to interview as many people as possible who were involved with the events of October, 1962. They wanted to publish as soon as possible. If the author did win his party's nomination, it was hoped that the book would show the candidate as a good and responsible leader.

The first thing that Catesby did was to show the invitation to his superiors at SIS to ask for advice. C was very enthusiastic. 'You must go, William, it will be a wonderful opportunity to add to our profile on this chap. It looks likely that he's going to be the next president.' C paused. 'I'm certain, of course, that you will be discreet to the point of blandness.'

The house on Palisades Beach Road was part of the exclusive and ludicrously rich enclave of Santa Monica Bluffs. Catesby couldn't wait to report back to Henry Bone. The place was an utter vindication of Bone's acid views on American style and taste. The house was more than the mere vulgarity of too much money and too little taste that simply made you smile, but a leaping vulgarity that left you breathless. There was a cocktail bar in every room and gold taps on every sink. But the sweetest irony, the one that Catesby couldn't wait to spring on Bone, was that the house was owned by a well-born English actor who was the son of a lord.

Catesby's room was one of the smaller ones without a view of the sea, but he was still pampered by the Hispanic servants – and did avail himself of the cocktail bar. It helped him sleep. He spent most of the next day closeted with the book editor who recorded everything that was said. Catesby was careful not to give away state secrets, but did reveal matters that were already in the public record with hushed confidentiality as if they were, in fact, top secret. The trick suitably impressed the editor.

Catesby was then left to his own devices until evening. He had a walk along the beach which was private to the enclave. A group of nubile young women in bikinis were playing volleyball. They were, like the cocktail cabinets, part of the hospitality.

After the first shock, the water was like cool silk. It was colder than the Caribbean, but not as cold as his native North Sea – even in a sunny August. It was a moonless midnight which made the stars even brighter and fiercer. He took a deep breath and dived deep into the dark. He wanted to return to that womb – the salt sea that had surrounded his native island and mothered every life form. He stayed under for a long time and heard strange sounds. Something made him feel that Alekseev's ghost was rising from the deep after a midnight swim of six years to join him. Catesby clawed frantically to get back to the surface. And when his head burst into the good night air, he realised that he was not alone.

'They told me that you had gone for a swim. I thought I would join you. I hope I didn't frighten you.' The voice was just as disarmingly feminine as it had been in that dreadful October, perhaps even more so. But there was a new inflection in the American's voice – one of reflection and melancholy. It was no longer the voice of a young man who hammered tables with fists and lisped angry orders.

'You surprised me.'

'Sorry I startled you.'

'It doesn't matter.'

'I also wanted to thank you for helping with the book. The editor says you were great.'

'I did my best, but we obviously can't tell the whole story.'

'Not in our lifetimes.'

Catesby laughed. 'That's as good as never. Dead people are awfully quiet.'

'I know – that's why they killed Oswald.'

'And why you tried to kill me – twice.'

'Being in power makes people brutal. We need to change that.' Kennedy paused. 'But at the time, I was trying to protect my brother. Can you understand that loyalty?'

'Yes.'

The two men were treading water and facing each other. It reminded Catesby of the night swim with Alekseev. And once again something dark and fatal hung in the midnight air. He knew that the man opposite was America's last chance.

'The same people who killed my brother want to kill me.'

Catesby noticed an odd quaver in Kennedy's voice – something ancient. It wasn't only his story, but a story as timeless as the murders of Absalom and Caesar. High office comes with a blood chalice.

'At first, I thought Johnson was behind it. Then I realised that LBJ hadn't the balls. The CIA, the Mafia? Sure, they had the balls, but not the competence. That's why you're still alive – not to mention Castro.'

Catesby breathed the sea air. He had never felt more alive.

'Jack was killed by big money, the Texas oil industry to be specific. They set up Oswald with a job that provided a sniper's perch. They used Oswald with his Russian defector background because they wanted to implicate the Soviet Union and Cuba. What those bastards really wanted was a backlash against the communists that would lead to war. It's why they hated us after the Cuba Missile Crisis. We didn't give them the apocalypse they wanted.'

'Is that what made you change?'

'I began to change before Jack's death. Cuba taught us both a lesson. We came so close to midnight. I saw what the other tough guys were like and they made me sick.' Kennedy paused. When he spoke again there was passion in his voice. 'We must stop this senseless slaughter in Vietnam.'

Catesby thought back to the incident in the US officers club in Berlin in 1961. He remembered all the lean young officers yearning to be let loose on Cuba, Laos and Vietnam. He wondered what their burning unquestioning eyes had seen – and if war had turned back on them and taken away their limbs and lives. Or if they had changed too – or only become hardened.

'There is something else I should tell you about,' said Kennedy, 'a confession.'

Something went click in Catesby's mind. It was a mystery that had never been resolved – a German mystery.

'I once made a secret visit that only Jack knew about. It was the result of a back-channel negotiation with a Russian called Georgi Bolshakov. Cloak and dagger stuff. I travelled to the North German port of Bremen in disguise – fake beard and brown contact lenses. In order to leave a false trail, a rumour was started that I was an Englishman. Galling, of course, for an Irish Catholic. I was secreted aboard a Polish freighter that took me to East Germany. You must have heard rumours about the trip?'

Catesby was genuinely surprised. 'Yes, but I didn't know it was you. I had a list of suspects, but you weren't on it.'

'We did a good job then. Our biggest fear was that the CIA would find out about the meeting – and then use it against us by leaks to their right-wing friends. So we exploited the rumour that a high-level Englishman was playing perfidious Albion and dealing with the Soviets behind our backs.'

More pieces slotted in. Catesby now understood Angleton's vicious personal attack on himself. Kennedy had fooled the CIA too.

'I suppose you could say,' said Kennedy, 'that it was an unofficial summit. But I didn't handle it particularly well – and neither did Khrushchev. Jack wanted me to make a pitch for a nuclear test ban treaty, but Khrushchev mocked the proposal. Later on, I must have come across as too aggressive. Khrushchev got fed up and emotional and said he was prepared to put nuclear missiles in Cuba to counter ours in Turkey.' Kennedy laughed. 'I thought he was joking – and I must have shown my contempt and disbelief. Maybe I provoked him into it.'

'I don't think so.'

'But there is something else that has always troubled me.' Kennedy paused. 'I was assured that only five of us would be present at the meeting, but there was a sixth man sitting in the shadows. It was one of the things that annoyed me. And I'm sure the guy wasn't a Russian or a German – it was his clothes and manner, cool and supercilious.'

'What did he look like?'

Kennedy gave a detailed description of the man. It was a perfect portrait of Henry Bone.

Catesby now understood why Bone had been so willing to take the rap. It was a double bluff. Catesby wondered if he would ever know all the details and conditions of Bone's invitation to East Germany.

'I'm getting cold,' said Kennedy, 'I don't want to die of pneumonia. Shall we swim back?'

'Yes, but why have you told me all this?'

'Because I want you to trust me – and consider yourself a confidant. It's my roundabout way of saying I want you to work for me as a foreign policy advisor – if I make it to the White House.'

Catesby laughed. 'I'm sorry, Senator Kennedy, but I'm not going to turn traitor by working for a foreign power.'

'What if London agreed?'

'We'll see.' In his heart Catesby knew that he could never live in America, but hoped with all his heart that Robert Kennedy would change it to a more gentle and thoughtful place.

As they swam to the shore Catesby saw the dark slim figure of a woman walking along the beach. She had a graceful elegance that was unmistakable, despite the calf-length Capri pants. When they came closer he saw the woman was carrying big fluffy towels.

Kennedy towelled himself warm and dry with the help of the woman. It was obvious that they were in love. And later, it was she who would tell the doctors to turn off the respirator and she who would thumb shut his eyes forever. Catesby began to walk away. He didn't want to intrude on their privacy. But before he left, Kennedy called out, 'Join us tomorrow night. After the vote count, I'm going to give a little talk at the Ambassador Hotel – and then some of us are going out for a bite to eat. Look forward to seeing you.'

Catesby was too far away to help, but near enough to see and hear what happened. Bobby had stopped to shake hands with a young Hispanic kitchen worker in a white smock. Catesby couldn't see more because a large man in a dark suit lurched up behind Kennedy and blocked his view. The shots were so close together that they sounded merged. It was a noise like two or three people beating simultaneously on metal panels with hammers.

There were now a lot of people shouting, 'No, no, no, no …' – and a chaos of flying bodies. Catesby was nearly bowled over by a big dark man crashing past. He caught a glimpse of a face that chilled him. He recognised it by the eyes: they were dead and cold. Catesby had seen their frozen lustre once before in the stairwell of a Washington hotel. The face around them was now puffed and pitted with disease and decay, but the eyes still belonged to Amleto. Meanwhile, people were swearing and someone was shouting, 'Close the doors, close the doors …'

A heaving rush of people, including a scrum of photographers, were surging into the kitchen and causing a crush that carried Catesby forward. Two huge black athletes, who were Kennedy's volunteer bodyguards, had pinned down a small wiry young man with frizzy hair. At first, Catesby didn't understand why they were thumping the thin young man. Then he saw the pistol. Catesby shouted, 'Get the other one too.' But his voice was drowned out in the loud confusion.

Catesby was now standing above Kennedy. The Hispanic kitchen worker was cradling Bobby in his arms. The bluish neon lights made the blood look like dark chocolate. For a second, Catesby hoped that a pot of chocolate had overturned in the chaos and that Kennedy was just winded.

Robert Kennedy looked up at the kitchen worker and whispered, 'Is everybody safe, okay?'

The worker replied in the soft rising and falling tones of Hispanic English, 'Yes, yes, everything is going to be okay.'

Flashbulbs were popping like mad. The young Hispanic took a rosary from around his neck and wove the beads through Bobby's fingers. More flashbulbs popped. Catesby now saw that the blood was real and forming a widening pool beneath Kennedy's head.

London. December, 1974

The brush pass had been carried out with cool and practiced professionalism. The touch was light, sure and almost unnoticed. And the conditions were perfect: an Oxford Street crowded with Christmas shoppers. At first, Catesby thought he must have imagined it. He vainly tried to spot a courier slipping away in the crowd as he shifted his shopping bag to his left hand. No one looked at all suspicious. But as Catesby reached deep into his overcoat pocket he touched the firm edges of an envelope that had not been there before.

Catesby smiled to himself and continued shopping. He would leave the letter until later. He had spent the day lecturing a new intake of field officers on 'tradecraft', especially covert exchanges such as dead letter drops. Catesby assumed that one of the recruits had played a prank. It had happened before.

The first thing that Catesby did when he got back to the flat in Pimlico was to light the gas fire and make a cup of tea. He was now in his late forties and life as a permanent bachelor seemed the most likely outcome. He limited himself to a single Huntley & Palmers digestive biscuit with his cup of tea. He liked being fit and had taken up long distance running again – and didn't want to carry an excess ounce on his long runs through Hyde Park and Kensington Gardens. To keep himself company on his runs he recited poetry – an eccentricity that got him noticed by passers-by. But he was reaching an age where it had begun not to matter. Catesby had lately become fond of Charles Sorley, a soldier poet who was killed in 1915 serving with the Suffolk regiment. He recited the verses again as compensation for not having a second digestive biscuit:

We swing ungirded hips,
And lightened are our eyes,
The rain is on our lips,
We do not run for prize.

We know not whom we trust
Nor whitherward we fare ...

'I suppose,' said Catesby. He looked hard at someone who wasn't there. The imaginary conversations had become a customary feature of his lonely evenings. 'I suppose, Henry, that you find this poem a load of sentimental tosh. But I like it, so up yours.'

Catesby tidied away the tea things and got out the Christmas wrapping paper. The most important present were the records for his sister. He knew that she liked Erik Satie and Maurice Ravel. He also knew they were the sort of composers that Henry Bone called 'purveyors of maudlin slush'. Catesby imagined Bone's thin lips curled in disdain and spoke aloud again, 'That's your opinion – and it's tedious.'

As Catesby began to unroll the wrapping paper, he noticed that he hadn't hung up his overcoat. When he picked up the coat, he remembered the letter. He found the envelope and removed it from the right pocket. Nothing was written on it, but he could see that it wasn't standard British stationery. He opened it. As soon as he saw the Cyrillic letters his heart skipped a beat. There was a photo too. It slipped out of the letter and fell face up on the carpet. Catesby's hands shook as he bent down to recover the photo. He knew who it was. His own eyes stared back at him. The eyes also belonged to a gawky girl of eleven who was trying hard not to smile. He held the photo as if it were the most precious thing in the world and began to read the letter.

Dear William,
Your daughter's name is Irina. The name means 'peace'. I hope you approve.

Irina is a lucky girl: she has three fathers. She bears Zhenka's name, Alekseeva; she was created by your seed – and my husband gives her the same love he gives our own children. Irina has two half-brothers.

Children. Their staring eyes so frightful. The running beat of new feet on wooden floors as you wait tensed for a tumble into tears that you can't prevent. The eternal disorder. The tired respite of evening when they whisper in semi-sleep. The paintings of birds and trams and sheep – and the stick insect witch I know is me. Waiting for their tender teasing riddles to unfold.

But now is evening so there is time for us. Moscow is frozen solid. The town is fixed in crystal – just like us. But I do not find this mysterious non-meeting a desolate one. When I listen to your unspoken phrases and silent words, I still hear your voice. You are a page that was not read, but I sensed its rage. In human closeness there is a secret edge that needs no words.

Until we meet again,
Katya

Acknowledgements

The first person I want to thank is Julia for her support, patience and understanding. Her son, Edward Manton, should be acknowledged for unwittingly contributing a visual image, which adds to the novel's appearance. I am also grateful to Frank Wilson. My big brother, who saw active service as both sailor and naval officer during every decade of the Cold War, supplied me with details and recollections that I am sure contribute to this book's historical authenticity.

Once again, I must give high praise to Angeline Rothermundt for her excellence as an editor. I also feel fortunate and grateful to have the support of Gary Pulsifer, Daniela de Groote and Andrew Hayward at Arcadia Books. All of you have made me feel valued as an author. Thank you.

Finally, I want to acknowledge the following books and sources. I would, however, like to single out the George Washington University National Security Archive as being especially helpful.

Aerospaceweb.org. 'Nedelin Disaster'

Akhmatova, Anna (ed. Roberta Reeder). *The Complete Poems of Anna Akhmatova*. Zephyr Press; Exp Upd Su edition, 2000.

Aldrich, Richard J. *The Hidden Hand: Britain, America and Cold War Secret Intelligence*. The Overlook Press, Woodstock and New York, 2002.

Bamford, James. *Body of Secrets*. Doubleday, New York, 2001.

Cuba Journal. The Mafia in Cuba (1902–1958) Source: www.cubamafia.info.

Davies, Barry; Gordievsky, Oleg; Tomlinson, Richard. *The Spycraft Manual: The Insider's Guide to Espionage Techniques*. Zenith Press, 2005.

Dobbs, Michael. *One Minute to Midnight*. Arrow, 2009.

Epstein, Edward Jay. 'James Jesus Angleton: the Orchid Man' from Epstein's *Diary* dated March 19, 1975.

Ford, Trowbridge H. Anatoliy Golitsyn: The KGB's Most Dangerous Defector. Codshit.com, Tuesday, 27 January 2004.
Fursenko, Aleksandr; Naftali, Timothy. *The Secret History of the Cuban Missile Crisis: 'One Hell of a Gamble'*. John Murray, London, 1997.
George Washington University. *The National Security Archive.* The following documents were accessed:
USSR, Memorandum, A. Adzhubei's Account of His Visit to Washington to the CC CPSU, March 12, 1962. (in original Russian with English translation)
CIA, Minutes, SECRET, "Meeting with the Attorney General of the United States Concerning Cuba," 19 January 1962 (Richard Helms)
DOD, Memorandum, TOP SECRET, "Cover and Deception Plans for Caribbean Survey Group," 19 February 1962 (Operation Northwoods).
Brig. Gen. Edward Lansdale, "Review of OPERATION MONGOOSE," Phase One, July 25, 1962.
"National Security Action Memorandum No. 181," Presidential Directive on actions and studies in response to new Soviet Bloc Activity in Cuba, August 23, 1962.
CIA, Minutes, TOP SECRET, "Minutes of Meeting of the Special Group (Augmented) on Operation Mongoose," 4 October 1962.
Chronology Compiled for The President's Foreign Intelligence Advisory Board (PFIAB), "Chronology of Specific Events Relating to the Military Buildup in Cuba," Undated [Excerpt].
DOD, Transcripts, SECRET, "Notes taken from Transcripts of Meetings of the Joint Chiefs of Staff, October-November 1962: Dealing with the Cuban Missile Crisis."
CIA Special National Intelligence Estimate, "Major Consequences of Certain U.S. Courses of Action on Cuba," October 20, 1962.
Secretary of Defense Robert McNamara, military briefing, "Notes on October 21, 1962 Meeting with the President."
USSR, directive, TOP SECRET, Malinovsky's Order to Pliyev, October 22, 1962.
"Radio-TV Address of the President to the Nation from the White House," October 22, 1962.
Dillon group discussion paper, "Scenario for Airstrike Against Offensive Missile Bases and Bombers in Cuba," October 25, 1962.

Prime Minister Fidel Castro's letter to Premier Khrushchev, October 26, 1962.
CIA daily report, "The Crisis USSR/Cuba," October 27, 1962.
Cable received from U.S. Ambassador to Turkey Raymond Hare to State Department regarding Turkish missiles, October 26, 1962.
DOJ, Memorandum, TOP SECRET, "Memorandum for the Secretary of State from the Attorney General," on Robert Kennedy's October 27 Meeting with Dobrynin, October 30, 1962.USSR, Cable, TOP SECRET, Dobrynin Report of Meeting with Robert Kennedy on Worsening Threat, October 27, 1962.
U.S. Navy, TOP SECRET/SECRET/FOR OFFICIAL USE ONLY, Charts/deck logs of anti-submarine warfare operations related to USSR submarine B-59, October 1962.
USSR, Memoir, "Recollections of Vadim Orlov (USSR Submarine B-59): We will Sink Them All, But We will Not Disgrace Our Navy," (2002).
Aspectos importantes contenidos en los informes ofrecidos por los jefes militares reunidos el día 24 de octubre de 1962 en el Estado Mayor General con el Comandante en Jefe Fidel Castro.
USSR, draft directive, Directive to the Commander of Soviet Forces in Cuba on transfer of Il-28s and Luna Missiles, and Authority on Use of Tactical Nuclear Weapons, September 8, 1962.
USSR, Directive, TOP SECRET, Prohibition on Use of Nuclear Weapons without Orders from Moscow, October 27, 1962, 16:30.
USSR, Directive, TOP SECRET, CC CPSU Presidium Instructions to Pliyev in Response to His Telegram, October 27, 1962.
USSR, Letter, from Chairman Khrushchev to Prime Minister Castro, October 28, 1962.
Cuba, Letter, from Prime Minister Castro to Chairman Khrushchev, October 28, 1962.
White House, "Post Mortem on Cuba," October 29, 1962.
USSR, Letter, from Chairman Khrushchev to Prime Minister Castro, October 30, 1962.
Cuba, Letter, from Prime Minister Castro to Chairman Khrushchev, October 31, 1962.
Bromley Smith, "Summary Record of NSC Executive Committee Meeting," November 2, 1962.

Bromley Smith, "Summary Record of NSC Executive Committee Meeting," November 5, 1962.
USSR, Memorandum of Conversation between Mikoyan and Cuban Leaders, TOP SECRET, November 5, 1962 (Evening).
USSR, Telegrams from Malinovsky to Pliyev, TOP SECRET, Early November (*circa* 5 November) 1962.
USSR, Ciphered Telegram from Mikoyan to CC CPSU, TOP SECRET, November 6, 1962.
President Kennedy's letter to Premier Khrushchev, November 6, 1962.
General Maxwell Taylor, "Chairman's Talking Paper for Meeting with the President," November 16, 1962.
Cuba, Order, TOP SECRET, Authorizing Anti-Aircraft Fire, November 17, 1962.
Cuba, Order, TOP SECRET, Rescinding Authorization to Initiate Anti-Aircraft Fire November 18, 1962.
USSR, Instructions from CC CPSU Presidium to Mikoyan, TOP SECRET, November 22, 1962.
Hungary, Embassy, Havana, Telegram, TOP SECRET, "The Essence of Soviet-Cuban Divergences of Opinion," December 1, 1962.
Great Britain, Dispatch, CONFIDENTIAL, British Ambassador in Cuba to Foreign Office, "The Cuban Crisis – Chapters I and II," November 10, 1962 (with minutes from FO's American Department as cover).
Greene, Graham. *Our Man in Havana*. Penguin Books, London, 1962.
Hamrick, S.J. *Deceiving the Deceivers: Kim Philby, Donald Maclean, and Guy Burgess*. Yale University Press, New Haven, 2004.
Hennessy, Peter. *Having it so Good*: *Britain in the Fifties*. Penguin Allen Lane, London, 2006.
Hepburn, James. *Farewell America*: *The Plot to Kill JFK*. Penmarin Books, April 2002.
The Independent: Obituaries. 'Aleksandr Feklisov: Spy handler for the KGB'. *Saturday, 8 December 2007.*
LiveLeak. 'The Nedelin Disaster'.
Mailer, Norman. *Harlot's Ghost.* Michael Joseph, London, 1991.
Mayakovsky, Vladimir. *The Bedbug and Selected Poetry*. John Wiley & Sons, 1975.

The Miami Herald. 'A nuclear secret in '62 Cuba crisis 100 Soviet warheads undetected by U.S.' By Juan O. Tamayo, 1998.
The National Post (Canada). 'Charade in Havana: Documents show Canadian diplomats gathered intelligence about Cuba for the U.S.' by Isabel Vincent, 25 January 2003.
New York Review of Books. 'Castro's Cuba: An Exchange'. Maurice Halperin, Carlos Ripoll, and Mark N. Kramer, reply by Arthur Schlesinger Jr. May, 28 1992.
The New York Times. 'Chief of Rockets Killed in Soviet; Moscow Reports Death of Nedelin in Plane Crash', October 26, 1960.
Presidential Studies Quarterly. 'Who ever believed in the "missile gap?": John F. Kennedy and the politics of national security.' 1 December 2003.
Orwell, George. *1984*. Penguin Books, London, 1990.
RussianSpaceWeb.com. 'Rockets: R-16 family: Nedelin disaster.'
Third World Traveler. Operation Paperclip Casefile, 8 August 1997.
Wilson, Edward. *The Darkling Spy*. Arcadia Books, London, 2010.
Wilson, Edward. *The Envoy*. Arcadia Books, London, 2008.
Wilson, Jim. *Launch Pad UK: Britain and the Cuban Missile Crisis.* Pen & Sword Aviation, 2008.
Wright, Peter. *Spy Catcher.* Viking Penguin, New York, 1987.

A number of real historic events are mentioned in this book and real places are mentioned. A few real names are used, but no real people are portrayed. This is a work of fiction. When I have used official titles and positions, I do not suggest that the persons who held those positions in the past are the same persons portrayed in the novel or that they have spoken, thought or behaved in the way I have imagined.